Ma's Diner

David Wilson

ISBN: 979-8-218-11375-9

"My, my, the clock in the sky is pounding away and there's so much to say."

-Mickey Dolenz

Dedications

To

James and Buddy

We had some great times growing up together. I'm surprised we were never arrested as a result of our shenanigans. Not even a traffic citation.

To Paul

You didn't hang out with us very often, but when you did it was certainly interesting. You passed away at far too young of an age. It made us all stop, think, and reflect, and possibly caused us to grow up a little in the moment.

You're still thought of to this day.

Table of Contents

Prologue

Ma's Diner is a sequel to my previous book, *Two Seasons*, in which we'll return to the tiny town of East Puddleduck, Maine, and see what 'Ma' Farnsworth and the other townsfolk are up to. Unlike its predecessor, the majority of the stories in *Ma's Diner* are nearly entirely fictitious except for one chapter, that being chapter five. And, in particular, one event within that chapter. Otherwise, the stories have been created almost entirely from imagination. In comparison, in my book *Two Seasons*, many of the stories were based on actual events set in the fictional locations and through the adventures of its created characters. However, even with the majority of the tales within this book being created from imagination, as I wrote each of them what I took from my memory were real places and actual people to base the stories on.

For example, when writing chapter five *(I'll try not to give up too much of the plot)*, where again another annual fair is the focal point of the story, my thoughts while writing this chapter traveled back to my childhood and memories of when I'd visit the Bangor State Fair each year. As I wrote this chapter I pictured the excitement of the fair that was held on the grounds of the old Bangor Auditorium and I visualized the layout of the fairgrounds, the horse racing track, the massive midway rides and games, the bright lights that lit the dark of night, and the building underneath the grandstands. It brought back fond memories of my youth that I was able to use to set the scene, and in my opinion, enhance the story.

In the upcoming chapter that details the little Friday night band at Ma's Diner, I recalled my days as a deputy sheriff in Piscataquis County, Maine. When circumstances would allow, I'd stop by the Monson General Store on

Friday evenings and listen to a group of local amateur musicians who would gather together for a jam session. I enjoyed taking a break from the stress of the job and joining others as we listened to the music. Anyone from town that owned a musical instrument was welcome to stop by and partake in the makeshift session, and the music was spontaneous as they would go around in a circle and each participant would choose the next song to play. I recalled this enjoyable time and used it as the backdrop for chapter 7.

For the chapters about Ma's vacation, I envisioned many of the locations that my wife and I have visited throughout the years, the experiences we've enjoyed, and the tropical locations that we've visited by use of our choice of travel, a cruise liner. I recalled places we've been, and excursions we've encountered as the setting for these particular chapters. I suppose this is a form of research for a book, only somewhat in reverse and I believe many authors of fiction utilize actual life events to enhance their stories. And I'm certain like many writers, along with performing research to base our stories, we've relied on an equally great amount of memory and past experiences in which to add detail. At times it was as simple as recalling a single person, place, or even something I'd taken note of and then picking my brain to create a story based on that one thing.

One major difference between the two novels is that in *Two Seasons*, as explained in its prologue, the stories were random in their timing as far as when each chapter occurred. In this novel, in comparison, the stories are in a basic chronological order spanning just about two years from the beginning to the book's end. And, as with many sequels, beginning where *Two Seasons* left off.

Two things that haven't changed between the books are the fact that as an inspiration I've continued to rely on the memory of my father's enjoyment of storytelling. Secondly, the fact that I've enjoyed creating the characters, and I've used *Ma's Diner* as a way to continue their character development, as well as introduce one or two new characters to add to the adventures.

I've also realized that having the freedom to create the majority of each chapter entirely from imagination, rather than base stories on events that occurred as was the case in *Two Seasons*, has been a bit easier than I'd hoped. I believe it was far more difficult to enhance a story that had been based on something that I'd experienced, or a story told to me by my father than it was to simply use my imagination to create a situation for 'Ma' to be part of, or to deal with. For example, as mentioned one of the tales included in chapter

5 is based on something that occurred that I was witness to. I had the full intention of including this story in *Two Seasons*, however, I hadn't had the ability to fictionalize it to the point that I felt it would be interesting to the reader. It wasn't until I had the idea to begin this book that I was able to give more thought to the memory of what had occurred and include it within the other imaginary events that take place in that chapter.

I've thoroughly enjoyed writing the two books and find it difficult to determine which novel I enjoy more, so I'll just say that I believe they're equal in my heart and soul.

I hope you enjoy *Ma's Diner*, and enjoy revisiting the matriarch of East Puddleduck as much as I've enjoyed writing about her.

And with that, once again, let's get started…

CHAPTER 1

Educating the Children's Choir

And just then, Bob farted.

"*Jeesus*, constable! I told you before not to be doing that in my diner!" Ma stormed up to the counter bar, keeping her nose upwind and facing Bob, directing her chunky pointer finger into the lawman's face. Bob Johnson had a look of caution as Ma commanded, "You don't ever break wind in here unless it's during the Bucksnort contest! Do you *hear* me?! And then only when I tell you to! Keep it up and I swear I'll sew your butt cheeks shut!" The police officer, with a pathetic expression displayed on his well-rounded face, simply nodded to Ma as he shoveled another spoonful of hot chili into his mouth and accepted his scolding.

Luckily for Bob it was just before the lunch hour, and the crowd was still a bit light in the diner on that Sunday with the churchgoers just beginning to stroll in. Old Marmaduke was the only other patron seated in a corner booth as the air began to clear, and he didn't seem to notice or care.

Joshua and Wally McIntyre wandered in and sat down next to Bob at the counter bar, and Joshua received the last waft as he turned and scowled at the constable before parking his own rear on the barstool, one down from Bob.

"Why don't you get that chili to go!?" Joshua blurted at the public safety officer. "You do the same thing every single day when you eat your lunch in here!" Bob just smiled and threw a wink to the mechanic and used car salesman, his cheeks now even puffier being all full of Ma's delicious food.

Ma set the boys up with silverware and paper placemats as the mayor, Rupert Wiggleswort, and his wife, Eleanor, strolled in and sat down at their usual center table. The diner was starting to fill as Smirnoff parked himself at an adjacent table while his wife, Cicely, put her apron on, preparing to assist Ma with the after-services crowd. Puut Voisine joined the big Slavic man at his table and Ruby 'Red' Mayflower slid into the front booth closest to the door along with Mable Johnson, who wanted nothing to do with her flatulent husband for obvious reasons. Val Doody also began to prepare tables in an effort to help out as her husband and selectperson, Paul Doody, sat with his board partner, Jacob Daley. Even Ma's nemesis, Mattie Daley, had decided to have lunch at the diner today, seated across from her husband, and it didn't take long before the dining room was chock full of townsfolk. Next to last through the doors were Runyon and El dragging behind, with the two taking a center booth along the front wall. Everyone in the diner had on their Sunday best. That is, except for Ma, who was wearing her usual floral-patterned sundress and food-stained apron over it.

As soon as they were to finish setting up tables with silverware and other condiments, Val and Cicely would duck into the restrooms to change out of their nice Sunday clothes and into something a bit more appropriate to help wait on the customers while Ma would be putting up lunch orders in the kitchen. In the evening the staff would typically increase to at least one additional local youth as the dinner crowd would be expected to be just a bit more than the noontime gathering.

Ma was turning to walk back into the kitchen after greeting everyone at the door with her usual head tilt with one eyebrow raised, and a grimace on her face when she spotted the big brown Cadillac wheel into the diner's gravel parking lot. "Bubblehead's here," she remarked loud enough for those seated closest to overhear, and Ma paused at the end of the counter bar to greet the pastor. Father Winkin exited his Caddy wearing his flowing Sunday frock and white collar. As he entered the establishment with his head held high, he stopped just inside the front door and looked down at Ma through the driving glasses that were perched on the bridge of his nose. Ma squinted up at him through hers and smiled, "Done for the day, preacher? Is it time to rest? It's the seventh day, you know. You shouldn't work too hard today."

"Bless you, my child." The response came with a bit of sarcasm, "I don't recall seeing you in the church today, Wilomena Farnsworth."

Ma closed her eyes and shook her head, "Nope, not today. I was too busy getting ready for the lunch crowd." Ma proceeded to let the pastor walk by to take a seat as she nodded to Val, a sign to have her come and help prepare meals in the kitchen. Ma turned towards the swinging kitchen half-doors as Val passed by the pastor.

"What are the kids watching today, father?"

"Oh, that's right!" Ma stopped and turned back around, pointing one finger into the air. "You're still showing the young-uns movies every Sunday, aren't you? You just can't keep your stupid hobby to yourself, can you preacher?" The old woman squinted and crinkled her nose, gazing up and waiting for an answer.

Father Winkin turned back to Ma, "There's nothing wrong with that." The preacher's usual arrogance displayed in his tone, "I don't see an issue with showing the children movies that have an educational or historical significance."

Ma, preparing herself for the verbal sparring walked straight back up to Percible, "Shouldn't they be learning about those things from a real person and not from a Hollywood movie, there preacher!?"

"Their parents don't mind. And additionally, it keeps their attention. You know most children today are a challenge to hold their attention for more than a few moments. I see no issue with showing them a movie as long as its subject matter is appropriate. We've been doing this for several weeks now with no complaints. None, except from you!" The reverend gave a quick nod in agreement with his own words.

Ma squinted and pointed her stout finger up at the pastor, "Well, I just don't think it means as much as a real person giving them the time of day!"

Percible extended his arm and placed a hand on Ma's shoulder to a wide-eyed diner owner, who frowned as she looked at his hand as if she were going to bite it off. "Don't worry, Ma. I don't show any movies to children under the age of ten years old and I make certain they're all watching something they can understand and will remember its significance when they grow older." The preacher noticed that Ma was giving him a look that let him know he needed to remove his hand, so he did as he continued, "The children are all primarily between the ages of ten to twelve years old, a very influential age, and they've watched a variety of important movies. They've watched *Schindler's List, Apollo 13, Ben Hur,* and *Roots* to name just a few. They've even watched that *Titanic* movie, of course with *that scene* edited out." The reverend continued quite proudly, "Each movie is teaching them a lesson that they'll hopefully remember and assist them in their future teachings at school. And it's not as if they're watching them unsupervised. For instance, today Myrtle Watson is with them while I grab a bite to eat here in your fine establishment."

Ma's scowl deepened, "You ain't buying these movies out of the collection plate, are you?!"

"Of course not!" Father Winkin scowled back at Ma, "I pay for them myself. I buy them all in DVD format and they're much cheaper if you just pick a title from the list in a catalog that I receive. I get discounts for the more I purchase, and the movies arrive just themselves with no cover art, just the disc itself in a paper sleeve. It's all very inexpensive and thrifty. I think the company I order from is called Bootleg…or something. I pay for them out of my own pocket, and I just add them to my personal collection after the children have watched them." The father was on a roll, similar to providing a sermon as he looked over to El and Runyon and smiled, speaking a bit more loudly and with a grin on his face, "I could watch a good movie over and over again and never grow tired, so it all works out for the best for everybody!" The two smiled and nodded back at the father.

"What are the kids watching today?" Wally leaned out past his brother Joshua and asked of the preacher.

Father Winkin turned to the auto repairman and said again, proudly, "Oh, today is that wonderful historical movie that lays out the famous Watergate scandal of the Nixon presidential era. It's a bit sophisticated in nature, but I believe the children will understand it. I'm sure that there shall be many questions afterward. A good, interactive discussion should take place." The preacher appeared quite proud of himself.

"I've seen that one. That's a good movie," came Puut's voice from his booth. *"All the President's Men.* I enjoyed that movie."

The preacher began a slow turn-a-round to Puut, his expression turning to a bit of concern and confusion as he frowned, "All the President's Men? No, no, no. I meant the one with Dustin Hoffman and Robert Redford. The one about Watergate."

The reverend stopped when El, seated directly beside where he was standing, looked up and chimed in. "Yeah, that's the one. *All the President's Men*. It's one of my favorites too."

"No, no, that isn't it." The preacher looked down at El and remarked, "You know, the one about Woodward and Bernstein of the Washington Post. The one with the secret informant that exposed what had taken place within the White House during the Watergate incident."

The father spun around as the mayor spoke from his table, with sarcasm, as he tucked his napkin into his collar under his colorful suit jacket, "Yes, yes. *All the President's Men*. That's the name of it just like El said."

The father's eyes widened as Ma tapped the preacher on the shoulder from behind and he turned back around with even more concern now showing in his expression. Ma adjusted her glasses and spoke in monotone, asking the obvious question, "And just what movie are you showing children, there preacher? *Hmmmm?*"

"I'm telling you, Ma. It's the one about the Watergate informant." The reverend was nearly whispering and spoke to her as if they were the only two in the diner.

"And what is it called?" Ma inquired again, her head tilting upwards and a smirk on her face as if both would allow her to hear better.

"It's called *Deep Throat*, obviously."

There was a simultaneous gasp from the patrons in the diner as Ma's eyebrows raised nearly to her hair bun. She gazed at the reverend out through her glasses into his, and straight into his eyes. She went silent for a moment as Smirnoff spit the water out he'd just taken a drink of, nearly into Puut's lap. Cicely's voice could be overheard as she held a kitchen towel up to her chest and said softly, "Oh, my God."

Eleanor Wiggleswort began to cough, and Mattie Doody let out a loud, audible sigh and said softly, "My goodness, those poor, innocent children."

Wally and Joshua nodded to each other with childish grins on their immature faces as Ruby and Mable stared at each other across their table, both a bit speechless. Finally, Ruby's open mouth turned to a devious smirk, and she raised an eyebrow at Mable, shaking her head slowly. Mable continued with the deer-in-the-headlights look plastered on her face, staring straight through Ruby. Constable Bob simply raised his eyebrows up and down as he stared into his bowl of chili and shoveled another spoonful into his mouth.

Ma opened her mouth to speak to the preacher, took in a breath, and then closed it again, her head still tilted. Her eyebrows lowered, then raised again as she pointed at Father Winkin, who was quite visibly more than a bit confused, and deeply concerned. Ma opened her mouth once again to speak and she asked, ever so softly, "Did you just say that you're showing those children the movie, *Deep Throat?*"

The preacher's head nodded as Marmaduke's French-accented, monotone voice could be heard across the dining room from his corner booth, "Them kids are certainly gonna learn something historical today. And you're probably right, there preacher. There's gonna be some interesting questions."

Ma grabbed her gut, put one hand on the preacher's arm, and doubled over as she burst out in uncontrollable laughter, tearing up and nearly losing her breath. *"Ahhh, ha, ha, ha, ha! Bwah, ha, ha, ha, ha!"* Gasp, *"Bwah, ha, ha, ha, ha!"*

"I don't understand!" The preacher looked up as Ma's boisterous laughing began to resemble the sounds of an ocean seal. The preacher looked around at a stunned diner crowd, none knowing how to provide an explanation to the pastor. "What's going on!?" The preacher asked in general, still looking around the diner and literally holding Ma up as she was laughing so hard she nearly fell to her knees onto the diner's floor.

Ruby began to stand up in her booth, parking her butt on the backrest and she held her hand above her head and tried to speak over Ma's laughing, *"Ahhh*h, father?" The Reverend, now with both his hands on Ma's arms in an effort to keep her from passing out, turned to Ruby. "That's a…*umm*…that's a movie about…*umm*…oh, dear…" All the men in the room had their attention fully on Red, all waiting for her description of the infamous flick. All hoping and anticipating that it would be graphic, and all smiling like children themselves. "That's a movie about…*umm*…well, you know…" Ruby began to bounce in place nervously as she attempted to explain. The menfolk straining their necks to get a glimpse of the front of her Sunday V-neck dress.

"Well, tell him!" Ma managed to get her laughter under control as she stood back up, still smiling wide. "Go ahead, tell the Bubblehead what he's showing the little cherubs!"

Percible had true concern on his face now as his attention was on Ruby, and not for the same reasons the other men's attention was. Red stopped bouncing and turned her expression towards Ma, responding sarcastically,

"Well, it was a mainstream movie! A lot of women went to see it too when it was at the theaters, and even some famous people had gone out to see it!"

"Yeah, but none of them were ten years old," Joshua mentioned, facing his brother and giggling.

Eleanor Wiggleswort, who was currently being fanned by her husband with the use of a paper napkin from across their little table, let out a heavy sigh and passed out cold in her chair.

Runyon chimed in, "Siskel and Ebert gave it two thumbs up!"

The reverend turned back to Ma, still holding onto her. "What is it? What are they all talking about?! What is *Deep Throat?* I don't understand! What's it about?" He pleaded with the woman.

"It's about sixty-one minutes long," Paul Doody mentioned. His wife Val flashed him a dirty look in response to his observation.

Ruby spoke back up, still looking straight at Ma, "He needs to know!" She looked at the preacher, "It's mostly about…well, it's about…well, it's about how to give a…*umm*…"

"Stop!" Ma barked, cutting Ruby off. Puut's smile widened as he stared intently at Red. Ma tugged Percible down closer to her to gain his full attention and she looked him straight in the face, "It's a pornographic movie, you Bubblehead!"

Father Winkin pulled back away from Ma and stood straight, "A what?! *A what?!*" He looked around the room to see that everyone was nodding. Well, everyone except for Eleanor, who was still unconscious. The mayor was no longer fanning her as his attention was intently on the matter at hand. The reverend looked back at Ma. "A *pornographic* movie?! It can't be!"

"Oh, it is!" Ma replied, waiving her arms off his grip and her demeanor turned a bit more serious, "And you're currently showing it to the entire children's choir!"

"But Ma! It just can't be! *Deep Throat* was the name of the Watergate informant!"

Ma snapped back, "Where do you think they got the nickname from, you dipstick?! From that dirty movie, that's where!"

"Dibs on the movie when you're done showing it to the kids!" Wally stood up and raised his hand.

Ma flashed Wally a look of warning, shaking her head as Joshua backhanded his brother in his gut. Wally sat back down and lowered his hand, flashing his brother a look and silently mouthing the word, *"What?"*

The mayor stood up, still disregarding his unconscious wife who was slowly slipping out of her chair and under the table. "Shame on you, Wally! And you too, reverend!" The mayor stood between the preacher and Ma, placing his hands on the lapels of his velvety suit jacket and speaking in his best politician's voice, "That's not a movie that needs to be circulating around this fine town! It's filth, that's what it is! Utter trash! Now, I suppose I can dispose of the movie properly…"

"*Shut up*, Rupert!" Ma barked sarcastically and pushed the mayor back down into his chair, "You ain't getting that movie either!" Ma then glanced over to Ruby, who was still standing in her booth, and gave her a "look."

Ruby, a bit surprised, responded wide-eyed at Ma, "What? I don't want it. I already have a copy."

Mas closed her eyes and shook her head. And at that very moment, if Puut's smile were to have gotten any wider, his face would have broken into two pieces. Not to mention all the men in the room were smirking at Ruby's comment. That is, all except for the preacher who was still pleading, "What am I going to do, Ma?!"

Ma's demeanor turned to one of reasoning, "Well, we probably ought to get over to the church and stop that movie for one thing. By now Myrtle's probably just as out cold over there as Eleanor is right here," pointing at the unconscious woman under the table. "Next, we're going to need to figure out what to do with a room full of kids that all at once just jumpstarted into puberty." The McIntyre brothers nodded to each other in agreement with the latter statement as Ma continued, "And you were right about one thing, there preacher, them kids will have questions!"

Percible fell to his knees, placed his head in his hands, and began to whine, "*Ohhhhhh*, I'll be defrocked for this, if not tortured and killed. Just like Frankenstein's monster, all the parents will hunt me down. They'll burn me at the stake. *Ohhhhhh*, I am alone and miserable. Only someone as ugly as I could love me now..."

Ma placed a hand on the pastor's shoulder and said confidently, "Don't start quoting movie lines, preacher. Now isn't the time."

Wally spoke up with eerie enthusiasm, "Especially not ones from *Deep Throat!*" Joshua grimaced and smacked his brother on the side of his head in response to his remark. Wally flashed his brother another "*what?*" look in response to being hit for a second time.

"Runyon!" Ma barked, "Get over to the church and turn that movie player off!" Her son nodded in acknowledgment and stood up to head toward the door.

Ruby pointed into the air and blurted out loud, "Especially before that final scene comes on!" Runyon stopped before he reached the door as everyone looked back towards Red, and the diner went very quiet.

"Final scene?" Father Winkin took his head from his hands and looked over at Ruby from where he was kneeling on the floor. He then peered up at Ma, "What final scene is she referring to?"

Ma flashed Ruby a look while everyone else in the diner, the women included, except of course for Eleanor, stretched their necks out to hear better what Ruby's description of "the final scene" might very well be.

Ruby looked straight at Ma, raised her eyebrows, and whispered loudly, "You know, the last scene…" Ruby used her hands to demonstrate an explosion, placing them in front of her in a double fist and then flicking them open wide, blurting out, *"Pewkew!"* The preacher's eyes widened, along with Ma's, and everyone else's in the diner too.

Mattie Doody placed her forearm over her eyes and sighed loudly, *"Ohhhhhh!"* She too passed out on her side of the booth while Jacob, who was busy staring at Ruby with a glazed look on his face, disregarded his wife's loss of consciousness as did Paul who was still seated beside Jacob. He also had turned around and was fully focused on Ruby Red.

Father Winkin looked back up at Ma and pleaded, "What does she mean by that?"

Ma shook her head and said calmly, "Nothing, preacher. She's just describing the…well, the…*ahhhhh*…the end of the movie where…where something happens."

Father Winkin's eyes widened as he listened to Ma and continued pleading, *"What?* What happens?!"

The preacher looked back over to Ruby and again she made the explosion motion with her hands and said softly, *"Pewkew."* Father Winkin looked back at Ma, his eyes begging for an explanation.

Ma finally said bluntly, "Well, *shit!* She's talking about the…well, you know! She means the big *organism* at the end of the movie! 'Scuse my French! You know, the deep throat part!"

The preacher looked around, still seemingly confused. However, everyone else in the diner certainly understood the meaning of the mispronounced explanation. Ruby was nodding her head in agreement with Ma's description. Runyon turned again to head out the door with the visual still fresh in his brain, and he tripped over his own two feet tumbling face-first to the floor.

El spoke up from his seat, "Could you describe it a little better, Ma? My memory is a bit fuzzy from when you and I last watched it some thirty or so years ago."

"Shut up!" Ma barked sarcastically at her other half.

Smirnoff opened his mouth and raised one hand to speak, however, Cicely immediately noticed and cut him off. "And you had better shut up too!" Her husband lowered his hand and closed his mouth with a disappointed look on his face.

Just as Runyon was picking himself back up off the floor and managed to get to his knees, the diner's front door flew open and smacked him in the noggin, knocking him sideways under the swinging double half doors into the kitchen. Standing in the diner's doorway was Myrtle Watson, who looked a bit frumpy to say the very least. Her hair was down from under her Sunday hat and hanging in her slightly sweating face, her eyeliner and makeup dripping downward a bit from the perspiring, and she was pointing one of her silk-gloved hands and glaring at Father Winkin. *"You!* How could you!?" You're sick! You should be ashamed of yourself!"

The preacher was slowly shaking his head at Myrtle's comments as if to say silently, *"It wasn't my fault."*

"How much of it did the kids see?" Ma inquired in monotone, "Are they in need of therapy yet?"

"Certainly not!" Myrtle responded, "I quickly sent them from the room during the opening credits! They were gone before the first filthy scene appeared on that television screen! They were out of the room before anything happened and never saw or heard a thing from that vile and disgusting movie!"

An evil smirk came over Ma's face. "You didn't quite say that you turned the movie off, there Myrtle." All patrons' eyes were wide toward the disheveled lady standing at the door. Well, except for Eleanor and Mattie's, because as you know, they were still both unconscious.

"Well, no…I didn't!" Myrtle said proudly, holding her head up high and attempting to locate an excuse. She replied in a slightly arrogant tone, straightening up, shaking her hips, and lifting her bosom with both hands from beneath her Sunday dress as if that would make all things proper. "I couldn't recall if I'd seen the movie before so I kept watching…out of sheer curiosity…about halfway through." Her voice lowered and trailed, "Until I needed a cigarette break."

"You don't smoke!" Ma pointed to the woman in the doorway and then turned her attention back to the pastor and assisted him to his feet. "Looks like you're off the hook there, preacher. It seems the children were spared. And, I hope you learned something from all of this!" The father nodded as Ma looked around the diner and stepped aside from the pastor, waving her stout finger around the room and scolding everyone as if they were all guilty of something. "Show's over! Literally! And you're all getting saltpeter and ice water in your meals today! And cold showers for all of you when you get home!"

Old Marmaduke chuckled to himself as he took another sip of his coffee, "*Heh, heh.* Some folks here might be in for a wilder-than-average night tonight. Whether they're with someone or not."

Ma flashed the old man a look and then glanced around the room again, pointing to both Rupert and Jacob, "And you two really should wake Eleanor and Mattie up!" Both men snapped back to reality and realized their wives were still unconscious and under their tables. The spouses began the effort to retrieve and revive the two ladies.

As Father Winkin was dusting his robe from where he'd spent time on the diner's floor, Myrtle Watson walked up to him, or a better description might be that she "slinked" towards him. Ma took notice as the preacher reared back and put his hands up, preparing to deflect whatever verbal thrashing that Myrtle was going to inflict on him next. As Myrtle approached, both Ma and the preacher noticed that the woman had a look of confidence on her face, with her head tilted just slightly downwards while looking up at the pastor. She had one eyebrow raised and a smirk on her face. Ma and the preacher looked at each other, then back at Myrtle, who was now directly in the father's personal space.

"And as for you." Myrtle said to the pastor in a low, eerily enticing growl, "I believe you need to return with me and watch the remainder of that movie." The preacher and Ma's eyebrows both sank as Myrtle glanced up to the ceiling, seeking her next excuse. She looked back at the preacher with horns nearly growing from her temple, and she said in a rather deviant voice, "You should be made to watch that *filthy* movie that you nearly corrupted those children with." She pressed a finger into the preacher's chest, "You should be forced to view that vile and disgusting film as punishment…in its entirety…and I'll be right there to make certain you watch the whole thing." Myrtle winked up at the preacher.

Father Winkin looked down at Ma, and with panic and despair in his eyes, he whispered, "Help."

Ma simply chuckled and winked at the pastor, "Serves you right, there preacher."

Myrtle grabbed the father by his arm and began to drag him from the diner. Ma slapped the preacher on his back to help him along as he failed to resist Myrtle's tugging, and she followed to the diner's doorway and watched as Myrtle dragged him out of the diner and nearly threw the preacher into the passenger side of his own Cadillac. She then hopped into the driver's side and took off back toward the church, spinning the preacher's tires and kicking up dirt and dust as they exited the parking lot. The preacher looked like a prisoner in a jail cell as he stared back at Ma through the window of his own car as it sped away.

Ma was chuckling to herself as she turned back to the diner crowd and noticed that everyone was staring at her. Even Rupert and Jacob, who continued to fan their spouses who had both returned to semi-consciousness, were both looking in the old woman's direction. Ma's smile turned to a scowl as she pointed and waved her stubby finger at everyone in the room again. And, just before disappearing into the kitchen, she exclaimed once more, "Saltpeter and ice water!"

Puut slid over to where Ruby was still seated on the benchtop in her booth, and he sat down beside her, looking up at the redhead with a wide smile still on his face. Ruby glared down at the Frenchman. "Forget it!" She swung her legs over his head to the front of the booth, giving him a teasing peek up her Sunday dress as Red jumped down and walked away to assist Ma in the kitchen. Puut's wide-eyed, straightforward gaze lasted several moments before Mable Johnson finally reached over and slapped the smirk from his face, and Puut got up to return to his own table to wait for his lunch.

*　　*　　*　　*

Exactly sixty-one minutes after arriving back at the church Father Winkin appeared once again at the diner's doorway. He looked exhausted, his thinning hair was messy, and his driving glasses cocked sideways on his face, one lens was cracked. His white collar was hanging off his robe which was now missing both sleeves, having appeared to have been torn clean away from the shoulders, and he was missing one shoe.

Most everyone that had been in the diner previously was still present, only semi-enjoying their lunches that were prepared by Ma. She hadn't had any saltpeter on hand, so she heavily salted everyone's meal and made them drink ice water, which they all required quite a bit of due to the salt that was causing everyone to experience severe dry mouth. The patrons all looked up in astonishment at the disheveled pastor now standing in the doorway. Ma was at the counter bar sprinkling more salt on Bob's apple pie, much to the lawman pleading for her to stop. She put the shaker down and approached the pastor. Wiping her hands on her apron she stopped in front of him and looked the pastor up and down, "What in the hell happened to you?"

The preacher, breathing heavily, opened his mouth to speak while looking straight ahead. Ma's eyes widened as she noticed he was missing one of his front teeth as Percible spoke softly, "I don't know. It's all a bit of a blur." He looked down at Ma, "I suppose in the words of Walter Eugene O'Reilly from the classic television show…I think I've been slaked."

Ma reached up and grabbed the pastor's chin, "Where's your tooth?"

Percible looked down at Ma through his broken glasses, "Does Ms. Watson own any horses?"

"I don't believe so."

"At one point the woman put a leather bridle in my mouth and cracked me with a whip. I don't know where she got either one of them."

Bob slid over to the next barstool when Ma gave him a head-toss and she guided the preacher to where the lawman had been seated, as it's the closest seat to the door. The preacher rested himself with Ma facing him from the service side of the counter bar. Ma filled a clean glass with ice water and handed it to the pastor, "Where's Myrtle at now?"

As the cold water stung the spot where his tooth once was earlier in the day, the pastor replied softly, "She's lounging in a pew smoking a cigarette."

Joshua, who had already turned to the pastor, inquired, "What happened to the movie?" Ma flashed Joshua a look, and he returned one with an expression of question on his face and a slight shake of his head.

Father Winkin reached into his bedraggled robe and pulled out a DVD, handing it to Ma. "Here it is. I don't ever want to see it again." Ma took the disk before Joshua could make a grab for it as the preacher looked over to

Ruby who was now standing near the end of the counter bar. The pastor spoke softly to Red, "You were correct…*Pew-kew*," as he made the explosion motion with his hands and then laid his head down in his hands on top of the bar.

Ma reached over and patted the pastor on his back. "Well there, preacher, I think you've learned something today. I think your habit finally caught up with you. I bet you're not going to show any more movies to the children, or anyone else for that matter, now are you?"

The reverend perked back up, sat straight, and spoke as if nothing had occurred out of the ordinary that day, "Oh no, I have a wonderful documentary to show the children next week." The preacher adjusted his broken glasses and spoke with confidence. "It's an educational piece on the dangers of global warming, I do believe. I chose it due to its title and it was highly recommended by the catalog company when I chose today's movie and placed the phone order."

Ma cocked her head sideways, crinkled her nose, adjusted her reading glasses, and asked in a cautious tone, "What's it called?"

"Behind the green…*umm*…something or rather. Yes, behind the green something!" He said proudly.

Ma closed her eyes and shook her head, "You better give me that movie too there, preacher. And that DVD player too."

CHAPTER 2

Catching Up

So, let's take a quick moment to catch up a bit, shall we? If you're just joining us, then this will bring you up to speed a bit on the tiny town of East Puddleduck, Maine, and its inhabitants. If you're a returning guest, having read *Two Seasons*, this will probably bore the Bejesus out of you.

Since we last found ourselves deep in the northern Maine woods very little has changed. East Puddleduck, just north of the slightly larger township of Skunksquirt, and just south of the Canadian border is still the quiet little town that it was when we last visited. Wilomena Bejesus Miller-Farnsworth, aka 'Ma', the town's 60-ish, pear-shaped matriarch still owns and operates the sole local diner where everyone congregates each morning, noon, and in the evening to grab a home-cooked meal and talk about the town. In other words, gossip. Ma is still as ornery and cantankerous as always. She still dislikes anyone not native of the town and is still considered the village's ringleader even though Rupert Wiggleswort, on paper, remains in charge as the mayor. And don't forget, the short and stout mayor is married to the boisterous Eleanor, who advises her husband on how to govern the town at the monthly meetings held in the tiny and aging municipal building. And Rupert's sister, Myrtle Watson, still organizes the children's church choir and works in the town office as the municipal clerk. That is when she's not watching movies with the pastor, as we just learned.

Ma remains at constant odds with Matilda "Mattie" Doody, and Ma still employs Val Daley in the diner as one of her managers, along with Cicely Smirnoff when she's not managing her little general store along with her husband, Smirnoff...errr...Smirnoff. Still, nobody can pronounce his first name, having been born in a far away foreign country and all. Mattie and Val's other halves, Paul and Jacob, remain as first and second selectpersons and bookends to the mayor, spending most of their days in his office talking about nothing in particular.

Speaking of Cicely and Smirnoff, they've managed to keep their general store in the red and even continue to operate an entire little haberdashery with the quaint little hotel rooms remaining available for rent on the second floor for all the "foreigners" that Ma doesn't want in her town. Ruby 'Red' Mayflower, our well-endowed and older than she'd prefer to be local beautician keeps her hair salon open a few days each week while continuing to assist in the diner on weekends and such. And Puut Voisine, our resident eccentric survivalist who has deep roots in Canada, still fawns over Ruby and continues to annoy Ma with his heavy French dialect.

The pandemic has officially ended. That certainly was a whole to-do, now wasn't it? The residents of the town all survived and after it was declared over and done with the mayor had Constable Bob mothball the box of masks and put them away back in the town office attic. Speaking of Bob Johnson, he's still our one and only locally shared police officer, covering both East Puddleduck and the abutting town of Skunksquirt. Ma still calls his wife, Mable, a "busybody" even though she employs Mable in the diner from time to time when the need arises. Bob continues to enjoy his daily free bowl of chili that he won during the "Bucksnort" competition, and he's still the favorite to win again this year even though most are hoping Ma will forget the idea of bringing that particular challenge back. My guess is that she'll ignore everyone's concerns and continue to hold her ill-fated contest anyway.

Ma's son Runyon has been dating a nice lady that his mother is well aware of, however, he hasn't brought her over for a formal family meeting and Ma's becoming a bit irked over it. You see, Runyon doesn't realize that his mother is aware of the mystery lady and, you know Ma, her patience isn't her best virtue. As we mentioned last time, Runyon's girlfriend isn't from town, and he has no idea how to break this news to his mother. More on this a bit later, as a meeting between Ma and the mysterious girlfriend is certainly imminent.

Ma still calls Father Percible Winkin, our local pastor, a "Bubblehead" and, as you just learned he seems to live up to the nickname. The father still has an issue with watching too many Hollywood movies and quoting many of them during his Sunday services and at other very inappropriate times.

Joshua and Wally McIntyre, the young and not-so-similar twins, continue to be hard at work in their automotive garage and used car emporium. The brothers have recently expanded the business and installed fuel pumps, and a new front-end alignment rack. The boys, along with Ma, the Smirnoff's, and Ruby Red are quite proud of their accomplishments as local business owners. Each keeps the town equipped with the basic necessities and offers plenty of locations for the scandalous chatter to flow freely and travel from place to place.

And, of course, there's still Old Marmaduke. We can't forget the village's voice of reason. He still hasn't cleaned up his yard and his homestead continues to decay daily. The town's wise man who lives on the border of the municipality in his aging log home, and property strewn with junked vehicles and other gas-operated machinery hiding in the tall grass and weeds, is quite content. He continues to eat his meals every day at the diner and attend every town meeting, seated in the back row and speaking only when necessary.

Now, if you recall, Ma had modified the town's "Welcome" sign with the words "Except for Foriners" added in bright neon, and she'd decided to make certain people would see it clearly, even at night, with the use of solar power. Since we last met the town did replace Ma's flashing neon unwelcoming sign that referenced her distaste for anyone not native with a new, less conspicuous hand-carved sign. This was a bit of a comprise between Ma and the town as they didn't want the flashing neon deterring all visitors, and Ma discovered that replacing the solar panel batteries was going to get costly in the long run.

So, we'll keep the update brief because the town and its residents really are just as they were when we last checked on them.

Let's get back to seeing what they're up to...

CHAPTER 3

East Puddleduck Gets the Internet

(Sort of)

"Order, order!" Mayor Wiggleswort declared as he brought the gavel down onto the piece of wood that he had sitting in front of him on the folding table. He'd lowered the gavel down gently as it had recently required gluing back together after a previous incident during the pandemic, and his sentimental instrument of power and authority had required repairs to the handle. As usual, the mayor had selectperson Daley seated to his left and Doody on his right, with Constable Bob in a folding metal chair off to the side of Doody. In the audience, several townsfolk were present for the monthly meeting to include the McIntyre Brothers, Ruby Red, El and Ma, Smirnoff and Cicely, Mattie Daley, Puut, Father Winkin, and Old Marmaduke.

"Good crowd tonight," Rupert declared as he looked over the audience. Ma just rolled her eyes, as this was the mayor's usual introduction as he continued, "First, and only order of business tonight is the internet."

"What internet?" Ruby inquired sarcastically, "We don't have access to the internet here in town. We're too rural, and you're too cheap."

"That's the point," the mayor stated. "We're set to finally have an internet connection all our own right here in East Puddleduck. One more step closer to modernization, and maybe we'll get some accurate, up-to-date news rather than all of that secondhand crap."

The tiny gathering perked up with a bit of excitement and enthusiasm. Everyone except for Ma, of course, who sat up on the edge of her seat. "What good will that do us? What good is the internet anyway? In fact, what the hell is the internet?!"

"Well, it's basically information right there at your fingertips. It would allow us to have more up-to-date communication with the outside world." The mayor attempted to explain, "We'll get the news, we'll have the ability to shop online, and we'll be able to talk to others right over the computer."

Ma lurched forward, rocking on her larger-than-average butt cheeks, and began to stand up as she pointed and barked, "Outside world! *Bah*! What do we need to talk to anyone outside of town?! We got the regular mail for that! You three had better not plan to use that contraption to invite more foreigners into town!" El reached up and patted Ma on the arm and she began to calm herself and started to sit back down.

Smirnoff, who was seated directly behind the angry woman, spoke up in his heavily accented voice, "Hey, Ma, just think we could e-mail family and friends that live far away in other states and for me, in my family's home country. No more waiting for letters in the mail."

Ma wiggled around in her seat, using her butt cheeks again in the assist, "E-what? What in the hell is that?"

Cicely smiled and responded, "E-mail, Ma. It's a form of electronic communication with others. Just like writing a letter to someone but you can read it right away. No waiting, no stamps, just type it on the computer and they see it instantly somewhere else in the world."

Ma squinted and glared at Cicely, not knowing whether to believe what she was hearing or not. Finally, after a brief silence, the grumpy woman pointed and growled, "You're full of crap! And I don't like being made fun of! You're on dish duty all next shift." Ma spun back around on her bum cheeks while Cicely stared confusingly, a surprised expression overtaking her face.

The mayor began again, "It's true, Ma. You can write to people anywhere plus get information on anything you want just like opening up an encyclopedia. All at the tips of your fingers."

Joshua, from across the aisle, turned to the upset diner owner, "You can watch movies and listen to music on the internet too."

"You can look up how to fix and build things." This remark having come from his brother, Wally.

Paul Doody was next, "You can get up-to-date news and weather without waiting, right at the click of a button."

Ma sat back in her chair with her arms crossed, perched on her bosom and she was shaking her head slowly. She then sat up straight and waived her plump pointer finger around the room. "You're all on dope, ain't ya?! You all smoked something funny before the meeting!"

The mayor whined, "No, Ma, it's all true. Everything they're saying. It's an amazing tool and we've waited a long time for this opportunity to have it. Now then…" Rupert picked up his notes from the table and adjusted his reading glasses, "I got this here memo from the telephone company explaining how this works. They call it a dial-up connection. It says here it will come straight through the telephone line. Now, seeing that we don't have a proper phone service and we're still working off the party line, the only direct line that we have runs straight to the town office and into Johnson's emergency phone that sitting on his desk. So, I say we start by putting the internet on his computer first and see how it goes. If it works out, we can expand on it later."

"How much is this going to cost!?" Obviously a question from Ma.

"It isn't going to cost anything," Rupert replied. "Not unless you start going crazy and buying things off the internet and charging it to the town. The telephone company said that municipal internet lines are free. We just need to figure out a schedule of who uses it and when. If it all works out we may even do away with that third-party telephone garbage and get real phone service here in town."

Bob leaned forward and looked to the mayor, whining in his response, "How am I going to get any work done with people coming in and out of my office to use the computer? That office is for official police business only. I got stuff in there that's secret service to the public and things."

The mayor, quite annoyed, looked straight ahead as he addressed the officer, "You're never in your office, Johnson! You're always in that cruiser of yours wasting gas or stuffing your face at Ma's Diner." The mayor turned his head and looked at the lawman, "And no one's going to mess with your gumball machine or jar of licorice sticks!"

Bob sat back, staring at the floor like a child as Ma's complaining continued, "Internet! *Bah*! Where does all that information come from anyway?!"

Wally leaned forward and replied, "It comes from the cloud."

Ma slowly leaned forward, glared back at the McIntyre brother, and groaned as she pointed, "You're asking for it, boy. You're looking to get slapped. And I'll come over there and do it, too."

"No, Ma," Wally whined, "that's what they call it. It ain't anywhere, it's just out there and they call it the cloud." Ma returned his comments by continuing to glare, slowly leaning back while giving Wally the "I'm watching you" sign with her fingers to her eyes and back at him.

Father Winkin, who'd been sitting quietly in the front row up to that point finally spoke up. With his head tilted back he peered down through his driving glasses at the mayor. "I understand there's a great deal of adult material to be found on the internet. Something to be concerned about I would expect, Mister Mayor?"

"And you ought to know all about that, there preacher, now wouldn't you?" Ma leaned forward and slapped the paster on his shoulder. The pastor didn't bother to turn around to acknowledge her observation, however, he did roll his eyes.

Jacob Daley spoke up, simply because he was feeling a bit left out of the conversation having not said anything thus far during the meeting, "We'll just need to be careful. We shouldn't have to worry about that, everyone here is an adult."

"That might just be the problem. And you're assuming a lot when you call everyone here an adult," Old Marmaduke observed from the back row with his arms folded, feet stretched out, and face down buried in his snowy white beard.

"Alright, alright! If there's no more discussion on the matter, then let's vote!" The mayor interrupted, annoyed with where the conversation was heading, "We'll put the internet into Johnson's office and come up with a schedule of who can use it, and when. In addition, everyone will need to be careful! And no buying stuff off the computer and charging it to the town!" The mayor looked around the room, "All in favor?"

Hands went up, even Ma's, but not without further comment. "The preacher here will require supervision during his turn." Ma looked up at the mayor, "And make sure your sister Myrtle ain't with him when he's on it."

Ma's comments brought chuckling from several in the room. Obviously not from the pastor, nor the mayor who scowled, shook his head, and brought the gavel down. However, not so gently this time, and he re-broke it into two pieces again. The mayor disgustingly shook his head and stared at the end he still had in his clutches as the head of the gavel bounced down onto the floor.

*　　*　　*　　*

It was just a few weeks later when Constable Bob and Ma were standing behind the mayor who was seated at Bob's desk in his rolling chair. They were all staring at a blank, blue computer screen with only the word "LOGIN" flashing in white letters at the top.

"What's that mean?" Ma inquired, leaning in, adjusting her glasses, and squinting.

The mayor glanced at his hand-written notes that were meant to explain the process, however, mostly they were just unintelligible scribbling. "We need to type our login and password in here, I think."

"What's a logging password?" Ma asked.

"No, Ma. A *login* and a *password*. Something that tells the computer that it's us and not someone else trying to use it. I set it up so we can remember it easily." The mayor glanced at his notes again, "Our login is 'East' and the password is 'Puddleduck'."

Ma turned her head down and gave the mayor a look. "That's genius. No one would ever figure that one out." Ma turned to the constable on her right, "Don't you know how to run one of these contraptions? It's yours, ain't it?"

"No, Ma, I don't. I always hand-write my police reports. I ain't never used a fancy computer like this. I ain't never even turned this thing on before." Ma shook her head and grimaced in response to the lawman as she looked back at the blank screen and squinted again, crinkling her nose.

The mayor reached over and typed the login and password, and then pushed the 'Enter' key. All three leaned in a bit, stared at the screen, and waited with cautious anticipation. After a moment or two, the computer began to make a noise through its tiny speakers.

"Buzz…buzz…buzz…ka-ding a ding a ding!"

Nothing happened. Ma, looking disgusted at the blank blue screen, looked to the mayor again. "Now what?"

27

"Well, I don't really know. I guess we wait. It must be attempting to dial up." The mayor squinted through his own reading glasses, excitedly waiting for the computer to do something, glancing at his notes and back to the screen again.

"Dial up who?" Ma asked in an annoyed tone, "Who's it trying to call?"

"Buzz…buzz…buzz…ka-ding a ding a ding!" Nothing.

"No one's answering," Ma commented. "Ain't no one home on the other end."

"Give it time!" The mayor barked back.

Ma continued to glare at the screen, "This is stupid!"

"Buzz…buzz…buzz…ka ding a ding a ding!"

As the three continued to watch, the screen began to change slowly from top to bottom from one color blue to another similar color blue.

"Looks like somebody's trying to answer. Still ain't doing much, though," Ma observed.

As the screen scrolled into view, instead of flashing, 'LOGIN', it now displayed the flashing word, 'SEARCH'. Ma grimaced and turned to the mayor again, "Search? Search for what? What's it looking for?"

Bob interrupted, "I think this is where you type in an address."

Ma's head snapped to him, "Who's address!? Not my address! I don't want everyone out there knowing where I live! Nobody said I had to put my address in there! I'm not getting burglarized by some foreigner named Claud over this internet thing by giving them my address! That's just foolishness!"

Bob attempted to explain, "Not Claud, Ma. The cloud. You see…"

The mayor spoke up, interrupting the lawman, "No, Ma. He means an internet address. Anything you want to look up. You can type anything in here and it'll take you to what they call a website, chockablock full of information."

"The mayor's right. You can look up anything and it's supposed to give you what you asked for. You can even look up recipes and such."

"Recipes huh?" Ma commented and looked back at the computer screen. "Okay, type in hotdogs. We're doing fried dogs with all the fixings for lunch at the diner. Let's see this fancy thing try to give me a better recipe than my own!"

Bob reached over to the keyboard and typed in the words, "tasty wieners." He pushed the enter key and the three waited, each staring again and expecting a delicious recipe for hotdogs.

From top to bottom, the computer screen slowly began to reveal the results. "Something's happening," Ma noticed. As the screen scrolled down, the first thing to come into view was the face of an attractive man with a long, black mustache. "Here comes the chef," Ma joked, "let's see what this genius knows about frying hotdogs."

As the screen continued to "reveal" the man, all three in the room reared backward, eyes wide and mouths dropping open. *"Good Lord!"* the mayor gasped.

"How's he gonna cook hotdogs all naked like that?!" Bob inquired, quite surprised with the results of the search.

The mayor continued, "Look at the size of that man's peee..*ahhh*...I mean, his…"

"No way in hell he's barbequing dogs what with that hanging out there." Ma cut the mayor off, speaking quite casually, "He needs one hand just to hold that thing away from the hot grill, maybe both." Ma's demeanor changed and she turned down to the mayor, "What kind of nasty crap is this?! We didn't ask to see a naked person with a huge Johnson!" Bob looked over at Ma, a bit puzzled, and she glared back yelling and pointing at the screen, "Not you, Johnson! His Johnson!"

"Type something else! Type something else!" The mayor screamed in a panicked voice while standing part way up, bending over the desk and striking several computer keys, ultimately hitting the escape key, quickly returning the computer to the blue 'SEARCH' screen.

Bob reached over and desperately typed in the words "pretty balloons" and struck the enter key. He leaned back, looking nervously at the screen as it went blank, searching for Bob's request.

"Pretty balloons?" Ma glanced at the officer and asked in a sarcastic tone.

"It was the most innocent thing I could think of."

"Something's happening," Rupert stated as he sat back in Bob's rolling desk chair, and they all stared at the screen again with Ma and Bob still crowded close to either side of the mayor. Once again, from top to bottom an image began to appear slowly, this time revealing a very attractive blond woman. All three leaned slightly towards the screen and their eyes widened as the mayor whispered, *"Oh, no."* The computer screen continued to reveal a very well-endowed and nude woman posing in front of a pool and palm trees. This time the website was accompanied by sound and animation as playful giggling could be heard, and when the woman finally came into full view she began "bouncing" up and down while holding certain exposed parts of her upper body while licking her lips.

The constable said in a low tone, *"Holy shit,"* as his eyebrows nearly touched the brim of his patrol hat. Ma flashed him a quick look, as she'd never heard the constable swear before.

"Well, one thing's for sure," Ma commented in a fairly monotone voice, "she's got it all over Ruby Red. Plus, she'll never drown in that pool as long as she floats face up." Ma's demeanor soured again, and she slapped the mayor hard on the back of his head. *"Whack!"* She barked, "What did we need this filthy contraption for?! Nobody needs to see this nasty stuff!" Ma glanced over to Bob, who was busy reaching into his uniform shirt pocket for a pen and notepad to write down the website's address. Ma leaned back, reached over, and pointed her chunky finger in his face nearly taking one of his eyes. She growled, "Don't you even think about it!" Bob lowered his pen in response and looked as if he might cry. Ma smacked the mayor for a second time on the back of his head. *"Whack!"* "Get that *shit* off that screen! We don't need to see her naughty parts anymore!"

"Ouch!" the mayor blurted out as he reached for the keyboard and struck the escape key again. "There's got to be other stuff on the internet, Ma. Clean stuff. We just haven't found it yet."

"You just be careful what you type in there next!"

The mayor quickly typed in anything in an effort to change the screen to something innocent, keying in the words, "mother and baby," hoping to see a nurturing website that included a loving mother and child. The three waited nervously for the screen to reveal its next hidden gem. Once again, from top to bottom, the screen slowly began to reveal a man who appeared to be wearing a baby bonnet. *"Oh, crap..."* Rupert voiced beneath his breath as the screen slowly revealed the man entirely, and discovered he was nude other than wearing what appeared to be a large diaper. This website had full video as the grown man, standing in an oversized baby crib, was approached by a statuesque woman clad in a leather thong and high heels. Her breasts were fully exposed and she was holding a baby bottle in one hand, and a riding crop in the other.

Ma's eyes grew as the sound could be heard from the computer's speakers, *"You've been a bad baby, haven't you? Naughty, naughty!"*

The mayor dropped his head face down to Bob's desktop. The lawman himself began to perspire as he stared at the screen. Ma slowly pointed at the computer screen, her finger shaking, "What-in-the-hell is she doing to that grown man that's wearing that diaper?!"

The mayor peered up at the screen, his head still resting on Bob's desktop, and he groaned, "Breastfeeding, I think."

Bob reached over and struck the 'Escape' key. The screen returned to the blue search mode. Ma lowered her head to the mayor's level and growled in a low tone, "Ain't there anything on this damn contraption that isn't dirty? Or are we just going to see naked people doing freaky things all day long?"

Rupert sat back up. "There has to be." As he reached for the keyboard once again Old Marmaduke strolled into the room. The wise man stood behind the three, looking at the blank blue screen, and waited with his hands in his coverall pockets. The mayor typed in the words "town meeting" and he hesitantly, with slightly trembling hands, pressed the enter key.

The screen, from top to bottom, slowly exposed a picture of the outside of what appeared to be a quaint little town hall from a distance. Elevator music played in the background as the video appeared to draw closer to the building. Ma, Bob, and the mayor sighed deeply in relief, looked at each other, and smiled in the accomplishment that they'd finally found something that didn't appear to involve naked people. Old Marmaduke stood and watched from behind as the video drew closer to the front door of the building and sure enough, above the door were the words "Town Hall." The video paused at the doors to the "town hall" and the music lowered, as what appeared to be the sound of many people moaning from inside the building began and quickly grew in volume. The smiles on Ma's, Bob's, and the mayor's faces all turned downwards as Marmaduke cracked a smile from behind. The video proceeded through the doors to a room full of men and women inside the building, all engaged in what appeared to be a group orgy. The camera angles zoomed in close, intimately close, to the writhing bodies and a man's voice overpowered the moaning, "...*Come join our town meeting, the mayor of Humptown is inviting you. Only ninety-nine cents per minute. Click or call now...*"

"*Jeesus Ke-riste!*" Ma yelled out. Bob put his hands over his own eyes as Ma reached out to both Bob and Rupert, trying to put her hands over both their eyes as well. Rupert's eyeballs rolled to the back of his head, he let out a sigh and fainted in Bob's chair, sliding down and under the desk to the floor below.

Old Marmaduke, smiling a wide, toothy grin chuckled from behind the three. "*Heh, heh.* That ain't how our town meeting traditionally gets underway.

Are you gonna add that to the next agenda, Mister Mayor?" Marmaduke stretched his neck out to see Rupert beginning to come back around under the desk.

"That's it! My eyes can't handle any more! I'm gonna have an aneurysm! Turn that shit off! *Turn it off now!*" Ma yelled and threw her arms into the air, "I knew this was a bad idea, but I had no idea!" Bob scrambled to pull the cord from the wall as the mayor raised his head back up over the desktop only to have Ma smack him hard again. *"Whack!"* "This was your idea! And it's the worst one you've ever had so far! No more internet! I forbid it in this town! I mean it!"

Just before Bob yanked the cord from the wall the computer's last words were heard as, *"...the Humptown mayor promises satisfaction...!"* as the screen displayed a close-up of a gentleman's *satisfying* moment.

"Aaaaggghhhh!!" Ma screamed as her hair fell from its bun and into her eyes that nearly popped from her head.

Marmaduke kept chuckling as he strolled casually back out of the office.

*   *   *   *

To this day East Puddleduck has strictly prohibited the internet from crossing into the town's borders, from the "cloud" or anywhere else for that matter. Ma won't even allow the word "internet" to be uttered in her diner or at a town meeting or you just might get whacked in the back of your head for it.

CHAPTER 4

Getting Ma Off the Ground

"Are you insane?!" Ma grumbled as she threw open the screen door to the porch and stomped towards the pickup truck in an effort to head to the diner to prepare for the hungry breakfast crowd. It was a warm July morning and Ma was running late as it was, with Runyon right on her heels.

"It'll be fun, Ma."

"The hell it will!" Ma nearly made it to the driver's side door when she stopped to turn around. "There, now you see?! All your jaw-flapping has made me forget my apron!" Ma stormed back towards the house, recalling having left the terminally food-stained sundress protection in the clothes dryer. She whipped the screen door back open and marched into the living room, stomping towards the laundry room just off the kitchen. As she passed by Elmer, who was busy performing his morning dozing on the couch, she took the opportunity to complain as the screen door's spring whined and the door slammed shut sounding as if her shotgun had been discharged. "Do you know what that boy is trying to get me to do?!"

El opened one eye and watched Ma pass by. "I ain't deaf. I've been hearing the conversation."

She stopped briefly when El decided to speak, "Huh, I guess you are alive. Well then, what do you think of his stupid idea? Me, going flying around up

33

in the air with that old sky jockey! I ain't never flown, don't plan to, and certainly not with that blind old idiot!"

El, determining that Ma wasn't about to leave him alone to relax, sat up on the couch. "Oh, c'mon Ma. Captain Ace ain't that old, and he's been flying for years."

"Ain't that old?! For *Chrissake* that name alone should tell you something! *Captain Ace!* He was old when you and I were young! He's ancient now!" Ma spun around to Runyon, who was just on the other side of the screen door as she walked back up to him and pointed her stubby finger at a hole in the screen near Runyon's face, "And, just pray tell, why'd you promise that old bush pilot that I'd go flying with him anyway?!"

"Because, Ma, he's a nice guy and his flying business hasn't been doing so good lately. I just figured if you went up with him, people would take notice and start trusting him again."

"And that's another thing!" Ma whipped the screen door back open between to two, straining the door's rusty spring once more. "If people don't trust him there's bound to be a good reason! He's getting too old to be flying around up in the air! I don't know how he even sees anything through them thick coke-bottle glasses he wears when he's on the ground! How in the hell does he even see the ground when he's up in the air!?"

"Maybe that's why he flies so close to the ground, Ma, to see it better," El groaned as he lifted himself off the couch and stretched his old bones. Fluffbutt the cat, who'd been laying on the back of the couch decided to stretch out as well, giving a big yawn and jumping down onto the warm spot that El had left to curl back up in. The cat was just ahead of Boris, their hound dog, who'd been at El's feet and hadn't been quick enough to get to the warm spot before the cat did. The old hound laid his jowls down on the cushion beside the cat, who took the opportunity to swat his nose as El continued, "Might be good advertising for the diner, you know."

"I don't need no advertising! Crashing and dying isn't going make my chicken fried steak sell any better!" Ma spun around again to finish what she'd returned to the house for in the first place and marched into the laundry room nearly knocking El back onto the couch as she shuffled past him.

Runyon and Elmer gave each other the "I don't know" shoulder shrug as Runyon came through the screen door and called out to his mother, "Awe, c'mon Ma! He ain't never crashed that you know of." Runyon attempted psychological warfare with his next comment, "Give the guy a chance. He'd do it for you if your business was slowing down and you were hurting."

Ma bent down and pulled her apron from the dryer, letting out a sigh and thinking for a brief moment before whining, "Dammit. Fine, I'll do it." Standing back up straight and turning back towards the living room, she stomped back in and waved her finger between the two. "But if I crash and die, I'm going to haunt the both of you, and I'll be pissed too!"

El let out a chuckle and began to tip backward toward the couch. Fluffbutt noticed and leaped back to the top of the faded cushions just in the nick of time before the old man's rear-end flopped back down into his spot, and El said softly as he dropped back down again and looked up at his son, giving a little wink, "This probably isn't going to end well."

*　　*　　*　　*

The day was clear and sunny as El, Runyon, and Ma pulled into the parking lot of Captain Ace's place of business on the Skunksquirt side of Moosehorn Lake. The lake itself borders both townships with East Puddleduck on the north side and Skunksquirt to the south. Some consider the town lines to go right through the middle of the 13-mile-long body of water. The Captain uses the lake to take off and land from one of his seaplanes, of which he has two Cessna 180, three-passenger single prop flying machines. Both having been built around 1981. As they pulled in underneath an old wooden sign that read "Ace's Scenic Flights" Ma noticed Rupert Wiggleswort standing next to his own vehicle in the parking area.

"What's he doing here?"

Runyon answered as he pulled the truck up next to East Puddleduck's mayor, "I mentioned to him that you'd be here today. He said something about wanting to get some photos of you in the airplane for next year's town report. You know, just in case he needed to dedicate it to you if you don't make it."

Ma, who'd been sitting between El and Runyon on the bench seat, turned to her son and gave him a look while growling, "That ain't funny, boy."

As Runyon shoved the stick of the old Chevy into neutral and pulled the parking brake, which made a loud ripping noise, he exited the driver's side and said under his breath, "I don't think he was kidding."

"What'd you say?!"

"Nuthin."

"Morning Ma!" The mayor greeted the less-than-happy diner owner, "Good day for flying, isn't it!"

"Shut up, asshole!" Ma pushed a whining Elmer out and jumped down from his side of the pickup truck. She was dressed in her usual floral-pattern sundress and swampers, nothing overly fancy. She'd put two hairpins in her bun to keep it tight in the wind. Ma walked straight up to the mayor and stuck her nose close to his face, "Are you going up there with me to get some good photos today?! *Hmmmm?* Said it yourself, didn't you? Good day for flying, isn't it?"

The mayor pulled his head back away from the woman and answered a bit hesitantly, "Well, no. I, *uhhh*…I thought I'd stay down here on the ground and take some action shots of you going past in the plane."

"I thought so!"

Captain Ace came walking out of a small hanger that had been built close to the lakefront near where his two Cessnas were parked in the water, each tied off to the separate ends of a long wooden dock. The Captain, a fairly small, thin old man, appearing to be at the youngest around 80 years old. He was dressed in brown coveralls that were too large for him, and untied brown work boots. He stood just under Ma's height and on his head he was wearing a leather aviator helmet that Ma recognized as one similar to what she'd worn during the three-wheeler incident. On his face, the Captain had a pair of thick bifocals and when he walked up to Ma he looked up at her through the glasses, and Ma saw a total of four eyes reflecting in the thick lenses and she wasn't certain any of them were looking straight back at her.

The Captain inquired, motioning towards Runyon, "Good morning, sir. Is it your wife that will be flying with me today?"

Ma turned slowly to Runyon and said in a monotone voice, "You've got to be kidding me." Runyon raised his eyebrows and flashed his mother the "I don't know" look.

The mayor intervened and placed his hands on the pilot's shoulders to formally introduce the two. "Captain Ace, this here is Ma Farnsworth-Miller. She'll be flying with you today."

The Captain responded by offering his hand to shake, extending it into the empty air between Ma and Elmer. The mayor's eyes widened as Ma turned to Runyon again, "I ain't going."

Rupert quickly attempted to change the subject, placing his arm fully around the Captain's shoulders and turning him towards the lake, "So there, Captain, which of those fine-looking aircraft are you taking Ma up in today?" The small group began to admire the two seaplanes at the lake's edge. Everyone, except for Ma, who turned to leave as El and Runyon stopped her and held tight to her shoulders to hold her in place.

Captain Ace peered in the general direction of his two seaplanes, and he spoke quite nonchalantly as he responded, removing a rusty wrench from his coverall pockets and using it to point in a general direction between the two flying machines. "Oh, those. Yes, well, we won't be taking either of those up today. Seems the one on the right wouldn't start yesterday and I spent the better portion of the day tuning up the engine with parts from the one on the left. Now, neither one will start for some strange reason that I can't figure out. No, we'll be taking 'old reliable' up today." The pilot turned and motioned to the hanger whose doors were closed, seemingly hiding behind them the airplane he was referring to.

"What do you mean, old? And how reliable are we talking?" Ma inquired with more than a bit of concern in her voice.

The five, led by the Captain, wandered towards the hanger. "Well, she hasn't been up in a while, but she flew just fine the last time she was." The Captain stepped just inside the hanger's walk-in door to activate a tall automatic door, and it began to lift. The pilot stepped back out, "And the good thing is that the fuel has a five-year freshness longevity guarantee so the carbs should be pretty clean, I think. Now, let me see…" The Captain scratched his chin with the wrench as the door stopped and jammed after raising only about a foot, just enough to be above the tall grass that had grown up in front of it over time. "It might be eight or nine years since she's been up. I suppose the gas could be a bit thick." He looked up at the mayor and waived his wrench, "Might need a bit of stabilizer in the tank first, that ought to do it. That's assuming I remembered to fill it when I put her away, of course."

Ma gave El a gaze, and he returned the look by shrugging his shoulders as the Captain gave the hanger's door a good swift kick with his work boot, and it began to rise again. The aircraft that the door had been hiding was a flying machine that looked as if it was placed in the hangar just after World War I and hadn't been moved since. The biplane had a single engine and propeller in front, two wings, one above the fuselage and one below, seemingly held apart by toothpicks, and had two open seats, one under the top wing and one directly behind it. The color appeared to be brown, however, the four spectators all gazing with their mouths open wide believed the colorization may be more from rust and age rather than actual paint.

"She's a 1932 Waco," the Captain stated proudly, a big smile on the old man's face. "She's a beaut, ain't she?"

Ma spoke first, "Looks like something the Red Baron flew when Snoopy was chasing him. And I'd put more trust in the doghouse that Snoopy was flying."

The Captain continued, seemingly ignoring, or simply not hearing Ma's remarks. "She's got 125 horsepower in the engine and holds 60 gallons of fuel, and she goes about 114 miles per hour at maximum speed. They were used mostly as training planes, and she's got controls in both cockpits."

"Well, that's good, in case you die up there and I have to land it," Ma commented sarcastically in a low tone before turning to Runyon. "There's no way in hell I'm going anywhere in that."

"Oh, c'mon, Ma. I'm sure it's safe. They probably made thousands of these back in the day."

"They discontinued this model in 1933." The Captain continued, "I'm pretty sure this one has its original engine if I remember correctly. Although, with that slight mishap in '62 near Mount Katahdin I'm not quite certain. We may have changed it out with another used one." The Captain lowered his head and scratched the top of his noggin with his wrench, "Who knew that mountain would end up being so tall?" Captain Ace looked back up, "Too bad for the guy that was flying with me. He forgot that he didn't have a parachute on." The Captain looked up at his treasure, "You can't wear any in this plane, the seat compartments are too small."

"That's it, I'm done!" As Ma again attempted to turn to run away and the three others, the mayor included, grabbed onto her and pulled her back again.

"Now, now, Ma." The mayor attempted to reassure her, "You'll be just fine. The Captain here has many years of experience."

"Sure, Ma." El wasn't sounding any more confident as he patted Ma on the back with one hand, holding her tight onto her arm with the other. "Just think, the Captain here has been taking people up on scenic flights for years. You probably couldn't get someone with more experience than him."

Ma, shaking herself free from the three, pointed her stubby finger at the old pilot, "Just where did you learn to fly anyway?!"

"Stunt flying!" The Captain blurted out, quite proudly. "Daddy was a stunt pilot in the circus and taught me when I was just a youngster. He flew an old 1918 Sopwith Dolphin…"

Ma cut the old man off, "And just which one was your father, Wilbur or Orville?!" El slapped her on her shoulder in response to the sarcasm. Ma returned the gesture with a scowl.

"Later on, I was hired to do some crop dusting for a guy who owned quite a bit of farmland in New Hampshire. I did that for several years until the day I got fired. I suppose on that day I was flying a bit too low…" The Captain pointed his wrench at El, "…And how was I supposed to know the old farmer would be screwing his neighbor's wife in the cornfield on that particular day?! *Heh, heh…*" He chuckled and looked back to the ground, "…I put a skid mark right across the farmer's rear-end and up his backside with my Thrush Commander in 1956." The old pilot lifted his head back up, "I guess it was pretty much soon after that I started my business right here. Just after the insurance company settled and the trial was over…"

"Well! Time's a wasting!" The mayor interrupted and blurted out, "Let's get you up in the sky, Ma!"

*   *   *   *

Ma was in the rear seat with her head sticking out above the tiny cockpit. She had an old leather aviator helmet on her head and thick, foggy goggles, a look she'd been seen in before. She had to remove her two hairpins and now had them sticking out underneath the leather helmet on both sides of her head which caused her to resemble a sad-looking Martian. At least this time there'd almost be no chance that a skunk would be spraying her, she thought to herself as she looked at the controls in front of her. In the tiny compartment area there were no gauges, just a long stick between her legs and a couple of levers and knobs in front of her and nearer the floorboard. In the seat ahead of her was Captain Ace, wearing his similar headgear. Ma stretched out her neck and looked around the old pilot to see that he had no more instruments on his side than what was in hers.

"How do you know how high up you're flying when you're in the air?!" Ma yelled, even though the engine hadn't been started yet.

"I look down!"

Ma sat back and whispered to herself, *"Oh, shit."*

39

"Okay!" The old man yelled to Runyon, who was standing in front of the aircraft, "When I say go, you give that there propeller a good turn!" Runyon reached up to the old, wooden prop and nodded. Captain Ace began cranking hard on the old, rusty levers and his body flopped in the seat as he tugged and pulled on the few controls he had in his cockpit.

"Holy crap! What are you doing up there, having a stroke?!" Ma yelled out.

"Okay! Give 'er a hard crank!" The Captain shouted and Runyon pulled the propeller down hard and fast, and it went around once under its own power. As it did so the engine blew fire and sparks which caused a sound similar to a cannon going off. Thick, black smoke poured from the engine compartment and surrounded the two seated in the plane and filled the hanger. Ma began coughing as it wafted out into the air from the hangar doors and the old man called back to her, "Points should be good and cleaned out now!"

"Terrific." Ma was hacking as the old man yelled out to Runyon to crank on the propeller again. Runyon did as he was told and the engine let out another loud boom, smoked even harder and the engine began to turn over as the propeller started to spin on its own. The airplane shook violently before the Captain gave it a bit of throttle and it slowly began to ease its way out of the hanger. As it passed through the door Ma spied El through the thick smoke off to one side, smiling and giving the "thumbs up" to her. On the opposite side, she saw the mayor snapping photos with a big smile on his face from behind the camera.

"She's a bit sluggish!" The Captain yelled out, "We're gonna need a bit more runway than usual to get her off the ground!"

"Runway? What runway?!" Ma screamed back at him.

The Captain turned his head to respond and pointed out in front of the plane. "That there field over there will work just fine."

Ma looked out ahead, stretching her neck out and squinting. She saw only trees and a house. "There ain't no field out there, you idiot!"

As the plane fully exited the hanger, the Captain turned the aircraft away from the lake. El, Runyon, and the mayor assembled behind as the aircraft pulled away and the smoke began to clear around them. The mayor asked the obvious question, "Where do you figure he's planning on taking off from?"

"I dunno," El responded. "I guess he's planning on using the main road over there.

All three traded dubious looks with one another as Runyon inquired of the other two, "Is that legal?"

Captain Ace turned out of the parking area onto the main road, barely making it through the signposts as he exited his place of business and pointed the aircraft straight down the middle of the main street. Ma's eyes were bulging as she heard the old man say, "Waco one to tower, requesting permission to take off."

"Tower?! What tower?! What the hell are you doing?! Who are you talking to?!"

The pilot turned his head, "Calling the tower to make certain the skies are clear for us to take off, of course."

"You don't have a radio, you whackjob! And there's no airport to talk to!"

"Well, certainly we have a radio! Ten-four tower, thank you!" The Captain increased the throttle and the engine roared as they moved faster straight down Main Street in the Town of Skunksquirt, Maine.

"Holy shit!" Ma screamed out as they picked up speed, causing several oncoming vehicles to quickly move out of their way, as horns honked, and drivers shook their fists out car windows and swore loudly at the two. One elderly lady looked up, as she was traveling the roadway in the same direction as the airplane passed by her, its lower wing barely clearing the top of her car. As she stared up in astonishment, Ma looked down at her with fear on her face and mouthing the words, *"Help me."* Still staring straight at Ma, the elderly driver veered to the right and struck a fire hydrant, breaking it from its base and sending water shooting into the air as if she were taking part in an animated cartoon.

The Captain nearly achieved full throttle as the airplane finally lifted from the road slightly, causing the plane's wheels to rise only about two feet from the ground, technically making the airplane airborne. "We'll be flying today at an altitude of about 9,000 feet!" The Ace called out quite casually as the aircraft lifted to a total of just five feet above the roadway. Oncoming vehicles continued to swerve as the airplane barely flew just above their tops. The pilot "flew" along the main road and turned left and right with it as the road followed the outskirts of Moosehorn Lake. "We're currently flying at an altitude of 6,000 feet and a cruising speed of 114 miles per hour!" The Captain called out, smiling, and enjoying what he believed to be the open skies.

"Hey, Dumbass! You're only five feet off the ground and going about twenty-five miles an hour! You just clipped a Buick and nearly hit a guy walking his dog!" Ma screamed.

The small aircraft bounced back down to the roadway. "Looks like we're in for a bit of turbulence, please keep your seatbelts on and the bathrooms will be closed for a bit!"

"Bathrooms?! What bathrooms?! Believe me, old man, I'm about to soil myself right here! What friggin' seatbelts?!" Ma pointed her finger at the back of the pilot's head, "You're going to end up hitting a deer if you don't get this thing up in the air!"

Captain Ace pulled back on the throttle and briefly lifted the airplane off the ground again, passing over another vehicle that was traveling in the same direction. "In just a moment we'll be above these clouds!"

"Clouds?! Those aren't clouds! That's the smoke from your own engine and a white Volkswagen Beetle you just bounced off the top of!" Ma seriously considered to herself that if the old bush pilot were to slow down again and touch the ground, she was going to simply jump out and hope for the best. And, just as she had this thought, Captain Ace lifted the plane up away from the road further, seemingly ruining her plan.

"If you look down you'll see that Moosehorn Lake got its name due to it being shaped like a moose's head!"

"If I look down all I can see, *quite clearly I might add*, is all of the *goddam* potholes on Main Street! And I'd appreciate it if you didn't hit any of them, you crazy, old goat!" Ma turned around when she thought she heard the wailing of a siren and she peered behind the airplane. For once she was relieved to see Constable Bob's cruiser, with its bubble flashing blue lights and siren screaming, following close behind.

Bob's eyes were wide as he leaned forward against his steering wheel and gazed out at the airplane he was chasing. He squinted and spied a fat woman's face looking back at him. "Holy cat crap, it's Ma! Hold on, Ma! I'll save you!" The police officer yelled out as if anyone could hear him. Bob grabbed his microphone and keyed it, "Puddlesquirt One to dispatch! I'm on Route 15 south on the west side! I'm chasing an airplane down the main road that's refusing to pull over! I need immediate assistance!"

"That shit ain't funny, Johnson," came the static response from the county dispatcher over the two-way radio. *"You've been smoking your own evidence this afternoon, haven't you?"*

*　　*　　*　　*

"I wonder how long they'll be?" Elmer inquired.

"I don't see them anywhere," Rupert observed as he used his hand to shade the sunlight, turning around in a circle as he looked up at the sky.

"I didn't see the plane get off the ground before they rounded the bend by the hardware store," Runyon noted.

El spoke again as he too gazed upwards and shielded the sunlight, "Well, they must have. You can't drive a plane down the main road, there's too much traffic. It shouldn't be long before they make a pass by us. Just keep looking up."

*　　*　　*　　*

"I'm telling you jerks, I'm chasing an airplane!" Bob yelled into the microphone, "I'm on Route 15 heading southeast out of town around the lake! I need help!"

"Uh-huh. Shift commander says he's going to take your radio away if you keep it up. Call us back when you catch it, and we'll send out the Air Force. In the meantime, we'll call one of them folks that chases UFOs for you for some advice."

Bob threw the microphone into the dashboard. *"Goddam it!"* He then reached down and turned the switch on his radio over to the public address system, activating the cruiser's external speakers, and he fumbled for the microphone again. He nearly drove off the road as he reached down and scooped the mike back up and he yelled into it and his voice amplified over the external speakers, *"Pull over, this the police! I command you to pull that aircraft over!"*

"Ten-four, tower. I'll lower my cruising altitude to 8,000 feet," Captain Ace called out.

"That ain't the tower, you moron! You're being chased by the cops! Pull this airplane over!" Ma screamed, desperately wanting to backhand the pilot however knowing better as he was the only one "in control" of the aircraft, and she didn't know how to drive an airplane down the open road, or at all for that matter. "You're going to kill us both! Pull over and take your traffic ticket!"

The Captain continued at around 45 miles per hour and his two front wheels were now fully on the ground again, with the tail end being the only part of the aircraft in the air. As the airplane rounded the next bend and continued to follow the roadway, a straight stretch of highway revealed a large semi tractor-trailer truck coming towards them about a quarter of a mile away. Ma pointed past Ace's shoulder, *"Truck!"*

The pilot squinted through his thick glasses and goggles. "Oh damn, another airplane in our path!" Ace pulled back hard on his stick and throttled up, at the same time attempting to hand crank the flaps. "My flaps are stuck!" He turned towards Ma, "Crank the flaps from your side!" He turned back forward, "Why didn't to tower tell us there was another plane in our airspace?! Pull the flaps!"

"Do what?!" Ma was in a panic, looking around her seat.

"Flaps, flaps! We need flaps!"

Ma reached both of her hands out the sides of her cockpit and extended her arms, flapping them up and down like a bird and bouncing in her seat, attempting to help the airplane gain altitude. "I'm flapping, I'm flapping!"

Bob's steering wheel was imprinting on his gut as he leaned forward again and lowered his eyebrows in confusion, watching as two fat arms flapped up and down out of the sides of the airplane. He then looked ahead and saw the oncoming semi-trailer, *"Oh, crap!"*

Captain Ace pulled back hard on the stick and gave it full throttle as the front wheels of the aircraft came off the ground again. He turned hard to the left and just as the truck passed by, he lifted the plane and turned the flying machine just enough to avoid a collision, putting the aircraft on a path out over the lake. *"Aaaahhhhhheeee!"* Ma's scream could be heard over the deep air horn of the truck that had locked up its brakes and was beginning to jackknife sideways on the narrow roadway. The rear wheel of the biplane struck the whip antenna on the truck's cab as the two passed each other. Both the semi-truck and Bob's cruiser came to a screeching halt sideways in the middle of the road, one pointing to the lake and the other in the opposite direction towards a hillside. The engine of the airplane echoed off the semi-trailer as it turned and flew out over the water.

* * * *

"Do you think they're lost?" Runyon asked as the three continued to look upwards towards the sparse clouds in the clear blue sky.

The mayor was using his camera's telephoto lens to search for the airplane. "No, I think he's just giving Ma a nice, long scenic tour."

"Is that them?" El pointed up.

The mayor shifted his lens to search where El had indicated, and he adjusted the focus, "Nope, that's an eagle."

*   *   *   *

"Up higher! *Get up higher!*" Ma screamed in a high-pitched tone as the old Waco aircraft hovered around six feet above the lake's surface. "You're making waves and scaring the passengers!"

"The pilot has shut off the no smoking sign! And the turbulence has calmed a bit!" Captain Ace called out casually, "We've now reached our cruising altitude of 9,000 feet!"

"The hell you have! Any lower and I'm gonna need a snorkel! Put me on dry ground, you dipstick!"

"In the event of a water landing, your seat cushion can be used as a floatation device!"

Ma looked down in a panic. "I'm sitting on a metal bicycle seat, you blockhead! How is that gonna keep a fat old woman afloat?!"

*   *   *   *

"I hear something," Runyon mentioned as the three men continued to search the skies.

Elmer pointed down the lake, "There, I think that's them over there." Rupert and Runyon turned and squinted. Off in the distance, they spied the tiny aircraft coming towards them. "Looks like he's flying awfully low, doesn't it?"

"Well, he was a crop duster, they tend to keep the planes low to the ground," the mayor responded as he raised his camera to focus on the incoming aircraft.

"That still looks pretty low. He's going to scare the Bejesus out of her middle name doing things like that."

"I'm sure she's having a good time," the mayor offered as he adjusted his focus and snapped a photo.

*   *   *   *

"Get this *goddam* antique flying machine up higher in the air before a fish jumps in here!" Ma was looking out and down as the front wheels of the aircraft skimmed the top of the water. She began bouncing and flapping her arms again, still not realizing that wasn't how it worked. However, she was desperate. "Get up higher! This ain't a submarine!"

"We need to stay low to avoid their radar!" Captain Ace called back to Ma.

"Radar?! Who's radar?! What radar?!"

"The Germans, of course! We're nearing Berlin and we don't want them to see us before we drop our bombs!"

"Berlin?! *Germany?!* Berlin, my *asshole,* you asshole!"

"Good idea, you sing out the German national anthem nice and loud and they'll think we're one of them as we approach! We'll have the element of surprise to our advantage!"

"We're not over Germany, you lunatic!" Ma screamed.

"Sig heil, Red Baron!"

"Oh, God, we're gonna die," Ma whined to herself as the Captain buzzed a pair of kayakers, flying only inches above their heads. The draft from the aircraft flipped both kayaks over and tossed their occupants into the lake. *"Sorrrry!"* Ma yelled out as she looked back at the two angry kayakers, both bobbing in the water and waiving their fists.

As they drew nearer the Captain's place of business, the old barnstormer lifted the plane to about 20 feet off the water's surface. Ma breathed a small sigh of relief in thinking that the Captain wasn't going to try for a water landing, seeing that this wasn't a seaplane. That is, until the Captain called out again, "As we approach the gate, please keep your seatbelt fastened until the airplane comes to a complete stop!"

This time Ma smacked the Captain on the back of his head. *"Thwack!"* "Oh, no you don't! You can't land this on the water, you old fool! There are no pontoons on this thing!"

"We won't be pulling up to the gate today, the tower says they're all full! Please wait for the portable stairs before disembarking the aircraft!" As the Captain made the announcement, he began to tilt the aircraft to one side.

Ma screeched as she grabbed onto the sides of her cockpit in an attempt to hang on, "No! Don't you dare! Do not turn this airplane over, you chowderhead!"

*　　*　　*　　*

"What's he doing with the plane?" Runyon inquired of the other two. The three were now making their way down onto the dock and watching as the antique aircraft was approaching, and apparently turning over in mid-air.

"Looks like he's doing some of that stunt flying," the mayor answered as he clicked his camera, obtaining the action shot he'd been seeking.

"Ma's gonna be awfully mad if he turns that thing over upside down," El remarked. "She's gonna be in a bad mood all the way home after this."

"What else would be new?" *"Click, click."*

*　　*　　*　　*

"Turn it back over! Turn it back over!" Ma screeched as the airplane continued along the lake completely upside down and only about 8 feet above the surface of the water. The old woman simply couldn't hold herself in place any longer, and just as the Captain began to pull the nose of the plane upwards, or rather downwards up towards the sky, Ma was ejected out over the lake.

"Please watch your step as you exit the aircraft!" The Captain called out as he gained a bit of altitude and eventually began to turn the plane back upright.

"Holeeeey shiiiiiiit!" Ma screamed as she hit the lake's surface and skimmed like a flat rock skipping across the top of the water, tumbling ass-over-teakettle in a general direction towards the dock, continuing to scream loudly all the way, *"Sonovabitchhhh! Goddammmit!"*

"I don't think that's how you're supposed to exit the plane," Runyon observed, and the three men watched as Ma tumbled towards them, her well-fed, flopping body surfing across the surface of the lake.

47

The mayor continued to snap his photos and chuckled, "*Heh, heh.* These are gonna be priceless!"

"You probably ought not to put those in the town report if you know what's good for you," El strongly suggested to the mayor, who stopped photographing and frowned in disappointment.

Ma finally slowed, stopped tumbling, and sank just before reaching the dock on the lake's edge up against a big old log that was half submerged at the shoreline. She flopped her arms over the log and rested her head down on it, spitting out a stream of water and gazing at the bushes lining the water's edge. Sitting in front of her, staring back from a piece of driftwood just a foot away was a skunk, its nose twitching in her direction. Ma, not moving her head, looked over at the creature through her water-filled goggles and she let out a heavy sigh. "Please, don't. I've had a rough afternoon." The tiny creature, seeming to understand, nodded in Ma's direction while still twitching its nose and standing on its hind legs. It then turned around and did what skunks do straight into Ma's face.

"Sonovabitch."

All three men winced from their vantage point on the dock just a few feet from Ma. Elmer remarked to the other two, "It must be something about the helmet and goggles they don't like."

*　　*　　*　　*

Twenty minutes later Captain Ace landed in the parking lot of the Walmart in Saint Blasphemy. Jumping down from his airplane in front of several state and local police officers, he proceeded to surrender to the "Germans." As he was being arrested the Captain demanded to be taken to the nearest American embassy, and he continually referred to the law officers as "Heiny Krauts" and would only divulge to them that his code name was "Snoopy."

And the county dispatch center owed Constable Bob an apology.

CHAPTER 5

It's Fair Time Again

"Hey, Ma, did you hear who's playing at the fairgrounds this year?" Runyon was standing in the kitchen of the main house, leaning up against the cast iron sink and nibbling on an apple. Ma was seated at the kitchen table, folding clean kitchen towels to take back to the diner before the lunch hour chores were to begin.

"Someone's playing at the fair? Nope, didn't hear anything." Ma didn't bother to look up as she kept folding, looking down at her towels through the reading glasses perched on the bridge of her crinkled nose, making certain the laundry bleach had removed most of the stains.

El's voice echoed from the next room where he was lounging, "That stage is kinda small, be better if someone played across from the diner!"

Still not bothering to look up, Ma barked, "Stop eavesdropping on other people's conversations! That stage doesn't need to be near the diner anymore to begin with! Nobody famous is ever going to play on it and we don't need any *foreigners* coming to town! They can keep them all at the fairgrounds next door, and out of East Puddleduck!"

Runyon interrupted the brewing argument, "Speaking of the fair, Ma, you ain't planning on ruining the animal contest again this year, are you?"

"I'll ruin anything that I want to!" Ma finally looked up, scowling, "The whole thing's rigged against me, it always was! And I ain't entering no stupid animal contest this year anyway! I never win, so I'm not doing it!" Ma calmed herself a bit, "This year I'm going to do something else."

"You ain't gonna put on a ski mask and rob yourself a ribbon, are you?" El called out from his comfy spot.

"Shut up! No! I'm entering the dessert-making contest! I don't know why I didn't think of this before. I make food for a living! There's no way that I won't win that one easily with something tasty!"

Runyon perked up, "That's actually a good idea, Ma. You're a sure win if you make some sweet apple pie or something."

"Of course, I'll win!" Ma finally looked up and pointed at Runyon, "Plus, I'm making sure of it!"

Runyon's demeanor soured, "Oh, no. What are you planning to do? You aren't going to kill the other contestants, are you?"

"No! Of course not! That ain't legal!" Ma leaned over from the table and swung open a cupboard door, reaching in and removing a small plastic case. She rocked herself to her feet, opened the case, and displayed the contents to her son. Inside was a medicine syringe large enough to vaccinate an elephant.

Runyon's eyes opened wide, "What are you gonna do with that!? You aren't going to drug the other contestants, are you, Ma?!"

"No, you fool! You know, you really are dumber than you look, aren't you?" Ma snapped the plastic case shut. "I happen to know that everyone's entry is kept in a kitchenette just behind the 4-H tables under the grandstands. Just before they start judging, they're all placed out pretty on them folding tables by those young volunteers. I plan to load up this here needle with hot sauce and inject it into everyone else's sweets so there's no way they won't pick mine as the best tasting one once everyone else's have been poisoned!"

Elmer appeared at the kitchen doorway, "That isn't very fair, Ma."

Ma snapped her head around, nearly shooting her hairpin from her bun. *'Fair!?* Do you think it was fair for them to do what they did to me last Christmas?! I was holding a nice holiday competition in my own diner when everyone spiked all my entries with booze and knocked me for a loop! I hope you two both remember all that because I sure don't!"

Elmer looked to the floor, scratched the back of his head, shook it slowly, and turned back into the living room. Runyon simply shrugged his shoulders and took another bite of his apple. A moment later he glanced out the kitchen window when he saw a pickup truck pull into the yard, and he tossed the apple core into the wastebasket. "Hey, Ma."

Ma snapped back around, "What?!"

"I got someone I want you to meet."

Ma stretched her neck out to see through the kitchen window and she spied a pleasant-looking lady whom she didn't recognize exiting the mystery truck. The younger woman was dressed in a pair of jeans and a pullover knit poncho over a sweatshirt with sleeves that extended past her hands. She had long, brown hair and was attractive in a normal kind of way, from what Ma could tell. She bounced down and out of the truck and skipped towards the front door, and before she could knock, Runyon called out, "Come on in!"

Ma squinted as the smiling visitor entered the kitchen and snuggled up to Runyon as he put his arm around her shoulders. "Ma, I'd like you to meet Priscilla," he said proudly, with just a hint of nervousness in his voice. "We've been seeing each other for a bit of time now."

Ma adjusted her glasses, squinted, and looked the young lady up and down. "Have you now," she said in a low voice.

Elmer appeared at the door again, back to Ma, and gave Runyon a look of caution. He motioned his head to Ma, silently preparing Runyon and his guest for the worst which might be yet to come he thought.

Ma took a step forward, stood straight, and faced the two. She first scowled at her son and then eased her expression just a bit as she looked the young lady up and down, holding her glasses as she did so. Runyon spoke hesitantly, "She prefers to go by Cilla."

"Nice to meet you…"

Ma whipped up her hand to cut the woman's words off as she began to walk around her, forcing herself between the young lady and Runyon. Priscilla's head turned as Ma walked to her rear and looked up and down again, "*Mmmm, hmmmm.*" The plainly attractive lady looked to be about Runyon's age in her 30s, naturally built, not too large or too skinny, Ma thought to herself. She continued her inspection of the girlfriend she'd suspected Runyon had been seeing for some time now. She came back around to Cilla's front and stopped. "*Mmmm, hmmmm.* I suppose you're the one from Skunksquirt?"

"Yes, Ma, she is…"

Ma held up her hand again, this time to Runyon, who appeared a bit surprised that his mother had apparently been aware of his girlfriend and where she lived. "I'm sure the young lady can speak for herself!"

"Yes, ma'am, I am."

"Dressed smartly. And wearing flat shoes, I see. That's a good sign." Ma said calmly with just a slight hint of sarcasm in her voice, "Do you work?"

"Yes, at the Maple Sugar Shack in Saint Sagacious."

"Ah, yes. I know the place well." Ma's demeanor was eerily calm. "Where are you from originally, my dear?"

"Skunksquirt. My family's native to the area."

"Are you Divorced?" Ma began to shoot off questions, still looking the young lady up and down.

"Never married." Priscilla kept up and fired every answer straight back.

"Kids?"

"No."

"Do drugs?"

"No."

"Parents?"

"One of each."

Alive or dead?"

"One of each, mother's alive."

"Live with her?"

"No."

"Been arrested?"

"No."

"Owe money to anyone?"

"No."

"Looking for money?"

"No. I do for myself."

"Fixed or fertile?"

"Fertile."

"Go both ways?"

"Ma!" Elmer warned, not having the ability to remain quiet any longer. The old woman turned to scowl at the old man. "We'll, Runyon deserves to know these things!"

"He probably knows already! The boy ain't stupid!"

Ma turned back and invaded Priscilla's personal space, looking up at her as she was a bit tall, like Runyon, standing about five-foot-eight to Ma's five-foot-nothing. Ma went quiet, staring straight at the younger woman. Priscilla stared straight down and back at her, straight-faced, and cocked one eyebrow. Ma did the same. Finally, Ma pointed her stubby finger up at the lady and blurted out, "I don't want kids running around here. No kids! They get underfoot, and you have to feed them three times a day. I ain't no substitute mother! I'm too busy!" As the old woman spun around to walk out of the kitchen, the young ladies' eyebrows raised.

Runyon leaned over to his girlfriend, who now had a look of confusion and amusement on her face, and he whispered, "I think she likes you."

El, casually stroking his long, red beard, chuckled and nodded, and then winked at the two younger adults.

Cilla let out a smile, reached out her neck, and called out, "I don't want them anyway, either!"

Runyon put his arm back around his girlfriend. He then recalled the conversation he'd started earlier and said to Cilla, "Wait here," as he started towards the living room. "Ma, I was telling you before, haven't you heard who's coming to the fair this year? It's that band you like, *38 Special!*"

Ma stopped mid-family room and turned around, pointing, "Do you have Rupert syndrome or something?! We don't get big names like that at the fairgrounds!"

"No, Ma, it's true. They do the smaller fairs sometimes. They did Blue Hill a couple of years ago. They're really coming up this way."

"38 Special?! *The* 38 Special?! The band with the brother of that guy from *Lynyrd Skynyrd?* The biggest southern rock band of the 1980s?! That 38 Special?!"

"Yes, Ma."

Ma stood silent a moment, still pointing up at Runyon and staring, one eye wide and the other half-closed. Finally, she blurted out before turning away, "You're full of manure!"

El spoke up, "Well, now, wouldn't that be something? It'd be a lot of fun to hear them in person and live. You know, Ma, they got that song that you like. You know, that one that he sings in memory to his brother."

Ma plopped her butt down on *her* recliner in the sitting room, groaning a bit, "Yeah, I know, *Rebel to Rebel.* I've nearly worn out the VHS tape that we have of their '99 Sturgis concert." Ma pointed at the aging video cassette player on the television stand beneath the Zenith. "That Donny Van Zant gives a good speech before he sings it. That's a nice song about his brother's memory. And it's a toe-tapper. All their songs are good." Ma looked up at Runyon, "You know, I was about your girlfriend's age when they were at their peak." Ma was beginning to reminisce, and her mood seemed to be improving.

El, still in the doorway, gave another wink to Cilla who'd been waiting patiently in the kitchen, motioning for her to come into the living room. Cilla smiled and walked past El, patting him on the shoulder as she went by and she took the opportunity to chime in, "I like that band. Maybe we can all go see them together!"

"Wouldn't that be something, Ma?" Runyon offered. "We plan to catch the show Saturday night, and you'll be there tending to the food shack anyway."

"Well…" Ma looked up to the ceiling after she pulled on the old recliner's lever, her feet flipping upwards and she bounced back in the antique lounger, launching Fluffbutt off the top where the cat had been laying and causing an indentation in the fake leather cushions. The cat obviously wasn't pleased. "It might be fun to see them in person. I like that Donnie Van Zant, he's a short, cunning little thing with a lot of energy when he bounces around on that there stage. I like that black hat he wears. It's not quite a cowboy hat."

"It's called a 'High Roller', Ma," Elmer observed as he eased back down onto his couch beside Boris, whose jowls were drooping over the edge of the cushions. "Just think, you'd be right there up front seeing him in person. Probably be the best time you've ever had at the fair."

Ma's demeanor turned a bit somber as she sat back up in her squeaky captain's chair and pointed at El. "You know, that's a strange thing that happened with his brother. Singing about a bird and asking if he were to leave, like dying or something, if would anyone remember him. And then right soon afterward he up and died for real in that airplane crash. That's some creepy stuff! There's some mystery to that!"

"Don't turn maudlin, Ma, let's just all go and enjoy the show together."

"I'm just saying." Ma leaned back and thought, nodding her head to the room, and looking up at the cobwebs on the light fixtures. Runyon motioned to Cilla and as they turned to leave Ma sat back up, seemingly forgetting what she'd been talking about. The two younger adults both turned their heads back as Ma addressed them, and once again Ma pointed, "And remember what I said about kids!" Ma looked straight at Cilla, "If you run out of them little rubber thingies, we still got plenty of balloons from last year's outdoor polka-band concert still hanging around. All different colors with little duckies on them. Snap one of them on his pecker before you get going!"

"*Ma!*"

*   *   *   *

At the Skunksquirt fairgrounds, the 4-H kitchenette is located inside and underneath the grandstands where the public restrooms and horse betting booths can also be found. On this day the kitchenette was locked up tight and under the strict security of a couple of young volunteers that were staffing an information table just in front of the doors. The teens were receiving entries for the food-judging contest throughout the morning while handing out fair programs and attempting to answer questions from fairgoers.

Ma's 'Other Diner', her mobile fried dough and burger trailer, was set up close to the grandstands. As she was preparing for the midway to open later after noontime she could see through the glass doors underneath the grandstand and wondered how she was going to gain entry into the room where the volunteers were guarding everyone's tasty contest desserts. She was anxious to inject them all with hot sauce and guarantee herself a first-place ribbon. The 4-H had several tables set up underneath the grandstands where other local folks were selling arts and crafts, and the two young volunteers were on patrol outside of the kitchenette that Ma was itching to gain access to.

Ma had dropped off her special dish earlier that morning, cinnamon pumpkin apple crumb cake. Since then she'd noticed several others stop and deposit their tasty entries including Mattie Daley's prized, scrumptious chocolate lava cake that Ma didn't want to chance losing the first-place ribbon to.

El was installing a new propane gas tank at the front of the food shack and Runyon was opening the swinging fiberglass service window awning. Cilla had volunteered to help Ma and she was inside the shack cutting up onions and peppers, preparing the condiments for the grill. Once El had the tank in place Ma could light the pilots to the grill and heat the oil fryer for her famous fried dough. Ma was standing beside Cilla preparing the dough, her hands and apron covered in white flour. As they worked, all three, Cilla, El, and Runyon kept noticing Ma staring over at the 4-H building.

"Whacha staring at, Ma?" Cilla asked.

Runyon answered his girlfriend as he tugged on the ropes to hoist the large fiberglass shutters up, "You don't want to know."

"She's looking to see how she's going to sabotage the tasty food contest," Elmer said nonchalantly as he finished screwing the gas lines into the regulator on the fresh propane tank mounted at the front of the shack just behind the trailer's tow hitch.

Ma ignored both and began speaking to Cilla as if she'd known her for years, and possibly understood how her mind works. Ma pointed to the grandstand doors, flicking flour into the air. "You see them two kids just inside the doors at that table? I need to get past those two and into that room behind." Ma pulled her horse-sized syringe from her apron pocket, "I got this right full of spicy hot sauce and I'm going to inject it into everyone's desserts, 'cept mine, of course."

"You're pathetic," Runyon observed while El just shook his head as he turned the handle to the fresh tank and set the empty propane tank off to one side.

Ma held the syringe up in front of her, "I bought the stuff from a catalog. It's literally called 'It'll kill you after your dead' hot sauce!" Ma chuckled as Cilla just stared at the deadly dessert-destroying weapon. "I just need to figure a way to get back in there before the judging starts later today and poison them other desserts!"

"She wasn't smart enough to wait and deposit her entry last," Runyon mentioned as he tied off the awning to the side of the open service window.

"Shut up!"

El stood up and stretched his back out, "Why don't you just try to win fair and square?" He then motioned to Runyon, letting him know it was okay to light the pilots in the food shack.

"Because!" Ma barked, "Nothing's fair at this stupid fair!"

Cilla stared at the grandstand's doors and the two kids seated at the table in front of the kitchenette. She folded her arms in front of her, then raised a hand to her chin, patted her cheek with her pointer finger, and closed one eye. She was deep in thought, "You know, Ma, you could just tell those kids that you forgot to put whipped cream or something on top of your dessert, and they'll probably let you into that room. Even better, take them something to eat too." Cilla now pointed at the doors, "They're just dumb teenagers, they're actions are controlled by their stomachs. A simple snack would distract them long enough for you to get in there and spike those desserts."

Cilla turned to look at Ma, who was staring back at her with a blank expression on her face. A moment of silence later and Ma's face displayed a larger-than-life, endearing smile, her eyes twinkled, and she responded casually, "Yes, my dear, my son will marry you." Ma then reached out the service window and whacked Runyon on top of his head with a metal spatula, yelling at him, "Why haven't you proposed to this sweet woman yet?!"

"*Ouch!*" Runyon yelled back as Ma smacked him again, wiping the concerned look off his face with the spatula, and he grabbed the top of his head. *"Jeese, Ma!"*

El had the same expression, one of confusion, as he stared at Cilla and then finally looked to his wife who was still hanging out of the front service window, "Oh great, she's one of you."

"It's genius!" Ma exclaimed as she leaned back in and put one arm around Runyon's girlfriend, pulling her in tight. She then knelt down to light the pilots on the grill and grease pit, still talking to Cilla, "You get those fixings to start sizzling and put a couple of dogs on the grill. I'll make up two nice, big fat fried doughboys and we'll take them to the young'uns to distract them while I squirt the hot sauce into everyone's desserts!" Ma stood back up, "Runyon! You go get me a can of spray whip from the corner store so it looks like I'm fixing up my crumb cake!"

Runyon looked up at his girlfriend, "You ain't really planning on helping her with this idea, are you?"

Cilla ignored her boyfriend and leaned into Ma, still looking to the grandstand's doors as she dropped the onions and peppers onto the heating grill and they began to crackle. "I'll keep those two kids busy and facing forward so they don't see what you're doing inside that kitchenette. You'll have plenty of time to squirt those desserts." Cilla winked at Ma.

Ma reached through the shack's service window again and whacked Runyon on his head for a third time. "Boy! If you don't marry this girl, I'm going to!"

"*Ouch!*" Runyon ducked and held tight to his aching head as he turned to walk across to the field just inside of the horse-racing track where the truck was parked to go retrieve whipped cream for his mother. As he walked away he glanced back at Cilla through the shack's rear door and waved a finger at her with a concerned look on his face. "You should watch what you do. Ma will get you in trouble if you ain't careful! She'll drag you down with her!" Runyon turned and held onto his aching head as he scurried away to do what his mother had directed him to, and before she could chase after him.

Elmer picked up the empty propane tank and began to walk past the service window to go along with Runyon. Looking back up at Ma, "It didn't take you long to corrupt this nice girl, did it?"

Ma waved her spatula at El and put her arm back around Cilla's shoulders, *"Bullshit!* She was born rotten just like me! Runyon knows how to pick 'em just like you did!"

El shook his head and continued towards the infield with the empty propane tank.

*   *   *   *

Cilla was busy doing her part to distract the two teenagers, one boy and one girl, inside the grandstands. She was asking them useless questions and watching them fill their bellies with the hotdogs that were dripping with fried fixings, and two huge fried doughs. Her plan was working to perfection, and Ma was inside the kitchenette under the ruse that her apple pumpkin crumb cake needed just a bit of whipped cream.

Ma was giggling to herself as she was turning each of the dessert trays around, squirting just a bit of hot sauce each time as she injected another section of pie, cake, or tasty pastry. She made certain not to squirt too much with each injection, and to also be certain that no matter where the judges were to bite into the treats they were going to get a blast of hot sauce to ruin the taste and solidify that her entry would be judged the best.

Every minute or two Ma would look back over her shoulder and out of the kitchenette door window to see that the teenage guards were back to her, and she spied Cilla giving her a wink each time to show that the coast continued to be clear. Ma saved the most sauce for Mattie's lava cake. She gave the chocolate sauce a good squirt and knew that when the cake was heated up in the microwave just before the judging, the chocolate lava wouldn't be the only hot ingredient. She made certain that chocolate sauce was going to set the judge's tonsils on fire. When she was done she pocketed the empty syringe.

"Thank you, Mrs. Farnsworth," the two teens said in unison as Ma exited the kitchenette, her covert operation having been completed.

Ma smiled, "Oh, no, thank you two," she said with a bit of sarcasm. "I don't know where my head was at, forgetting the whipped cream like I did." Ma flashed a deviant little smile to Cilla, who returned it back to her. She then remarked to her partner in crime, "Come, my dear, we should get back to the food shack and get ready for the midway to open. There's still lots of work yet to do." And the two conspirators left, giggling like schoolgirls to each other as they returned to "Ma's Other Diner." The two ceased their merriment as they exited the grandstand doors. They both stopped and stood straight as they spied El and Runyon standing with their arms folded in front of the food shack, both glaring and shaking their heads at the two. Ma's face turned sour as she threw up her arms, *"Bah!"* She stomped back into the shack, "Mind your own business!"

*　　*　　*　　*

Mayor Wiggleswort was walking around the folding tables in the area underneath the grandstands. Several of the tables had been cleared and set up with the seemingly tasty entries for the pending competition. Rupert was one of three appointed judges this afternoon and he was leaning over the attractive treats to get a good whiff of each. Right on his velvety coattail was Constable Bob, the second judge. Bob had a childlike grin on his chubby cheeks as he looked over all the sugar and other "special" ingredient-filled goodies. The third judge was Charles 'Chuck' LaFleur. Skunksquirt's mayor was a smart-looking fellow in his late 40s, a tall, dark-haired, square-faced gentleman that many local ladies considered quite easy to look at, and Rupert hated him for it. Not to mention that in comparison, Mr. LaFleur was probably better at running a township than Rupert ever was, having more of a background in municipal government. He'd been a town manager for the larger town of Saint Sagacious in his past, and Rupert's background prior to his appointment solely consisted of selling used cars.

Also, in comparison, the statuesque mayor of Skunksquirt was smartly dressed in a nice white dress shirt, black suit pants, and shiny black dress shoes to Mayor Wiggleswort's purple velvety sports coat, purple pants, pink shirt, and shiny yellow shoes. Bob had on his usual clean white uniform shirt, blue uniform pants and shiny black faux leather police gear, black suspenders, and shiny gold badge.

Strolling around in the barn-like structure, admiring the arts and crafts while waiting, was small a crowd of locals and the contestants themselves. Everyone was anticipating the judges' sampling and ultimately announcing a winner to this year's contest. The contestant's desserts had been chilled, heated, or otherwise prepared moments in advance for the three judges to sample. Ma and Cilla were standing close by the tables, smiling at each other often as both had their better halves to either side, still with their arms folded in disgust in knowing what was about to take place.

"You should be ashamed," El leaned in and whispered to Ma.

"Shut up!"

Runyon opened his mouth to speak, and Cilla elbowed him in the gut to make certain no words would come out. Runyon returned the gesture with a frown.

"Well folks, it's about time we got to the sampling," Rupert stood up and declared. "We've got a big evening with the concert coming up later on at the stage out front, so let's get started." The announcement from East Puddleduck's mayor was met with applause from the contestants and onlookers. "I'd like to thank our young volunteers from the 4-H for setting this all up for us." Additional applause went towards the small group of teens standing nearby, all in their green logo T-shirts.

"Everything looks scrumptious," Mayor LaFleur smiled around to the contestants, all but one who were ladies primarily of the older generation who all smiled back at the handsome mayor. Rupert noticed and grimaced, as he'd never received the same swooning from the ladies that LaFleur always did when he spoke.

"Now, we'll be handing out three ribbons today," Rupert continued, "first, second, and third prize, and one honorable mention." Additional, semi-pathetic applause came in response to his words.

Bob grabbed three paper plates and handed one each to Rupert and Chuck. He then handed out plastic forks to the other two as Eleanor Wiggleswort, who couldn't compete due to her husband being one of the judges, volunteered to cut and distribute the samples. She began with Ruby Mayflower's red velvet cake and velvety rich frosting. Eleanor cut each judge an equal and ample amount as they extended their plates for their samples. The three judges smiled at each other, and each took a nice big bite of the cake as Ruby Red stood nearby with her hands clamped together in front of her, and she bounced just a bit in place in nervous anticipation of how the judges would like her entry. Menfolk noticed her body in motion, not to mention her tight V-neck T-shirt and equally snug jeans and high heels. Puut was strategically positioned close to her rear, literally, and staring lovingly with a huge smile on his mustached face.

The initial moment of taste went quite well for the three decision-makers. Bob sounded off first, *"Mmmm-mmmm."*

"Very nice," Rupert said with his mouth full of cake and sweet, rich frosting.

Mr. LaFleur just smiled and winked at Ruby with his mouth full and Ruby winked back. Luckily, Puut hadn't noticed as he was still staring elsewhere.

As the velvet cake began to saturate their taste buds, Ma's hot sauce began to kick in. Mayor LaFleur experienced it first and his smile quickly turned downwards as the spicy liquid penetrated his palate. Ruby noticed his demeanor change and she stopped bouncing. "What's wrong?"

Chuck, who didn't want to appear hurtful, attempted to work through the heat, discomfort, and overall horrible taste in his mouth as he attempted to re-establish a smile. However, he only had the ability to provide a nervous look and he responded through his mouthful, "Nothing, nothing at all. It's very good." The suffering mayor managed to utter no more as he involuntarily spit the cake from his mouth.

Just then it hit Rupert, who began to perspire. Ruby, and others, noticed his expression take a turn. Ma and Cilla were trying their hardest not to smirk, chuckle, or laugh as they watched their diabolical plan taking effect.

Ruby's expression soured and she began to get a bit upset, dropped her arms, and remarked to Rupert, "Whatsa matter? You don't like it either?!" Rupert attempted to crack a smile to ease her concerns. It didn't come as he began to break a full sweat, his eyes watered, and he started to cough and choke.

Bob's sense of taste discovered the hot sauce last as his squinting, cheeky expression of joy suddenly changed to a wide-eyed stare. The officer frantically looked around the table for a glass of water. There wasn't any. Bob managed to swallow his hot cake and then cleared his throat and coughed out, "Can I have a glass of water, please? Or any liquid will do." He remarked as politely as possible, "Cake's a bit dry." His lie was met with spastic nodding from the other two in agreement.

"Someone better bring them a trough," Ma whispered to her cohort. "They're gonna need it before they're done."

After a bit of cold water, and reassuring Ruby Red's pouting face that her cake was just fine, the judges happily moved on to the next entry. Cicely Smirnoff had submitted a nice carrot cake with thick, rich, buttery frosting. Eleanor distributed a hearty slice to each judge and with renewed energy, the three sampled. Again, each first bite seemed just fine, and the judges smiled at one another. Cicely, hugging onto her hubby, watched the three closely. She let go of her husband and stood straight when she noticed Rupert's face turn first.

Grimacing, squinting, and perspiring, the mayor inquired with a full mouth, "You didn't happen to add some spices to this, now did you, Cicely? It bites back a bit."

"Of course not!" She replied angrily as she also noticed Mayor LaFleur tearing up while still attempting to politely smile.

Bob attempted to pretend that he was wiping his mouth with a napkin while actually spitting the cake into it, only to be discovered when he removed the napkin and his tongue was still hanging out. Panting heavily, he couldn't help but say in a low voice, "Holy doggie-doo, that's hot!"

Mayor LaFleur forced a swallow and managed to clear his throat, "Secret Russian recipe, perhaps?"

Smirnoff grabbed Cicely before she could lunge at the judges and he spoke in his heavily accented voice, "Yes, it's called judges are going to get punched in the face if they ask again." Cicely shook her shoulders and Smirnoff released his grip as she frowned deeply and crossed her arms, huffing in disgust.

Bob finally forced a smile through the sweat that was now visible on his temple, and carrot cake spit from his mouth out as he simply said, "Tasty." He chugged more water from the small bottle he'd been provided and quickly accepted another from one of the 4-H volunteers, and he quickly emptied the second one as well.

Ma leaned to Cilla, "You and Runyon probably should get more water for these three, or we'll be calling an ambulance." Cilla nodded and grabbed her boyfriend, yanking him out the door as they went to retrieve a much larger supply of water. They returned moments later having filled two 5-gallon pales from an outside spigot near the food shack, placing a metal ladle in each bucket.

Rupert had taken his suit coat off before moving on to the next entry. This one being from the only man to have submitted a treat, 'Sloppy' Joe Bottoms. Joe owns a small bakery in Skunksquirt, "Sloppy Bottoms Bakery," and daily he supplies Ma's diner with breakfast donuts and pastries. This day, he'd prepared homemade raspberry pop tarts, now chock full of hot sauce thanks to the two smirking criminals.

Bob, being quite familiar with Sloppy Joe's donuts and other goodies, took the first bite into a big, fluffy pop tart. The raspberry and hot sauce squirted out the sides of the pastry, onto his hand, and into his mouth as he nearly ate the entire tart whole truly believing it would be delicious. The hot sauce hit Bob's taste buds instantly and he spit the entire pastry back out, staining his white uniform shirt as the filling dripped down from his chin. Bob then made a face that was similar to what you'd expect after sucking a lemon and he reached for one of the water buckets, threw out the ladle, picked the entire pale up, and began chugging.

Unfortunately for the other two, they had taken bites at about the same time that Bob had and were both now in similar agony. Rupert began fighting Bob for the pale of water and LaFleur was coughing and hacking, doubled over and his face covered in raspberry hot sauce. The stunned crowd stood watching, and as LaFleur's coughing eased he looked up, managing to hack out, "Did all you people do your cooking in the same kitchen?"

Sloppy Joe, looking bewildered and scowling, glanced over to Ma. She noticed and looked back with an "I didn't do it" expression on her face, shaking her head and eyebrows raised.

*   *   *   *

Several more high-octane desserts and several more pales of water later and the three judges were standing in front of Mattie's entry, the chocolate lava cake. Bob, with sweat pouring over his face and his uniform stained with every color of frosting, pie, cake, and pastry that he'd yacked back out. Mayor LaFleur was down to his sweat-stained T-shirt that was now untucked from his dress pants, and he was wiping his brow with his formally white, however, currently stained dress shirt that he'd shed. And Rupert, who was now fully crying and down to only a T-shirt, undershorts, dress socks, and his yellow shoes. He'd taken the rest of his clothes off and was standing nearly nude, sweat pouring over his less-than-attractive body.

The crowd all stood, each staring blankly at the display in front of them. Even Ma and Cilla were somewhat concerned. Ma leaned back into Cilla and said softly, "Only two entries left. I hope none of them dies before they get to mine."

Old Marmaduke slid through the crowd and stood behind the conspirators, as he'd been observing the disaster from the back of the gathering. He leaned into Ma, "You did something to everyone's desserts, didn't you?"

"No, I *didn't*."

"Yes, she did," El turned his head and replied casually in a low voice.

"Shut up!" Ma whispered loudly.

Marmaduke spoke again, "You should be ashamed of yourself, Ma."

The three judges looked at each other in despair. Eleanor reluctantly handed each a helping of Mattie's chocolate lava cake. Each hesitantly accepted the paper plate full of danger. Rupert looked down at the cake, then up at Bob, and with fear in his eyes he remarked, "I'm never doing this again." Bob nodded as each of the judges scooped a portion of the cake and lava onto their plastic spoons. Each waiting to see who would be brave enough to try it first. Onlookers were stretching out their necks for a view, everyone now with a morbid sense of curiosity to see what reaction this train wreck of a dessert was going to cause the three. Ma's eyes were wide with anticipation of what Mattie's hot sauce-filled lava cake was going to do to each of them. The judges held their spoons to their mouths and each nodded to the other, indicating they'd all go at the same time, and they each cautiously inserted the lava cake between their aching gums and closed their eyes.

Mayor LaFleur's eyes opened wide as he looked down at the plastic spoon still on his tongue. His eyes rolled to the back of his head and the tall, handsome man fell over backward to the floor, quite unconscious. *"Thump!"* The spoon still sticking out of his mouth when he landed.

Expressions in the room turned to ones of surprise and shock from all, and audible gasps could be heard from the tiny crowd. All except for Mattie, who'd been suspecting the entire time and she glanced over to Ma with a deep frown on her face. Ma's eyes were wide as she watched the mayor of Skunksquirt pass out and fall to the dirty cement floor.

Next was the mayor of East Puddleduck. Rupert, spoon in mouth, grimaced and began to bawl uncontrollably, hopping from his left foot to his right and waving his hands in the air as if he were attempting to take flight.

After a few brief moments of this, East Puddleduck's mayor removed his T-shirt and underpants, crying and bolting butt-naked from the grandstands and out onto the midway. Everyone's heads and bodies turned and watched as he ran between Ma's food shack and the tent that houses the ring toss-onto-a-bottle game where he found the spigot and hose. Still hopping up and down without any clothes on except for his bright yellow shoes and socks, the crying mayor turned the spigot on and threw the hose to Eleanor, who'd followed quickly behind. She began to hose his exposed, pear-shaped body down while he stood with his mouth open wide, tongue hanging out and arms flapping in the air still crying like a child who'd lost its mother.

"There's something we never need to see again," Elmer observed casually to Runyon and Marmaduke.

The tiny crowd was forced to look away, all standing back up straight and turning their attention to the remaining judge, Bob Johnson. Mattie was still glaring at Ma, knowing good and well that she'd sabotaged everyone's contest entries. Bob had taken his swallow of the lava cake and was staring off into space, sweat now pouring from several fat parts of his body. As he stared straight at nothing, he dropped his hands and leaned forward. The spoon and plate full of lave cake fell to the floor while his arms dangled at his sides.

Cilla leaned into Ma, "Is he dead?"

Ma spoke up, "Constable! Wake up!" She approached Bob, snapping her chunky fingers in his face. "Wake up, boy!" Only a moment later Bob seemed to snap back to reality and looked straight at Ma, their eyes about level to each other with Bob bent forward. "Wake up! You got one more entry to shovel in! And you're the only one left." Bob frowned and looked around as Ma continued, "LaFlower's on the floor, and Rupert's naked on the midway! You're all that's left!"

"I can't, Ma," Bob whined.

"You've got to! You gotta finish what you started!" Ma looked back and motioned for Cilla to bring the bucket of water. Cilla grabbed a plastic cup, filled it, and handed it to Ma. "Here!" Ma blurted and handed Bob the water. "Drink up! And don't be a baby, there's only one left and it's mine! You know you're in for something good from me!" Ma leaned down and cut a big slice of her apple pumpkin crumb cake and flopped it onto a paper plate. She grabbed a plastic fork, stuck it into the cake, and handed it all to Bob, who was still leaning over and giving Ma the, "please don't make me do it," look. "Eat!" Ma barked and Bob reluctantly lifted his arm to accept the plate.

And just then a young voice from the crowd called out, "Hey, where's the whipped cream?!"

"What?!" A surprised Ma called back and turned to see the two young volunteers who had been staffing the information tables earlier emerge from the tiny crowd.

One of the teenagers, the young girl, pointed, "The whipped cream? Where's the whipped cream you needed to put on that cake earlier when you asked to be let into the kitchenette? There ain't no whipped cream on that cake."

Ma scowled at the youngster, "Mind your manners, kid!" As she said this Cilla slid through the small crowd and over beside the young girl.

"I knew it!" Mattie Daley yelled out, pointing, and pushing through the crowd to get closer to Ma. "I knew it! You did something to all the other desserts, didn't you, *Wilomena Miller?!*"

"No, I didn't! The kid doesn't know what she's talking about!" Ma barked at Mattie and then looked straight back at Bob, shoving the paper plate into him. "Eat!"

Mattie looked over to the 4-H volunteer. The teenager opened her mouth to speak again, and Cilla reached out and pulled the girl into her. Gently but firmly she wrapped her arm around the child's neck to stop her from speaking and placed her other hand over the child's mouth. Cilla then turned her head to Runyon and with a half scowl, half smirk on her face she blurted out sternly and directly, "Yes! I will marry you!"

Runyon, with an entirely shocked and terrified expression on his face, turned to his father and spoke in a tone that nearly posed the statement as a question, "I didn't ask her?" Elmer shrugged his shoulders and raised his eyebrows in response.

Ma gave Bob a direct and dirty look, with her face still only inches from the lawman's. Ma grabbed another plastic fork, cut a piece of her cake from the plate he was now holding, and pinched his nose to force his mouth open, shoveling the bite in. The officer closed his eyes tight as the morsel hit his taste buds. Bob opened his eyes back up to Ma staring and scowling through her reading glasses, and Bob's expression turned to one of bewilderment. He swallowed the bite hard, his Adam's apple working the crumb cake down to his stomach, this time without the burning sensation. In fact, it was without any sensation at all.

"Well?!" Ma asked in a low tone with the onlookers all quietly staring, everyone waiting for Bob's response. All except for Runyon who was staring straight with a blank look on his face and wondering what had just occurred.

Cilla still had a tight hold on the teenager who was struggling against her grip as Bob looked straight at Ma and said in a whisper, and with a slight lisp from the previous hot sauce damage, "I can't taste it."

"What?!"

"I can't taste it, Ma. I can't taste anything. Whatever was in all those desserts has burnt my tastebuds off."

"Hah!" Mattie shouted out, Ma's head snapping around to her. "You finally did it to yourself! He can't declare you a winner if he can't taste your crappy apple crumb cake!"

Ma's head snapped back to Bob, their noses nearly knocking into each other. Ma's scowl deepened as Bob gave her an "I'm sorry" look on his aching face. Ma's right eyebrow raised, and her left eye began to twitch. She raised her hand, pointed her stubby finger, and began to open her mouth, and then thought to herself while blurting out, "LaFlower!" Ma and Bob's heads turned to look down. On the floor still out cold was Mayor LaFleur, with Puut kneeling and holding his head while Ruby fanned the unconscious man with a napkin, both giving Ma a dirty look. The old woman and the lawman looked back at each other, Ma squinting and frowning, her eye still twitching and Bob wincing as if he expected to be smacked. Ma's head then turned to look out the grandstand doors for Rupert whom she spied running, naked, through the midway away from the grandstands with Eleanor trotting close behind his exposed behind.

Ma simply dropped her head in defeat, *"Goddamit."*

Mattie began an evil laugh as the onlookers began to disperse. The competition was over. The contestants all shook their heads in Ma's direction as they left, however, her actions didn't really surprise any of them at all. Cilla finally let go of the teenager, who flashed her an angry look as she shook herself off.

Runyon turned to El, "What's going on?"

"Well, you're Ma just lost another contest and Bob will never taste food again." El motioned toward the floor, "That guy's probably dead." He then motioned to the doors, "And Rupert's not wearing any clothes and running laps around the fairgrounds looking for more water." El then looked up at his taller son. "Oh, and you and Cilla are apparently getting hitched." He chuckled and wandered back outside towards the food shack. Runyon still stood in place, seemingly in shock and continuing to stare blankly.

Cilla hugged onto Runyon's arm and said calmly, "C'mon, loverboy, we need to get your mother out of here before they make us clean up this mess."

"I can't taste anything," Bob whined again, still bent over and face to face with Ma. "I can't go through life without tasting anything. I love food. Especially yours. Help me, Ma."

"Oh, quit your complaining. It's just hot sauce, it'll wear off." Bob began to stand back up as Ma looked around. "I can't believe I didn't win." She looked over to Cilla, who shrugged her shoulders at the old woman. Ma then looked at Runyon and noticed him staring into space, "What's wrong with him?"

Cilla looked at her fiancé and smiled, "Nuthin. He'll be fine."

Runyon looked at his Mother and said softly, "I didn't ask her."

"Heh, heh," Ma chuckled and shook her head as she wandered back towards her food shack, carrying her plate of apple pumpkin crumb cake with her, and taking a bite herself with a plastic fork.

*　　*　　*　　*

The Skunksquirt fairgrounds stage sits in front of the grandstands on the opposite side of the horse racing track, about twenty feet back into the infield that the track surrounds where the fairgoers park their vehicles. The stage itself, a twenty-by-twenty concrete slab was built four feet high from the ground and has steel girders in each corner raising up to a metal-framed roof to keep the weather off whoever is performing. It certainly isn't anything fancy, but it works for most of the small shows that thus far have performed on it.

With the band's equipment all set up, it didn't appear to have left a great deal of room for the members of the legendary *38 Special*. However, they were known for playing smaller venues and apparently didn't feel the need to have the big light shows and glitz that other bands traditionally rely on. The band was known for just showing up and playing the good old southern rock music that had made them famous.

The anticipation of a big name was paying off and the fair was experiencing more patrons than they'd ever had in the past. Excitement was high and cash was flowing throughout the midway at both the games tents and food joints. The band's tour bus had arrived around 4:00 p.m. and many local folks were watching the roadies set up the tiny stage with steel guitars, amplifiers, a large drum set, and the band's logo strung behind the stage on a huge fabric curtain. The band's road crew had also set up a small soundboard and spotlights just in front of the grandstands, all pointed toward the small stage.

At 6:00 p.m., just one hour before the concert was set to kick off, the fairgoers began taking up spots both standing near the stage and others grabbing seats in the grandstands. The midway had completely ceased operations as excited local townsfolk gathered on the horse track. Ma, not wanting to have anyone blocking her view, shut the food shack down at 5:30, and she and El secured a standing spot directly in front of the stage. By 7:00 p.m. nearly two thousand people were standing around the track, and the grandstands were seated to capacity. The annual fair hadn't experienced such a famous visitor in the past and this was gearing up to be a successful booking for the community that might just lead to more big names in the years to come.

As Ma admired the equipment on the stage and the band's signature winged Pegasus on the huge tapestry hanging just behind the drum set, she mentioned to her other half, "We'll open the shack back up just after the concert's over. It should be around nine or ten o'clock. We'll clean up with this crowd. I'm guessing most will be smoking something funny that'll give them all the munchies. Fries will sell best later tonight." El returned a nod in agreement as he looked up and admired the band's instruments and equipment. Ma gazed up at the steel girders, steel trusses, and metal awning over the stage, "Looks like they made a few improvements to the stage since last year." El glanced up as Ma continued, "I don't seem to remember that metal roof up there. I wonder how it'll sound with those bass and steel guitars bouncing loud music off from it."

"I dunno, Ma."

Looking straight up above her to one of the steel trusses, Ma spied what appeared to be a large bird sitting on a girder. She pointed, "What's that? Looks like a big, fat pigeon. That can't be real, can it?"

Elmer glanced up. "Nope, it's probably not. Probably one of those decoy things to keep other birds from nesting up under there."

"Whatever it is, it ain't moving. You're probably right. Good idea too, the band probably wouldn't appreciate being crapped on by a roosting pigeon."

Ma continued to gaze up at the bird as Runyon and Cilla pushed their way through the growing crowd. "Got a spot saved for you two right here," Ma said, being aware of their arrival while continuing to stare upwards.

Runyon, appearing a bit more relaxed than earlier, glanced up, "Whacha looking at, Ma?"

"That bird up there. It can't be real, can it?"

"Naw, must be a decoy or something."

"I said the same thing," El added.

Cilla was next, "It don't even look real. It ain't moving, either."

Ma looked back down, massaging her aching neck from straining to look at the bird, "Probably made of plastic or something."

Constable Bob came swimming through the crowd which was now packing in numbers in front of the stage and back across the track to the grandstands. Ma noticed him pushing his way through and it was quite apparent that he'd put on a clean uniform since the earlier contest. The big lawman made it to the stage and turned his back to the cement as Ma addressed him, "Get your taste buds back yet?"

Bob scowled, "Yes, I did. No thanks to you and your stupid ideas."

"I knew you couldn't stay away from food long, taste buds or not. What brought them back?"

"A raspberry snow cone and push-up ice cream."

Ma shook her head, "What are you doing here, anyway?"

Bob stood his tubby body up straight and tall, "I'm the security for the concert. I'm here to make sure no one gets out of hand or starts a mosh pit."

"There ain't no mosh pits at a southern rock concert," Runyon noted sarcastically.

"What would you do anyway if someone did get out of hand?" Ma asked, squinting, and adjusting her glasses, "Wave a hotdog at them?"

"I can handle myself!" Bob frowned at the diner owner who'd poisoned him earlier in the day.

"Well, just make sure nobody crowds me or tries to get in my way!" Ma replied back, "You got any bullets in that gun?" Bob simply scowled and shook his head at the old woman in return for her comments. Not that he could hear her comments very well with the crowd at capacity and growing louder in wait for the band to take the stage. Bob looked around and a nervous rush overtook him as he spied throngs of people packed in like sardines halfway around the horse racing track to each side, all the way back and up into the grandstands.

Ma was standing up tight against Cilla and explaining to her, "the good old days," when the band was at their career's height in the mid-80s, and she was a bit younger when the spotlights suddenly lit the stage through the evening's dark, and the crowd began to cheer loudly. People who'd been seated in the grandstands were on their feet and the clapping was thunderous as the band members bounced out onto the stage, smiling, waving to their fans, and grabbing their instruments. Ma was cheering along with everyone with a huge smile on her face as the bass player and two lead guitarists swung the instrument's straps around their heads and prepared themselves to begin playing the music. Ma swooned when all of a sudden, walking up from the back steps and out onto the stage, was a smiling Donnie Van Zant wearing his signature black hat and a microphone in his hand.

"Oh, my God! Oh, my God! It's him! It's him!" El was giving Ma a look as she tugged hard on his arm, her eyes glued to the stage. She was like a schoolgirl, *"It's him!* It's Lynyrd Skynyrd's younger brother! *It's him! Oh, my God, it's him!"*

"Yes Ma, it's him!" El yelled back, his words drowned out by the cheering crowd as he attempted to release himself from Ma's grip.

Ma was gazing up at the band's lead singer, her eyes glassed over and a creepy grin on her face that both Runyon and Cilla took notice of. Cilla smiled and poked her fiancé in the gut, amused by how Ma was reacting having seemingly been instantly shot backward many years to a younger, more carefree time.

"How y'all doing this evening?!" The lead singer's voice was loud and boisterous as it blared out through the amplifiers, and the crowd loudly cheered, whistled, and applauded in response.

"Oh, my God! It's him!" Ma yelled again and turned to El, "He spoke!" Ma bounced up and down like Ruby Red does every time she gets excited, only with much more disturbing results in her floral pattern sundress and swamper boots.

"Calm down, Ma!" El yelled, "Just enjoy the show!"

Runyon pointed up, leaned into Cilla, and yelled, "Ma's right, that bird must be fake! It ain't moving to the sounds of his voice through those speakers!" Ma also peered up and noticed the fat pigeon-like bird hadn't moved, her childlike demeanor only changed for a moment as she glanced at the creature, however, quickly returned as the lead guitarist, Don Barnes, struck the first chord to *Rockin' Into the Night*.

Ma screamed like a banshee when the song began, startling El, Runyon, and Cilla. Ma threw her arms in the air and started swinging them back and forth above her head, much like hundreds of other fans were doing, only a bit more concerning in nature with her underarm fat flapping in one direction and her boobs through her sundress going in the other direction. Bob's eyes widened as he watched Ma's body jiggle to the music, his back still to the stage and thinking to himself that he might be in over his head with this crowd, in his honest opinion. In glaring at Ma, in his mind, he could only compare what he was seeing to a big dancing circus bear or fat hippo playing in the river Nile. Bob had to shake his head and force himself to look away to clear his thoughts and regain his focus.

Now that the music was playing loudly, and the bass guitar was reverberating off the steel construction of the stage, many standing close enough to have the ability to look up under the awning including the band members were all noticing the motionless bird sitting on the steel truss. Folks were glancing up and pointing as most, if not all, also believed the feathered creature to be a fake. As Ma bopped to the music and contemplated reaching up to touch her idol, which she literally could have done, she noticed that the musicians were also glancing up quite often at the very still bird as they played music and sang.

As the first song came to a close and the crowd went crazy again with cheering and applause lead guitarist and vocalist, Don Barnes, spoke out, "Well, looks like we have a lively crowd here tonight in Maine, don't we Donnie?!"

"We sure do!" His bandmate responded into the mike, and the cheering grew even louder. Ma's voice was certainly not going to last the evening with her screaming along with the rest of the fans. Ma also had the ability to whistle quite loudly through her fingers, which pierced El's eardrums each time she did so.

El leaned behind Ma and Cilla over to Runyon, who put his ear in close so he could hear his father over the crowd, "Your Ma's gone nuts!" Runyon smiled and nodded in agreement and then went back to enjoying the show.

The music began again, and the band cranked up the volume with *Wild Eyed Southern Boys*. While Ma was swinging, bouncing, and flapping to the music she continued to glance up at the motionless bird. She also continued to notice the lead vocalist doing the same, even as he knelt at the front of the stage and allowed a few people to sing along to the chorus while he held out his microphone. Ma also noticed that the Van Zant brother was moving closer to her.

Now, you'd have thought that being such a huge fan of the band, and this, without a doubt being their biggest hit song, Ma might just have known the words to it. And, the lyrics, especially the chorus, certainly aren't difficult to remember. However, the truth was that Ma was just really caught up in the moment, not to mention the fact that she was truly terrible at recalling song lyrics. You see, she's one of those shower crooners who simply makes up anything that goes along with the tune rather than takes the time to learn the actual words to a song.

In other words, Ma didn't know the words to *Wild Eyed Southern Boys*, and the microphone was nearing her.

Ma was admiring the long black leather jacket and cowboy hat that the bassist was wearing when she turned back to find Donnie Van Zant's microphone stuck directly in her face at the start of the chorus again. The singer was staring straight down at Ma with a big, sexy smile on his face waiting for Ma to bellow out the words. Ma had no time at all to think, and it was obvious she put no thought into the following words that she sang out loudly for everyone to hear;

> ♫ *"Cause she loves those*
> *Big, fat battery-operated toys*
> *They remind me of big fat boys*
> *Those big thick, vibrating toys!"* ♫

Mr. Van Zant pulled the microphone back, winked at Ma, and laughed the next, and correct, lyrics into the microphone. Other members of the band and about one thousand, seven hundred people also broke out in laughter. Constable Bob winced. El leaned back to Runyon and yelled into his ear again, "Picture that the next time you're in the house when your Ma's singing in the shower!" Runyon gagged and looked as if he might be sick to his stomach.

The band continued and the southern rocker began his signature skipping across the stage, poking his long microphone stand into the air as he went along the tiny stage with amazing agility considering the small space he had to work with.

The band completed the song without further incident and carried on with more hits and more pointing, glancing, and starting at the bird to which the creature remained motionless. Ma continued to look up every few minutes while thoroughly enjoying the music, waiting for the moment that she knew was to come in which Donnie Van Zant would bellow out his signature song, *Rebel to Rebel.* She knew the signs to listen for too, having watched her VHS of the band at Sturgis in '99 many times over. She knew that he had a speech that he'd give just before the song where he'd talk about his late brother, and the tribute song would follow.

It was only a couple of tunes later that she finally heard the words she'd been waiting for. The vocalist began by addressing the crowd, "Boy, we've got a rowdy bunch out here, haven't we?!" The crowd, Ma being the loudest, began to cheer. "We're going to slow it down a bit. I'm going to sing a song about a man who's no longer with us…"

Ma nearly fainted with joy.

"…So, if you don't mind here tonight, Skunksquirt! I'd like to dedicate this next song to my brother, the late, great Ronnie Van Zant of the Lynyrd Skynyrd Band!"

The cheering, applauding, and downright yelling was deafening, and Ma's smile was so wide that her face nearly cracked into two pieces.

The first guitar lick began and the bass backed it up as the lyrics began. When Donnie Van Zant reached the first chorus, Ma's eyes teared up, "…*Rebel to rebel…*"

Ma, oddly enough, knew these lyrics well and along with the audience, they were all chanting the words along with the band as they sang loudly. Runyon and Cilla were hugging each other tight, singing and swaying. Even El had his arm around Ma as she was watching the lead singer smile big as he sang his tribute song to his own brother.

As the song continued and the second chorus rang out, just at that moment, at that very moment, Ma happened to glance up as the bird that had been motionless on the vibrating steel beams since the concert's onset finally took flight. The bird spread its wings, leaped, and buzzed the stage straight past the vocalist, and the entire band watched as it made a complete circle just over their heads. Mr. Van Zant's eyes bulged as it flew in front of him when it came around again and swooped down and out of the front of the stage, just over Ma's head, and took flight straight out over the audience and off into the open air. The entire band, even though their expressions said it all, remained composed and played on.

As for Ma? Well, not quite so much.

"Jeesus Ke-Riste!" Ma screamed and watched the bird buzz just above her head. She ducked and turned as the feathered creature flew out and past her. "Did you see that?! *Did you see that?!* I told you! I told you! I told you there was something to that whole, free bird thing!" Ma grabbed onto El and shook the old man with one hand while pointing into the night air with the other. *"It's him!* He's inside that bird! It's his brother inside that bird! It's *Lynyrd Skynyrd!"*

Runyon and Cilla noticed Ma having a fit while El attempted to calm the woman, "Ma! It's just a bird!"

"No, it ain't! *Oh, my God!* It was him!" Ma was frantic, jumping up and down, "It's his soul inside that pigeon!"

Bob was taking notice of Ma and he too became a bit concerned. He yelled out over the crowd and the music, "Ma! Whatsa matter?! Are you having a stroke or something?!"

Ma turned and grabbed the law officer by his collar and pulled him down to her. *"It's him!* He's inside that bird!" Ma pointed to the metal truss with one hand, still with the other hand choking Bob's collar, "He waited for his brother to sing that song, and then he flew off!" Bob's eyes were wide with befuddled concern as he looked up into the air at an empty, star-lit sky over the crowd, seeking Ma's UFO.

Runyon grabbed his mother and pulled her back, "Ma, it's just a song and a bird!"

Ma snapped around to Runyon, "Exactly! It was him! *Oh, my dear Lord!"* Ma grabbed Runyon's shoulders hard and pulled his face to hers, "All those pigeons that I killed last year! How many people did I murder?!" Ma was frantic with a wide-eyed, glazed-over gaze in her eyes. Her superstitious side was now in overdrive. "Those poor pigeons! *Oh,* what did I do?! Whose souls have I tortured?! What if I did something to our own family?! What if I murdered your Aunt Grizelda's soul?!"

"She ain't dead yet, Ma," Runyon reminded the distraught woman.

"I need to take chicken off the menu!"

Due to Ma's fit, neither El nor Runyon, Cilla, or Bob had noticed the music had ceased completely and the crowd was now focusing on the crazy woman at the foot of the stage. "Excuse me, is everything okay?!" A voice blared over the amplifiers. All but Ma turned to look up to see the members of the band were all standing at the stage's edge, looking down at Ma who was still gazing off into the dark, night air. Donnie Van Zant, with a smile still on his face, spoke through the microphone again, "Ma'am, are you okay? You aren't having a heart attack or something, are you?"

"What?!" Ma snapped around and looked up at the singer, still crazy-eyed and she responded frantically, *"No! Yes! Maybe! I don't know!"* Ma pointed behind her in the direction the bird flew off into. "Did you see that?!"

The crowd had all gone just as silent as the music as the band member's voice continued to be loud through the microphone and speakers, "Yes, ma'am. We all saw that. Are you sure you're okay?!"

Ma was trembling, El now holding onto one of her arms, and Bob the other. *"What?! I dunno! Yes. No. Maybe!"* Ma was spinning her head around, her eyes wide, looking for the bird to return.

Elmer looked up at the band, "She'll be fine. Ma here owns the local diner and she's a bit superstitious. She just worries about things like what she just saw."

Bob glanced up, "She's just concerned that was a sign to stop serving chicken on the menu."

The lead singer chuckled into the microphone, "Well, I certainly hope that doesn't happen!" As another band member brought over a cup of water and handed it down to El to give to Ma, the band's frontman continued, "Nothing like a big plate of southern fried chicken!" Mr. Van Zant stood back up and turned to the lead guitarist, "Ain't that right, Don?!"

Don Barnes stood back up and approached the mike stand while putting his guitar back on, "You got that right!" He pointed down to Ma and addressed the audience, "Let's all hear it for this nice lady here and her southern fried chicken!" The crowd erupted in applause and cheering, and once again the electric guitar rang out as the music cranked back up. Ma looked up to see her favorite southern rock singer smiling down at her and winking before turning his attention back to the audience to complete his signature song and begin the next tune, *Trooper with an Attitude.* A song that Bob fancied in particular, and he bopped his head along to the lyrics while continuing to perform his official duties.

"You gonna be okay, Ma?" El leaned into Ma's ear and asked.

She smiled back, "Yeah, I'm fine." Ma's nerves calmed and she returned to enjoying the music, however, she did look around quite often to see if the bird was flying back before the concert was over.

It didn't.

*   *   *   *

The concert concluded later in the night with a three-song encore. The band had rocked the Skunksquirt fairgrounds to its limits, leaving every single fan more than satisfied.

As the lights went down on the stage and people flowed back onto the midway, Ma opened the food shack up again. She smiled from behind the grill as she glanced out of the rear door and over to the infield to see the big tour bus pulling out as the band headed to its next gig somewhere else. Ma began humming *Wild Eyed Southern Boys* to herself while Cilla, standing next to her and doling out French fries to hungry patrons, smiled at the silly old woman.

*   *   *   *

As the weekend came to a close, so did the fair without further incident. Although, the committee that makes the plans for the annual event did ban Ma from entering fair-related contests for the next three years. We'll see how that works out for them.

And Ma did take the band's advice and she continues to serve southern fried chicken at the diner. However, she does stop at the fairgrounds whenever she finds herself in the town of Skunksquirt for any reason, and she peeks up underneath the stage awning to see if the bird has returned to nest.

To this day it hasn't.

CHAPTER 6

Groundhog Day

"This is the dumbest idea you've had yet," Ma remarked to the mayor from her second-row seat in the tiny town office public meeting room. As usual, during this mid-winter monthly meeting, Mayor Wiggleswort was wearing his bright-purple velvety suit jacket specific for town gatherings, purple suit pants, and a bright yellow tie perched on his nice white shirt. Seated to either side were board members Doody and Daley, and Constable Bob in a metal folding chair off to one side.

"It isn't dumb, Ma, it's good, clean fun. We could use a little fun around here. The winters are long and cold, and folks are getting anxious and looking toward spring. Sometimes we need something a little different to give us a pick-me-up," the mayor explained to the ever-complaining resident diner-owner.

"Oh, it's different, alright!" Ma wiggled to the front of her chair on her butt cheeks, sat up, and pointed to the town's other leader. In her signature sarcastic tone, she responded, "You do realize, don't you, that someone has already thought of Groundhog Day? It's been around for a while now, in case you hadn't noticed."

"We know that Ma," Rupert whined. "We can't come up with every new idea. And why should one town somewhere in Pennsylvania have all the attention?" The mayor looked around the room at the small crowd, "What's the name of that place, anyway? Puntatoony? Puntatoxy?"

"It's Puxatony. And the groundhog's name is Phil," a monotone Marmaduke spoke out from his usual seat in the back row, his head down, arms crossed, and legs stretched out.

Daley looked at the mayor, "We can't use a groundhog too, Mister Mayor, can we?"

Constable Bob leaned forward and looked down the folding tables to the mayor, "That'd be copying someone else. That'd be cheating."

Ma rolled her eyes in response to the stupidity she was bearing witness to. The mayor, staring up at the ceiling and scratching his chin with his duct-taped gavel, "You're right, we need a different animal. And we can't use the shadow thing either. We need something more original."

Ma couldn't take it anymore and rocked herself to her feet, crinkled her nose, raised an eyebrow, and addressed the board members, "Original?! Are you serious?! You're all talking about stealing a national holiday as it is! How original is that?! Is it the goal in life of you three to always make the rest of us look stupid all of the time?!"

Doody spoke up, "It's only for us, Ma. We're not looking to get the country involved. It'll be our own little day near the end of winter to look forward to." He turned to the mayor, "You know, they say that thousands of people show up in Poontang, Pennsylvania to see that groundhog come out of its hole every year. Just think what we could do here."

"It's Puxatony." Again, from Marmaduke.

And again, Ma rolled her eyes and sat back down, throwing her hands in the air and whispering to herself, "I can't wait to hear what they do with Gobbler's Knob."

Doody continued, "We could do a whole thing around it. You know, a big breakfast, banners, and get all fancied up and stuff! Mayor, you could get all dressed up in a nice suit!"

The mayor looked down at his current attire, wondering to himself why it wasn't good enough. After a moment or two, he perked up suddenly, having had an epiphany, "Hey, Ma! Does that bear still visit the diner each week?!"

Ma responded, quite nonchalantly, "Yeah, he wanders out of the woods every Wednesday morning and sits his hairy ass on the diner's rear steps until I come out and give him a stack of hot waffles all covered in maple syrup. I've never seen anything like it, just like clockwork. Ever since he followed me and El out of the woods that year he's been like flypaper once a week. I suppose eating waffles was a better idea to him than hibernating for the winter." Elmer smirked and nodded in acknowledgment of Ma's words.

The mayor looked left and right at his tiny board, "That's it! We'll use Ma's bear to tell us if springs coming! It'll be our original idea!" Daley, Doody, and Bob all nodded and smiled in agreement, endorsing the mayor in the belief that he'd thought of something brilliant, not to mention to further stroke his ego which was what they were all best at doing on a daily basis.

Ma flashed the mayor an "Are you kidding me?" look out over her reading glasses and responded, "You do realize there, Einstein, that it's called Groundhog's Day for a reason, right? Not, big-ass bear day." Ma glanced over in her row to the McIntyre brothers who were seated at the opposite end and staring back at her. Both shrugged their shoulders in stereo. She looked at El, seated beside her other side, and he too gave her the "I don't know" look. Ma glanced behind her and everyone else in the room shrugged their shoulders at her. Ma turned back to the board in disgust, shaking her head.

The board members, seemingly ignoring Ma's comments, expanded on their idea with Doody asking, "What are we looking to have the bear do? We can't have it seeing its shadow like Puckylucky Phil does. That wouldn't be very original."

"It's Puxatony." Marmaduke's monotone hadn't changed as he reclined in his seat, his face buried behind his long, white whiskers.

"Oh, this is exciting!" Ruby bounced from her seat in the third row, "Our own version of Groundhog Day!" The McIntyre brothers both turned to stare at the general area of Ruby's chest as her excitement was quite obvious. Both with dumb, childlike smiles on their faces. Ruby took notice, glancing over to the boys and blowing them an air kiss.

"Why don't you just wait for the bear to do something and then decide if that signals an early end to winter or not?" Smirnoff mentioned from directly behind Ma in his heavy Slavic-accented voice. The old woman slowly turned around in her chair, giving Smirnoff the "really?" look, her eyebrows raised. The tall man blew Ma an air kiss in return, amused by the conversation in the room. Cicely too raised her eyebrows, an indication that she also was amused by the ridiculousness of the situation.

"That's a good idea!" Mayor Wiggleswort pointed his gavel at the room, "We'll wait for the bear to do something and then decide if winter's ending!"

Ma turned back around slowly, "Hey, Nostradamus! When the bear does something, does that mean that winter is ending soon, or going on six weeks longer?"

Rupert looked up, searching for the answer in the burned-out bulbs on the light fixtures, "Well, I suppose if he does something that means there's more winter coming. If he doesn't do anything we'll call it an early spring. I think that's how it works with Perplexity Phil."

"It's Puxatony."

Ma rolled her eyes again, her tone becoming increasingly more sarcastic, "And who's the lucky *asshole* that gets to hold the bear up in the air like they do with that groundhog in Gobbler's Knob?"

Constable Bob took Ma's comments seriously and turned to the mayor, leaning backward in his chair to see him better. "I think we should just stand back and watch. I don't think the bear will let us pick him up. That might make him a bit grumpy."

This time it was the mayor's turn to roll his eyes at the lawman's comments.

"What's the bear's name, Ma?" Paul Doody asked.

"Shithead." Ma's casual response drew chuckling from several in the room.

"*Shithead?*" Doody turned to the mayor in a panic, "We can't call him Shithead, that'd take away from the significance of the day! Who's gonna come to Ma's diner to see 'Shithead the Bear' predict an end to winter?"

"That's true." The mayor responded, still looking at the ceiling, "We'll need to come up with another name for him."

"You can't rename my bear! And we don't need anyone coming to my diner for any of this!" Ma barked, "We ain't advertising this as anything! Absolutely no *foreigners*! I'm warning you, Rupert!" Ma was pointing and shaking her plump finger at the town's leader.

"Call him Petey!" Ruby Red offered all smiles from the edge of her seat, proud of her contribution to the overall concept.

"*Hmmmm*, Puddleduck Petey," The mayor said in a low voice. He then looked out at Ruby, "I like it! Puddleduck Petey it is!"

Ma glanced over to Ruby and gave her a dirty look. Ruby glanced back at Ma, shrunk back in her chair, and silently mouthed the word "sorry" to the agitated woman. Ma turned back front. "Hey, *idiots!* Has it occurred to any of you that the bear only comes out on Wednesdays? What are you going to do next year when Groundhog Day isn't on a Wednesday?! What if he decides next year to hibernate? Does someone plan to go into the woods on a Saturday and poke the bear to come out of his den? I'd like to see that! I bet you'll see him do *something* then!"

"Well," Rupert whined, "we'll just have to hold our holiday on a Wednesday each year, that's all. And I don't see that bear giving up a good thing at the diner as long as you keep feeding him." The board members nodded in agreement as they all cautiously looked out at Ma.

The old woman sat back up on the edge of her seat, adjusted her glasses, and said in a casual, however arrogant tone, "So, let me see if I have this straight. You're going to have people at the diner staring at a big black bear on Groundhog Day. Then, you're all going to wait for the bear to do something. Something other than sitting on my back steps eating a short stack of syrup-covered waffles. And, once the bear does something, you'll all declare winter to be over or not. A bear on Groundhog Day?! A big-ass bear doing something other than seeing his shadow like that little rodent does in Knobbler's Gob? Do I have this all correct? *Hmmmmm?*"

"It's Gobbler's Knob." Again, Marmaduke.

Ma snapped her head around to the side, "Shut up!" She then turned back to the mayor, lifting one eyebrow, and waiting for his answer.

The mayor looked at Ma and nervously responded, "Well, yes. That's the general idea."

"And you think people from all over the country are going to ditch Punkintony Phil for this?!"

"It's…"

Ma stood up and spun around with amazing agility, her faded floral pattern dress twirling around her pear-shaped body, and she shook her chubby finger at Marmaduke, "I'm warning you! Don't!" Old Marmaduke flashed a smile and blew Ma an air kiss as she turned back to the mayor for his answer.

"Well, yes! I believe this will catch on…locally."

Bob spoke next, "Ma, do you think you can get the bear to sit on the front steps so we can all sit in the diner and watch him? You can't see the back steps from the diner's windows."

"Of course, I can! That hungry bear would sit inside at one of the booths wearing a bib for them waffles if that's where I decided to serve them! He's a pain in my ass!"

"Gee, Ma, do you think you can get him to wear a bib on Groundhog Day? That'd be something!"

Everyone in the room rolled their eyes at the Constable's remark.

*   *   *   *

Groundhog Day. It was bright and sunny, the temperature was up a bit to a balmy 34 degrees Fahrenheit. The diner was packed early with people having arrived before the bear's usual Wednesday arrival time of 6:30 a.m. The McIntyre's had put the town's wooden street barricades out at the edge of the road with a notice saying that no one would be allowed in the diner's lot after 6:00 a.m. so that nobody would wheel into the diner while Puddleduck Petey was enjoying his waffles and scare him away.

Over the past few weeks, Ma had been leaving waffles closer and closer to the front door in an effort to coax the bear to the front steps after finishing up his breakfast in his usual spot on the rear steps. This day, she'd be placing the bear's entire stack of syrup-covered waffles on the front steps of the diner. Inside, Runyon and El had moved the booths away from the front wall and everyone was standing at the diner's windows to get a view of Puddleduck Petey and wait for the bear to do something, an indication that winter would continue for six more weeks.

Ma had finally shined up to the idea of the event and had even gone so far as to put a sign on an easel just inside the diner's doors that read the following;

> **Come to the Diner on Groundhogs Day.**
> **Show Up Early, No Admittance After 6:00 a.m.**
> **Winters End to be Predicted!**
> **See If Shithead the Bear Does Something.**

A few times the mayor had attempted to cross out the bear's formal name and write in "Puddleduck Petey." However, Ma continually changed it back.

Rupert had studied the traditional Groundhog Day ceremonies and how it was handled in Puxatony, Pennsylvania. He had on a black tuxedo, velvety of course, and a top hat. He's also made his select board members, Daley and

Doody, wear tuxedos as well, renting all three from Choppie's Secondhand Shop in Skunksquirt. Unfortunately for the other two, the store hadn't three tuxedos on hand so Jacob and Paul's ended up being bright sky-blue leisure suits, with top hats to match. Rupert had his sister, Myrtle, create a fancy paper scroll and she'd written on it a proclamation that the select board had endorsed, declaring this day as East Puddleduck's official Groundhog Day. The proclamation explained the event that was to take place in which everyone would watch and wait for "Petey the Bear" to do something that would predict the end of winter. The mayor read the proclamation out loud, standing in the center of the diner while Runyon and Ma watched for the bear from the kitchen windows and kept their eyes towards the wood line where the furry creature traditionally emerged from each Wednesday morning.

Ma had the diner's window blinds down, open only enough to peek through as she didn't want her bear spooked by the small crowd of onlookers. She wanted her favorite furry friend to eat his waffles in peace. Constable Bob had come prepared, though, with a canister of bear spray added to his duty belt in the event the bear did get spooked and tried to enter the diner. Not that Bob knew how to use bear spray, nor would he even have the courage to use it in the face of danger. The truth was, Bob would most likely be the first one to jump out a window or hide in the restroom if the animal was to become aggressive.

Ma was serving breakfast buffet style from the counter bar this morning with waffles obviously being the special of the day, and most of the patrons were standing while enjoying their early morning meal. When Rupert completed reading the proclamation from the chair he was standing on, which still didn't cause his short stature to touch the ceiling even with the top hat, he continued to address the small crowd, "Now remember everyone, we've promised Ma that we won't scare Puddleduck Petey."

A voice very much resembling Ma's echoed from the kitchen, cutting the mayor off, *"Shithead!"*

The mayor glanced towards the kitchen, rolled his eyes, and continued, "So, please try not to crowd the front window when shit…, I mean the bear comes around and keep your voices down. And please leave room for myself and my select board to get the best view so we can observe and see if Petey does something."

"Here he comes!" Runyon's voice called out as he and Ma spied the bear exiting the woods and sauntering towards the diner, his large hairy backside swaying back and forth as he walked along. As he neared the building the bear's head bobbed in the air and his nose twitched. Ma smiled and recognized her red hunting hairpin in his jaws that the bear had kept since he and Ma had their first encounter.

Ma entered the dining room with a big plate of syrup-covered waffles and she cracked the front door open and slid the plate out onto the front step as others began to crowd the windows. Ma took a spot at the diner's glass front door with the blinds down. She used her hand to peek through two of the blinds as she saw her bear coming around the corner of the diner, its nose leading him to his breakfast.

Rupert, Paul, Jacob, and Bob were closest to Ma, peering out of the front windows as others surrounded them. "He's coming," the mayor announced, "everyone quiet down now."

Ma watched as her big hairy friend approached the front stairs, placing its huge paws on the second of three steps as his twitching nose located its target. The bear gently laid the hairpin down out of its mouth beside the tasty plate full of sweet waffles. The huge mammal sat back on its hind end and used the stairs as his own personal table as he reached his large paws out and carefully picked up the plate, holding it against his chest and beginning to chow down on the waffles getting syrup all over his snout, on his paws, and dripping down his furry frontside.

The spectators were in awe of the majestic creature. Patrons had their necks stretched and people were taking turns at the windows to get a glimpse of the bear through the blinds. Ma chuckled to herself at the front door as she watched her friend satisfy his hunger. She whispered and shook her head, "Such a glutton." When the plate was empty and the bear had licked it clean, he dropped it and began to lick the syrup from his paws, sitting back and up straight, giving a nod to the chef that he spied through the blinds. Ma smiled and nodded back.

"Okay, folks, let's see what Petey does next," the mayor whispered.

"*Shithead!*" Came a loud whisper from the front door, "And this time I meant you and not the bear!"

Up against the front windows now along with the town leaders and the lawman squeezed together were Puut, Ruby, Val, Cicely, and Mable. Behind, looking over and around their shoulders were Smirnoff, the McIntyres,

Father Winkin, Mattie, and Eleanor. Other townsfolk were behind them, each attempting to see what, if anything, the bear would do to predict the winter's weather. El and Cilla hugged up to Ma to see through the front door and Runyon had his nose up against the kitchen's front window looking from the opposite side to the big bear.

The sun was rising from the east and it cast a shadow from the bear to the ground beside him under the diner's front windows where most everyone was watching from. As the bear finished cleaning the syrup off himself he peered down to the ground, apparently noticing his own shadow.

"Oh, no!" Constable Bob whispered loudly, "He sees his shadow!"

"We can't count that!" Doody whispered in desperation, "That's Punkeetunkees thing!"

"Puxatony." Came from Marmaduke, who was sitting in his usual corner booth away from the excitement, enjoying a hot cup of coffee and a plate of waffles.

"Just wait!" The mayor whispered loudly, "He'll do something else! Give him a bit of time."

"Oh, crap!" Ma whispered loudly. All heads turned to her, all eyes wide.

"What?" The mayor asked in a low voice.

"His tea! I almost forgot his tea!"

"The bear drinks tea?"

"Well, yeah. All that syrup sticks to his mouth and the waffles dry him out," Ma said casually as she reached over and knocked on the kitchen's swinging doors. "He prefers tea over coffee, with a bit of honey added, of course."

Runyon handed a large tin cup with hot, steaming tea through the swinging doors and Ma cracked open the front door and carefully, however quickly, set the cup on the top step. The bear's nose perked up again and he reached over with his massive paws and picked up the cup, sat back, and tipped the cup upwards chugging the tasty thirst quencher.

"Is that the something we've been waiting for?" Doody asked the mayor.

"No, you fool! He's just enjoying a cup of tea! Ma says he does that every week," The mayor whispered back annoyingly as "Puddleduck Petey" finished his tea and dropped the tin cup to the ground. The mayor continued in a low tone, "Okay, folks, he's either going to do something now, indicating a longer winter, or he'll just walk away and springs around the corner."

The big bear rocked on his hind end and continued to sniff the air, grunting happily for a few moments as everyone watched with anticipation. The bear seemed to notice everyone spying on him and he raised one paw, waiving in the air.

"He ain't doing nuthin! He's just playing! And he sees us!" Daley blurted. The mayor quickly *"shooshing"* him.

The bear then dropped to all fours and stepped sideways to the front windows. He reared up on his hind legs and placed his front paws on the sills directly in front of the mayor, Paul, and Jacob. The three, and everyone, reared back, a bit surprised. The bear sniffed close to the glass, and they all leaned back in cautiously. Petey then let out a loud grunt, jumping everyone behind the windows. Ma chuckled to herself.

"What's he doing?" Bob asked with a bit of concern in his voice.

"He's just saying hi," Ma replied. "He ain't gonna hurt you. He's just curious is all. Like some other dumb animals that I know."

Finally, after several tense moments of the bear sniffing and grunting at the onlookers with his paws up on the windowsills, "Shithead the Bear" lifted his right leg up high.

"Looks like he's gonna pee on your diner, Ma," Joshua McIntyre noticed.

Ma strained to see out the door window at her furry friend. "He better not if he knows what's good for him. Nobody pees on my diner and still gets breakfast served to them!"

The mayor looked a bit concerned as he hoped that a bear peeing on the diner wasn't the "something" they'd been waiting for.

Finally, with one leg still in the air and while doing a balancing act, the huge animal let out a big, loud bear fart. Onlookers winced as Ma's eyebrows tilted down, and with a puzzled look on her face, she responded to the bear's breaking of wind, "Huh. Waffles don't usually do that to him."

"He farted! He farted!" Ruby bounced and whispered loudly, "That's something, isn't it?! Ma just said he doesn't do that! That's our sign!"

Ma leaned back away from the door and looked at the small crowd, specifically at the mayor. "Well, there you go, Mister Mayor. There's your something you've been waiting for. A big bear fart."

Mayor Wiggleswort, desperate for the bear to do something else, watched as "Puddleduck Petey" jumped down on all fours, turned and picked Ma's red hairpin back up in its snout, and waddled back towards the woods. "Oh, damn," he whispered under his breath and dropped his head.

The crowd moved away from the windows and circled around the mayor. Rupert, appearing a bit disappointed, tossed the proclamation onto one of the tables. "Well, folks, it's official. I suppose winter's going to last another six more weeks. The bear's ass has spoken."

"Well, that's a great way to tell the weather," Puut commented in his heavily French-accented voice. "What happens if he shits out a whole berry pie? A three-day nor'easter?"

Ma walked up and put her arm around the mayor's shoulders as others began to help El and Runyon place the booths back up against the windows. "I told you this was a stupid idea. You should have stayed with the groundhog thing in Pennsylvania." With puppy-dog eyes, Rupert nodded to Ma in response. "I'll get you a hot cup of coffee. Unless, of course, you want some tea with honey to go with your waffles?" Ma chuckled as she went to get the mayor a fresh cup of coffee. After a step or two she stopped and turned back to the town's leader, "And please don't fart in here, six more weeks of winter is enough, let's not go for twelve."

After the diner was set back up to normal everyone sat down while Val and Ma served up fresh hot coffee and a bit more breakfast, and the townsfolk somberly discussed the topic of winter possibly lasting longer than anyone was prepared for.

*   *   *   *

The next Wednesday "Shithead the Bear" returned for more waffles. From that day on, and each year thereafter, East Puddleduck's end of winter would be determined on the Wednesday nearest to Groundhogs Day by a waffle-eating, tea-drinking black bear at Ma's Diner. The season's deciding factor forever being whether or not "Puddleduck Petey" has flatulence after he finishes his breakfast.

CHAPTER 7

Speaking of Auntie Grizelda

The lunch crowd was light in the diner on that late spring day as El, Runyon, and Constable Bob were all seated at the counter bar enjoying their mid-day meals. Bob had just about half of his fried hotdog drowned in relish, mustard, and ketchup inside a nicely toasted bun stuffed into his mouth. El had chosen the fish chowder with fresh haddock and Runyon was crunching down on a bacon, lettuce, and tomato. Ma was standing on the opposite side of the counter leaning up against the kitchen service window facing the three and reading a letter she'd recently received.

El looked up from his soup spoon, "Who's that one from?"

"Grizelda."

"Jeesus. Is that old cow still alive?"

"Yep, and complaining as always," Ma responded to her other half casually as she continued to hold the letter close to her face, appearing to be having a difficult time reading the writing. She adjusted her glasses and held the letter out away from her to see if that would bring it into a better focus.

"Who's Grizelda?" Bob asked, getting his words out around the hotdog before biting down on it.

"That's Ma's older sister." El answered back, wiping chowder from his beard with his napkin, "She's an ornery old goat. Meaner than Ma."

Bob smiled and nodded as Ma said quietly, "Shut up." She then lowered the letter momentarily and looked at Bob, "He's right, though. She is an old goat. And uglier. And only a half-sister."

"She's about a hundred and ten now, ain't she?" As El slurped another spoonful of warm chowder.

"At least. Mother had her at an early age. She was probably a mistake too. And she looks a lot older than she really is. All those years of being a crab to everyone, especially to me, took its toll. It says here her last divorce was just finalized."

"How many did that make?"

"Seven that I can count. So many that we never even met the last one. I feel bad for the ones we did meet. They were all nice guys until they hooked up with that old crusty old bird."

El slid his empty bowl away from himself and dropped his napkin onto the counter. "She must've been a looker at one time to get all those men." He chuckled towards Bob, "She'd scoop one up, marry him quick, and then drain him dry. She'd leave them holding onto nothing but an empty bank account, and then she'd move on to the next."

"True enough. I guess you can't begrudge her style," Ma mumbled from behind the letter.

"She certainly never did anything for free," El added.

"Whadya suppose made her so mean, Ma?" Runyon inquired as he snacked on his side of crispy potato chips.

"Life, I guess." Ma lowered the letter and looked at El, "You know, one time when I was just a youngster she put Calamine lotion in my father's Pepto Bismol. He found out one night when he had the drizzles and drank half the bottle. His asshole exploded from both ends for hours. Old grizzle face blamed me and when I tried to speak up she drug me by my hair to the pond out back of the house, threw me in, and threatened to drown me. There was nothing I could do, she was older and bigger than I was at the time."

"*Cripes*, Ma, that's rough," Bob mentioned as he spotted hotdog mustard on his black uniform tie and tried to use his napkin and ice water to remove it.

"Hey, Ma! Can I get another coffee over here?" Puut's voice rang out from his corner window booth where he was enjoying a toasted ham on rye, holding up his empty cup.

"Wait your turn!" Ma never lowered the letter as she responded, "There's three ahead of you over here!" Puut frowned as he lowered his cup and took notice that Ma didn't seem to be waiting on anyone seated at the counter bar, and he pondered for a moment on just how long he'd be made to wait for his coffee.

"Hah!" Ma blurted and jumped the three seated at the counter. "Says here the last one took his money with him. Seems this one didn't take to the idea of her leaving him and he got himself a good lawyer. No alimony!" Ma lowered the letter, revealing a smile, "Serve's the old bat right! I'm sure she has enough anyway all tucked away somewhere. Lord knows she didn't spend any of it on anyone else, the old tightwad!"

"It's true," El continued, "to look at her you'd think she lived on the streets."

Puut wandered up to refill his cup from the coffee maker behind the bar on the kitchen window counter that Ma was continuing to lean against. As usual with townsfolk, Puut was unable to ignore the conversation. "So, why does she write to you, Ma? If you two don't like each other?"

"I'm all that's left, I guess. And she thinks that I like her for some strange reason. Either that or she's trying to get something out of me. Nothing to give and I wouldn't offer anyway! Truth is, she's been so mean to everyone all through her life that nobody will listen to her now. I think she'd write these here letters knowing good and well that I don't necessarily read them just to have someone to write to."

"She visited us a few years back," El interrupted as he held up his cup and Puut refilled it with hot, fresh java. "What a terrible weekend that turned out to be. She drove up from where she lives…" El looked toward Ma to complete his sentence.

"Lewiston," Ma mentioned while continuing to read to herself.

El continued, "She was rotten to us the entire time. It was almost as if she doesn't even know she's doing it. We were all miserable by Monday morning and pretty near ready to bury her in the cow field out back of the house."

"Awwwe, shit!" Ma blurted and lowered the letter, wrinkling it in her fist. "That old wench is coming back here again for another visit!"

Runyon looked up from his sandwich that was halfway between his plate and mouth, "No!"

"There goes Christmas, and it's only June," El mumbled as he put a spoonful of sugar in his coffee.

Even Bob, who hadn't ever met Ma's sister in the past, threw a bit of a look of fear towards her as he continued to wipe his stained necktie, "Say it isn't so!"

"Why's she coming here? We don't want to see her! Isn't there something we can do to stop her from coming?!" Runyon had lost his entire appetite and shoved his plate away from himself, "Why does she feel the need to come ruin our lives just because hers sucks?"

Bob chimed in, "When does the letter say she's coming?"

Ma uncrumpled the letter and scanned it again. "She writes here the first Friday in June." Ma lowered the crinkled letter and gazed up at the ceiling in thought.

Puut noticed as he turned to return to his booth, "That's today, Ma."

The old woman's eyes widened as she looked at Puut and then scooped the letter's envelope off the bar and looked at the postmark. *"Goddam* slow post office! This was sent three weeks ago!"

"Can't we run out and modify your sign at the edge of town?" Runyon inquired of his mother, "Can't we change the name of the town or something? Or at least make it say something like no mean old ladies allowed?"

"*Heh, heh*, we'd need to kick several out of town if we did that," El chuckled and looked straight at Ma, winking when he said this. She returned his comment with a scowl.

Runyon stood up from his stool, picking up his plate to take to the kitchen. As he walked by the end of the bar he did some wishful thinking, "Maybe we'll get lucky, and she'll get lost on the way here."

*　　*　　*　　*

Friday nights typically enjoy a full diner, and this evening was certainly no different. Val and Mable were handling the dining room while Ma was preparing meals in the kitchen and giving pointers to her assistant cook, Father Winkin's young nephew, Stanley.

Ma had begun another tradition recently in that each Friday evening several local townsfolk would occupy a corner in the dining room and play live music, as the town was lucky enough to have several amateur musicians who toyed with a variety of instruments. Nothing fancy, mind you, but they didn't sound all too bad. Ma had come up with the idea due to the fact that

Runyon had been picking the acoustic guitar for many years and it turned out that his fiancé, Cilla, had a sweet singing voice. Runyon had begun strumming the guitar in the diner one evening and Cilla joined in with vocals. After that, others began showing up to participate and Ma had made the decision to officially make it a Friday tradition. Now, for a few hours each Friday evening, local townsfolk played and sang at the diner. Ma was particular, only allowing country and southern rock music to be played, and it had to be something she enjoyed, and not too loud as to drive paying customers out.

This evening Runyon was on his guitar, as usual, and Puut was on his banjo while Joshua McIntyre had a small, electric drum. Wally McIntyre had been practicing the electric guitar and had a small amplifier set up. El was on the whiskey jug and even Myrtle Watson had been convinced to bring the church's tiny electric keyboard to the diner and was playing along as best she could. The cramped corner of the diner was packed tight with want-to-be musicians and the tradition had steadily grown over the past few weeks since Ma had been allowing it. One of her better ideas too, no doubt, as everyone seemed to enjoy the music as they ate a meal or simply listened while sipping coffee. Runyon had let his mother know early in the day that this evening would be special, and that Bob Johnson was going to surprise her with something, however, he wouldn't tell her what the "something" would be. Ma was skeptical that Bob would be surprising her with anything other than his usual bottomless stomach.

At the moment Cilla was banging a tambourine against her leg and singing *The Weight,* a song made famous by *The Band,* with the diner's "band" having just completed Charlie Daniel's version of *Simple Man.* They'd even started the evening with a couple of tunes by Zach Brown, a favorite of Ma's as we all know. They didn't sound professional by any means, however, they didn't sound terrible either.

Rupert and Eleanor were toe-tapping at their usual center table, eating their pulled pork dinner, and gently bopping their heads side to side. Marmaduke was doing the same in his booth while sipping on a cup of Joe. Father Winkin was seated with Ruby Red, whom Ma had warned sternly not to get too excited over the music and never to throw her brazier to the makeshift stage, and Puut was happily seated next to her hoping she would. Cicely and Smirnoff were sharing a rack of ribs, and the music, at the table next to Rupert and Eleanor, and Bob was at his usual spot at the counter bar enjoying his chili. The one free bowl per day that he'd earned a year prior. His head also bopped to the rhythm of the music.

When the song concluded and the little band received applause from the patrons, Cilla skipped to the kitchen and opened the swinging double half-doors. "Hey, Ma! Can you take a break and come out here a minute?"

"I suppose." Ma turned from the dishwasher that she'd just loaded up and followed Cilla back out to the dining area, taking her apron off and tossing it on the counter bar as she exited the kitchen. When Cilla went by the bar just behind Ma she tapped Bob on the shoulder, a signal for him to follow. Ma squinted and frowned at the lawman, who was flashing Ma a cheesy grin and he winked at her. As he stood up he removed a small metal tube from the inside of his summer police jacket. Ma adjusted her glasses, "What's that?"

"You'll see," the constable replied as he removed his coat, placed it on his barstool, and followed Cilla to the musician's corner.

"This one's for you, Ma," Cilla called out as all the patrons turned to the diner's owner and smiled. Ma still had her scowl on her face in wonderment as she waited impatiently. She did, however, adjust her glasses and squinted in an effort to hear better.

On Cilla's signal, Joshua began the beat with the little electric drum and Runyon began the guitar's part. Ma adjusted her glasses again and felt she may just recognize the song but wasn't quite certain yet. As the mystery song began, Bob put the piccolo to his smiling lips and began the familiar and famous introduction to Marshall Tucker's *Can't You See*, with astonishing precision and talent.

"Good, Lord," Ma whispered to herself in the lowest of voices as Bob peeped out the notes on the half-sized flute. Ma broke into a smile as Rupert got up and walked over to her, placing an arm around her shoulders. Ma turned to him as the other musicians joined in for an extra-long introduction, as Bob was in the moment, eyes closed, and hips swinging as he fluted out. Ma tilted her head to Rupert, "Where'd he learn to do that?"

Rupert leaned into Ma, smiling, "He says his maw made him when he was young. He's been waiting some time for this. He's been practicing."

Everyone in the diner was clapping to the beat and toe-tapping as Cilla began to sing; *"Gonna take a freight train…"*

Ma began to toe tap and both she and Rupert bopped to the beat. Ma began clapping her hands along with everyone in the diner as they all sang the chorus out loud. Cicely and Smirnoff stood up from their table and began to dance in place to Ma's tune, still singing along to each other. Puut and Ruby did the same which put Puut at Heaven's Gate. Rupert even threw a glance at Ma, and she nodded, and the two began to dance in place. Everyone sang and danced, and Wally even managed to get in a guitar solo mid-song. When the familiar tune reached the final chorus everyone stopped, clapped to the beat, and sang out, repeating the chorus several times over.

Bob rounded off the song by closing it on the piccolo, the same as the band that had made the tune famous, and the diner's patrons returned the efforts with an ovation. First to the little band and then turning to Ma, who was all smiles and clapping along. *"Awwe,* go on! You're all just looking for a free meal!" Everyone laughed as Ma threw a wink at Bob, amazed by his hidden talent. Bob winked back, waving his piccolo in the air with a huge smile on his chubby cheeks.

There was so much jubilee in the diner that no one had noticed the old lady who had wandered in and was standing just inside the front entrance. The tiny band's members noticed her first, having been facing in that direction, and they went silent as their smiles turned downwards and the joyfulness quickly faded away. Others turned to see what they were all staring at. When Ma turned along with Rupert, she saw her at the doorway. The woman looked to be in her seventies, her frumpy gray hair poorly done up and looking as if it might be a wig. Her frowning face wrinkled, and she had on far too much makeup in an obvious attempt to hide her age. Her maybe five-foot stature and thin body was wearing an ugly sweater top and an old red skirt down to knobby knees. Multi-colored socks were scrunched just above her two dirty white canvas high-top sneakers. She was carrying a gaudy brown pocketbook strung over one arm on a faux gold chain. In her other hand was an old, torn suitcase with a faded floral pattern that resembled many of Ma's sundresses.

The diner went entirely silent, and Rupert leaned into Ma. "Who's the homeless woman?" Ma just stood and stared, scowling. Rupert took a step toward the woman. "I'm sorry ma'am, but the nearest shelter is…"

Ma grabbed Rupert's shoulder, held him back, and began to walk past. "She ain't homeless, not yet anyway. That's my stupid sister, Grizelda." Ma continued past the mayor, walking straight up to her sibling. Ma was only a bit taller and the two looked each other in the eyes, both frowning.

After an uncomfortable moment of silent scowling Grizelda spoke first, "Whoever that band is you hired, they suck. How's it going, bitch?" As she dropped her suitcase on the diner's floor.

"Oh, shit," El said softly. Then, just loud enough for everyone to hear, "We better all get back to business." The patrons, the little band included, began to disperse back to their seats and other duties as they attempted to avoid the confrontational reunion that was about to take place.

"What the hell are you doing here, Grizelda?" Ma asked of her sister.

"Just wanted to feel the love," her older sister said bluntly as she began to walk past Ma and through the diner. As she reached the Wiggleswort's table she picked up the mayor's fork just as he was grabbing for it, and she looked closely, "Silverware's dirty. You might want to get a new dishwasher." She dropped the fork back down and Rupert frowned, looking up at the woman as she continued with Ma right on her tail.

Ma pointed at her sister's backside and growled, "If you came here just to be an asshole, you can get right back in your car and point yourself south!" Grizelda put her hand up to waive Ma off and continued strolling through the dining room.

El walked up to the less-than-pleasant old woman and attempted to be polite, tipping his head, "Grizelda."

The less-than-welcome visitor returned the politeness in a monotone voice, "Dick." Ma rolled her eyes and shook her head. El continued past to take a seat next to Bob at the bar. Grizelda looked to her left to the booth where Father Winkin, Puut, and Ruby Red were now seated again. She addressed them all, tipping her head to each, "Sky Pilot…Moustache…Tits." They all scowled, each in awe of the woman's rudeness. Percible looked at Ma through his driving glasses, mouth open. Ma looked back, closing her eyes, and shaking her head at him, a makeshift apology for her ignorant sibling.

Grizelda continued to the corner booth where Old Marmaduke was seated and waiting for his coffee to be refilled. He didn't speak and continued to look straight ahead, seemingly ignoring the woman. Grizelda stopped and said back to her younger sister, "This one looks like he needs a coroner. Smells like it too."

"Okay! That's it!" Ma reached out and grabbed Grizelda by her shoulder, spinning her around, "What are you doing here?!"

Runyon and Cilla walked past without addressing the visitor. Grizelda leaned out past her sister and mentioned as they went by, "Finally got a piece of ass there boy, I see. It's about time, and a cute one, too."

Cilla began to turn around, obviously prepared to do battle. Runyon put his arm around her and dragged her on towards the kitchen, "It ain't worth it."

Ma leaned out into Grizelda's face, blocking her view from the two, "I said! Why are you here?!"

Grizelda looked back at her sister, silent for several moments while Ma waited for an answer. Finally, Grizelda took in a deep breath, sighed heavily and her shoulders slumped, "Willie, I'm here because I'm dying."

Ma snapped her chunky finger into her sister's face, "That ain't funny, Griz! Don't get my hopes up or try to play on my feelings just to get a free meal or a room for the weekend!"

"It's true Willie. I haven't got long." Grizelda's voice was somber, "Sit," as she motioned to an empty booth and the two women sat facing each other.

Val walked up, having overheard, and leaned down to Ma, "I'll take over for a bit." Ma looked up and nodded. Val walked over and tapped Ruby on the shoulder, a signal for her to get up and help her.

Ma scowled, "You better not be screwing with me, Griz. I don't have time for foolishness. Don't try to play me like one of your husbands. I ain't as dumb as they all were."

"I'm not. It's true, Willie. I just wanted to come back one more time, you're the only family I got left." The woman appeared to sound sincere, "And I know I haven't been a good sister to you."

"That's an understatement."

"I know. I've been mean and haven't treated you very well." Grizelda leaned over and took Ma's hands, "I never spoke highly of you to anyone. I never invited you to any of my houses during any of my marriages. I've never taken the time to truly get to know your family here. I don't even really know your husband, Delmar, or your son, Bunyon."

Ma chuckled a bit, mostly out of astonishment rather than sympathy.

"I know that I tried to get Mom and Dad to give you up for adoption, many times. I even tried to recruit foster parents on my own."

Ma frowned.

"I know I set your car on fire…twice…once with you in it…"

"That was you?! I still have the scars!"

"I even stole your antique brass teacup set that Mom gave you the last time I visited."

"I want those back!"

"And do you recall that time mom and your dad took us whale watching in Bar Harbor when we were kids? You didn't really slip when that whale blew snot all over us from his blowhole as he surfaced near the boat. I pushed you overboard. And it wasn't a coincidence either that the boat was missing all of its floaty survival rings that day. I tossed them overboard at the dock before we left for the open sea."

Ma's expression had turned to a half scowl, half "really?" look on her face.

"And the bow and arrow incident when you were six wasn't entirely accidental…"

"Okay! I get it!" Ma pulled her hands away, "You stunk as a sister! Terribly. Maybe even criminally!"

Grizelda stood up and faced the booth, "I know! That's why I'm here! I want to make it up to you! You're my sister."

"What are you dying of, anyway?" Ma looked straight down at the table as she asked the question and fidgeted with a sugar packet, speaking softly.

"I can't pronounce it. Who can nowadays with everything that can kill you having a name that you can't enunciate? It's all medical terms and all Greek to me. And the doctor says what I got is rare."

Ma's expression began to turn back to one of endearment. She didn't have words. The diner was silent as well without anyone having the ability to not eavesdrop in the small establishment, however, each attempted to hide the fact by continuing to carry on as if nothing was out of the ordinary. Cicely and Smirnoff were staring at each other in silence. El and Bob's heads were staring down at the counter bar. Val was forcing back tears as she set a fresh coffee down for Marmaduke, who was staring out the diner's window. The mayor and Eleanor couldn't force down another bite and Rupert placed his spoon down, shaking his head, and reached for Eleanor's hand. Puut and Father Winkin stared at each other, both speechless and Mable sat quietly in thought. Others in the dining room were quietly contemplating the fragility of life. Even Joshua and Wally, seated at the counter bar, were silent and picking at their plates, neither having the urge to eat at that moment.

Ruby, who was quite unaware, exited the kitchen carrying a tray of clean silverware and bumped the counter bar forcing a spoon to drop to the floor, making a noise that broke the silence. Grizelda's head snapped in her direction, "Hey, fire crotch! Can you *please* keep it quiet?! I'm trying to have a sentimental moment here! Go back in the kitchen and comb the ginger out of your hair!"

Poor Ruby's eyes went wide as Ma stood up and faced her sister, "I knew it! *I just knew it!* You just can't be nice, can you?! You're not here to make peace! You're here to spout off one more time and get sympathy that you don't deserve from people you don't even know!"

Father Winkin quickly stood and approached the two, placing his hands on Ma's shoulders to keep her grounded as he addressed Grizelda, "How long have you been given, my child?"

"Six months," Grizelda responded and looked up at the pastor, grimacing. "And what do you mean, my child? Are you blind through those glasses? I'm not a child."

"I'm sorry, that's not long, my dear. You should try to make the most of the time you have left," The preacher remarked as Ma wiggled her shoulders and turned to walk away.

"What'd you have in mind there, sky pilot? Feeling a bit frisky, are we? Are you looking to get a piece of this before I go? Got a thing for the younger ones, now do you?" Grizelda's tone had turned sarcastic as she smirked up at the preacher and winked.

"Oh, good Lord!" Ma stopped and whined.

"Certainly not!" Father Winkin blatted, tipping his head back and looking down through his driving glasses, placing his hands to his chest in defense of himself, "I was just trying to be nice in your time of despair and sorrow!"

"Best ride you'll ever have," Grizelda mentioned as she propped her breasts up through her sweater with each hand, beginning at her belt line where her aged and sagging boobs appeared to start from.

"Jeesus, Grizelda!" Ma turned back, "Are you stupid or something?! He's a priest!"

Grizelda turned her attention back to her sister and whispered loudly, "Exactly! It's probably been a while for him. He's probably hornier than an antelope!" She looked back up to the pastor again, "Whaddya say, there preacher? You want me to straighten your skin flute? Ever seen *Deep Throat?*"

Father Winkin let out an audible gasp as Ma blurted out, "That's it! I'm done!" The diner's owner stomped back and waved her finger in her sister's face, "Grizelda, you get your ass out of my diner! This just ain't the place for you! If you are dying, then I'm sorry for you! But it's time for you to go! And

I mean now! Right now!" Ma pointed to the door and then turned back to head into the kitchen. She grabbed the still-stunned preacher by his arm, dragged him backward to his booth, and sat him back down, leaving Grizelda to stand by herself. The other patrons hesitantly went back to eating, drinking, or hiding behind their menus.

Grizelda called out to her sister just as she made it to the kitchen, "Fine! I'll leave! Now!" As Ma marched into the kitchen and the swinging doors closed behind her, Grizelda took one step towards her suitcase when she suddenly stopped in her tracks. A few patrons were peeking as they saw Grizelda stand straight, her eyes bulged, and her body stiffened. Her eyes then rolled a bit and a slight, creepy grin came across her face. Grizelda's eyes rolled entirely, and she fell straight backward. *"Thump!"* Down to the floor she went, her eyes closed on impact, however, the creepy grin remained.

A few stunned patrons remained seated. Val, the mayor, Father Winkin, Runyon, Cilla, and Puut got up and surrounded the woman. Constable Bob knelt and checked for a pulse from her now limp wrist. He looked up at the mayor and slowly shook his head. Runyon looked to El who was observing while still seated at the bar. El gave Runyon a casual "oh well" look, raising his eyebrows and frowning. Others were, for the most part, indifferent to the situation as no one knew exactly how to react to the nasty woman's poorly-timed demise.

Ma, upon hearing Grizelda hit the floor came back into the dining room and stopped, the kitchen's swinging doors striking her backside. "Okay, who did it? Who laid her out?" Ma squinted and scowled, looking at Father Winkin, "Was it you, preacher? I can't say that I blame you after what she said to you."

The preacher looked at Ma with wide eyes, his head shaking like a cat coming out of the rain. "I never touched her!"

"Ma, she's dead." Bob looked up at the diner owner and said in a soft voice, "She just keeled over all on her own."

"What?!" Ma scowled and adjusted her glasses, walking up to the group, reading their faces, and then looking down. Elmer followed as Joshua, Wally, Smirnoff, and Eleanor were slowly getting up from their seats as well. Ruby was holding back at the counter bar. Mable was seated close to the group and Cicely stood beside her table. Old Marmaduke continued to sip his coffee from his corner booth, continuing to stare straight ahead at nothing. Ma looked to the constable, "Are you sure?!"

"I'm pretty certain, Ma."

Rupert said softly, looking at Ma with endearment, "We're sorry for your loss, Ma."

Ma looked up from the body to Rupert, "Huh, what? Oh. Well, I ain't! She was a horrible person! It's just like her too, dying on my diner floor like this. If I didn't know any better I'd say she planned it!" Patrons sighed in relief to her words as it was apparent that no one was overly sad to see the crabby visitor's untimely expiration.

"I thought she said her doctor told her she had six months left?" Runyon observed.

Old Marmaduke, still seated and holding his coffee to his lips, "Someone can't tell time."

"We should find out who her doctor was and make sure no one goes to see him for anything," Cicely remarked. "He obviously isn't very good at giving an accurate diagnosis that I can tell."

Ma looked over at her, "You're right. Seems to me that doctor could have been a little better at predicting when her end was coming. Probably should've warned her against traveling, too."

Puut chimed in, "I bet he charges way too much to tell you you're dying too." Everyone nodded in acknowledgment, and it was apparent that the conversation was turning quite casual, even though a dead person was lying on the diner's floor.

Bob looked up, still holding the deceased woman's wrist, "You know, some of them big city doctors don't even tell you in person. They make their staff give all the bad news whiles they collect their paychecks."

Ma looked down and continued in a casual tone, "Well, we need to get her off the floor. This ain't good for business. Someone might come in and think she ate something bad."

Mayor Wiggleswort inquired while staring down at the body, "Do we need to call someone? Maybe do an autopsy or something and see what caused it?"

Bob laid the woman's hand back down, "I'd say it was either what she had wrong with her, or the floor when she hit it."

Ma snapped her head up, "Well, that's good enough for me! The constable's diagnosis here is official enough. Now, where to put her until the funeral?" Ma clasped her hands together, looked up, and thought for a moment before pointing at the McIntyre brothers, "Do we have any salt left over from last winter in the town shed? We could throw her on that. That'd keep her fresh for a few days until the funeral! Nothing fancy, mind you. I'm sure the preacher here can come up with an express service. She didn't have family other than me so let's keep this simple and quick. Her ex-husbands certainly won't care. They'll all probably do a jig when they find out."

Father Winkin, from behind the mayor looked down at the body through his driving glasses with his head tilted back and said with a hint of disdain in his tone, "I say we just throw the horny old toad in a hole and call it good!" He gave a stern nod to his own statement while everyone else in the diner turned to stare at the preacher with a bit of amazement in their expressions. The father looked around the small crowd standing with him, *"What?"*

Rupert tapped Bob's shoulders, "Get up and call Buster's funeral home in Saint Blasphemy and get them over here. Mean-spirited or not, we can't just throw her on a salt pile or dig a hole." Ma scowled and shook her head in disagreement as Rupert turned his attention to the preacher. "I'm sure you can come up with a nice, short service. We can't be known as the town that didn't care."

"Since when?!" Ma's voice rang out.

Rupert put his hand on Ma's shoulder, "Don't worry, it'll be short and sweet. A couple of Hail Mary's and a hymn or two and it'll be over. Besides, we haven't had a funeral in town for a long time. It'll be good practice for Father Winkin in case he needs to do a real one sometime for anyone we actually care about."

Ma acknowledged with a quick nod, as she agreed that the preacher could use some practice. She turned to the McIntyre's, "You two go get your tractor and scoop her up." She turned back and looked down, "I ain't paying for no coroner's taxi ride, the front-end loader is good enough." Ma began to return to the kitchen and turned to Bob, who was struggling to get his large body up off his knees and back to an upright position, "Hey! H.R. Puffinstuff! Can you play taps on that piccolo?"

*　　*　　*　　*

It was a dreary Sunday afternoon, although fitting weather for a funeral. The skies were overcast, and a bit of drizzle was in the air. The tiny church was filling with parishioners, all in attendance for the service. Inside the mood was somber and the setting appropriate. Candles were lit and Myrtle Watson was softly playing hymns on the Sears and Roebuck off to the side of the altar. On the altar itself was the "casket" sitting on top of a white sheet that was draped over a folding table. The coffin had been constructed from three wooden fruit crates from Smirnoff's store that he'd had out in the back. One crate had been cut in two for either end, and two others hollowed out to make the middle. Inside was the dearly departed, a bit taller than the coffin. However, they made her fit by bending her legs at the knees, as Smirnoff had only the three crates to work with. The McIntyre boys had built the casket and Father Winkin had lined it with a clean white bedspread and pillow. On the altar were a variety of plastic floral arrangements that Mable Johnson had gathered from the cemetery over the years at each season's end and stored in the mortuary crypt. She'd cleaned them up nicely and arranged them for the service. There were several Mother's Day arrangements, three from Memorial Day and one Valentine's Day bouquet with a pink balloon and hearts. On the table next to the casket was a framed, and only picture that Ma had managed to locate of Grizelda that had been packed away in storage long ago. It was a photograph of a younger Grizelda, possibly in her twenties or thirties, and she was scowling at the camera and holding up her middle finger.

Everyone was dressed in their Sunday Best, even Ma, who was standing outside with Elmer next to the church's signboard wearing a newer clean floral pattern dress and flat shoes. She had on white gloves and a large-brimmed summer hat. Elmer was wearing a blue suit and tie, shiny black shoes, and his hair all combed nice and slicked down with Vitalis hair tonic. Ma proceeded to walk inside while El continued to admire the handwriting on the sign;

> **Sunday Services to be Held at 2:00 p.m.**
>
> **In Remembrance of**
>
> **Grizelda Gertrude Bonefat Porter Flanders Juarez**
>
> **Cobbledink Cockburn Smith**

Runyon and Cilla strolled up behind El. Cilla was dressed all nice in a bright yellow dress and flat shoes to match. Over her dress was her knit poncho. Runyon had on a spiffy-looking brown sport coat over a dress shirt, corduroy pants, and clean loafers. Runyon, with his arm around Cilla, read the sign and commented, "Why so many last names?"

Elmer responded, "Ma couldn't recall who the last husband was, just the lot of them, so she had the preacher put them all on here." The three proceeded to walk into the church and located Ma, who was standing at the altar and staring down at her sister. Elmer put his arm around Ma, "Are you okay?"

Ma looked at him as if he'd asked a dumb question, "Yeah, fine. Just checking out the makeup job. That coroner never should have let that Bubblehead assist." The four looked down at Grizelda. She still had the creepy smile on her face, too much red rouge on her cheeks and bright, fire engine red lipstick, blue eyeliner, and thick, peach foundation under it all. "Still, quite a bit less than she usually had caked on her ugly face," Ma turned away to take her place in the pews. El leaned in and took notice, raising an eyebrow and nodding in agreement.

The house was full of townsfolk close to Ma and the family, and they all settled in as Father Winkin, dressed in his usual flowing black robe and white collar, approached the pulpit and laid the good book down. He looked down at Ma and smiled before raising a hand to begin the ceremony as the organ music went quiet off to the side. Ma looked up and politely smiled at the preacher.

"My friends, we're gathered here today to pay our last respects to Grizelda, *umm*...Grizelda...*errr*, Porter, Cobblecock, Flandersdink...*errr*, something or rather." The pastor looked out over his flock, "As we say goodbye today to this woman, we must remember that death isn't the end..."

"It is in this case," Ma whispered, interrupting the pastor. Elmer flashed her a look and shook his head.

"*Ahem*...As I was saying." The preacher looked down at Ma, "Death isn't the end, it is a beginning. Today it is but a celebration of life..."

"Amen! I'm celebrating the fact that she's gone!" Ma blurted. Elmer "*shooshed*" his wife as others giggled.

Father Winkin attempted to ignore Ma's outburst, "And as this good and, *errr*...decent woman makes her journey and walks through the heavenly gates above..."

"Or the elevator ride in the other direction..."

"Ma!" Elmer thumped his wife on the shoulder and whispered loudly. Ma returned the gesture with her usual scowl. More giggling could be detected among the parishioners.

"Well, she weren't no saint!"

"Just behave!"

Ma looked back up to the pastor, "Sorry. Please, continue on preacher."

The smirking and chuckling from the room ceased again as Father Winkin nodded in his usual arrogance down at the bereaved and attempted to regain his train of thought, "As I was saying, as I walk through the shadow of the valley of death…I mean…" The Father was beginning to fluster as Ma had interrupted his prepared speech that he'd attempted to memorize one too many times, and now he was lost for words. "Umm…*ahhh*…Hail Mary full of grace who feared no evil. Trespass not through the Garden of Eden and ignore the apples…" Father Winkin shook his head and said under his breath, "*shit.*" He looked up, "Oops, sorry. I meant…Oh, hell! For Goodness sake, does anyone want to come up and say something about the deceased?!" The preacher inquired in a sarcastic tone and then looked down through his driving glasses at Ma, "Something *nice* maybe?" The preacher scanned the room. It appeared no one had anything to say. Father Winkin looked back at Ma.

She just shrugged her shoulders, "I got nuthin."

Finally, Father Winkin slumped his shoulders and sighed, "Oh, fine then." The preacher raised a hand again, closed his eyes, hesitating several moments as he checked his thoughts, and then began again. "On the day this lady finally died, nobody came to pray. This preacher shall say some words, and then we'll chuck her into the clay." Several in the room failed in their attempts to hold back their chuckles at the terrible reference to the famous ballad. The pastor was attempting his best to be serious, however, he had little material to work with, not really having known the dearly departed other than what he'd encountered in the diner only days prior. Ma kept her head down and she smirked as the preacher continued to struggle for the appropriate words, "The game of life is hard to play, and Grizelda knew she was going to lose it anyway. The losing card she finally lay, so this is all I have to say…"

Ma leaned into El and whispered casually, "Theme song to *M*A*S*H*."

Father Winkin's voice grew louder as he held a hand high and continued, "My friends, let me quote the Leviticus Ten. Drink the not, nor the thou sons with the, lest yea die. Nor congregate at the corner tabernackle…"

Ma leaned over to El and whispered, "More *M*A*S*H*. Father Mulcahey's drunk sermon." El just shook his head in response and gave her the signal to shush with his finger to his lips. Ma glanced around the room to view many in agony in their attempts not to laugh out loud.

The preacher paused, as if in deep thought when in reality he was struggling for words, and then he began again, gazing out over everyone, "…Grizelda was a good bowler, and a good woman. She was one of us. She was a woman who loved the outdoors…" The preached looked down at the body, "…And bowling. And as a surfer, she explored the beaches of Southern California, from La Jolla to Leo Carrillo and up to Pismo."

Ma's expression soured as she attempted to determine just what the preacher was referencing now.

"She died, like so many young women of her generation, she died before her time. In your wisdom, Lord, you took her, as you took so many bright flowering young men at Khe Sanh, at Langdok, and at Hill 364. These young men gave their lives, and so would Grizelda. And so, Grizelda Cobblecock…*errr*…Flandersdink…something or rather, in accordance with what we think your dying wishes might well have been, we commit your final mortal remains to the bosom of…*ummm*…or local cemetery, which we think you may have loved so well."

"What in the hell was that?!"

"*Shhhhhh*, Ma!"

"It was the eulogy scene from the Big Lebowski," came Rupert's voice as Eleanor backhanded him in his gut to keep him quiet.

The preacher continued, "God is pretty busy. It's not reasonable to expect him to concern himself with the individuals. Therefore, don't pray to God to solve your problems. God wants brave souls." Father Winkin grew louder, "He wants winners, no quitters! If you can't win, at least try to win! God loves tryers…isn't that right, Robin?" The father looked straight at Wally McIntyre, who glanced at his brother with a confused look on his face. Joshua simply gave his brother the "I don't know" expression in return.

Ma leaned into El, smiled, and whispered loudly, "I know that one, it's Gene Hackman's sermon scene from the *Poseidon Adventure!*" El shook his head at his wife in apparent disgust to the unorthodox proceedings.

Father Winkin walked out from behind the pulpit and approached the fruit-crate coffin, closed his eyes, and raised one hand, pointing it out palm up and in a calmer voice, "She…she saw things you people wouldn't believe.

Attack ships on fire off the shoulder of Orion. She watched C-beams glitter in the dark near the Tannhäuser Gate." The preacher opened his eyes to a bewildered audience, "All those moments will be lost in time, like tears in rain." He looked endearingly down at the makeup-covered corpse lying inside the farm crate and said softly, "It was time to die."

Ma, with another bewildered look crossing her face, turned around and looked to Cicely and Smirnoff who each shrugged their shoulders. She then looked over to the McIntyre brothers who were seated in the same pew on the opposite side of the room. Wally leaned forward and glanced back, "*Blade Runner*, the tears in the rain speech."

"Anyone got a dove they can release?" Uttered a monotone Marmaduke, seated in the last row with his head down, arms folded, and legs stretched out.

Ma stood up and clapped her hands together, "Well, that's good enough for me. Good job, preacher!" She winked at Father Winkin, who seemed relieved that someone had brought a close to the ceremony before he'd been required to come up with additional material. Ma scanned the room, "Let's move this along." She looked over at the McIntyres, "Did you two dig a hole yet?"

"Yes, Ma. Got a spot dug out in the far corner of the cemetery," Joshua replied as he stood up and approached. Others in the room began to stand to leave, all a bit confused as to whether the funeral service had actually concluded or not, and where to go next. Joshua handed Ma a piece of paper. "We found this is your sister's stuff when we brought her over to the church. We thought you might want to read it."

Ma took the paper and looked at it with a puzzled expression and then she addressed the room, "No need to assemble at the cemetery as far as I'm concerned, the boys here can take care of that. Let's all head up to the diner for some after-the-funeral refreshments. Special of the day will be crab cakes in honor of the deceased." Ma began to read the paper that had been handed to her, adjusting her glasses a bit. Others meandered, some waiting on Ma and others congratulating the pastor on a successful service. As Ma read into the body of the mystery letter she began to tear up.

El noticed first. "You okay, Ma?" He asked as Ma's head began to drop as she read further. El looked up at Runyon and shrugged his shoulders.

"What's going on?" Runyon inquired as he and Cilla became concerned. Ma's head was fully down, and she lowered the letter to her side.

Others began to take note of Ma's emotions and started to circle around, each concerned for their matriarch. El remarked to everyone softly, "I think the weight of the loss has finally hit. Her heart is dropping. It was only a matter of time and circumstance." El began to put his arm around his spouse while others lowered their heads out of respect.

"It's okay, Ma, let it all out. We understand," Rupert remarked as Eleanor approached and put her hand on Ma's shoulders, which were now shuddering to her apparent sobbing. Ma's emotions were beginning to affect the others in the church as several began to tear up, not so much for the deceased but rather for Ma's current state of apparent sadness. Bob Johnson was showing it the most as tears began to stream down his chubby cheeks, his wife Mable putting her arm around the big man.

Ma's shoulders began to bounce more as her head remained down. El looked up and put one hand out, "Let's give her some air." He attempted to tug on her just a little to get her to go with him to the door, "C'mon, Ma." As he did so Ma's head began to come back up, and she revealed that she wasn't exactly crying from sadness, she was also smiling. Ma's face was tear-stained as her crying and laughing were both causing her eyeballs to waterfall. Ma sighed heavily and pulled her glasses forward with the hand the letter was in, and she began to wipe her eyes with her other hand.

"She's gone goofy from the service," Wally whispered to his brother.

"What is it, Ma? What did the letter say? Why are you smiling?"

Ma's voice cracked through the weeping, "It was Grizelda. It's her last will and testament. She kept it with her in that stupid suitcase." Ma adjusted her glasses back after wiping away the tears, and she displayed an even wider smile, "She was rich! And she left everything to me!" Ma held the letter up, "All that money she fleeced out of all those husbands! Plus, her life insurance policy! I'm the beneficiary! It's at least twenty-thousand total!" Ma burst out in laughter that she could no longer control.

Cilla leaned into Runyon and whispered, "That ain't exactly rich." Runyon lifted his eyebrows to his fiancé, realizing the same.

El pulled his arm away, "*Jeese*, Ma, you're terrible. We thought you were weeping over your loss."

Ma scowled at her husband, "My loss? I didn't lose anything! Grizelda was a mean, rotten person! I'm getting payback for all those years of her trying to get rid of me! She had it coming!"

"Oh, c'mon, Ma. She couldn't have been all bad." Rupert joined the conversation, "Look at all the people that showed up here today to pay their respects."

"Pay their respects?!" Ma's demeanor changed to her usual cynical attitude, and she pointed at the altar. "Look at what you put her in! I can feel the love just oozing from those fruit crates right now! Admit it, none of you liked her any more than I did and most of you only met her that one time for no more than five minutes! I'm taking the money and running!" Ma gave a stern nod and began to walk towards the door. Just before reaching it, she stopped and turned back, giving her attention to the McIntyre brothers. "Don't forget to drop that crate in the cemetery and throw some dirt over it." Ma began to turn back to the door and stopped herself, dropping her head and then spun around once more, "Just do it respectfully!"

After Ma exited the church, the remaining few went silent. Following several moments of folks looking at each other while swaying side to side, kicking the floor, and rocking on their heels, Elmer let out a chuckle which had a trickle-down effect and everyone began laughing. Once the tension had eased Joshua gave a head nod to Wally to help him take care of the dearly departed. Father Winkin closed the crate cover as the boys removed the casket. Everyone bowed their heads in respect as the two carried the makeshift coffin through the church past them all and out the doors to the waiting front-end loader.

It was Bob Johnson who made the suggestion that would finally empty the church. "Them crab cakes are sounding pretty good."

CHAPTER 8

Ma's Vacation

Runyon was placing the last of the egg cartons in the bed of the pickup truck as just minutes earlier he and El had performed the morning collection from the hens in the chicken barn. This was a daily task as Ma not only required but also insisted on fresh eggs daily in the diner. Ma was taking an inventory with pencil and paper as Runyon gently placed the delicate cargo in the truck when she reached out and held one carton aside for the house.

"Whacha plan to do with the money that Grizelda left to you, Ma?"

"I have a few ideas," Ma casually replied as Cilla skipped up behind her. Ma grabbed another carton from the truck and handed it back to her, "Here, put this in Runyon's fridge. I'm sure you two can use it."

"Thanks, Ma!"

The old woman continued, "I think I'll spend a bit of it having you build out the further wall of the diner and make a little more room in there, and maybe change out some of the older fixtures in the kitchen like that crappy dishwasher." Runyon nodded in response to her ideas.

"That's a good idea, Ma," Elmer's voice was heard as he exited the barn with a full steel milk can, struggling a bit and dropping it to the ground as Runyon noticed and jogged over to help his father. Runyon, even though he was on the thin side, had the strength of several as he hoisted the hundred or so pound can, carrying it back and lifting it into the truck being extra careful not to drop it and damage the eggs. Meanwhile, Elmer checked his own aching back and continued, "We could use a couple more booths and a proper place to play the music on Friday nights."

Ma stopped counting and waived her pencil between Runyon and Cilla, "And you two!" Both perked up and noticed Ma's directness as she scowled at the couple and then pointed her pencil at Runyon's tiny cabin, "That ain't no place for the two of you to live in. You'll need a proper house somewhere else!"

The younger ones both looked nervously at each other, Runyon wondering if his mother was kicking him out of the tiny cabin they'd built on the homestead. Ma cracked a bit of a smile and pointed her pencil directly to her son, "So, I'm going to have you and Elmer put that thing over on the west side of the property where it overlooks the creek bed, and you get a good sunset. I'll hire you and the boys to do some building so that you and my future daughter-in-law here will have more room to move around. You need a proper-sized house with a nice kitchen."

El's face formed a smile, as he'd suspected this was coming as Cilla put her arms around the big-hearted diner owner, being careful with the eggs, and blurted out, "Thank you!"

Ma allowed Cilla to hug her for only a moment. "Alright, alright. Don't get mushy!" Ma gently pushed her away and glanced at Runyon, "It's only right that you have a nice-sized place to put your wife on the homestead and a place out of my earshot to call your own."

Runyon leaned into his mother and said softly, "I didn't ask her."

"Shut up!" Ma barked and looked to Cilla, who was all smiles, "And you and me need to start planning the ceremony and let me know what you need." Cilla nodded to Ma in agreement.

As El walked past Runyon, the boy leaned into his father and whispered, "I didn't ask her."

"You should probably do what your Ma says and shut up, boy. Haven't you learned yet that you don't make the decisions? If your wife says you're getting married, then you're getting married." Runyon stood back up with a befuddled expression on his face.

"You know what else you should do with that money, Ma?" Cilla spoke up as Ma squinted and listened. Cilla gently poked Ma in the shoulder, "You should do something for yourself! Something you've never done. Take a vacation or something. Go somewhere. Maybe go on a cruise! You'd enjoy that."

"A cruise?" Ma adjusted her glasses, "A cruise to where? Like on a big boat or something?"

"Yeah, Ma, a big cruise ship. That'd be fun and relaxing for you. You deserve it with everything you do for everyone else."

Runyon and El shook their heads to one another as Ma pondered the suggestion, and Cilla continued, "I've looked into them, it's just like being on a big floating city. You wouldn't have to do anything. You get a room of your own, they feed you all day long and there's even stores and a casino on them ships. They have fancy shows every night and all kinds of games. They even have bingo!"

Ma was taking in the information, scowling in deep thought, and staring at the sky. "A vacation, huh?" She snapped around to Runyon and El, "What do you two think?!"

El rubbed the back of his neck, "I dunno. Them big boats go pretty far away. Plus, you'd need to fly just to get to where they're parked. They have a lot of people on them fancy ships. You know how you are around people you don't know. You're not too good around people you do know."

"Cilla's right about all of them things those big boats have, Ma," Runyon offered as he took the carton of eggs that Cilla was reaching out to him. "But Pa's right too, you aren't so good around crowds, not even small ones."

Ma crinkled her nose at the two and turned back to Cilla, "Where do them big boats go?"

"Warm places. Toasty warm. Like the Caribbean."

Ma squinted, "The what? The carribeaner? I got one of them on my keychain. Is that where they're made?"

"No, Ma, the Caribbean," said Runyon as his mother turned back to him. "Way down south past Florida. It's really hot down there."

"Hot? Like here in the summer? How hot? Like in the seventies hot?"

"More like nineties hot. All of the time, too."

"I ain't flying." Elmer said softly, "I ain't too keen on hot places, neither."

Cilla spoke again, "C'mon, Ma, you'd like it!" Ma turned back to her future daughter-in-law. "Don't listen to either of these two grumps, you deserve it, and your room on the ship would be nice and air-conditioned when you needed to get out of the sun. And you don't have to fly, them ships go out of Boston and head straight for the warm weather!" Cilla pleaded, taking Ma's arm, "Oh, c'mon, Ma! A nice, week-long cruise where they visit a different place every day! You'd love it!"

Ma looked up at the sky again and thought for a moment while El and Runyon stood, somewhat disgusted by the idea, knowing what Ma was like around people in general. Cilla's eyes and smile were wide as she waited for Ma to make a decision, flashing Runyon a dirty look, and then back to Ma with her smile. Ma finally looked back down at her, "I got three conditions!"

"What?"

Ma spoke sternly to a concerned Cilla, "First, that Val and Cicely agree to run the diner while I'm gone! They're the only ones I trust entirely, and they won't wreck the place!" Ma turned to Runyon, "Second, you get Marmaduke to watch the homestead here and tend to the animals. He'll make certain everything here at the house is taken care of and he'll also make sure that the diner gets what it needs! He'll do it all for a cup of coffee at the most if I know him well enough."

Runyon looked confusingly at Ma, "Why not me...."

"Third!" Ma turned back to Cilla, whose eyes were wide, and her hands clasped in front of her. "You and Runyon go with us! I ain't going with just this old idiot of a husband!" Cilla raised her arms high and screeched, nearly jumping into Ma's arms as the old woman turned back to the men, "This'll be your wedding gift. Plus, I'll feel better having you two younger people with us to keep us safe and make sure we're doing everything right and proper and staying out of trouble! This old fart would just get us lost in a foreign country." El looked up and frowned at his wife.

Cilla kissed the scowling woman several times, "Thank you, thank you, thank you!"

"Okay, get off me." Ma pushed the grateful younger lady away.

Runyon, giving a disgusted look leaned into El, who was shaking his head at the thought of it all, "I never asked her to marry me."

"Shut up, boy."

*　　*　　*　　*

Ma had trusted Cilla to make the arrangements, not having time to bother with it herself, including packing the appropriate clothes for the four travelers and arranging for a reliable rental car from the McIntyre's. Of course, Joshua wasn't about to charge Ma for the vehicle and made certain he and Wally gave them the best vehicle on the lot, giving the big sedan a good once-over before handing over the keys. They did, however, leave the hand-written advertisement for their used car lot in the rear window, written using a bar of soap.

Cilla planned out the trip for the four of them by booking a six-day, seven-night cruise out of Boston with two stops in the Bahamas in both Nassau and Freeport. Cilla had booked her future in-laws into a balcony room and herself and Runyon into an adjacent interior room, which was a bit less expensive and was good enough for the two of them. She was just excited to be included and on her first ever cruise.

The drive to Boston was a bit awkward with Ma not having been out of the northern Maine area for quite some time, and there was plenty of back-seat driving from the grouchy woman as Runyon was at the helm and using the car's fancy GPS that Ma had decided to argue with quite often during their journey. Not to mention the swearing she directed at the many other vehicles that passed by them during the drive. The further away they traveled from East Puddleduck and crossed over the state lines, the worse everyone else's driving was, according to Ma's loud and verbal opinions.

As they arrived at the Boston harbor and pulled into the cruise terminal parking area they received their first glimpse of the massive, colorful cruise ship. The three others still hadn't any idea of just what Cilla had packed for them to wear, however, both El and Runyon were a bit skeptical as to what may be in their luggage if it were to be anything like what Cilla had dressed them in for the drive to get to the pier. Runyon, who was accustomed to a plain T-shirt, jeans, and sneakers, exited the vehicle wearing a button-up sleeveless, bright orange tropical shirt with pictures of multi-colored palm trees on it, khaki short pants to his knees, and brown sandals. El was dressed in a bright blue Hawaiian shirt with pictures of motorcycles on it, tan short pants, and blue plastic clogs. On both of their heads were baseball caps. The one on Runyon's head with the saying, "Next Stop, Bahamas," and El's with the quote, "I Brake for Bahama Mamas." Ma and Cilla both had on sundresses. The one that Ma had on was bright orange with a tropical floral pattern and Cilla's was a bright yellow with a banana pattern. Ma, for the first time ever had on a pair of flip-flops, along with a big-brimmed sunhat, and thick-lensed, clip-on sunglasses over her reading glasses. Cilla also had on large-lensed sunglasses, not of the clip-on type, though.

As ridiculous as El and Runyon felt they soon realized as they exited the vehicle that everyone else parked at the terminal that were preparing to board the ship were all wearing the same similarly stupid-looking clothing that the four of them had on. El and Runyon gave a look at each other in amazement that so many people could purposely look that ridiculous all at the same time, and they shrugged their shoulders at each other.

"Look at the size of this ship!" Ma exclaimed as all four looked up at the "Queen of the Seas" as the name indicated on the bow. "It's huge! How many people does this thing hold?"

"Around two thousand passengers and the same number of crew," Cilla mentioned as she shaded her sunglass-covered eyes with her hand and looked up at the massive hull towering above them. "It's eleven stories tall."

"Uh-huh. Ever see, Titanic?" El remarked. Ma scowled at the old man and whacked him on the shoulder in return. Elmer exclaimed his displeasure and held his aching arm as a porter approached the foursome and asked if he could take their luggage.

Cilla leaned into Ma, "They take care of everything for you on this trip. You won't have to do anything. Just tip the ones that help you."

"Tip them? Everyone?!" Ma asked.

"Yes, most of them. It's customary to tip the people that help you get on the ship. Once you're on board your tips are included, or you can just tip the ones you want."

El flipped the porter a quarter, "There you go, son." The porter caught the coin, briefly stared at it, and then flashed El a look.

"I think it's supposed to be more," Runyon observed.

"That seemed fair." Ma squinted and looked to Runyon, "How much more?"

Cilla spoke up, "A couple bucks to five is about right, I think."

Ma snapped her head to Cilla. "Five bucks?! All he did was pick up a couple of suitcases and throw them on that rolling cart!" Ma turned to the porter and pointed with her stubby finger, "Are you gonna unpack them for me and wash my dirty underwear too?" The porter's eyes grew wide as he stared at the finger in his face.

"Ma!" Runyon yelled out.

"Well, shit! For five bucks he should be rubbing my aching feet!" Ma's comments weren't going unnoticed by the many people in the parking area as Ma turned to Cilla and said in a softer voice, "By the way, I like these flippity-flops. I didn't think I would, but they're pretty comfy." Cilla smiled and nodded as Ma spun back around and pointed again, raising her voice once more, "We don't take tips in my diner! Much less for only tossing a suitcase! Hells bells, I had to pick up a dead woman's suitcase off my diner floor and nobody offered me a quarter! How many more of you are there before I get on this tub?! I'll end up broke before we leave the dock if I need to dish out five bucks every time I sneeze, and you guys say Gazuntite?!"

"It's fine, ma'am," said the porter with his arms raised in front of him in defense of himself. At that point, the poor guy just wanted to get away from the crazy old woman and her equally insane family.

Ma wasn't allowing him to leave peacefully as she spouted off when the man turned to assist another traveler, "What do you do for ten bucks? Wax my upper lip for me?! My husband here could use a manscape, there's twenty in it for you!"

El put a hand on Ma's shoulder. "Take it easy, Ma. This is all new to us. Let's just get on the boat."

*　　*　　*　　*

Ma was a bit pale and clammy, with one hand on her stomach, *"Ohhhh, Jeesus. I think I'm going to be seasick,"* she whined and leaned against Runyon, holding her other hand to her mouth and letting up a quiet burp.

"Ma, we haven't left the dock yet." Runyon pushed his shoulder up and knocked his mother back upright. She returned the gesture with a scowl. The four were seated in the waiting area of the cruise terminal along with hundreds of other excited passengers, all waiting to board the ship. El was asleep in his seat, arms folded in front of him, his baseball cap down over his brow, and his bare legs and clogged feet stuck out in front of him.

Ma reclined and folded her arms too. "How long is this going to take? Half of the vacation will be over before we get on that boat!" Ma's frustration was quickly overtaking her queasy stomach.

"We have number '235' and they're on '196'." Cilla looked up at the digital ticker and observed. "They've got lots of people at that long service counter, though, so it shouldn't take too long." Cilla leaned forward and turned to Ma, "Now, don't forget Ma, they take lots of pictures of you on the trip, beginning right here in the terminal, I think. All week long they'll be snapping your photo, lots of times and mostly when you don't want them to."

"That's bullshit."

"It's what they do, Ma. They snap you all day, every day, and then put the pictures all up on a tack board with everyone else's on the boat…"

"…And let me guess, then they want me to pay for them all."

"Just the ones you want, Ma."

"That's bullshit."

"…*Two thirty-five*…" The intercom blurted out.

Ma whacked Elmer in his sleeping gut, causing him to jump as she rocked on her buttocks and up to her feet. "C'mon Captain Ahab, it's time to go!"

"*Jeese, Ma!*"

After checking in at the counter the four were on their way, exiting the terminal and beginning their walk across the long glassed-in gangway to the ship's entrance on the Promenade deck. As they entered the big, colorful room Caribbean music could be heard emitting from the steel drums being playing next to a huge liquor bar. The four travelers were in awe, gawking around and up, as in the center was a massive glass elevator and the decks were open for several floors above them. There was also a grand, lighted staircase to either side of the elevator. As they took their first steps into the massive room, a smiling lady photographer stopped the four. "Welcome! Can I take your first photo on the boat?" She spoke in an accent that Ma didn't recognize.

"Oh great, here we go," she said sarcastically to El, who just chuckled.

Cilla bounced in front of the camera with Runyon in tow, "Yes, you sure can!" Ma smiled as she watched Runyon stand tall and smile with his fiancé tight on his arm as they stood behind a makeshift boat anchor bearing the ship's name, and a scenic tapestry behind them of a warm Caribbean location, and had their photos taken.

Next, the photographer turned to Ma and motioned her to the photo set. "Nope," Ma said, closing her eyes and putting her arm out.

In her foreign accent, the lady photographer replied, "Oh, c'mon, my lady. You're first time on a ship? Don't you want photos to remember it'all?"

"I'll remember it just fine."

"Just one photo?"

"I said no."

"It won't hurt at'all. A nice photo of you and your husband." The lady photographer was smiling wide.

"Oh, fine!" Ma realized she wasn't going to see any more of the boat until she stood in front of the camera and had her picture taken. She tugged El into the photo scene with her and Ma smiled wide, a nice, big fake smile. As the photographer snapped the picture, Ma displayed a nice, big fat middle finger straight over the anchor and at the photographer. "There! Thank you very much! Let's go!" Ma dragged El out of the scene and along behind her. Elmer had to hold onto his baseball cap as he was being pulled into the Promenade deck, which was overly crowded, and very loud. Ma stopped and observed the big bar in front of the glass elevators and she leaned to Cilla, "You need to keep me away from that thing! If I have one drink I'll be passed out under the boat."

"That's going to be a challenge, Ma. There's a bar around every corner. Lots of places to eat, too."

"We'll see about the food. I'm a bit picky if it ain't mine," Ma said as the other three turned to look around the massive ship's deck and wandered out of her arm's length. Ma spun completely around too, slowly, and admired the decorations, pictures, paintings, and bright lights. When she turned back she was met with a plate of drinks in her face, and a tall, fine-looking uniformed waiter holding the tray.

"Drink of the day for you, ma'am?"

Ma squinted at the plate of multi-colored, cold refreshments. "Huh? Oh, okay. Yes, what's the drink of the day?" Ma looked at the waiter's nametag and decided against attempting to address him by name as she couldn't pronounce it, let alone read what it said. His accent was something similar to Smirnoff's, she thought.

"It's fruity, ma'am. You'll enjoy it." The smiling waiter leaned down to her, "I just need your room key."

"What?" Ma looked down at the card key she'd received when checking in at the terminal. She'd hung it around her neck on a lanyard the cruise staff had provided to her so she wouldn't lose it. Ma removed her lanyard and handed it to the waiter, "Do you mean this thing?"

"Yes, ma'am. This is how you pay for everything on the boat, and it's the key to get into your room."

"Huh? Okay." Ma accepted the instructions well. Better than usual than if she were receiving them from someone she actually knew. The waiter handed Ma the drink and a receipt, and walked off to the next passenger, thanking her as he left.

"Yes, okay." Ma mumbled to herself, *"Jeesus,* there's a lot of *foreigners* on this tub." Ma cocked her eye at the tiny receipt, "I thought everything on this boat was free." Ma squinted harder as she lifted the fruity drink close to her mouth. The receipt came into view as the drink touched her lips, and she yelled out, *"Holy shit!* Twelve bucks?!" Ma looked around for her husband, whom she spotted through the crowd. "Elmer! Come over here and look at this!" Ma held up the receipt as others began to take notice, as Ma was louder than the crowd of people, and the steel drum music. "Twelve bucks for a fruit drink! A *goddam* fruit drink!"

Runyon and Cilla, who'd been listening to the steel drums and sipping on their own drinks, turned when they heard Ma call out. They both quickly started shuffling toward Ma to quiet her down as the loud woman walked up to El on the other side of the room, brought her expensive drink to her lips again, and took a sip. Ma stopped, eyes widened, and she turned around and spit the drink back out and straight onto Runyon's shirt. *"Pewtew!"* "Holy shit! This has alcohol in it! A lot of it!"

"Yes, Ma." Runyon replied in a disgusted tone, "It's the drink of the day. They all have alcohol in them." Runyon attempted to locate the stain on his colorful shirt to wipe it off with a napkin. He couldn't find it.

El wandered up behind his wife as she stared at her expensive drink and lowered her voice a bit, "Twelve bucks for a shot of rum and flavored water?"

"That one's cheaper than most others too. The drink of the day is usually a buck or two cheaper," Cilla pointed out. "It's the non-alcoholic stuff that's free, except for the soda. You gotta pay for that, too."

"That's bullshit." Ma shook her head, holding up the hourglass-shaped plastic cup. "Amazing." She handed the drink to El, "Here, you finish it."

"Ain't you gonna have a drink or two on the trip, Ma?"

"Maybe one or two, we'll see. Not at those prices, though! Where's our rooms, anyway?" Ma looked around as if her stateroom was close by.

*   *   *   *

"Oh, *my God.* I'm gonna puke." Ma was standing at her balcony glass doors, looking out with both hands up against either side of the frame.

"Ma, you're looking out at the pier parking lot," Runyon remarked as he entered his parent's stateroom with Cilla just ahead of him. "We haven't moved yet."

The old woman turned around, "I just know this tub is going to bounce up and down on that ocean, and I'm going blow chunks."

"You won't even feel it, Ma," Cilla said as she sat on the edge of their bed, all smiles. "These rooms are nice, aren't they?"

"It's like sardines in a can with a window."

"Bathrooms a bit tight," El remarked as he exited the tiny washroom. "Not much room for the smells to go." The other three crinkled their noses at his remark, expecting the worst. "If you fart in here everyone's gonna know it."

Ma pointed towards the hallway between their rooms, "You ain't got no windows on your side?" She was being serious.

"No, Ma," Runyon answered, a bit sarcastically, "there's not too many windows in the interior rooms."

Cilla stood and put her arms around Runyon's and looked him in the face, "It'll be nice and romantic for us." She looked over at Ma, "It'll be romantic for you in here too."

Ma rolled her eyes and responded in her sarcastic tone, "Oh, *Jeesus*. Does *that* look romantic?!" Ma motioned to her other half, who was now lounging on the cramped stateroom couch, his arms folded and hat down over his eyes. Ma turned and looked out the balcony again, belching as she looked out over the parking lot as her stomach went queasy once more.

"Take it easy, we still haven't moved yet, Ma."

"I just know I'm gonna be sick!"

*　　*　　*　　*

It was just about 6:00 p.m. and the four were seated in the main dining room. They were all admiring the décor in the elegant supper-eating area as the smartly dressed waiters were pouring glasses of ice water and placing baskets of warm dinner rolls on their table. El undid his fancy cloth napkin and tucked it into his shirt as the other three gave him a look and put theirs in their laps. The oversized dining room was full of hungry passengers and many wait staff were running about. People were carrying on conversations and glassware was clinking while Caribbean music played over the speakers mounted in the ceiling. It was a busy and loud place.

"See, Ma. We said you wouldn't feel the waves," Runyon said as his menu was placed in front of him by one of the wait staff.

"Yeah, I suppose you were right. I can't feel the boat moving so much." Ma glanced out the big picture windows they were seated next to and watched the waves going by as the ship steamed forward, and then she picked up her menu and adjusted her glasses. She looked around and whispered, "How many waiters do they have for each table? There's a swarm of them in here."

"Looks to be three per table, Ma," Cilla observed as she stretched out her neck and looked around.

"Three? *Hmph*, that's two, too many," as she looked around the room. "One per table at the diner is more than enough. No wonder these cruises cost so much, you gotta pay for way too many waiters!"

"There's a lot more people here than in your diner, Ma," El mentioned as he looked over his fancy menu.

"Can I start you off with an appetizer?"

The smartly dressed waiter startled Ma from behind as she jumped in her seat. *"Jeesus!"* she blurted out as the man rounded to the end of their table in full view of them all. "Don't do that to me or you'll be cleaning up my seat!" Ma yelled out and pointed up at the man.

"I apologize, madam. My name is Sefu, and I'll be your head waiter for the entire week." The polite, clean-cut gentleman said in his native accent, "May I start you off with an appetizer, Mrs. Wilomena?"

Ma looked confusingly over to Cilla, "How'd he know my name?!" She looked back up, "Seafood? Is that your name?" Ma crinkled her nose and stared over her glasses.

"Sefu."

"See-food?" Ma adjusted her glasses.

"Sefu. It's Swahili."

"I don't care what kind of fish you serve here." Ma looked over to Cilla, "Imagine that, they serve fish on a boat. Go figure."

"No, Ma. That's his name. And it's his job to know yours, that's why they assign the tables so they can learn your name before you get here. It's all part of the experience."

"Hmmm." Ma glanced back down at her menu. She held the menu out and squinted, peering through her reading glasses perched on the bridge of her nose with the sunglasses flipped up as she looked over the list of appetizers. Her eyebrows sank as they came into view:

Iced & Smoked Fresh Oysters
Apple Mignonette
Butter & Mace Stuffed Mushrooms
Parmesan Pearl Bone Marrow & Hand-Cut Beef Tartare
Parsley Shallot Salad
Parmesan Pillows

Ma slowly lowered the menu and looked up at Sefu with a blank, slightly agitated expression, "What in the hell are these?" Cilla looked away and chuckled as El and Runyon kept their heads down, glancing at each other across the table, knowing good and well what was to come.

A smiling Sefu responded, "Madam, they're the appetizers. They're all very good. You should try one."

"First off, chuckles, don't call me madam. I ain't the head hooker of this haram!" Ma made a circling motion on the tabletop with her finger. Cilla blurted out a laugh, holding her napkin to her mouth to conceal the outburst, and continued to look out the window at the ocean passing by. "Second, I ain't buying whatever it is your trying to sell here." Ma glanced back at the menu, "Bone marrow? Are you serious? Pillows?" Ma lowered the menu again and looked at El who still had his head down. "Mace? Ain't that the hot stuff Fat Bob Johnson carries on his belt?"

El couldn't help but chuckle, "Yup, it is."

Ma held her appetizer menu out to Sefu and said politely, however sarcastically, "We'll skip the appetizers and go directly to the main course. Can we have the menus for that, if you please, Seafood?"

Another outburst from Cilla and Elmer. Runyon kept his head low and placed his hands over his eyes, trying his best not to laugh. Sefu left the table to retrieve the main course menus. El looked up at his wife, "*Jeese*, Ma. You need to try to be more polite. He's just being nice and doing his job."

Ma folded her arms and looked straight down at her silverware. "I know. I just ain't used to all of this fancy crap."

Sefu returned moments later with four more menus. He hesitantly handed one to Ma. She looked up at the nice-looking and smartly-dressed waiter, "I'm sorry, Seafood. I'm just not used to all this fancy-pants, high society food and stuff."

"It's Sef…no problem *mada*…I mean, Mrs. Wilomena. Please, try one of our delicious dinner entrees."

Ma held the new menu out in front of her and squinted, grimacing, and sighing as she made out the list of items:

Ricotta Ravioli
Tiger Shrimp Creole
Featured Vegetarian
Salmon Fillet with Citrus Rub
Pork Chop with Caramelized Onion
Flat Iron Steak
New England Lobster

Ma began to giggle to herself, bouncing gently in her chair. "*Heh, heh. Heh, heh.* Oh, goodness." Ma sighed again and looked up, "I'm not sure if I want to eat a salmon that's been rubbed, or what the cook was rubbing, but I hope the fish was happy before he went." Ma handed the menu to Sefu, "I'll take the steak. Medium. I don't know what you'll put in it, but it's probably better if I don't."

"Excellent choice." Sefu happily took the menu back and received the orders from the other three.

As Sefu left the table Ma continued to giggle and asked no one in particular, "Crazy, isn't it?" She started to wipe the tears of laughter from her eyes under her glasses when suddenly she was startled again.

"Bottle of wine?"

"*Jeesus!*" Ma jumped as the man behind her shoved a wine list around her shoulders between her and El. Ma snapped her head around to see a shorter man, similarly dressed the same as their wait staff in black pants, a white dress shirt, and a black vest. "If you boys don't quit that I'm going to pee in my dress!"

"Sorry, madam."

"Oh, here we go again," El whined.

Ma pointed back and up at the man, whose name she couldn't pronounce from his nametag, nor did she recognize the accent. "I'm warning you! Stop calling me…*ahhh*, forget it!" She grabbed the wine list and adjusted her glasses.

"A bottle of wine might be nice." Runyon was attempting to change the subject and distract his mother, "What do they have Ma? Anything we've heard of?"

"Well, I'll tell you one thing, I've heard of these prices! They're called highway robbery!" Ma looked up at the wine person, "Forty-five dollars for something called a penis gringo?! Are you nuts or something?!"

"That's a Pinot Gringo, madam."

Ma turned to El, "Look at this! They got something called a 'Smoking Loon' for thirty-five bucks! I can smoke a loon for free with my shotgun! And look here! A simple Chardonnay costs forty bucks!"

Cilla reached over and grabbed the wine list, handing it back to the waiter, "Water will be fine." The man tipped his head and happily walked away.

El grabbed the napkin-covered basket off the table, "Here, Ma. Have a roll, they're free with dinner."

Ma took one of the several types of rolls, held it up, looked carefully, and then pounded it on the tabletop. "Yup, just as I suspected, hard!" Her three dinner companions laughed.

As the four waited for their meals and were engaging in "cordial" conversation, once again Ma was startled when a photographer stuck her camera between her and El, pointing it at Runyon and Cilla, "May I take your picture?"

"*Jeesus!*" Ma jumped sideways from her seat and grabbed a fork, pointing it at the photographer, who leaned back just a bit as Runyon and Cilla hugged up close to each other in their seats for their photo. Ma looked at El, "They better quit doing that! My heart can't take much more, and I didn't bring enough pairs of under britches to change into every time they startle me!"

The photographer, again dressed similarly to the wait staff came around between Runyon and Cilla as Ma followed her with her arm, continuing to point the fork at the innocent photographer. The lady then asked Ma in her accented voice, "Your photo madam with your handsome husband?"

El perked up and smiled at the compliment as Ma lowered the fork and said in a sarcastic tone, "Oh, yes." Ma snuggled up to El, and as the photographer focused and snapped the picture Ma stuck her middle finger up across the table straight at the camera. "There, now scram!" The surprised photographer moved on to the next table.

"Dinner is served!"

"Sonofabitch!" Ma jumped from her seat again. And again, Ma lifted the fork back up as Sefu placed her plate down. "I'm not telling you again, stop jumping me!"

"I'm sorry *mada*…I mean, Mrs. Wilomena."

Ma looked down as her plate was placed in front of her. The steak was no larger, or thicker than a cellular telephone. Garnished with seven string beans, as Ma counted them, a sprig of parsley, and a dollop of what appeared to be mashed potatoes. "What the hell is this?! We said no appetizers! This can't be my dinner!" Ma stuck her fork into the tiny, flat steak and waved it at Sefu, "In my diner, we serve up USDA prime that's bigger than the plate it comes in! This is a pathetic dog chewy toy!" Ma looked over to Cilla's plate which contained a tiny lobster tail and she pointed at it with her steak, "And where did that tiny crawdad come from? We got bigger bugs swimming around in our toilets back home! That ain't no New England lobster! A Maine lobster would eat that puny thing as a snack!" Ma glanced at El's plate, not having the ability to make out what the tiny portion was. "What the hell did you order?"

El poked at his mystery dinner, "I ain't sure."

"Hey, Ma." Runyon received his mother's attention as he stared at his little mystery meal, "I saw a buffet-style burger barn on the Promenade deck."

Ma threw her baby steak down and stood up, "Well then, that's where we're headed!" She smiled at her confused waiter, "Nothing against you, Snafu, we just ain't used to these fancy things, and we're hungry! Let us know when you get some proper food in here and maybe we'll be back later in the week." The remaining three stood up, placing their napkins down and they all left the elegant dining room to many staring passengers and wait staff, who were all either amused or a bit embarrassed at the show they'd been witness to as the Mainers headed for the ship's burger joint.

*　　*　　*　　*

As the four sat at a table on the open Lido deck enjoying the outside ocean air and starlit skies, they chowed down on their appropriately portion-sized burgers all dripping with fixings and fries on the side as they watched other cruise passengers walking by, eating, or swimming in the nearby pool. Ma smiled at her companions and said, "Now this is a proper meal!"

Ma spent much of the first part of the night in her tiny stateroom bathroom, praying to the porcelain God. She ultimately felt the gentle waves after all.

At around midnight, she ordered room service, a toasted ham and cheese. It helped settle her stomach.

CHAPTER 9

Sailing to Nassau

For the next two days, Ma and her cohorts would enjoy life on the ship as they sailed along the vast ocean toward the Bahamas. The four would spend time lounging under the sun-drenched skies on the Lido deck checking out the various trinkets and specialty shops on deck 2, and even taking in a show in the grand theater. When Ma walked into the two-story auditorium located at the bow of the ship she first thought they'd left the vessel when looking around the highly decorated and massive theater, wondering how they'd managed to fit such a large stage and auditorium inside the boat. They'd also spend time checking out and sampling the various buffet-style eating establishments on a number of decks that seemed to be located around every corner. However, the burger stop on the Lido deck remained their favorite. All four began to form a nice suntan and the other three made certain that Ma didn't get burnt, prompting her to use plenty of tanning lotion and reminding her to turn over often when she lounged under the sunlight on deck 10. Ma had even taken to sitting outside on her balcony to watch the ocean go by without becoming seasick and also enjoyed the child-free area on the Serenity deck near the stern.

The most challenging part of the cruise was acclimating themselves to the heat, however, the clothing that Cilla had either ordered by catalog or picked up at Choppies was working out quite well. El and Runyon had accustomed themselves to their Caribbean attire and they were blending in with other passengers, who were also wearing similar multi-colored clothing. El had even taken to wearing sunglasses, something he'd rarely had on his head in the past, and the baseball cap. Ma poked fun at his knobby knees exposed by his short pants quite often.

On the fourth day, the ship arrived in Nassau, Bahamas. The sky was clear and the temperature was a balmy 92 degrees when the ship docked. As the four stood at the rails on the Lido deck, along with many other excited passengers, they watched the crew as they tied the ship off to the massive pier where two other cruise ships were already docked. Ma looked out at the little town before her and admired the pale-colored buildings and rooftops on the shops and houses, and the palm trees and Caribbean foliage. She noted just how busy the area seemed to be with both tourists and locals.

"Now, remember Ma," Cilla began, "it's way different here than at home. You and El should stick close to us. Do you see that area of shopping places down there?" Cilla pointed to the shops nearer the ships just off the pier. There appeared to be several street blocks of little shops and liquor bars. Ma lifted her eyeglasses with the clip-on, flip-up sunglass lenses and looked where Cilla had indicated. "Them ones are safe to shop in. They got all kinds of junk for you to haggle the price over." Cilla pointed out past the pier to the village, "Don't get too far out over that way, though. It's not as safe the further you wander out."

"What time is our excursion?" Runyon asked of his fiancé.

"Excursion? What's that?" Ma looked up through her flip-ups and from under her sunhat.

"It's an outing, Ma. Cilla planned it for us. We're going to take a boat to our own private island for the day. We're going to sit on the beach, hop in the ocean, and have a nice lunch. She even arranged for a couple of cabanas."

Ma, looking up and holding her sunhat in the warm breeze, "What's a cabanana?"

"It's a beach tent to put your lounge chair under to keep the hot sun off you." Cilla responded, checking her wristwatch, "We've got a little over an hour before the bus gets here to take us to the boat."

Ma smiled at her future daughter-in-law, "You thought of everything, didn't you?"

Smiling, "Yes, Ma, I tried. We can shop for a bit and then go find our bus that'll take us to the charter boat and out to the island. Did you put your bathing suit on under your sundress and bring suntan lotion?"

Ma opened up a big, burlap beach bag that she'd picked up in one of the ship's shops and stuck her face in it, rummaging through it with one hand. "Yup, I got some of that squirty oil in a can right here along with a couple bottles of water, some chewing gum, hard candy, half-a-bag of chips, some cash in that floaty thing on a string that you made me buy, extra sunglasses just in case I lose the ones on my head, another set of reading glasses, a bathing cap, two hairpins and a tampon in case the cash gets wet.

El and Runyon each made a face, not entirely understanding what Ma meant by the last item and the description of its potential use.

"And I got my new, fancy bathing suit on that you helped me pick out of that catalog." Ma hiked her sundress up in the front, exposing the bottom portion of her polka-dotted one-piece.

"Ma! Put your britches down!" El spouted.

Still holding her sundress up, she turned to El, scowled, and stated quite casually, "Whatsa matter with you? I ain't naked under here." El grabbed Ma's sundress and released her grip from it, dropping it back down.

Cilla turned Ma back around by her shoulder. "Now, Ma, remember, folks here will try to sell you everything and anything. You don't have to buy it, and especially don't buy anything that they say is a funny cigarette."

Ma squinted at Cilla, "I don't smoke tobacco anyway."

"That isn't exactly what they'd be trying to sell you, Ma," Runyon remarked. "She meant marijuana."

"They got that here, too?!" Ma asked, wide-eyed behind her dark sunglasses.

"Yes, Ma, and they'll try to sell you it right out on the beach. And they'll call it lots of things to try to get you to buy it. Weed, grass, gange, special cigarettes, and lots of other names too. Don't let them sell it to you."

"And remember Ma," Cilla continued as she adjusted Ma's hat straight, "the fruity drinks here have alcohol in them too, just like the ones on the boat."

Ma turned to El. *Jeesus.* Too many things to remember." El agreed with a raise of an eyebrow and a nod in response.

The foursome made their way to the Promenade deck and disembarked the ship by gangplank. At the end of the short catwalk and just on the pier was the photographer. Just off the gangplank was a painted sign in the shape of a ship's rescue ring to have your photograph taken from behind that read "Welcome to Nassau." Ma shook her head as she walked the gangplank as if a pirate was going to toss her over, and she scooted in front of El and dragged him to the sign. Before the photographer could even ask, Ma stood the two behind it and blurted, "Just take the damn picture!" And, as before, just as the photo was being snapped she flashed her middle finger along with a big smile and continued onto the pier with Elmer in tow. After Runyon and Cilla gladly had their photos taken the four wandered through the Custom's gate, displaying their ship identification cards as passports to the new country, and continued to the shops that were close to the ship and just off the pier. Ma and Cilla picked up a few trinkets to tuck into their beach bags to take home with them, a necklace here and a bracelet there. Even Runyon found himself another baseball hat with a logo that read, "I Be Jammin' in the Bahamas."

Finally, after wandering the area for a while Ma found herself under a shaded area nearer the ship where many others were waiting for their individual charter buses to take them to their various day excursions. Ma sat down and took her hat off. "*Jeesus*, it's hot here," as she waved the hat in front of her sweating face.

El plopped down beside her, groaning as he lowered his rear end to the wooden bench, "It sure is. These here silky shirts and short pants make it a bit easier, though."

"Isn't it gorgeous?" Cilla remarked, smiling large and looking around. "Our bus should be here soon. Where'd Runyon go?"

Ma squinted and looked through the crowds, spotting her son approaching carrying a cardboard tray with four small round containers with straws sticking out of each one. Ma pointed, "Here he comes. Looks like he bought himself four coconuts for some reason. The sun must be getting to him."

Runyon wandered under the awning and Cilla grabbed one of the hollowed-out coconuts, giving her fiancé a kiss. "Thanks, hun."

Runyon handed a coconut to his mother. "Here, Ma. You need some liquids. Don't drink too fast."

Ma reached for her drink, frowning, and admiring the hollowed-out Caribbean fruit full of something frosty and cold. "Thank you. What's in it?" She sipped the straw and her eyes widened, "*Holy shit!* That's strong!"

"I said go slow, Ma. That's a Pina Colada. Lots of Caribbean rum in that. Take it easy." He handed a drink over to Elmer, who stood halfway up and bent over to grab it, nodding to his boy before parking his butt back down again and sampling his cold treat.

Ma took another sip. "Tasty drink. Fruity like bananas and stuff."

"Wouldn't take too many of these to put you under a table, there Ma," Elmer observed as he grinned and sipped.

"Ain't that the truth."

The buses arrived moments later and the four, along with other various ship passengers were on their way to their private island. Ma had some choice words for the bus driver as she wasn't accustomed to just how fast they drove on the busy streets of Nassau in an oversized minivan that consisted more of rust rather than metal. It seemed as if there were little to no traffic laws and speed limits didn't appear to exist. Ma did take notice that the further away they got from the pier, even though the country was quite beautiful, it still showed signs of poverty in certain neighborhoods. Ma eased up a bit on her attitude towards tipping and had El give the driver and their knowledgeable host, who talked to the visitors about the history of the island, a few bucks when they arrived at their charter boat. They proceeded to board a small charter that had a visible capacity of around 50 people with at least 75 dubious tourists and headed out to their island paradise destination. Ma's stomach took a bit of a beating on the twenty-minute trip. On the small charter, she felt the waves quite a bit more than on the ship.

They disembarked the tiny charter onto a tropical island of endless crushed shells and sand beaches that went far into the crystal-clear blue waters. Palm trees, hammocks, and cabanas stretched out under the bright, blue skies as far as their eyes could see. Just back from the beach was a large, covered patio with a restaurant, bar, and souvenir shop, plus a lavatory and changing rooms.

"Okay, I admit it," Ma claimed as she stepped off the pier and into the warm, soft sand, "this is incredible." Ma kicked off her sandals and threw them in her bag. The other three removed their footwear as well to enjoy the hot sand in their toes.

"Yep, sure is something," El remarked. And just as he said this a young, tanned, well-endowed, and skimpy bathing-suited lady walked past him. Her booty protruded around her tiny thong and her buttocks and boobs jiggled and bounced as she continued past. Runyon noticed as well, and Cilla elbowed him in the gut.

"*What?* It's kinda hard not to notice the scenery."

"You have scenery right here." Cilla pointed up and down her better-than-average, however not quite as endowed or large-bootied body. "C'mon, let's get us a cabana and a hammock before they're all taken. Your dad needs to get comfortable." El smiled and nodded to his future daughter-in-law in response to her kind words and caring.

They began to stroll the beach for a shaded spot near the water and Ma was dragging a bit behind. She was looking down at her feet in the sand, watching her steps and trying not to fall over in the soft granules when a tall, well-built, and tanned young man holding a tray of colorful drinks cut her path off. "Complimentary drink, madam?" The waiter asked in his deep, Caribbean-accented voice. Ma looked up at the dark-skinned, muscular man, who only had on a tight, tiny bathing suit.

"*Oh, my,*" Ma softly exclaimed as her wide eyes looked up at the man's muscular chest, and Ma briefly forgot what she had been told about the fruity island drinks. She smiled, "Yes, thank you," as she grabbed the tallest glass and watched the man leave, checking his backside as she chugged what she believed to be fruit punch. "They certainly build them nice here," Ma mumbled to herself as she quickly finished her drink. It was far too hot out to notice how warm the cold drink was going down. Ma caught up with the others, limping as her feet sunk into the sand with each step. Runyon and Cilla were laying out their beach towels onto two lounge chairs under a cabana tent near the ocean's tide line. El was under two palm trees in a large, woven hammock, the trees offering him plenty of shade. Ma dropped her beach bag and held up her empty glass, "This was tasty." She looked around, "When that nice boy comes back I think I'll have another one. I noticed the potty's close by in case I need to tinkle."

"Ma, those drinks have alcohol in them," Runyon noted.

"What?" Ma squinted at her empty glass. "Alcohol? I didn't taste any booze in this."

"That's because it's hot out, Ma," Cilla said as she laid out in her lounge chair face-first and held up a bottle of tanning oil, Runyon's hint to apply some to her backside. "You need to be careful with those. Go slow."

"Got an empty hammock here," El remarked from under his baseball cap, pointing to another one beside him that had been tied off to two more palm trees. The second hammock was underneath a nice, big palm leaf-covered tiki hut.

"What? Me? In one of those?" Ma picked her bag back up and approached the waist-high hanging hammock. She dropped her bag again, "How do you get in one of these?" She looked over the contraption, "Where's the steps?"

El responded from under his hat, "There ain't no steps, Ma. Just swing a leg up and over."

Ma stared at the woven rope lounger, "You've got to be kidding? Swing my fat leg over this thing?"

"That's how it's done."

Ma looked over the situation and grabbed the hammock, preparing for the worst when she heard a familiar voice behind her. "Complimentary drinks for you good people?" Ma turned to see Mr. Skimpy-Suit holding another tray full of refreshments.

"Yes, I'll have one," Ma smiled and reached out.

"Ma, go easy on them."

"I know what I'm doing. Mind your own." Once again, Ma retrieved the tallest glass as the handsome islander smiled at her. Ma smiled a toothy grin back. The waiter then handed the other three each a refreshment before seeking his next thirsty beachgoer. Ma took a big sip and set the glass down on a small plastic table next to the lounge chairs. "Hand me this when I get up here," she said to no one in particular and then turned back to attempt to mount the hammock.

El lifted his hat back up above his brow. He didn't want to miss this show. "Need some help there, Ma?"

"Of course not!" Ma looked over the situation once more and took hold of the sides of the swinging rope bed. Cilla raised up on her elbows and Runyon sat up to watch as Ma attempted to swing one leg up over onto the mesh ropes. She swung her chunky leg backward and then up and over. *"Unggh!"* Her leg landed on its target and Ma hesitated for a moment to wait for the contraption to stabilize again before attempting to go further. She then jumped up off her other foot and tried to land face first into the mesh, only to flip it completely over and she landed in the sand, face up, on the other side. *"Thump!" "Shit!"*

"Jeesus, Ma. Are you okay?" El sat up straight in his hammock and inquired.

"I'm fine!" Ma didn't move as she stared straight back up at the tiki hut's roof.

Runyon and Cilla began to get up and Ma put her arm up in the air, staring straight upwards. "Stop! I can do this by myself!" Ma weebled and wobbled back to her feet, dusting the dry beach sand off her sundress. She then picked her drink back up and slurped another straw full before returning it to the little plastic table and preparing her second attempt at the swinging hammock.

"Maybe you shouldn't drink any more alcohol before you get up in there," El suggested.

"Shut up!" Ma stood back to the hammock this time and reached behind herself for two tight grips on the sides. She bent her knees slightly and then launched herself up and backward, attempting an acrobat move. *"Unghhh!"* Ma's butt landed briefly on its target before the hammock flipped again, and once again Ma went to the sand, this time face first. *"Thump!" "Sonofabitch!"* Ma paused only a moment and then rolled over onto her knees, yelling out, "Don't get up!"

Not that anyone was.

Three more attempts and three more sips on her drink…and three more soft landings in the sand and Ma finally allowed the other three to assist. El had a hold of her under one shoulder, Runyon on the other, and Cilla between her legs with them both up in the air.

"This is embarrassing! Don't drop me!"

"Just keep quiet and don't wiggle so we can get you in here and we can all relax! People are starting to stare at us like we're Circus de' Soiled or something!" El said to his other half as between the three of them they tossed her. Ma finally landed in the hammock, gently swinging as the others stood guard for the hammock to slow down, making certain the old woman wasn't going to fall out again.

"Hey, this is nice!" Ma smiled and adjusted her hat, gazing out over the ocean as Runyon handed her drink back to her. "Lovely!" Ma removed the straw and guzzled the rest of her drink while the other three went back to relaxing in the hot sun once again, having all worked up a sweat from helping the portly woman get into the hammock.

"I'm telling you, Ma, you need to go easy on those," Runyon mentioned as he lounged back into his chair, adjusting his beach towel. Cilla returned to tanning, laying down on her stomach again and El quickly hopped back into his hammock and pulled his hat back down over his eyes. All three looked up when they heard the noise, El lifting his hat, Runyon sitting up, and Cilla propping up on her elbows. They looked over to see that Ma's eyes were shut, her arms dangling over the side of the hammock, and her empty glass in the sand. She was snoring loudly, passed out cold.

El lowered his hat again, "Well, we tried to tell her to go easy on them."

*   *   *   *

"Hey, Ma! Wake up!" It was Runyon's voice as Ma snapped back to the world of the living. Ma's eyes popped open and she startled, causing her hammock to rock, and once again she flipped out and down into the sand. *"Thump!"* Landing on her hands and knees.

"Goddamit! What happened?! Where am I?!"

"You slept all day," El groaned as he assisted Ma up by the arm to a standing position and picked up her beach bag to hand to her.

"What?" Ma wobbled on her feet and adjusted her cockeyed sunglasses.

Cilla brushed the sand off Ma's sundress. "You passed out from your fruity drinks and slept there in the shade all day. But don't worry, we kept the suntan oil sprayed on you so you wouldn't burn."

"You snored something awful," Runyon offered.

"What?!" Ma's head snapped around, "I missed the whole day? I missed going in the ocean? I missed lunch?!"

"Yeah," El handed Ma her bag, "it wasn't bad either. Some kind of rice and bean thing."

"What?! *Dammit!"*

"The kids told you to slow down on the drinks. You know how you are. C'mon, the boat to take us back to the ship is waiting."

Cilla wrapped her arm around Ma's and began to lead her back to the pier, smiling, "Don't worry. There's always tomorrow when we're in Freeport. And we've got the rest of the evening to enjoy."

Ma looked out at the crystal blue waters and whitecaps on the waves as she staggered through the sand back to the charter boat. As she gazed out over the ocean and limped along, she felt disappointed in herself for wasting such a beautiful day.

"Sonovabitch."

*   *   *   *

Upon returning to the ship the four enjoyed life back on the Lido deck and the burger joint once again. It had been "Elegant Night" on the ship, where every passenger was expected to wear their finest fancy garments, have their photos taken, and eat in the fancy dining room together. However, when Ma discovered that her floral-pattern sundresses weren't considered 'formal' enough, she refused to participate. Not that they wanted to do the dining room thing, anyway. Later that evening, with renewed energy from her daytime nap Ma attended a show in one of the smaller lounges and laughed to a late-night comedic show, although she did abstain from any more fruity drinks for the remainder of the night. She also ordered another toasted ham and cheese at midnight from room service. This time ordering two plates and forcing El to stay up late with her as they enjoyed them on the balcony of their stateroom, feeling the warm breeze and watching the ship sail away from Nassau in the moonlight, and onto their next destination.

CHAPTER 10

Freeport

On the fifth morning of the cruise, the dining room was sparsely populated with sleepy-eyed passengers. Every morning up to that point Ma and her family had enjoyed their daily breakfast at the buffet on the Lido deck where it was served about mid-ship. This day they'd decided to try the fancy dining room again where they'd heard about a sit-down breakfast being served. Ma, seated next to the windows and across from Cilla, was staring out at the village of Freeport in the Grand Bahamas. The ship had docked sometime during the wee morning hours while they'd slept, and the four were waiting for the boat to clear Customs and allow the passengers to disembark for their daily outings, tours, and shopping trips.

"Looks kinda like the place we were just at," Ma remarked as the two men stretched their necks out past Ma and Cilla to see the town below them. "Where are we going today?"

"We're heading to another private beach where there's lots of swimming in the ocean. We've got a charter bus taking us there," Cilla replied with a big smile. "There's also a shopping center just outside of the beach area! You'll love it!"

Ma looked at Cilla and couldn't help but smile along with her, momentarily, and then her smile turned downwards. "Wait? Another bus?

Oh, great. Do they drive like idiots here too?" Cilla simply nodded back at her in response.

Sefu appeared behind Ma, startling her as he'd done before. "Good morning, Mrs. Wilomena!"

"Jeesus!" Ma exclaimed and jumped in her seat. She instinctively attempted to grab a fork from the table, only to bring her hand up holding a spoon. Sefu moved to the head of the table and Ma threw a scowl at him, "Stop doing that!"

"My apologies, Mrs. Wilomena. It's so nice to see you all back here again." Ma rolled her eyes and placed the spoon back down on the tablecloth. Their smiling waiter inquired politely, "May I start you all out with coffee, or perhaps a glass of orange juice?"

"The coffee here sucks," Ma answered back, not quite under her breath as Elmer elbowed her gently in the side, receiving a frown for his efforts. She responded again to their smartly dressed waiter, "Juice will be fine, Seafood." Everyone nodded their heads to let Sefu know that it would be orange juice all around the table. And like magic, a waiter with a carafe full of juice appeared and filled their glasses, which strangely enough didn't surprise Ma.

The waiter with the breakfast menu did.

"Sonofabitch!" Ma jumped as the menu appeared over her right shoulder from behind. Ma picked her spoon up again and looked up at Sefu, who was still at the head of the table as another of his wait staff distributed the breakfast menus to everyone. Sefu gave Ma the "sorry" shoulder shrug. Ma gave him a look back and waved her spoon at him before putting it back down. Ma grabbed her menu from the waiter's hand, adjusted her glasses, and squinted;

Carab Oats Porridge
Shiitake Mushroom Soup
Scrambled Tofu on Toast
Asian Pancake Rolls
Muesli
Piccolo Poached Eggs
Frittata

Ma took a moment and looked the menu up and down, *"Mmm, hmmm."* She lowered it a bit and looked up over her reading glasses at Sefu. His eyebrows raised in anticipation of her response to the breakfast choices. "You're not serious," she said in a monotone voice. "Shitty mushroom soup?" Ma looked at El, "And apparently Fat Bob Johnson will be visiting our table to serenade your eggs with his piccolo." She glanced back up at Sefu, "And what in the hell is a *frit-ta-ta?"*

Sefu, with his hands tucked behind his back and bent forward just a bit to answer her, smiled and explained in his pleasantly accented voice, "It's an egg-based dish, deliciously filled with your choice of meats or vegetables."

"Sounds like an omelet to me," Ma said in monotone, still glancing up over her reading glasses.

"Ah, yes, Mrs. Wilomena. It is very similar to an omelet."

"Then why not just call it an omelet?"

"Because it's a frittata."

"You just said it was an omelet."

"It's like an omelet."

"Then call it an omelet."

"It's a frittata, not an omelet."

El turned to Ma, "You're not winning. He's pretty good at this."

Ma looked over at Runyon and said sarcastically, "So, would you like a frigging ta-ta, or an omelet?"

"I'd prefer quiche."

Ma glared at Runyon, squinting her eyes. This time she located her fork and held it up to him, "You're looking to get poked." Runyon smiled a toothy grin as El and Cilla chuckled.

Ma glanced at the menu again, and back to Sefu, "What the hell is mooselick?"

"Muesli. It's cold oatmeal, Mrs. Wilomena."

"Then why not just call it…"

"Give it up, Ma," El interrupted. "It isn't worth it."

Ma lowered her breakfast menu and looked to Cilla, whose smirk remained as she said it to her future mother-in-law before Ma could even get the words out, "Breakfast buffet on Lido?"

Ma nodded and held her menu back up for the waiter to take away.

Sefu smiled and nodded. He wasn't surprised.

*　　*　　*　　*

Ma spotted the photographer before exiting the ship's gangplank. Today, the camera lady was standing just beyond the custom's checkpoint in front of a huge "Welcome to Freeport" sign, snapping photos of the excited passengers. As soon as the four cleared the country's Customs station Ma dragged her cohorts over to the sign. Today, with the three others knowing what was to come, both Cilla and Runyon joined Ma's photo with Elmer. The four smiled wide as they each presented the one-finger wave to the camera before moving on and officially beginning their day.

As Ma boarded the tiny charter bus, having a bit of difficulty with her beach bag as she climbed inside and banged it against the doors, she said to the smiling driver, "Keep it under 60, and crank up the air!" Ma flopped down on the nearest empty seat and El slid in beside her. As the bus sped through the streets of Freeport Ma tried her best to snap a few photos of the sights while parked at the traffic lights and stop signs along the way. After every stop, a familiar voice could be heard echoing through the bus, *"Goddammit!"* as Ma noticed in her digital display that most of the photos either turned out fuzzy, or she had her thumb in them.

After twenty or so minutes the tourists arrived at their destination. They disembarked in front of a restaurant and sports bar on the ocean's edge. On the opposite side of the road was a large bazaar with several blocks of novelty and trinket shops. Cilla hopped off the bus beside Ma, "What do you want to do first, shop or lay out on the beach?"

"Let's have the boys grab us a good spot on the beach and you and me do some shopping over there."

"Good idea!" Cilla turned to her fiancé, "Go get us four chairs under the cabanas and we'll catch up with you in a bit!"

Runyon frowned, "Don't break us by buying stupid stuff!" Cilla just waved her hand, fluffing him off, and the two brightly dressed women proceeded to wander toward the shopping area.

"Heh, heh. You don't know much about women and shopping, do you?" El remarked as he grabbed his son by his colorful Caribbean shirt and began to pull him toward the beach, "C'mon, I need a lounge chair. It's too hot to mess around here." The flip-flopped men made their way through the food and drinking establishment's walkway, past the changing rooms, and down onto the beach.

The bazaar was busy and colorful with tiny, open-front shops lined together, each full of every kind of native souvenir imaginable, and plenty of local folks ready to sell them to the tourists. The two hadn't even fully crossed the road before shop owners were all waving at them to come and enter their little establishments and spend money on things they didn't need. "Let's just start at one end and work our way through," Cilla leaned into Ma and mentioned. Ma nodded back in agreement.

Ma quickly realized as they entered their first shop that the locals were going to try to sell her anything that she either stopped to admire or simply laid her eyes on. Each shop appeared to be no larger than your average public restroom, with tables crammed inside as souvenirs and clothing were strewn about and dangling from the makeshift tapestry walls. Each time Ma paused to pick up and admire something cute, someone immediately attempted to sell it to her. Cilla stayed close to Ma to make certain she didn't end up with a wheel barrel full of trinkets that the local folks managed to talk her into buying before leaving the shopping area for the beach.

Ma wandered into one shop in particular and took an interest in a small, turtle-shaped decoration, hand-carved from a coconut shell. Ma picked it up to admire it as Cilla leaned into her, "That's cute." Ma looked up and nodded to her when she was immediately startled from the other side by the shop's proprietor.

"You want to buy that little turtle, my lady?"

"*Jeesus!*" Ma jumped and turned around to see the colorfully sun-dressed shop owner behind her. "It's a good thing I'm wearing a bathing suit under this! If you do that again I'll need to jump into the ocean over there to clean out my britches!"

"I'm sorry, my lady." The pleasant and smiling, however, pushy woman responded, "Do you want to buy that little turtle?"

"How much?"

"Ten dollars."

Ma's eyes widened momentarily, and then she squinted through her clip-on sunglasses at the little turtle she was holding and looked back up at the woman again, "I'll give you fifty cents."

"No, no, no, my lady. Ten dollars," she smiled and repeated.

"Fifty cents," Ma said.

"Eight dollars."

"Seventy-five cents."

"Seven dollars."

"Eighty cents." Cilla was trying hard not to chuckle as she stood close by and admired a bright blue sundress hanging on the cloth wall that separated this tiny shop from the next.

"Six dollars."

"You're not understanding the concept of this," Ma said casually. "One dollar."

"Five."

"One dollar."

"Six-fifty."

Ma's head pulled back, "You're going in the wrong direction."

The two cordially haggled back and forth for a moment or two more, the shop owner not going lower than five dollars and Ma not going above a buck. Eventually, Ma would give up on the efforts and purchase a keychain from the lady for two dollars. She'd then stroll to the very next booth where they had another, identical little coconut turtle that Ma purchased for three bucks. In the shop next to that one, the same turtle had a sticker price of two-fifty.

"Sonofabitch!"

After strolling the bazaar for a bit and making their individual purchases, the two excited shoppers began to make their way back to the beach. As they walked through the shaded sand passageway between the sports bar and the changing rooms and emerged onto the hot beach, Ma spotted something in the sky over the ocean as she removed her flip-flops and shoved them into her beach bag. "What's that up there?"

Cilla looked up as she used Ma's shoulder to steady herself and remove her footwear. "They're parasailing."

"What's that?"

"It's where you fly above the ocean tied off to a power boat. A parachute behind you keeps you up in the air. Runyon and I are planning to do that a little later today."

Ma began to limp her way down to the water's edge to look for their other halves, "Why would anyone do that?"

"It's fun, Ma. You can see a lot from up there. You float in the sky and take in the sights."

"Is it safe?"

"Of course. It's just like being in a playground swing, except it's up in the air."

"Hmmph." Ma stopped, held her sunhat in the breeze, and looked up through her sunglasses again, watching the parasailers as they glided through the air. "Doesn't look as bad as that disastrous fiasco that Captain Ace put me through."

Cilla paused to look up, "Nope, not at all. You should try it. It might make you feel better about what happened. You know, increase your confidence. You'd have fun up there." Cilla turned around at the water's edge and began looking around the beach into the rows of cabanas. "There's the boys over there!" She pointed and Ma stretched out her neck to see Runyon sitting up in a lounge chair under one cabana, and El passed out in the one just beside him. Cilla waved her arms to Runyon, who spotted her and waved back, and the two women began walking the beach the short distance to reach the boys. Ma kept looking up in the sky at the parachute as she hobbled and tripped through the soft, ocean-drenched sand.

"Ma's gonna go parasailing!" Cilla remarked as she plopped down onto her lounge chair.

El, who'd been sprawled out on his chair, arms and legs hanging over the sides and hat down over his eyes, lifted his hat and opened one eye, "Excuse me? Parasailing? You've got to be kidding."

Ma dropped her beach bag into the sand, and it clanked as if it were full of car parts. "Nope, I'm thinking about it." Ma looked up and saw the parasailer drop in the air a bit when the boat turned around, and she said softly and hesitantly, "Maybe."

"I don't think you ought to be doing that, Ma," Runyon observed as he finished applying tanning oil to his arms and swung sideways in his chair to start oiling up Cilla.

"Why not? It ain't like Captain Ace's kamikaze flying service!" Ma looked up again, "Is it?"

Cilla spoke up as she pointed to her back, and Runyon began applying tanning oil, "No, it's safe. Just as long as you're not scared of heights or nuthin."

"I ain't scared of heights!"

El lowered his hat back down, "You ain't thrilled with them, either. It's up to you, but I don't believe that'll end well if you go up there. Just saying."

Ma flopped down on her lounge chair and out of the direct sunlight. *"Jeesus,* it's hot. Where's the drink people? Don't they come around here like at the other place and serve us cold drinks?"

"You aren't going to drink yourself unconscious today, are you, Ma?"

"Nope, no booze." Ma dug into her beach bag, grabbed her can of spray tanning oil, and began hosing her arms as she sat up in her lounge chair. El began to cough as the spray wafted inside their cabana. "I'd like some lemonade or something today. Just something to keep me hydrated."

And just at that very moment, the man's voice startled Ma, having come from the side of the cabana and out of her sight. "Cold drinks for you folks?"

"Jeesus!" Ma jumped in her lounge chair, inadvertently pointing the can over at Runyon, who'd turned to look up at the waiter standing next to El's side. She sprayed oil all over Runyon's face, causing him to choke and cough before Ma pointed the can back at the beach waiter as if it were one of her dinner forks. "I'm not kidding! Stop doing that unless you want to see me use this beach as a kitty litter box and crap right here in the sand!"

The waiter, a bit overdressed in the hot sun wearing a pair of cut-off casual pants and a white shirt with the sleeves rolled up, rounded the cabana, and faced the four. "Sorry, madam." The well-tanned and not bad-looking fellow was holding a tray full of cold and frosty drinks.

Ma lowered her weapon and looked up, "You got anything without alcohol in it?" The waiter handed Ma down a pink lemonade. Runyon and Cilla each chose a rum punch and El decided on a cold, locally crafted brew. The four lounged back in the hot shade and enjoyed watching others wade out into the ocean.

Ma, Runyon, and Cilla spent the next hour or so going back and forth from their plastic lounge chairs to the ocean where they'd cool off in the blue-green waters and watch small fish swim by their legs while El would remain in his comfy spot under the cabana.

After returning from the ocean for the third time the three were re-applying tanning oil, each seated on the edges of their chairs when a very fit young man approached wearing only a speedo. Both Ma and Cilla took notice of the well-built local lad. In fact, Ma was heard saying under her voice as she stared up at him, *"Oh, my."*

"Is anyone ready for some fun today?" The young man said to the group in his Caribbean accent, "We have jet skis, banana boats, paddle boards, kayaking, and of course, parasailing."

"Banana boats? Is that something you eat before you go parasailing?" Ma inquired, quite seriously.

"No, my lady."

"We want to do some parasailing!" Cilla spoke up, motioning with her hand between herself, Runyon, and Ma.

A calm voice emitted from underneath El's hat, "That ain't gonna end well for one of you."

"Shut up!" Obviously Ma.

"Of course, my lady. If you all come with me I'll arrange for it."

Ma rocked herself back to her feet and, along with Runyon and Cilla, they began to follow the fit young lad. "Watch our stuff," Ma directed to El.

"Uh, huh." Elmer responded from under his hat, "Have fun. Try not to fall out of the sky." Ma looked back and gave El a frown as she limped in the sand behind the others.

*　　*　　*　　*

The oversized powerboat floated gently on the waves several hundred yards from the shoreline as Ma stood underneath a metal awning at the stern, wearing an extra-large life preserver. Two local islanders, both dressed only in swimming trunks, finished tightening up the harness that surrounded Ma's pear-shaped body. The boat driver was a thin, young man of color with long cornrows in his hair and wearing a red, green, yellow, and black crocheted Rasta hat on the top of his head. He was bopping his head to the steel drum Calypso music playing through the boat's radio speakers as he looked back and watched Ma being prepared for her parasailing experience. As Runyon and Cilla watched from their boat seats, Ma scowled as the two young men pulled and tugged on the straps. "What the hell is all this crap for? I thought I was just going swinging in the air behind the boat!?" Ma glanced behind her and watched the colorful parachute, which was currently anchored to the metal awning, wave in the breeze. Ma noticed a metal bar swinging below the awning that was secured to the parachute and it appeared to have several straps attached by carabiners that extended to what looked similar to a playground swing seat laying on the deck of the boat.

"You are, Ma," Runyon answered. "That's just safety equipment to keep you in your seat."

"Safety equipment!? How dangerous is this?"

"Not at all, my lady," one of the tanned islanders said in his accented voice as he jerked hard on a chest strap, and Ma gave out a little grunt as her boobs were pinched. There were no words to describe what Ma looked like in her bulky life preserver, bright yellow harness, and blue polka-dotted one piece with large flip-up sunglasses on her face and her hair up tight in its usual bun.

"Now, here's what will happen," the young man received Ma's attention and she looked up through her clip-ons, which were two sizes, too big for her reading glasses. "When the boat goes, the parachute will lift, and the wind will take you up into the air. The faster the boat goes, the higher you will go. If the boat slows, you'll come down gently. If the boat turns, you'll come down." The man held up a single, blue and yellow rope in his hand. "You'll be attached to the boat with this and when it's time to come back, we'll pull you back to the boat and you'll land right back here on the deck."

Ma pointed, "That tiny piece of string is going to keep me attached to this boat!? That's what's going to keep me from dying?! That's a cat toy!"

"No, no, no. That is a strong rope!" The boat driver called back to the concerned woman, "No worries, my lady. Everything is going to be irie."

Ma scowled, "Irene?" She looked back up at one of the men who was now connecting her harness to the swing seat. "Who's Irene? Does she own the boat or something? I'd like to speak to her about the safety briefing!"

"No, mon. Irie. Everything's gonna be irie!" The boat driver repeated to Ma, smiling wide as he attempted to calm the woman.

Ma looked down at Cilla, "Is he blind or something!? I'm not a man and I don't see any Irene on this boat!" Ma looked back at her safety staff, "I don't think he should be driving the boat until he gets his eyes checked! He ain't been smoking them funny cigarettes, has he?"

"No, Ma." Cilla corrected her, "It's just the language. Irie means okay. He means everything will be okay."

"Okay, my lady. Now, just sit down here and wait. Once we get going you will float gently into the air. You will have fun! Look around and see the beauty of the island while you're up in the air! Now, when you're up there, if you want to go higher you need to give us the thumbs up. If you want to go lower, thumbs down. Okay?"

"Oh, this will be something!" Cilla said to Runyon as she dug into her beach bag and located her camera. She called back to Ma, who was parking her butt on the stern deck and holding her straps tight. "Wave to me while you're up there, Ma, and I'll get some good photos!"

The boat driver received his signal, and he pointed the vessel into the wind. The parachute filled up with air and Ma waited, calling back to Cilla, "I probably won't do too much waving. I think I'll be hanging on tight and trying to enjoy the ride!" Ma's tush bounced gently on each wave as the boat increased in speed. Ma smiled and waited for her parachute to lift her "gently" into the air, as she was told it would.

And then it happened.

"Holy shiiiiit!" Ma screamed when her stout body lifted off the deck and quickly shot backward up into the air when the boat driver went full throttle. Immediately, she gained altitude as she watched wide-eyed in terror as the boat seemed to leave her behind, and she flew straight upwards. *"No, no, no, no, no, no, no!"* She cried out as she went higher. *"Screw this! Take me back down! Take me down!"* Ma screamed and clutched the ropes tightly, locking her eyes closed as she continued her skyward direction, *"Stop! Stop it now!"*

"What's she saying?" Runyon asked as he shielded the sun from his eyes and gazed upwards, watching his mother appear smaller and smaller at the end of the rope as she flew higher into the air. "She didn't seem so happy when she lifted off."

"Don't be dumb," his fiancé answered, as she too watched Ma climb higher into the sky. "We can't hear her. That's why he told her to use hand signals."

Ma's grip on the ropes was causing her hands to go numb and she cried out for no one to hear, "Put me down! Put me back down! What's the matter with you *assholes?!* Take me back down!" She opened her eyes and looked down. Her eyeballs bulged as she gazed at the single tiny rope that was connecting her to the boat that now appeared as small as a mouse on the ocean's surface some 300 feet below her. *"Are you all stupid?!* This is too high! My ass is going to touch the moon! Take me down! Now!" The old woman was scared silly and frantic, "I need a fruity drink! I need a fruity drink! Send some alcohol up here! Have NASA send me up a bottle of whiskey!"

*   *   *   *

El, who was sitting up on his elbows, looked up through his sunglasses from under his ball cap as he watched his wife sail by high up in the clear blue skies. *"Heh, heh.* That ain't gonna end well." He rested back again, however, kept his hat up so he could continue to watch the catastrophe that he knew was taking place.

*   *   *   *

"I'm dead! *I'm dead!*" The old woman, not having the ability to pry her hands from the ropes, continued to scream out, "Put me down! *Put me down!* I don't want to be up here! I'm going to get hit by an airplane! I'm going into outer space! I'm not an astronaut! Take me down before I land on the moon!"

As the boat and its passengers kept their eyes up they seemed oblivious to Ma's predicament, believing she was having the time of her life. The driver began to turn the boat around, causing slack on the rope and Ma quickly dropped from the sky down towards the ocean. "What's happening?! *Hey!* The parachute's popped a hole!" As the water drew closer, Ma screamed again, "*Goddammit!* What the hell are you doing?! Take me back up! I'm going to crash! *Take me back up!*"

Just as Ma's feet touched the warm ocean water, the boat completed its turn and the line went taught again, and Ma shot back up into the air. "*Shiiiiiiiit!*" She cried out as the parachute climbed back higher, "*Sonofabitch!* This ain't funny! Don't do that again! My bladder can't take this! I'm going to spray pee all over the place! I'm going to crop dust the ocean! *Cut it out!*"

Ma reached the maximum height for a second time and after a few more moments of yelling and screaming, she took a deep breath as she stabilized at the same altitude, and she felt as if she were floating. As she glided along Ma began to calm a bit and looked out and around at the view. She pulled herself up and adjusted her tush in the swing as she spoke to herself out loud, "Huh, this isn't so bad, I guess, once you get used to it." She began to relax and admire the sights of the island's colors, the tops of palm trees, the nearby village, the ocean, and the sky. She even cracked a smile, however, when she glanced down at the boat again she frowned and let one hand go of the ropes just long enough to extend her middle finger to the boat's occupants.

*　　*　　*　　*

Everyone was continuing to gaze upwards, even the boat's driver who had turned around and glanced up at Ma, each shielding their sunglassed eyes with their hands. Runyon asked the question, "What's she doing?"

"Looks like she's giving the signal to go higher," Cilla observed.

"She's as high as she can go," the boat's operator answered.

"At least she seems to be having fun."

*　　*　　*　　*

"Jeesus, this is high up," Ma said to herself as she felt the warm air going past and she glided across the sky. Ma had found her center and she was enjoying the experience for the moment. She began looking for specific and familiar things. She thought she had spotted El on the beach, even though there were hundreds if not more tourists lounging on the sun-drenched sand. She spotted the restaurant and bazaar and even felt she could make out the ship in the distance. Ma leaned forward just a bit and glanced down at the clear ocean below as she began to make out the shadows of shapes in the water. She made out coral reefs, sandbars, and schools of fish. She also spied something larger that appeared to be moving in the water. *"Holy crap!"* Ma let one hand go and pointed down, yelling out to the boat still believing that someone could hear her, "Do you see that!? Sharks! I told you! There are sharks down there!"

*　　*　　*　　*

"What's she doing now? Cilla inquired while spraying more tanning oil onto her arms and on Runyon's shoulders.

"She's pointing down." One of the boat's staff noticed and then turned his attention to the driver, "She wants to touch the ocean again. Slow the boat down!"

*　　*　　*　　*

"What the hell are you doing?!" Ma cried out as she clutched the ropes hard and began to plummet toward the water. *"Jaws* is down there in the water! Go up! *Go up!* I don't want to be shark bait! I've seen this movie! The asshole gets eaten! Take me back up! *Take me back up!"* Ma dropped from the sky and hit the ocean hard. *"Splash!"* Ma's feet, legs, and rear end dunked under the water.

The experienced boat driver expertly increased his speed just as Ma landed, and only momentarily was she in the water when she began to rise back up again. The toothy, smiling boat operator was looking back as the others were also smiling, pointing, and laughing. Ma shot back up just out and above the water's surface, and then again the boat slowed, and she took another dip. *"Splash!"* Water spouted up around her as her plump booty went under, and immediately back up again.

"Goddammit! I'm not a friggin' bobber with a fish on! Cut it out!"

Ma cried out as the boat sped up and slowed three more times, and three more times Ma took a hard dip into the ocean. *"I'm going to kill you all if I live through this!"* She screamed, and as Ma's body raised back up out of the water again, a swimming dolphin jumped from below her feet in the same direction and nearly hit Ma's toes as it leaped out of the water. Ma's eyes popped from their sockets as she looked down and then back to the boat. "Did you see that?! *Did you see that!?* I told you, *you assholes!"* She screamed loudly, "I told you there were sharks down there! You just tried to use me as chum! You're trying to feed me to a great white! You're trying to use my ass to get your pictures in the papers!" Another dolphin jumped to her left and one to her right. *"Oh, my God!* They're swarming! A pack of sharks are swarming below me! *Up!* Go back up!" Ma became a bit delirious and began losing touch with reality. *"Oh, my God!* They're trying to kill me! Feed the fat woman to the sharks! Call Chief Brody! Call Hooper! Call Quint! You're gonna need a bigger boat!" Ma began to swoon and, between the fear of thinking that she was being used as chum bait and the motion of the ride itself, she passed out, her head and arms dangling in the wind.

One of the men signaled the driver as the other began to reel the rope back and pull Ma back towards the boat. Slowly, Ma began to draw closer as the boat decreased its speed on the ocean waves. The two men grabbed onto her as she landed gently back on the deck of the power boat, and they held her in an upright, seated position. Runyon and Cilla were on their feet as Ma slipped in and out of consciousness, her eyes only half open. *"Hooper drives the boat, Chiefy…Polly does the printing…smile you sonovabitch…"*

"She's quoting *Jaws,"* Runyon looked up at Cilla, both were now bent down and holding Ma upright by each shoulder.

"Ma, are you okay?" Cilla gently shook her arm as the parasailing staff began to unbuckle the harness.

The old woman continued to swoon, looking around at everyone with glassy eyes. "Pippet, where's Pippet? Okay, we'll drink to our legs." Ma stared straight forward and began to sing in a low voice, *"Show me the way to go home, I'm tired and I want to go to bed…I had a little drink about an hour ago and it's gone straight to my head…"*

Runyon and Cilla looked confusingly at each other, then back to Ma.

"…Here lies the body of Mary Lee, she died at the age of a hundred and three. For fifteen years she kept her virginity, not a bad record for this vicinity…" Ma trailed off and, as the men removed her life preserver over her head, she fell backward out of Runyon's and Cilla's hands to the deck. *"Thump!"*

*   *   *   *

"You three tried to kill me!" Ma blurted as the four, including El, waded up to their waists in the warm ocean waters after their parasailing excursion had ended. "Even you!" She splashed water at El, who gave Ma the "I didn't do anything" look from under his ball cap.

"Oh, c'mon, Ma," Runyon whined as he held Cilla up in the water with one arm under her back and the other under her thighs while she floated face up. She had an arm around his neck and Runyon turned circles in the water with his fiancé as she enjoyed his attention. "There wasn't any shark. It was a dolphin, and you completely missed out on watching me and Cilla having a good time up there, being all passed out in the boat the whole time."

"Bullshit! That was a great white and it nearly bit my feet off!" Ma realized she was again in the water and began to nervously look around. "Oh, crap! What if it's still looking for me? What if it's still hungry? I won't deny that I'd make a tasty meal for one of them big bastards!" Ma seemingly and nearly immediately lost her train of thought as she looked back to the shore, "Speaking of that, when's lunch?! I'm hungry. I certainly hope it isn't fish."

Cilla looked at her waterproof watch, "In about twenty minutes. And it's jerk chicken."

Ma began laughing, looking at El, who was wading out while holding his arms around himself as if it was cold when in fact the temperature now was in the mid-90s. "Did you hear that? They're serving you up for lunch!" El frowned in response and splashed Ma back with the palm of his hand.

"This is so relaxing," Cilla mentioned as she gazed up at the clear sky and Runyon continued to float her on top of the water.

Ma watched with a smile as the two younger ones enjoyed the ocean. She turned back to her soggy, much older other half and her smile turned downwards, "You feel like doing that to me?"

El, not looking up from his fish gazing and in a monotone voice, "Some things don't float as well as her and water isn't going to make it any easier to hold you up."

"Are you calling me fat?!"

"Nope, you said it yourself, you'd make a hearty meal for them sharks, not just a skinny beef jerky snack."

"Shut up!"

$$* \quad * \quad * \quad *$$

After their day of parasailing and ocean frolicking on the beach ended, the four returned to the ship to shower off the tanning oil and sand, and they enjoyed their evening on the ship as it departed Freeport for the open seas once again.

And once again, it was a burger joint supper on Lido and a late-night toasted ham and cheese in her cabin for Ma.

CHAPTER 11

A Day at Sea

The sixth and final full day of the cruise was again spent at sea, the ship having left the Island of the Bahamas and now it was pointed back towards the States. It was a sunny and hot day as the ship sailed through calm waters. On this day the foursome had their usual buffet breakfast under the clear skies on the Lido deck. During the meal, they planned their day's activities which would begin with Ma, Cilla, and Runyon laying out in the sun on deck 10 while El participated in an important after-breakfast nap in his cabin. Cilla had also arranged for her and Ma to visit the spa after lunch while leaving the menfolk to fend for themselves. Later in the evening, they'd all relax in the piano bar which they hadn't done as of yet during the cruise. There was even talk about visiting the fancy dining hall for supper, however, this idea remained up in the air by breakfast's end.

On their way back from their morning meal they wandered through the ship's casino as they'd done many days prior, as this was an easy shortcut to several other locations on the ship. Now Ma wasn't a gambling person, however, having another full day to themselves and throughout the week having already seen and done most other activities that she'd set out to do, she hesitated while strolling through the casino on this morning.

"Looking to play one of the games, Ma?" Runyon inquired as he noticed his mother stop behind him to admire the rows of bright and loud slot games.

Ma was studying one of the colorfully lit electronic games, squinting and adjusting her glasses. "I dunno. I'm not one for being a fan of losing money in one of these contraptions." She was staring at a slot machine that had a combination of numbers, letters, and Egyptian symbols on its electronic game screen. The display confused her as the symbols scrolled quickly and appeared to provide an example of a winner, telepathically begging players to sit down and deposit their money.

"They're not rigged or anything, Ma, in case you're worried about that. They're just games of chance. You either win or you don't." Cilla rested her arm on Ma's shoulder, "Give it a try. What do you have to lose?"

"Money, that's what!" Ma barked as she continued to stare at the game.

"I'm heading to the room," El mentioned as he continued on toward his cabin for his strategically planned morning nap. Ma flashed him a look as he went by.

"Go on, Ma. Give it a try," Runyon remarked. "We'll stay here a few minutes and spend a couple bucks, try our luck, and see what happens. You never know, we might get lucky."

"We'll, I'd need to find one that I can figure out." Ma continued to wander through the casino with Cilla and Runyon in tow. Other passengers were already playing this morning and, along with the slot machines themselves, caused it to be plenty loud in the large gaming room. Ma finally stopped at one game in particular that had a big colorful and brightly lit picture of a fluffy cat that she thought to herself resembled Fluffbutt just a bit. "This one here looks good." Ma sat down on the stool and faced the game, "How do I play it?"

Cilla put her arm around Ma and looked up at the directions on the big electronic display above the gaming screen. The game display itself had many blocks of pictures with various smiling animated cat breeds, cat toys, what looked like cat food, goldfish, and a picture of a diamond cat collar. Four rows of five blocks appeared to make up the slot-type game. Above the game screen was the big, colorful electronic display with animations, directions, and explanations of other perks if the player's attempt was a lucky one. "Looks like the more of the same cat you get in any direction, the more you win. And if you get three or more of those diamond cat collars, you might win big."

"I don't know about these electronic things. How many ways can I win?" Ma inquired as she looked up at the display, "Is it just one row straight across like the old-time slot machines?"

Cilla reached up and tapped a spot on the screen that read "Ways to Win" and it displayed all the colorful zig-zagged lines going in every direction and covering almost every block, reflecting all the various ways the game could be won. "Looks like a ton of ways to win, Ma. It just depends on how much you bet."

"*Jeesus*. That's confusing. I guess I'm just gonna have to keep it simple. I'll just push some buttons here and see what happens."

"Good idea, Ma." Runyon observed and pointed, "Now remember, you plug your room card into the machine here to make it work and it'll keep track of what you're spending. And just because the game says it only costs a penny, don't be fooled. Depending on what kind of a bet you make, and how many ways you want the game to try to win for you, you could end up spending more than you planned on."

"Yeah, yeah." Ma fluffed her son off with her overconfidence, "I'll figure it out. I ain't stupid, you know!"

"Okay, Ma." Runyon gave Cilla a smirk and motioned for the two of them to leave Ma to her game.

"Have fun!" Cilla said, patting Ma on the shoulder as she wandered off to find her own game to play.

The old woman gave the machine another once-over from behind her reading glasses and plugged her card key into the appropriate slot. The screen scrolled and displayed the message "Welcome Wilomena!" Ma squinted at the screen and chuckled, "*Heh, heh*. It knows my name." She looked to the player next to her immediately to her left, a pleasantly plump older woman much like Ma herself, who had a fake smile on her face and was obviously not impressed with Ma's discovery. Ma frowned and turned back to the game.

Next, the machine asked how much money she wanted to wager. She glanced down at the flashing buttons below the game screen on the control panel. Ma squinted again as she noticed the many combinations of bets, from '1X', '2X', and so on up to 'Maximum Bet' with several options in between. Ma noticed that not one of the buttons indicated how much the bet was going to cost her, so she began by pushing the '1X' and watched the game display as one colorful line displayed through the middle of the blocks, indicating that a win could only be achieved if her symbols were all the same on that one single center line. Ma then pressed 'Maximum Bet', looked up, and watched the game screen light up with the colorful lines going in every direction all over the game's blocks, reflecting many ways a win could be achieved. *"Hmmph,* that seems like better odds," she remarked and left the 'Maximum Bet' button lit and tugged on the slot's lever mounted on the side of the machine. "C'mon, Fluffbutt!" She released the lever and watched as the pictures scrolled and scrolled on the electronic display. Ma's eyes went up and down, attempting to keep up with the quickly moving blocks. Ultimately, the display slowed and stopped revealing many different animated cats, a few numbers, a picture of a goldfish in a glass bowl, and one diamond cat necklace. Ma looked to the lower left of the screen at the 'Win' box, which displayed a big fat zero, and then at the lower right to the 'Credit Spent' box, which displayed '25¢'.

Ma's voice was a bit louder than she realized, "Twenty-five cents?! I thought this was a penny game!" Ma looked up at the game and scowled, "I just lost a quarter in you and didn't win garbage!" Ma's voice was heard over the sounds of other nearby slot machines and several players looked over to the upset gambler, including the now seemingly annoyed woman seated beside her. Ma frowned and adjusted her glasses. She looked over the buttons and this time she pushed the choice marked, '2X'. She watched as several colorful, zig-zagged lines appeared, representing several potential ways to win. She pulled the slot lever and again the electronic display scrolled. Ma's frown remained as she watched the quickly moving blocks finally slow and stop, and many colorful cats and other symbols were displayed in the blocks. This time, however, a line appeared through five brown, smiling cats, and music played. Ma smiled and looked down at the 'Win' box, it displayed a whopping, '5¢'. She looked over to the 'Credit Spent' box, it displayed '10¢'.

"Goddammit!" Ma blurted, "I just lost another nickel! Even when you win, you lose this stupid game!" The unimpressed woman next to Ma attempted to ignore her and on the next try, Ma pushed the '5X' button and pulled the lever without looking at the odds. The game scrolled and scrolled. When it slowed and stopped she watched as bells went off and two lines flashed colors in different directions on the game screen. Ma looked down at the '5¢' spent on the left and then saw '25¢' in the 'Win' box on the right. "That's better," Ma chuckled and pointed at the game, looking around her immediate vicinity to see that other passengers were not paying much, if any, attention to her, including the stuffy lady seated beside her. This caused Ma to frown again,

and she went back to her game. Still high on her twenty-cent profit, she depressed the 'Maximum Bet' button and pulled the lever. After her head bobbed up and down watching the game screen scroll and finally stop, she looked down to the left to see another big, fat zero in the win box, and then to the right to the '25¢' in the spent box.

"Sonofabitch!"

"Drink for you, ma'am?"

"Jeesus!" Ma startled and jumped in her seat, spinning her head around to see one of the casino's wait staff carrying a tray filled with alcoholic beverages. Ma scowled at the tall, pleasant-looking lady who spoke in another unfamiliar accent. "What?! No. I'm all set. Except for maybe peeing in my pants!" The waitress smiled and nodded, moving on to the next player. Ma noticed the pompous lady next to her glancing and frowning before returning to her own game. Ma crinkled her nose and scowled back in return.

Ma pushed the '5X' option again where she'd had the most, and only luck thus far, and yanked on the slot's lever. She again watched the display scroll, accompanied by the game's usual musical sounds. This time when the scrolling ceased, loud bells and whistles began emitting from the machine, and the upper display began flashing bright colors, catching Ma off guard and causing her to startle more than usual. *"Holy shit!"* As she jumped backward off her stool and pointed at the machine, Ma's unfriendly gambling partner annoyingly glanced over to her with a look on her face that resembled an expression someone might display after smelling a foul odor. Ma looked straight back at her and pointed her chunky finger at the slot machine, "Did you see that?! It's having a fit or something! That wasn't my fault! I'm not paying for it if it's broken!"

The similarly aged woman tipped her head forward and glanced over her reading glasses that were chained around her neck, and remarked with a bit of arrogance, "It means you won something." The woman pointed to the upper display screen. Ma squinted and looked up where there were now instructions directing her to choose from several animated cats for additional chances of winning more money. Ma squinted down at the 'Win' box and saw that her play had earned her $100.

"Holy crap, a hundred bucks!" Ma blurted.

"If you press one of the cats you might double, or even triple your money," the fellow gambler remarked, remaining with her more-than-slightly pompous tone.

Ma began to sit back down, "Oh. Yeah. Okay, I knew that." She glanced back over to the woman, who was wearing a similarly colored sundress, and to be honest, there wasn't much of a difference between the two women at all. Ma smiled, "Thank you." The woman smiled back, not quite sincerely, and once again returned to her own game. Ma studied the upper display screen and noticed there were several pictures of animated cats to choose from, each representing a level that her current winnings would multiply if she were to win again. Each choice also came with several free plays the game would provide to Ma, again with the additional chance to win even more money. Still a bit confused, Ma decided to use the "eeny, meenie, miny, moe" system, and she made a choice.

*　　*　　*　　*

"Sounds like someone won big," Runyon observed as he stood behind Cilla, who was currently playing a cowboy-themed electronic slot game. Loud bells were going off elsewhere and echoing throughout the casino, indicating that a player had won something substantial at one of the games.

"Maybe it's Ma. Wouldn't that be something?" Cilla remarked, without taking her eyes off her game.

"Doubtful. I just hope she doesn't lose too much money or we're going to hear about it for the rest of the trip, and all the way home."

"Hear about what?!" Ma startled the two as she walked up behind the couple.

Cilla turned around on her stool, "Did you win anything, Ma?"

"These games are rigged! They're bogus. All they do is take your money! I didn't win anything except for this stupid little piece of paper!" Ma waved a dollar-sized piece of paper in the air out in front of herself. "This is all that came out of that damn machine when I was done playing! And it made a ton of noise before spitting this out at me! I had to leave, it was too loud for me!"

Runyon took the paper from his mother and began to read it as Cilla continued, "You don't get money from the machines, Ma. This isn't like Vegas or anything. If you win the machine gives you a voucher to take it over to the teller counter to collect your money." Cilla pointed and Ma glanced over to a glassed-in counter area along the casino's back wall where several staff were assisting other players.

"*Jeeze*, Ma! This says you won five-thousand dollars!" Runyon's eyes were wide as he held the paper close to his face and noticed the amount. He held the paper out away from his face and then pulled it back in to make certain he'd read the amount correctly.

"What?!" Ma turned back and looked up at Runyon.

Cilla snatched the paper from Runyon's hands and looked at it. Her eyebrows raised as she too read the amount, "He's right! Five-thousand bucks! Wow!"

Ma snatched the paper back, holding it up to her face, and squinted through her reading glasses. "Are you sure?!"

"Yeah, it's true. You won a bunch of money!"

Ma continued to look over her golden ticket, "I thought something was up when all those bells went off and the old crone beside me got all stuffy and started swearing like she was mad or something, and then got up and left. Five thousand, huh?" Ma finally made out the amount on the small piece of paper, "That'll buy a few cups of coffee, now won't it?" She looked up at Runyon and smiled, "It pretty much pays for this trip!"

"Good job, Ma!" Cilla smiled along with her future mother-in-law. "You see? You can get lucky once in a while. Do you want to try for more?"

"Nope!" Ma said with confidence, "I want my money. I have no idea what I'm doing and would probably just lose it all if I kept going. I don't even know how I won this." Looking back again at her valuable voucher, "Let's cash in and get out of here."

"Okay, sounds good," Cilla remarked as she spun back around to finish the play that she'd begun when Ma showed up. Cilla pushed the 'Spin' button, something that Ma had never noticed while using her slot's lever, and all three watched as the pictures of cowboys, cowgirls, and other western symbols scrolled electronically. When the scrolling ceased, bells and whistles went off and lights flashed.

"That's what my machine did!" Ma blurted and pointed.

"Ha, ha!" Cilla yelled out and clapped her hands together as she spun around and smiled wide up at her fiancé. Runyon looked down at the game screen and smirked as he read the number in the 'Win' box. It read '$1,000'.

*   *   *   *

The ship's spa was located on deck 11. Ma and Cilla were both lying on their stomachs next to each other on the adjacent massage tables with only a towel covering each of their backsides. Ma was staring down at the floor through the table's face cradle with her arms dangling over the edges of the table.

"Why is my head in a toilet seat?!"

"It's not a toilet seat, it's just a place to rest your face and still have the ability to breathe while they work on you." Cilla had chosen a relaxing hot stone therapy for the two and she was resting on her elbows and waiting for their session to begin. Cilla was watching the two lady therapists prepare the stones and massage oils. "You're going to enjoy this, Ma. It will relieve your stress and increase your blood flow."

"Increase it to where? My blood flows just fine!" Ma continued to lay flat with her head stuck in the cradle, talking to the floor, "I feel like a drunk person getting ready to blow chunks into a crapper. It's making my stomach queasy."

"Don't worry, it'll be fine. They take warm stones and place them on your skin to start the flow. Then they'll use the stones to help massage your muscles. Just relax and enjoy it."

"I don't like the idea of someone putting a burning rock on me! I was at a campfire once when I was a kid and the fire pit rocks got so hot that one popped and shot a chip into my shin! It burned something awful! I was only twelve and I had to pour my entire can of beer on my leg to cool it down. I still have the scar from it!"

"These rocks aren't that hot. They're just warmed up and they're smooth. It'll be fine."

"Okay, are we ready?" The pleasant masseuse asked Ma in her accented voice as she approached the table and rolled Ma's towel down away from her shoulders.

"Hey! Keep my ass covered! I already feel like a beached whale laying here! I don't need someone walking in and seeing my backside sticking up in the air! I don't want any rocks in my butt crack either! It isn't a flower garden!"

Cilla chuckled as she rested down and settled in for her massage, placing her face through the cradle as her masseuse prepared to begin by placing a warm towel on her back. "Oh, this is going to feel good!"

Ma felt something hot touch the skin on her back, *"Hey! Holy shit!* Owe! Take it off! These damn things are hot! You lied to me! You're trying to fry me like a strip of bacon!"

Cilla jerked back up on her elbows as her masseuse turned around, somewhat startled. Ma's masseuse lifted the warm cloth back up. "That's just a hot towel, Ma," Cilla observed. "She's just softening your skin first before she starts."

"Huh? What? Oh, okay. Sorry." Ma attempted to relax as the towel was placed back down. "Okay, this is nice I guess."

Several minutes later the pair of masseuses removed the warm towels from the ladies and Ma's therapist placed the first warm stone near the base of her spine. Ma cringed and stiffened as it touched her skin. *"Ahhhhh! Goddamit!* That thing is hot! You're trying to burn my butt cheeks off!" The masseuse placed a second rock just above the first. *"Jeesus!* This is torture! You're trying to brand me like a bull! Why'd I let you talk me into this?! Take them off! *Take them off!"*

Cilla couldn't help but start laughing as she kept her head down and enjoyed her warm rock session while Ma squirmed, her head stuck in the toilet bowl and her body unable to navigate the table from under the rocks. The masseuse carefully placed the third rock on Ma's back, and she barked, *"Oh, my God! Stop it!"* She then let out a blood-curdling scream, *"Ahhhhhhhhhhh!"*

*   *   *   *

"Did you hear something?" Runyon inquired of Elmer as the two strolled past the swimming pool on the Lido deck, each cradling their own Bahama Mama rum drink.

Elmer stopped and looked around. "I heard it. It kinda sounded like your Ma. It sounded off in a distance somewhere."

Runyon glanced around as he took another sip of his drink. He noticed a few other passengers had also appeared to have heard the commotion and were seeking the cause of the strange noises. Runyon squinted and listened hard, "It can't be Ma, they're way up on deck eleven inside the spa somewhere. Maybe a shark just caught a seagull or something."

The two shrugged their shoulders at each other, sipped their drinks, and kept strolling.

*   *   *   *

"Sonovabitch! I'm going to be scarred for life! This isn't a massage, it's a torture chamber! You're all with the Spanish Inquisition! If you're trying to get a confession out of me, I did it! Al Capone's vaults! JFK! The Lincoln assassination! Whatever it was, I did it! *Stop! Ahhhhhhhhh!"* Ma bellowed loudly again as the masseuse placed another warm rock on her backside just below her neck. The three other women were finding it difficult to control their amusement. Even Ma's masseuse was giggling while she continued placing warm rocks on the spastic woman's back. She'd never had a customer whine so much about a warm rock spa treatment.

"Ahhhhhhhhhheeeeee!"

*　　*　　*　　*

El and Runyon looked at each other as they stopped at the ship's bow and listened intently over the other normal sounds of the sailing vessel. They could still hear distant screaming over the sounds of the passengers and festivities taking place outside on other decks. El looked out over the rail at the ocean behind them and raised one eyebrow. "Maybe it's whale song. You know, like a humpback or something. It's hard to tell where it's coming from."

"You're probably right."

They both strolled on the exterior catwalk on the outer edge of the ship's deck. At one point El spotted something strange out of the corner of his eye through the sunlight two decks above. He pointed, "Hey, look at that, some big fat woman is running naked down the stairs on deck eleven."

Before Runyon could get his head tilted upwards to see what El had spied, Ma quickly waddled inside to the interior stairs on deck 10. She continued to run away from the spa located one deck above, having to briefly dart outside to get to a set of stairs that would take her down, as she didn't want to stand naked in the elevators with anyone while waiting to get down to the deck where her cabin was. She was done with people trying to torture her with hot rocks and she'd bolted from the spa long before the treatment had been completed, having jumped off the table while her masseuse had been retrieving more stones. Unfortunately, she'd caught her single towel on the massage table before sprinting out the spa's doors and everything was hanging out and flapping in the ocean breeze as she stomped barefoot down the stairs.

"I don't see anything. Are you sure you saw a fat, naked person?"

"Ayah, I do believe so." El tilted his head back down and rubbed his aching neck with one hand as he began walking again. "You certainly see and hear some strange stuff on this tub."

"I've heard about them nude sunbathers on deck eleven. You wanna go up and see if the rumor's true?"

"Nope, not if they're all anything like that. That looked too much like your Ma when she's in her birthday suit."

The two stared strangely at each other momentarily before shaking their heads, sipping their drinks, and moving on.

*　　*　　*　　*

Ma frowned and shook her shoulders back and forth while seated in her chair in the fancy dining room. Cilla looked across at her and smiled, "They feel better, don't they?"

"Yeah, maybe."

"I told you it wasn't going to be so bad. It took your stress and tension away, didn't it?"

"I'm not so sure about the stress part. My legs still hurt from hiking seven flights down those stairs back to my room!"

"I hope it was worth it," El said in a monotone voice as he tucked his napkin into his shirt. "The whole *goddam* ship heard you screaming out like that."

Ma gave her husband a dirty look.

"The crew even tossed a life ring overboard thinking someone had jumped off the ship, and they even called the Coast Guard," Runyon offered.

"And we had a hell of a time explaining to the captain why you were streaking all naked like that down all those stairs and up the hallways. Not to mention trotting right past the daycare center on deck nine. A lot of them kids are gonna need therapy."

"Shut up!" Ma blurted out, "You don't know what it was like! I was being tortured! You assholes were trying to kill me again with hot rocks! My back probably looks like a tic-tac-toe game! It ain't my fault the friggin' towel got hooked on that table! I'm lucky I was able to get up in the first place with burning rocks all over my back while my head was stuck in a crapper seat!"

"Speaking of torture," Runyon mentioned, not paying attention to his mother's complaints, "why are we back in here anyway? You don't like this fancy place. The burger joint would've been fine tonight."

"Because I have a plan." Just as Ma said this Sefu appeared, cautiously, at the head of the table making certain not to startle Ma. She looked up at the smiling waiter and flashed a huge smile back at him. "Seafood! My favorite person!"

"Ah, welcome back Mrs. Wilomena. It's so good to see you all again. I hope you stay a bit longer this time." The pleasant waiter began to waive a hand to his staff, a signal to bring the menus to the table. Sefu also prepared himself mentally for the results once his guests viewed the choices.

Ma held a hand up, surprisingly empty of its usual fork. "No need for menus, there Seafood." Runyon and Cilla flashed Ma a puzzled glance. El shook his head and began to take his napkin from his shirt, fully expecting to leave the dining room for the burger joint on Lido. Ma, continuing to smile wide at Sefu, spoke calmly, "We will all have seven of those pathetically thin steaks, all stacked together like pancakes, medium please unless someone else here wants them well done. Surrounding the steaks we all want a half-dozen of those crawdads that you call lobsters, with hot butter on the side. Each plate should have two baked potatoes all smothered in sour cream and bacon, and four sides of whatever vegetable you have. Feel free to flop into a plate whatever other kind of meat you have in that kitchen, and a nice big basket of warm dinner rolls, please. We'll finish up with four heaping bowls of vanilla ice cream. Chocolate if you don't have vanilla."

The other three stared at Ma in amazement as Sefu responded, "Excellent choices, Mrs. Wilomena! Right away!" As Sefu left the table to take care of her order, Ma looked around at her dinner companions with a big cheesy grin on her face, and she nodded confidently.

"Nice job, there Ma," El remarked and tucked his napkin back into his shirt.

"I didn't know you could do that," Runyon said to his fiancé, who simply shrugged her shoulders in response.

"Of course, you can!" Ma barked, "It's our cruise and we paid for it! Besides, I figured we deserve one good sit-down meal where someone else serves us before this boat ride is over. How bad can the food really be? If we don't like it, we know where to go."

"Well, you know your food better than anyone else, Ma. It sure sounds like it'll be good."

As they waited for their meals, Ma and her hungry family enjoyed small talk. Before the food arrived the passengers in the dining room were presented with a speech from the ship's captain thanking everyone for cruising on his ship. After the captain's presentation, the wait staff provided further entertainment as they sang and danced for the passengers. Sefu managed, after some coaxing from the others, to get Ma up from her chair to dance with him and his wait staff. When the meals finally arrived they were prepared just as Ma had ordered. After sampling the meal Ma looked up and gave a smile to her head waiter in approval. Sefu smiled back and nodded to his fellow restauranter and throughout the entire meal, and for the first time that week, nobody startled Ma out of her seat as she enjoyed her meal and her company. When it was over Ma gave Sefu a big hug and a hundred-dollar tip for putting up with them for the entire cruise.

Following dinner, with their bellies full, the four wandered towards the piano bar on deck 3. On their way, they strolled through the area of the midship that Ma referred to as "photo alley" where picture boards lined the walls. Thousands of photographs that had been taken of passengers throughout the cruise by the ship's photographers were available for passengers to browse through and purchase. Along with other passengers, Cilla and Runyon began searching for the photos that had been taken of them throughout the week. Ma perused the picture boards, halfheartedly seeking her photos. Cilla found them first, along with her own pictures, and handed Ma's stack to her. Ma and El looked through the snapshots with Cilla and Runyon looking over their shoulders. Runyon shook his head and Cilla chuckled as Ma thumbed through the stack of glossies, each one highlighting colorful, Caribbean scenes in the background with Ma flipping the camera the "bird" in the foreground, mostly frowning in each one. Ma stopped at the Freeport photo and declared, "I like this one best!" Ma held up the picture, it was the photo of the four together on the pier where they'd all performed the smiling, one-finger salute for the camera. Ma looked over her shoulder at Cilla, "I want this one! It's going up in the diner for everyone to see and admire. We're a good-looking bunch!"

"Good choice, Ma."

*　　*　　*　　*

♫ *"Sweet Caroline!"*
"Bah, bah, bah!"
"Good times never felt so good!"
"So good, so good, so good!" ♫

The foursome sat at the bar that circled the piano along with other passengers either seated with them or at tables throughout the room, all loudly singing along to the song, swaying side to side and smiling at one another. Genuinely, all were having a great time on their final night of the cruise. Ma, enjoying a fruity drink with the others, was singing as loud as anyone else. Ma looked up and admired Runyon and El's straw fedora hats perched on their heads, another souvenir they'd purchased earlier in the week and something they'd both most likely never wear again along with the other garments they'd been made to wear on the trip, as Ma thought to herself. But who knows, she thought again as she admired her Caribbean sundress, maybe they'd all dig these colorful clothes out again one day and take another vacation similar to this one to another warm, tropical location.

And with that musical-filled evening coming to a close, so did Ma's first official vacation ever.

*   *   *   *

"How was the trip?" Marmaduke inquired as he sipped his coffee from his spot next to Constable Bob at the counter bar during Monday's lunch hour. Ma was standing behind the counter facing the two, wiping her hands on her stained apron, watching, and waiting for Old Marmaduke to finish his coffee so she could refill it. She was still a bit chilly on this late spring day in comparison to the tropical islands where she'd just arrived from the day prior, and she showed a bit of a suntan on her face and arms.

"The ride home sucked. And waiting to get off that tub took all morning long. We didn't get in until pretty late last night." Ma dropped her apron back down and grabbed the coffee pot, filling the old man's cup as he lowered it from his snowy-white beard. Old Marmaduke tipped his head as a thank you.

Bob spoke through his bean chili-filled cheeks as he stared intently into his lunch bowl and scraped the sides with his spoon, "Oh, c'mon Ma. It couldn't have been all bad."

"No, I've got to admit, I had a good time for the most part." Ma refilled Bob's cup too as she spoke, "It was unbearably hot, though. And lots of foreigners on that boat and everywhere we went on them islands. Dozens of them. I wasn't used to all that."

"That tends to happen when you're in other countries." Bob was being serious as he shoveled the last spoonful into his mouth and looked up at Ma.

Ma gave the lawman a look and responded sarcastically, "You don't say? You know, if you were any brighter we wouldn't need lightbulbs in here." She looked back at the old man, "Thanks for keeping things stable at the house." She pointed a stubby finger at Marmaduke as she turned to replace the coffee pot to its burner with her other hand, "Fluffbutt looked a little peaked when I got home, though!"

"The cat ate just as well as anyone else while you were gone."

"I'm glad to be home." Ma looked around her and then back to the old man, "Things look pretty stable here. Diner's still standing."

"Cicely and Val did a fine job here," Bob offered. "They even fed Shithead the Bear his waffles last Wednesday. They remembered a little late and he showed up scratching at your back door." Bob pointed with his spoon, "That bear is getting pretty greedy and eats more and more every week it seems."

Ma squinted and frowned at the constable, "Reminds me of someone else I know."

"You missed the monthly town meeting," Marmaduke remarked. "Wiggleswort had no idea what do to with all that silence without you in the second row to argue with him. Lasted all of five minutes before they tabled the entire agenda and adjourned. They didn't dare make a decision without you."

The mayor, from his usual center table, flashed a look to the backside of Marmaduke, raised his hand, and began to open his mouth. Marmaduke lifted his head, stared straight up, and responded without blinking as if he'd telepathically sensed the mayor's reaction, "You know it to be true, Rupert. Don't deny it." The mayor frowned and lowered his hand, grumbling to himself as he returned to his lunch. Ma chuckled as she wiped a clean drinking glass with a kitchen towel after holding it up and checking it for spots.

"You also missed that fool, Voisine, going on one of his illegal spring turkey hunts!" Bob stated as he intently checked his bowl for any speck of chili that might still be remaining. "He went up in the town office's attic and stole that old Woody Woodpecker mask, dressed himself all up in brown khaki, and gorilla-glued turkey feathers all over his hunting vest. He even tied a set of tan-colored truck nuts under his chin to make it look like a turkey waddle before sneaking out into your field across the street here early last Thursday morning."

Ma giggled and shook her head, "Not surprising. What'd you do about it?"

Bob looked down and fiddled with his spoon, "Nuthin." Bob looked back up and said with arrogant pride, "I was busy at the time."

Ma pointed her stout finger at the lawman, "Horse manure! I bet you were sitting right there eating a nice, big breakfast that Val fixed up for you and did nothing as you watched that Frenchman sneak into that field, didn't you?!"

"Maybe," Bob replied sheepishly.

"Ain't no maybes about it! You never even tried to pry your lazy ass off that barstool and wouldn't have known what to do with him if you'd caught him."

"He didn't get anything, anyway," whined Bob in his own defense. "He just looked stupid trying it."

"Well, it's good to see the town didn't fall apart without me," Ma remarked as she turned and began to walk through the kitchen's swinging half-doors. She stopped for a moment, turned back, and flashed a smirk, "But I bet you all missed me while I was gone!"

Bob glanced up and flashed Ma a big smile on his puffy cheeks. Marmaduke took another two-fisted sip of his coffee, staring straight ahead. Rupert continued to grumble to himself at his table.

CHAPTER 12

Planning a Wedding

Cicely and Ma were seated across from each other in the booth closest to the kitchen, each working on peeling potatoes that were stacked in a small crate at the end of the table and preparing them to become home fries for several days to come. Cilla and Ruby Red were standing behind the counter bar, both leaning on their elbows on top of the counter and facing the dining room. It was just after closing and Runyon was cleaning the kitchen from the day's mess-making. El was sipping on his cup of stale, old coffee in the booth adjacent to Ma with his backside to hers. Mabel Johnson, who'd been helping out in the diner on that particularly busy evening, turned to the others after locking the bolt on the diner's door formally closing the establishment for the night.

Ma glanced up at Cilla, "You know, now that it's quiet, I wanted to talk to you about planning your wedding."

An echo came from inside the kitchen, *"I never asked her!"*

"Shut up!" Ma stretched her neck out and bellowed before leaning back and continuing with her potato peeling. "It's still going to be in the church, isn't it?"

"Yep, sure is," Cilla smiled wide. "Nothing big, though. There's no need to make a big production of it. Let's make it just close family and friends, okay?"

"Well, you know everyone from town will be there," Ma remarked as she squinted and peeled. "This is a big thing here. Something that doesn't happen every day in East Puddleduck, someone getting married, you know."

Ruby flashed a big smile and turned her head to Cilla, "Especially seeing that it's Ma's family getting married." She gave the bride-to-be a shoulder chuck. "You know Ma will do it up right for you."

Ma continued peeling without looking up, "Don't worry, we won't make a huge thing of it. Just let me arrange for a small ceremony and to do the reception here in the diner afterward."

"Of course, Ma." Cilla turned to Ruby, "You're still going to be my maid of honor, right?"

Ruby put an arm around Cilla, hugging her and resting her head on her shoulder, "You can count on it!"

Cicely looked across the table as she flipped another peeling onto the air, "Who's Runyon's best man, Ma? Is it going to be Puut?"

"Nope." Ma looked up and pointed her potato peeler at Cicely, squinting through her reading glasses, "Can't you just imagine that dumb Frenchman standing up there next to Runyon wearing all his khaki with a duck, or maybe something worse on his head? He'd probably be wearing deer urine as cologne." Ma went back to peeling. "Nope, it'll be Runyon's childhood friend, a kid he grew up with. Runyon's already phoned him and made sure he'll be there. He moved to the Portland area with his own bride quite a number of years back." Ma looked up, "Kid's name is Sacrilegious Boudarelli. We called him SacBob for short." Ma leaned back and tilted her neck, "Do you remember SacBob?"

"Ayah, good kid," Elmer responded from behind his cup.

"Yes, he was." Ma looked back to Cicely, "The Boudarelli's had a chicken farm in town for many years before they retired to one of those old folk's homes somewhere in northern Penobscot County. SacBob grew up on the farm. He was a hard-working kid. A big kid too." Ma puffed her shoulders, "You know, rugged. All that working on the farm for his folks. He was a nice kid, too, for the most part. Up until he fell into that nasty stuff."

"Drugs?" Ruby inquired from the bar.

Ma looked up, "Nope, manure. A few of the Boudarelli's chickens got out of the pen one night when he was about twelve. While he was chasing them around the yard the following day, SacBob tripped headfirst into a steaming pile of cow crap. It toughened him up a bit, but he wasn't as nice to the other kids who started making jokes about it to his face once word got out. Not to mention, the stink still lingered on him a while even after his folks scrubbed him up in the pond. He bullied up a bit after that and pounded a few of the other kids when they poked fun at him. Runyon always came to his defense though, and stuck up for him. They were always good friends."

Ruby glanced at Cilla and encouraged her, whispering, and giving her another chuck on the shoulder, "Go on, ask him," motioning her head towards the dining room.

Ma perked up, "Ask who what?"

Cilla gave a nervous glance to Red, stood up, wandered over to El's booth, and slid down into the bench seat across from the old man. El lowered his cup and smiled at his future daughter-in-law, "What's on your mind?" In the next booth, Ma frowned, turned her head, and stretched her neck to hear better.

"You know," Cilla spoke softly, "my mom will be at the wedding."

"Ayah, we're all looking forward to meeting her."

"But with Dad gone, I was wondering." Cilla stared down at the table as she spoke and fiddled with the napkin, "I was wondering if you wouldn't mind…"

Ma smiled and turned back to potato peeling as El interrupted the young lady, "I'd be honored to walk you down that aisle." He winked, "But I ain't giving you away." Cilla's eyes widened as she looked up at El and he continued, "Pretty much the opposite, we're taking you in."

Ma smiled wider as looked down and kept peeling, as did everyone else who overheard the sentimental old man.

*　*　*　*

"Listen here, Bubblehead! I don't want you screwing this up!" Ma was pointing her stubby finger at the preacher, standing at the base of the altar and looking up. Father Winkin leaned with one hand on his podium and looked down at the old woman with his head tilted back, gazing through the reading glasses perched on the bridge of his nose.

"I don't know what you're talking about," the preacher answered in his usual pompous tone, turning his nose away from the conversation.

"Oh, yes you do!" Ma was crinkling her nose and waving her finger at the town's religious leader, "Absolutely no movie quotes during the ceremony! Not one! You had better do this up right or your ass will meet my boot!"

The father turned his head back and flashed a sarcastic grin to the old woman, "Of course, I'll do it up correctly. I know what I'm doing. It's a wedding, isn't it? A celebration! A joining of two people!" The preacher's voice began to raise as he looked upwards, "Two people joined as one for eternity...!"

"Save it for the wedding!" Ma barked as Myrtle Watson entered the church carrying fresh flowers for the altar's vase. Ma swung around and pointed at the startled woman, "And you!" Myrtle stopped and her eyes grew wide. "You had better learn the marriage march on that Sears and Roebuck! And you better not mess it up!"

Myrtle flashed Ma the "who, me?" look and shook her head. Ma swung back to the father, continuing to point her pudgy finger, "I ain't kidding there, Bubblehead! This better be the best you've ever performed! I don't want anything ruining Cilla's special day!" The preacher closed his eyes and turned his head, seemingly ignoring Ma's concerns, which only achieved to aggravate the grumpy woman even more.

"Where's she today?" Ma swung her frowning head back around when Myrtle posed the question.

"What?! Why?! Who wants to know?!"

"I want to speak to her," Myrtle's tone was just as arrogant as the father's had been. Myrtle closed her eyes, turned her head slightly, and put a hand to her chest after setting the fresh-cut flowers down next to the altar. "I want to offer the girl some advice before the ceremony."

Ma marched straight up to Myrtle and stuck her nose in the woman's face, "Advice?! Advice on what?!"

"Marriage, of course."

Ma pulled back and burst out laughing, "You?! Give advice on marriage?! You can't be serious!" Ma continued as Myrtle bent down away from her and began to fluff the flowers in their vase, "You were only married for all of one week! And you'd only met the man less than thirty days before that!" Ma looked up at the preacher again, "What possible advice could she give to anyone wanting to get hitched?! How to lose a guy in less than forty days?!"

Ma pointed back to Myrtle, who stood up and faced her, appearing visibly offended, "About the only advice you could give anyone is how to have secret, kinky sex! With leather accessories!" Ma looked back up at Father Winkin, "Isn't that right, there preacher?!"

Father Winkin's eyes popped open wide behind his glasses, and he let out an audible gasp as Myrtle looked Ma straight in the face, blushing and flustered. "How's your whip?!" Ma blurted, and Myrtle turned to scurry away from her as fast as she could, entirely embarrassed. Ma stayed right on her heels and waddled behind the fleeing woman all the way to the church's doors, yelling all the way, "Maybe you should start one of those Avon clubs where the women get together all dressed in kinky lingerie and order sex toys from a catalog! I'm sure the preacher wouldn't mind if you bought some new accessories for the next time you two decide to watch *Debbie Does Dallas* together!"

Myrtle stopped at the church's entrance and spun around, "I never!"

Ma pointed straight at her nose, "Oh yes, you have! In fact, I bet that chain on your reading glasses around your skinny neck isn't even for them spectacles, is it?! I'll take bets that it's probably a set of nipple clamps!"

Myrtle let out a loud, *"Ohhhhhh!"* Nearly fainting as she turned and ran out into the parking lot.

Ma circled back to Father Winkin, who was holding his arms to his chest in a defensive stance and his arrogant expression had turned to one of absolute horror and shock, and he was unconsciously, slowly shaking his head while Ma barked at him. "And I mean it, preacher! No mess-ups on the wedding day! Get it together and act professional!"

Ma bolted out the door after Myrtle, who was frantically attempting to flee the scene and get into her car. The preacher's eyes were still wide, and his mouth gaped open as he stared towards the door, entirely flabbergasted. He could still hear the echoing of Ma's voice coming from outside. *"Myrtle! Wait! I need to see your catalog! I need a big, long vibrator. One of those ones with the rabbit ears! My cake mixer's broken again, and I need to whip up a fondue for the wedding!"*

* * * *

Elmer was supervising the effort to move Runyon's tiny cabin to the west side of the property. Runyon, the McIntyre boys, Puut, and Old Marmaduke were all participating in the chore. Truth be told, Marmaduke was too mostly observing and offering his expertise, along with some rusty tools, in an attempt to get the job done.

As Ma had suggested, they were moving the little log cabin to a spot further away from the main house where the two soon-to-be newlyweds would have a bit of privacy, plus the room to expand on the tiny structure itself. Ma had chosen a location on the property that faced the west and would provide the couple with a better-than-average view of the evening's sunsets when the weather was clear.

The McIntyre's had already assisted in clearing and dragging a new road where only a goat path had existed before, and now the small crew was using fresh-cut cedar trees to move the building. The logs had been cut just a bit longer than the width of the cabin and they'd stripped the bark by hand with a couple of old Witherby log peelers that Marmaduke had laying around his property. They'd also moved the logs into place with two cant dogs that the old man had lying around. However, first, they'd been required to make new handles for the tools due to the fact that Marmaduke had left the old log hooks outside for too many years and the handles had rotted, and they'd splintered and broken the moment the men began attempting to make use of them. Marmaduke had also brought a rusty chain to tow the building, which had already snapped twice for the same reason the log hooks had failed. It too had been left outside in the weather in the tall grass of the old man's palace for many years too long.

The tiny crew had jacked up the little cabin and placed the logs underneath and out in front, as they'd planned to log-roll the building to its new location using a small tractor. The reliable, building-moving maneuver consisted of continually placing the logs out in front to keep the cabin up off the ground and moving forward with the tractor pulling the building along on the chain. The process was going fairly well with Runyon on the tractor and Puut, Joshua, and Wally grabbing the logs as they rolled out the rear of the building and moving them back to the front while El and Marmaduke followed beside and called out non-helpful suggestions from the comfort of Puut's side-by-side ATV. In reality, El and Marmaduke's directions were far better than what Ma would've been providing, hence the plan to make certain she was working in the diner on the day that the men had scheduled themselves to move the building.

The tiny cabin currently consisted of only two small rooms, a living-kitchen area, and a bedroom. It had worked just fine as a bachelor pad for the so-far single Runyon. However, now, Ma was adamant that the building be moved and expanded upon to allow for a decent-sized kitchen, a separate living area, and an indoor bathroom. Ma wasn't about to have her daughter-in-law using an outhouse on a regular basis and possibly suffering a late-night encounter with a moose, as Ma had done in '75. As soon as the McIntyre's had completed the road and cleared a flat spot to place the building, Ma had been quick to hire *Flushies Plumbing and Septic Service* out of Fort Brethren to drill a proper well and put in a septic system for the house. Ma had made certain the young couple was going to have all the necessary and modern conveniences. Runyon himself would perform the indoor plumbing, having quite a bit of experience from all the work he'd done at the diner each time there was an issue. El and Runyon had already cut and set extra cedar poles to eventually direct the electricity out to the new location, however for now the couple would rely on gas lanterns for light, a gas stove, fridge, and hot water heater. Plus, a generator for the occasional electrical needs. The home itself would be an ongoing project that Runyon and Cilla would complete on their own and, if they weren't going fast enough, they were sure to be "encouraged" by Ma.

After the successful move of the building and later on that warm day in late May, they had the cabin all up and mounted onto new cedar posts. The small crew had set the logs they'd used to roll the building into place as the underpinning for the planned new construction, which would be performed in the days and weeks to come.

Hot, sweaty, and tired, well, at least four of them, the six were resting on an outcropping of rocks on the edge of the hill that looked down into a small valley and stream below. They were admiring the view to the west where the sun was just beginning its descent and enjoying ice-cold iced tea from a five-gallon cooler that Ma had prepared for them and sent along with a stack of plastic, disposable party cups.

Puut, looking out at the sunset, gently slapped Runyon on the back. "So, my crazy friend, you're really going to do it, eh? You're getting married."

Runyon stared into his cup of iced tea and swirled the ice chunks around, "I never asked her."

"You better get your head around it, boy," El remarked. "It's happening faster than you think. And you're Ma's making certain of it. She's taken quite the shine to your better half. We all have. She's a good girl and comes from a good family."

"El's right," Marmaduke agreed in his heavily accented voice as he looked to Runyon, holding up his cup and winking at the betrothed man. "You had better get in the right headspace if you want to make it work. Marriage is a job."

"Whacha mean?" Wally inquired, his youth and immaturity showing in his tone.

"What I mean is that marriage takes a lot of work. There's rules!" Winking at Wally as he continued, "Like always pretending to listen to the woman, even if you ain't listening."

"And the quieter you are, the better." El chimed in from the opposite side of Runyon, whose head swung as his father spoke. "Don't worry, she'll always do all the talking for you."

Puut nodded in agreement.

"And she's always right, even if she ain't." All heads swung back to Marmaduke as he and El began bouncing advice off each other from opposite ends of the six men seated on the rocks.

"And put the toilet seat back down, sometimes." El raised his head and looked at the sky as he spoke, "But sometimes keep it up. It'll give her something to complain about. And they love to complain."

Puut continued to nod to each comment as Runyon, Joshua, and Wally's expressions were each closer to fear, apprehension, and disappointment.

"Never complain about her cooking, even if it don't taste good."

"Don't tell her she can't buy it, whatever it is."

"Always pretend to be happy to see her, even if you ain't."

"Don't ever tell her that she makes bad choices. Remember, you were one of her choices."

Runyon's, Joshua's, and Wally's heads were bouncing back and forth like a ping-pong match. Puut just kept gazing at the sky and listened intently.

"Don't leave the milk jug empty in the fridge. Nor the orange juice, neither."

"Always hold her hand in the store. It keeps her from grabbing more stuff and throwing it in the cart."

"Remember, everything will always be your fault, even if it ain't."

"A headache always means no. And she don't really have a headache."

"Maybe always means no."

"Yes sometimes means no. They change their minds a lot."

"You can't ever yell at her, not unless the house is on fire, and she needs to get out."

"And memorize the term, 'yes, dear'. You'll be saying it over and over again."

"Don't leave your dirty magazines laying around. Find a good hiding place. And don't ever let her catch you playing with it. Once you're married, it's hers, not yours."

"No more peeing in the shower, it ain't a toilet anymore once you're hitched."

"Always open the bathroom window. And think of the toilet bowl as a bullseye. Always aim for the bullseye unless you want to clean the bathroom and listen to more complaining."

"Don't ever wipe your greasy hands on her clean kitchen towels. Nor on the dirty ones, neither."

"Don't leave your dirty drawers on the floor anymore. That's what the new wicker basket is for. And get yourself a new wicker basket."

"Avoid skid marks unless you want to do the washing."

Wally leaned into his brother and whispered, "I ain't ever getting married." Joshua silently agreed.

"And don't ever tell her that she's fat, even if she's moving in that direction." Marmaduke's final word of advice before nodding his head and quenching his thirst.

El opened his mouth to speak and then realized he didn't have any more advice to provide. He looked over to Runyon, who was staring blankly and appeared a bit pale in the fading sunlight.

"Are you okay?"

*　*　*　*

Ma was inconsolable as she sat in the front row pew of the church. To her sides were Elmer, and Cilla's mother, Henrietta Wadsworth, both attempting, and failing, to comfort the old woman. Ma was dressed in a brand new, pink floral-patterned sundress, frilly pink gloves, and newer flat-bottomed shoes. On her head was a large-brimmed sunhat. Elmer was in a black tuxedo, rented from Choppies, and shiny black dress shoes. His red hair and beard were all trimmed up nicely. Cilla's mother, an average-sized lady in her later

50s, who had dark brown hair similar to her daughter's and a care-worn face and hands from obvious years of hard work, was clothed in a nice yellow dress and hat to match. Both El and Henrietta were trying their best to calm Ma's nerves.

It was Cilla and Runyon's wedding day, and Ma was already bawling long before the ceremony was scheduled to begin.

The tiny church was filling with East Puddleduck's residents, all close friends to the Farnsworth-Miller side of the family, as well as several friends and family to Cilla's side. Everyone was dressed smartly, even the McIntyre Brothers and Puut Voisine, who had all been warned sternly by Ma to dress themselves respectfully for the occasion. Even Old Marmaduke had, for the first time in years, donned a suit which consisted of brown corduroy that he'd had tucked away in one of his closets. It'd needed an airing out as it was a bit mothball-smelling when he dug out of storage, and it displayed a couple of age holes in the elbows that Myrtle Watson had offered to patch up for him.

Cicely and Smirnoff arrived and the tall Slavic man, dressed in a gray suit and pink bowtie, sat down in the pew behind Ma. "What's wrong with the old woman?"

"She can't stop crying," El answered and turned his attention back to Ma, "It's going to be okay. You aren't losing your boy today, you're gaining a daughter."

"…*Ooohh, hoo, hoo…*" Ma's head down, a handkerchief to her tear-stained eyes, "…*Sniffle…sniffle…it's not that…hoo, hoo hoo…*"

El looked up and shook his head at Smirnoff, not having the ability to calm his wife. Smirnoff leaned forward and put a hand on Ma's shoulder, "Well, then, what is it?"

Ma raised her head and looked towards the altar, "What if that idiot boy says no?!...*Bwah, haw, haw!*" Ma buried her head in her handkerchief again.

Cicely, wearing a long, violet dress with a sunhat and gloves to match, leaned forward next to her husband. "Don't worry, Ma. He won't say no. It'll be fine!"

"But what if he does?!...*sniffle…siffle…sob…*" Ma turned her teary eyes to El, "Can we keep her and toss the moron out?!...*Bwah, haw, haw!*" Ma closed her eyes tight and leaned into El, who put his arm around her as he continued to shake his head to the others, looking at them with an "I don't know" expression displayed on his face.

Off to the side, Myrtle was busy doing her best to softly play what she believed to be appropriate music for a wedding ceremony on the Sears and Roebuck. She was playing most of the correct notes from what others could tell. On the altar standing at the podium Father Winkin was dressed in his flowing black frock and white collar. He was practicing his lines into the air and not paying attention to much of anything else at that moment. Runyon, standing near the preacher, was rocking on his heels and appearing quite nervous. His long, black hair had been pulled back into a ponytail by Ruby earlier in the day at the salon along with many other townsfolk getting their hair done up in preparation for the wedding, and his handlebar mustache and sideburns had also been neatly trimmed. He was wearing a black tuxedo, similar to the one El had on. The pants were just a bit short for his long legs and his bright white socks were poking out the bottom before they disappeared into his clean, black dress shoes. He was quite anxious and the only thing calming him a bit was talking to his friends, SacBob and Puut, whom he both had standing next to him on this day.

"Hey Sac, I'm awfully glad you made it for this."

"Wouldn't have missed it my friend," the equally aged and smartly dressed man replied. Runyon's childhood buddy was wearing a blue suit and tie, a white dress shirt, and a flower in his lapel. The man looked a bit younger than his actual age in his mid-thirties, had short blonde hair and no facial hair to speak of. He wasn't as muscular as Ma had spoken of him being, or what Runyon had recalled.

Runyon looked his friend up and down, "I still can't believe how thin you are, Sac. You've lost all your weight since I saw you last, and some of your bulk too."

Sac looked at the floor, "Yeah, I know. I lost it all the hard way. It was the juice."

Runyon's expression turned to surprise, "Awe, no, Sac. You weren't into steroids, were you? Was it a side effect? You aren't going to die from it, are you? I've seen pictures of those pro wrestlers that have shriveled up and croaked after using that stuff."

"No, no, it wasn't steroids," Sac replied sarcastically as he looked up at his friend. "Prune juice! The wife put me on a liquid diet when I got up to 300 pounds a few months ago. It's all she'd let me have, nothing else all day long. I had the shits something awful for weeks. She'd read about that *Hollywood*

Diet thing and thought she'd come up with a cheaper solution. I dropped over a hundred pounds."

Runyon and Puut simply raised their eyebrows in response. Puut wasn't quite as smartly dressed, however, he still appeared quite dapper in a dress shirt, leather vest, clean newer blue jeans, brown boat shoes, and absolutely no khaki or face paint. He leaned forward past Sac to speak softly to Runyon, "You're really going through with this, eh? Taking the plunge?"

"I guess so…" Runyon looked down to the first row of seats, "If I don't, Ma will kill me and throw me off a bridge."

"Oh, who are you kidding?" Puut continued, "You love the girl. Just like Ruby loves me." Runyon and SacBob glanced at Puut and flashed the "really?" expression as Puut stood tall with a cheesy grin on his face, truly believing in his own words. "When you've got a love like that, it's forever."

"I ain't so sure about that, Puut. You ask her out all the time and she says no all the time. And you've proposed marriage to her at least seven times."

With the same cheesy grin and in his heavy French accent, "She's just playing hard to get. She'll come around. The woman loves me."

Just as he said this Ruby appeared at the doorway to the Sunday School room, waving her hand towards Elmer. Ruby was dressed in a tighter-than-Ma would've preferred pink dress, low cut at the chest and high cut above her knees, which didn't go unnoticed by the menfolk. Especially Puut, who forgot his train of thought and stared intently with his cheesy grin turning to a stupid, adolescent one when Ruby stretched her body out of the doorway and leaned forward to get El's attention.

"I gotto go, Ma. It's time," El remarked to his other half, who'd calmed a bit and she nodded. El looked across the row and motioned to Rupert, who was easy to spot in his bright purple velvety suit coat, dark purple pants, and violet dress shirt. His thinning and slick-backed hair had so much tonic on it that it shined in the church's bright lights. Rupert noticed and flashed El the "who, me?" look and pointed at his chest before getting up to shuffle over. El remarked to Rupert as he stood up, "You stay here and keep Ma calm until I get back. She's a wreck today. I gotta go walk the bride down this here aisle. You wait here with her until I get back and keep her grounded."

Rupert nodded and timidly sat down next to Ma, carefully taking one of her hands and at the same time hoping she didn't punch him for the gesture. "Don't worry, Ma. It's going to be just fine. Just look around, the church is all done up nice…" Ma, eyes still teary, looked around and agreed by nodding.

"…And just look at all the people that have shown up. It's a big to-do for us all…" Ma nodded in agreement again. "…And Father Winkin will give a fine ceremony…" This time Ma looked at Rupert after glancing at the preacher and frowned a bit, somewhat skeptical of that prediction. The next statement, which may have been more thought out had the mayor known why Ma was crying in the first place, and most likely wouldn't have been uttered, especially not in the form of a joke. "…And Runyon probably won't run from the altar…" Rupert gave a smile to Ma as the fatal statement exited his mouth.

Ma's eyes teared fully again and she buried her head in her hanky. *"Ahhhh…Bwah…ha…ha…ha!"* As she cried out, literally and loudly.

Cicely leaned forward and whacked the mayor on the back of his head with a cardboard hand fan she'd brought along because it matched her dress.

"Ouch! What?! What did I say!?" Rupert turned to see who'd hit him and Smirnoff frowned at the mayor, leaning forward to place a hand on Ma's shoulder, attempting to calm her again.

Myrtle began the traditional wedding march as Ruby scurried to the alter from the side room and took her place as the Maid of Honor, adjusting her tight dress to her body when she arrived. Puut, with the same stupid grin remaining on his face, whispered over to her, *"Psssst.* Hey, Ruby, how about we make this a twofer?"

Ruby, who had bent over to adjust one of her high heels, looked up, "How about I kick you right in your twofer!?"

Runyon reached over and backhanded Puut in his gut in an attempt to return his attention to the ceremony at hand. Puut refocused, however, he contemplated any type of physical contact with Ruby, even one that resulted in him getting kicked in his balls, as a positive step in the right direction.

"Oh, God. Here we go," Father Winkin whispered to himself, patting his brow with his frock sleeve. His usual pompous demeanor had been overtaken by his nervousness about being required to perform a good and proper ceremony or face Ma's wraith.

Runyon smiled wide as everyone turned their attention to the back of the church where Elmer was arm-in-arm with the bride. Cilla, smiling herself, was dressed in a long wedding gown, traditional, with a white veil covering her face. Elmer stood tall and proud with a big smile behind his thick, red beard. Behind the two was Boris, Ma's hound, with Cilla's train in his jowls. Once the bride and father-in-law-to-be began their march towards the altar, Boris followed behind and kept her gown off the floor.

"Heh, heh. I taught him to do that," Ma mentioned to the mayor, smiling through her tears at the sight of the bride. Her mood seemingly improved at that moment.

As the two slowly marched to the music towards the altar, with each step they took the sobbing from one person in particular began again, and quickly became more audible and noticeable to the others in the room.

"…Sob…sob…sniffle…ohhhh, hooo, hoo…"

Many wedding watchers began to turn their heads toward the direction of the sobbing.

"…Ohhh, hooo, hooo, hooo….sniffle…awwwww, hooo, hooo…"

More heads turned, including El's and the bride, as they slowed their pace in the aisle. Boris even came to a stop just behind them and turned towards the sound of the crying.

"…Sniffle…ohhhh, hooo…awww…Bwah, haw, haw!…"

El and Cilla stopped entirely, as did the music. Ma finally stood up, spinning her pear-shaped body around, and blurting out, "What in the hell is your problem, Constable?!"

Constable Bob, his uniformed belly jiggling as he sobbed and cried, had his wife's arm around him in the next-to-last row. His eyes were shut, eyelids puffy and his face tear-stained. Mable, dressed all nice in a light-orange sundress, frilly gloves, and large-brimmed orange sunhat, looked up. "Sorry, Ma. He's just a big softie. He gets so sentimental at these types of things."

"I'm going to grab him by his softies and give him what-for if he doesn't shut up! He's interrupting the ceremony!" Ma bellowed, pointing at the lawman. Both Rupert and Cilla's mother, Henrietta, gently tugged on Ma to get her to sit back down in her seat.

Bob sucked it in, forced open his eyes, and looked at Ma, mouthing the word "sorry" to her, patting his glassy and bloodshot eyes with his hanky as he did so. Ma reluctantly turned back and parked her heiny as Myrtle began again on the Sears & Roebuck.

El, Cilla, and Boris resumed their march to the music. When they arrived at the altar, Cilla kissed El on the cheek as he lifted her veil. El proceeded to sit back down beside Ma while Rupert returned to his spot beside Eleanor, who was all smiles and staring up at the bride and groom. Cilla and Runyon stood facing each other in front of the preacher, holding hands, although Runyon's hands were clammy and trembling a bit. Father Winkin had regained his composure and he smiled at the betrothed couple. Holding his bible open in his hands, he looked out over the crowd. "Dearly beloved, we are gathered here today…"

"He does!"

"Ma!" El whispered loudly and stopped her from standing, his hand tight on her arm.

Ma, squatting and tugging against him, "I'm just making sure the boy doesn't screw this up! I'm just helping in case he forgets the correct answer!"

"No, you're not! Sit back down!"

"I am too helping. He ain't that bright, you know!"

Cilla chuckled in response to Ma's efforts. Runyon looked like he was about to pass out. The preacher looked down at Ma through his driving glasses, *"Ahem!* May we please continue?"

"What?!" Ma's head snapped to the altar. "Oh, yeah, go ahead." Ma waved her other hand towards the preacher and placed her butt back down in the pew. However, El continued to keep a firm grip on her arm.

"We're gathered here today to witness the connection of souls between Runyon Farnsworth Miller and Priscilla Wadsworth." Father Winkin looked endearingly to the two, "The bond of marriage is not a casual one and should not be taken lightly…"

"Get to the part where he obeys her!"

"Ma!"

"Shhhhh!" Came from Cilla's mother, who now had a hand on Ma's other arm. Even Runyon flashed his mother a look while Cilla simply continued to chuckle. Puut was now forcing back a giggle as well. Ruby was beginning to worry and SacBob didn't know what to think, however after being away from town for so long his memory was improving on just how boisterous and cantankerous Mrs. Farnsworth-Miller could be.

Ma tugged against both El and Henrietta and blurted, "Stop interrupting me!"

"You're the one interrupting!" El shot back at his wife, "This ain't your wedding! It's theirs!"

"Ahem!" The preacher intentionally cleared his throat loudly and glared down at Ma, "As I was saying…!" The preacher looked back down at his notes that he'd written on a three-by-five index card he had tucked inside his bible. "Marriage is the joining of two hearts as one…"

"And the boy must obey!"

"Ma!"

"Get to the part where death rips him apart if he don't!"

"Ma! Sit down!"

"Let go of me! You're keeping me from the ceremony! I need to make sure he says yes and obeys!"

"Oh, for Goodness' sake!" The preacher yelled out arrogantly as he slammed his Bible shut, swung his head, and yelled, "Would you *please* just sit down and shut up!" Audible gasps could be heard as Father Winkin immediately returned to reality. His eyes, as well as everyone in the room, widened and his demeanor turned to terror as he realized what he just said, and to whom he'd just said it to.

Ma's eyes were bulging as El and Henrietta tightened their grip on her arms, fully prepared to hold her back to keep her from leaping to the altar and tearing the preacher limb from limb. Even Smirnoff reached forward and gently placed his hands on her shoulders.

"Ma's gonna kill him," Wally McIntyre leaned and whispered to his brother Joshua, who nodded his head.

Ma, with a more-than-surprised expression pasted on her face, had no immediate response to the preacher's strong words. A moment of silence in the church resulted as Ma scowled, squinted, and crinkled her nose. A bit of smoke could almost be seen emitting from her ears. Her expression ultimately softened just a bit as she sat back down. After a brief thought, she almost admired the preacher for having the backbone to challenge her. She continued to scowl at the preacher as Smirnoff and Henrietta relaxed their grip on her, and she gave the pastor the "I'm watching you" sign by placing her chubby fingers to her eyes and then pointing at him.

The nervous pastor, hands trembling, looked back down at his Bible and his eyebrows raised once again as he noticed that when he'd inadvertently closed the book he'd lost his place, and his crib notes had shot out when he slammed the Bible shut and were now on the floor somewhere. His eyes quickly darted to the floor around him. He didn't see the notecard anywhere.

"Is there a problem, Father?" Cilla whispered.

The preacher's face snapped back to her, "Huh? What? *Ummm*....of course not, my child." The preacher forced a smile on his face, and then lowered his head and whispered, ever so softly, *"Holy shit."* The preacher slowly looked back up and turned his head to Runyon, and, in a move to stall for time he whispered to the groom, *"Ummm,* how are you doing, my boy?"

Runyon, who'd been staring into space turned his head to the preacher, and seemingly returned from the fog he'd been lost in. He leaned into the preacher and whispered back, "What? I don't know…*I never asked her…*"

The father's head reared backward, his eyebrows raised, and he whispered, "Yes, well, we're a bit beyond that now, aren't we?" Father Winkin stood back straight, glancing over to Cilla who luckily hadn't quite heard Runyon's remarks as she continued to smile at the pastor, who cautiously smiled back.

"What did he say?!" It was Ma's voice again.

The preacher glanced over at the old woman, "Nothing." Father Winkin then looked back out over the church full of friends and family, all patiently waiting for a wedding ceremony. He looked side to side at Ruby, SacBob, and Puut, who were all nervously smiling. He glanced back to the floor where his notes had been lost as he took a deep breath and prepared to begin again. Regaining his composure he set his bible down, raised both hands, and held them near the couple's shoulders. He tilted his head back and again smiled at the two. Both smiled back. People in the church smiled. Ruby, Puut, and SacBob smiled. Boris, who'd been lying at the foot of the alter, lifted his head and smiled. "Runyon, my boy." The pastor, perspiring a bit, looked straight at the nervous bride-groom and took a deep breath, "For Priscilla…*umm*, for Cilla…" Runyon's eyebrows raised. Everyone on the altar was holding their breaths and waiting, eyebrows raised. Everyone in the audience was on the edge of their seats, holding their breaths and waiting, eyebrows raised.

"For this young lady…For Priscilla…" Another deep breath, "…You better watch out. You better not cry. You better not pout. Do you know why I'm telling you why?" The preacher stopped, eyebrows raised, apparently waiting on an answer as Runyon just stared at him, confused and blinking his wide eyes. The preacher continued, "She'll be making a list, she'll be checking it twice…" Again, Percible hesitated, apparently waiting on a response.

Runyon, still quite befuddled turned and glanced at SacBob, and whispered, "Was that a question?" Sac just shrugged his shoulders.

Puut leaned forward past the two and responded out loud to the preacher, nodding, "She'll know when he's been naughty and when he's been nice."

Still sweating, however calming a bit, the preacher let out the breath he'd been holding and repeated the words softly, "Naughty and nice."

Ma rolled her eyes along with her head. El looked at her and slowly shook his noggin in a signal for her to keep quiet and Ma scowled back at him in response.

The preacher turned to Cilla. "My dear Priscilla, for Runyon…for the boy…will you watch him while he's sleeping? Will you know when he's awake?" Cilla's eyes widened, "…Will you know if he's been bad or good..?"

Cilla turned slowly to Ruby, who glanced at the bride, shrugged her shoulders, and then leaned past her to face the preacher, stating softly, "He'll be good, for goodness sake."

The preacher repeated in a low voice, smiling, "For goodness sake."

Heads in the audience turned to one another, many with bewildered expressions on their faces. Joshua and Wally began giggling. Ma turned her head to El again and whispered, "Oh, for *Chrissake*! He's quoting Christmas songs!"

"*Shhhhh!*" Responded El and Ma scowled again, shaking her head.

"Actually, Ma, the politically correct term is holiday music," Jacob mentioned, leaning forward in his pew to respond from across the row."

"Shut up!"

The preacher, seemingly on a roll, looked back to Runyon and nearly sang the words more loudly, even swinging his hips just slightly, "And curly head dolls that cuddle and coo, elephants, boats and kiddy cars too…little tin horns, little tin drums, rudy-toot-toot, and rummy tum tums…"

"*Percible!*" A voice rang out. And surprisingly enough, it wasn't Ma's this time as the preacher's head snapped to the side to catch Myrtle Watson shaking her finger in the air in his direction, while many more onlookers began smirking and laughing, including Runyon and Cilla. "Don't you even think about reciting the next verse!" She warned.

"Sorry," The preacher said softly to no one in particular as he refocused and looked to Runyon, "Do you have the ring?"

SacBob dug into his pockets and removed one of the two rings that Runyon and Cilla had picked out at Frankie's Pawn Shop in Fort Behemoth. He handed it to Runyon, whose shaking hands accepted the symbolic, sterling silver jewelry. Runyon turned and took Cilla's hand again and held the ring near the appropriate finger.

Percible continued, regaining his pompous demeanor, "The ring is a symbol of eternity. Because of the ring, there is no beginning and there is no end. Because the ring is a circle."

Everyone in the pews smiled, endearingly.

"It's not a triangle. A triangle has a corner. A triangle has an end. The ring is a circle, it has no end. It's a promise of your love forever, for all eternity."

Most smiles continued. Ma's began to turn downward a bit. Joshua and Wally began giggling again as the old woman glanced over at them and then looked back up at the altar.

"Because it's a circle…"

"Stop quoting *Chuck and Larry*, you asshole!" Ma's voice rang out.

Percible flashed Ma a sarcastic grin and motioned to Runyon to place the ring, and Runyon slid it onto Cilla's finger. "Do you, Runyon, take Cilla to be your wife?"

Without hesitation, "Yes", as Runyon looked into Cilla's eyes.

"*Ohhh…Bwah, haw, haw! Ohhhh…ohhh…ohhh….he…said…yes! Oh…hooo…hooo…*" It was both Ma and Constable Bob crying loudly, in unison.

Father Winkin turned his head to Cilla, "Do you have the ring, my dear?" She responded by turning to Ruby, whose mascara was staining her teary eyes.

"Huh? Oh, yeah!" Ruby dug her hand into her dress cleavage and began to fish. "Hold on." The menfolk all stretched their necks out to see better as she fondled and searched, going from one fake boob to the other, and in between. Puut nearly passed out unconscious as she dug down further. "Wait, I have it, I know I do." Finally, she produced the ring, "Ha! Here it is!" She held it up for Cilla to snatch out of her hand.

Puut, lightheaded and trembling, nearly tripped on his own feet backward from watching the show. He caught himself, almost knocking over a vase of pink daffodils in the effort. "Thank you, Lord," he whispered out loud.

"Amen." Percible had responded without realizing it, having been standing closer and having had a slightly better view. He wiped the sweat from his brow again on the sleeve of his frock. He recomposed himself and motioned for Cilla to slide the ring onto Runyon's finger. "Do you, Priscilla, take Runyon to be your husband?"

"I do." She smiled into Runyon's eyes.

The preacher raised his arms again to the two and looked to the crowd, "If there's anyone here who objects to this…"

"Skip that part!" She bounced up before anyone could hold her down to her seat this time, even though both El and Smirnoff had reached out with their best attempts. Everybody on the altar gazed down at Ma. "Everyone here knows *damn well* that if I hear a peep from any of them to that question, I'll throw them in my woodchipper and serve up what's left of them in my diner!"

"Oh, that's disgusting," Mattie Doody inadvertently blurted out, then realized she'd spoken at the wrong moment. She looked up at Ma who was glaring at her and shooting daggers. "Oops, sorry."

Ma turned back and glared at the preacher, "Get along with it! And I'm warning you! If you start quoting the Chipmunk Christmas song, I'm gonna come up there and beat you!"

"Well…fine," Father Winkin uttered under his breath as he rolled his eyes. It was apparent that was going to be his next move until Ma's warning had now put a halt to it. He shook it off, and the preacher raised his hands again. "Ladies and gentlemen, I now pronounce them man and wife!" He nodded his head to the couple as cheers erupted from the churchgoers, and the two newlyweds kissed.

Runyon, after the kiss to his new bride and she hugged him tight, moved his lips to her ear, and whispered as the clapping and cheering continued, "I told you this wouldn't be a normal wedding."

Cilla pulled back and looked straight at her new hubby with a huge smile on her face, "It's okay. Normal is boring."

And then they kissed again.

Myrtle Watson would be the one to catch the bridal bouquet later during the post-wedding festivities at the diner, beating out all of the eligible women, including Ruby, who'd made a good dive for it.

CHAPTER 13

Breakfast at Ma's

Ma woke as the first sign of light began to peek through the bedroom window shades, her internal clock was spot on as it was just about 5:00 a.m. She sat up as El turned over onto his side and let out a sleeping grunt. Ma rolled her fists over her eyes, reached over, and pulled the string on the little lamp she had sitting beside her on the nightstand. She looked down to the foot of the bed where Fluffbutt was sitting up proudly and staring back at her, seemingly with a smile beneath its whiskers. Ma scowled and looked around the bed, as she knew what this meant and she spotted the dead mouse on Elmer's side by his feet and knew immediately what the cat had been up to during the night. She'd been chasing mice again and brought a "gift" to her owners.

"Goddamit." Ma whispered, "Looks like you had some piss and vinegar in you last night, didn't you? Your furry little rump had to go and chase mice all night, didn't it? Why do you have to do that?" Fluffbutt's hind end raised into the air and her tail puffed out as Ma spoke, and the arrogant fat cat let a chattering meow out of her as if the two were carrying on a conversation.

"Ouch! Jeesus, Ma!" Elmer groaned as Ma whacked him on his backside through the blankets.

"Time to get up, Sleeping Beauty!"

193

El groaned again as he turned over just enough to face his wife with only one eye open. What he saw was Ma staring back at him with her morning scowl on her face. El looked up to see Ma's hair all up in rollers and picks, all held together with an old hair net. He moaned, "Why do you bother to do all that to your hair when you know good and well you're going to roll it all up in a bun and shove a stick through it?"

"Shut up and get up! My beauty routines are none of your concern!" Ma threw the covers off her side and rolled out of the bed, forcing Fluffbutt to jump down to the floor and prepare to follow the old woman into the kitchen. "And get that mouse off the bed while you're getting up!"

El glanced down with his open eye and spotted the present the cat had left behind. He then looked to his side of the bed and his head snapped back, and he opened both eyes wide when he came face-to-snout with Boris. The hound was staring his droopy eyes straight at El and patiently waiting for either to get up and feed him, a bit of drool exiting his jowls.

"I don't know which one looks worse in the morning," El whispered to the dog.

"What'd you say?!" Came a voice from Ma who'd just stomped out of the room towards the kitchen.

"Nuthin."

"And don't fart when you get out of that bed! It's disgusting! Save it for the toilet where those smells belong!" The same voice echoed from down the hallway.

"Why not? You do it all night long and don't seem to mind," El whispered as he threw the covers back.

"*What?!*"

"Nuthin."

By the time Elmer had lifted his tired body up out of bed, disposed of the cat's newest toy by tossing it out of the bedroom window, and walked down the hallway to the kitchen, Ma had fresh coffee percolating on the stove. She didn't make breakfast at home during the week due to the fact that she needed to get the diner open, and she and El could grab their first meal of the day there. Ma had early morning townsfolk to prepare for and make sure they all got to work on time with their bellies full. The first cup of coffee at home was simply to get her and Elmer going.

"I need some fresh eggs from the barn this morning," Ma said while setting a fresh cup of joe down on the kitchen table in front of El as he slid into his usual chair.

"Ayah."

Ma parked herself opposite with her cup in hand and took her first sip of many for the day. "Did you hear all the caterwauling last night around midnight? It sounded like it was coming from the barn somewhere. We must have a big ole hooty owl out there somewhere."

El lifted his hot coffee to his mustache, "Ayah, either that or Runyon and Cilla were having a good time last night in their cabin. They're newlyweds, you know." El winked at Ma from over his cup, and a grin formed on his tired face.

"*Oh, good Lord!* Do you have to say things like that so early in the morning?! I don't need that in my head all day long!" Ma grumbled and turned away from her husband, disgusted. After taking another sip of her coffee she turned back. "Speaking of those two, Runyon had better remember that I need him to fix the bad burner on the cook stove, and she's due to start work for me today on the breakfast shift. They better both be on their game this morning!"

El was staring straight into his coffee cup, "They'll remember. You don't need to worry." Just as he said this Ma detected movement outside. She pushed against the kitchen table to lift herself up and peered out of the window over the sink. Through the morning mist of dawn, she spied Runyon coming from the barn carrying a crate of eggs that he gently slid into his truck. Ma squinted and saw Cilla waiting in the passenger side of the idling pickup. Cilla spied Ma peering out the kitchen window, and her new daughter-in-law smiled and waved. Ma smiled and waved her hand back in Cilla's direction, her saggy bingo wings on her underarm flapping along with her hand. Ma's smile turned down when she turned back to El and saw him grinning the "I told you so" grin from behind his coffee cup.

"Shut up!"

*   *   *   *

When the old Chevy rolled into the diner's lot, Ma and Elmer saw that Sloppy Joe Bottoms' minivan was already parked out front, and the bakery owner was standing at the rear of his vehicle with the double doors open. Ma spied the stack of bread racks in the van all filled with fresh-baked goodies. She pulled into her usual parking space, and she slid down out of the truck from the driver's side, holding the truck's door tight to help keep her steady on her feet as she landed. "Whacha got for me today, Joe?"

Sloppy Joe winced when he turned to answer the old woman and caught a glimpse of her polka-dotted granny panties when her sundress momentarily hiked up as she slid out of the truck and before they dropped back down to her knees. Sloppy Joe himself was dressed in his white baker's uniform and he shook his head like a cat to remove the visual before responding, "All good stuff, Ma. I got some plain and chocolate donuts, some with glaze, and some with filling. Got some bear claws too. Today's muffins are blueberry, chocolate chip, and pumpkin seed. I tried making cannoli, but they came out looking more like eclairs. I'm not sure what happened."

Ma stretched her neck out beside Joe to see what he had in the truck. "Oh well, it's all good. You can't be perfect like me all of the time. Bring what you have inside and fill up the display on the counter. And don't forget to leave me a slip. The breakfast crowd will be here soon along with their appetites." Sloppy Joe nodded in response as Ma continued towards the diner's front steps.

Elmer had gone ahead and as he entered the diner he discovered Cilla setting up breakfast stations. His daughter-in-law had a nice clean apron over her T-shirt. She also had on a pair of newer-looking jeans and clean sneaker shoes. She looked quite professional, he thought to himself. Cilla turned to El and smiled as he greeted her back, "Morning sunshine." El pushed open the kitchen's swinging half-doors and found Runyon on his knees in front of the gas stove. He had one of the burners apart and was looking over the fixtures. "Need any help?"

"Naw." Runyon answered without looking up, "Looks like the pilot was just dirty. That Stanley kid is too messy when he's cooking. The burners are all caked full of grease."

Elmer nodded and let the doors close as he opened the diner's door for Joe, and the baker entered with a bread rack full of donuts and pastries. On his way by the counter, El removed the glass cover to the pastry display while Joe set the rack down and began to load the fresh, tasty cholesterol-filled goodies onto the trays. Ma was close behind as she hurried into the kitchen to begin her prep work after glancing over to her newest employee and smiling. In the kitchen she found Runyon finishing up at the stove.

"Is it bad?"

"Nope. Just tell that Stanley kid to not be so messy when he's whipping his spatula around between the stove and fryolator."

Ma squinted and stared at the stove while nodding in agreement. "I'll take care of it." Next, she took a moment to check her 'birthday' list she had pinned to the wall while grabbing her clean, however terminally food-stained apron from a hook right beside it. Ma kept track of everyone's birthdays on a hand-written list. If a patron whose birthday it was visited the diner on their special day, which was almost certain to happen, she'd provide them with a free cupcake and birthday candle. Ma squinted and adjusted her glasses as she looked at her scribbling and compared it to a small calendar she had tacked up next to it. "It figures. Looks like Fatboy Johnson gets a cupcake to go with his free chili later today."

Runyon picked up the few tools he'd used to clean the stove and threw them back into an old, rusted toolbox. He stood back up, pushing himself against his dented toolbox while groaning like an old man. He asked as he wiped the front of the stove clean with a greasy rag, "We don't have to sing happy birthday to him do we?"

"No, we ain't singing happy birthday! Does this place look like *Ruby Tuesdays?!*"

"What?" Ruby inquired as she entered the kitchen.

"Huh?" Ma turned to see who'd spoken.

"You said Ruby Tuesday. I'm Ruby," spoken as if Ma didn't know who she was, "and it's Tuesday. You have me on the schedule for this morning, plus this coming Friday and Saturday."

Ma turned to look at her calendar again. She leaned in, squinted, and scowled, then shook her head when she discovered Ruby was correct in the coincidence. Ma threw her hands up in the air and walked over to light the fryolator. She turned to face Ruby again and pointed her spatula just as Ruby dropped a pen and pad of paper in the pockets of her pink mini-dress that she'd worn to work this day. The skimpy waitress attire that she'd specially ordered was cut high above the knees and the buttons on the chest were undone quite low, not to mention the high-heels that exposed her pink painted toenail feet, which matched her glittery pink fingernails. Ma frowned, "Go show Cilla how to set up stations properly, she's out there winging it!" Ma waived her spatula up and down, "And quit wearing stuff like that in my diner! People are here for breakfast, not a live peep show! If you drop that pencil and bend over you're gonna give everyone a stroke when they all see your panties smiling back up at them, or your big hooters fall out!"

Ruby flashed a grin and blew Ma an air kiss as she exited the kitchen. Ma glanced back to Runyon, who had a childish grin on his face. That is until his mother's gaze wiped it off and he headed out the back door to deposit his tools into his truck.

Ma just shook her head in disgust and lit the grill.

As Runyon tossed the toolbox into the bed of his pickup, which made a loud clanging noise when it landed, the mayor's car pulled up beside him and parked. Runyon glanced over as Rupert exited the driver's compartment wearing a velvety dark blue leisure coat over a bright blue dress shirt and dark blue pants. His tie was orange. Runyon just shook his head at the mismatched sight as the mayor looked his way while waiting for Paul Doody to exit the passenger side, and Jacob Daily emerged from the rear seat. Doody and Daily were each wearing white, short-sleeved dress shirts and tan khaki pants. To Runyon, they both looked like a pair of bookends.

The mayor stood on his tiptoes to see over the top of his car, "Hey Runyon, can you take a look at the rain gutters at the town office? I think they're clogged full of leaves. Myrtle says the water's trickling in again after every rainstorm and dripping on her typewriter."

"Ayah. I'll take a look at it after breakfast if Ma hasn't got something else first."

Jacob leaned into the mayor and whispered into his ear while Paul nodded his head, apparently having telepathically overheard what Jacob had said. The mayor also nodded and turned back to Runyon, "And while you're at it, can you have a look at the public restroom toilet? It won't stop running."

Runyon was expressionless as he watched, and he offered the next observation while waiving a pointer finger between the two selectpersons, "Do either of them two talk out loud, or do they just wait for you to speak in their place, there Jeff Dunham?"

Rupert frowned, shook his head, and turned to enter the diner with his select board members in tow, and he stopped just inside the diner's doors. Not because Ma was blocking his way at the end of the counter bar, but because he'd stopped to smell the fried sausage and bacon that she had just begun sizzling on the grill. The mayor closed his eyes and smiled, his nose turned upwards into the air. He opened his eyes back and grinned, *"Mmmm, mmmm!* It sure smells good, Ma."

Ma wiped her hands on her apron, her expression was emotionless. "Uh-huh. I see you, plus the Skipper and Gilligan didn't waste any time getting here this morning."

"Well, we got business to attend to over breakfast," the mayor answered confidently. "We need to discuss this month's meeting agenda and talk over Stella Babadook's building permit application."

Ma's demeanor remained constant, "Isn't Stella only looking to put up a tiny metal shed for her gardening tools? What in the hell kind of permit does she need for that?"

The mayor, caught a bit off guard, replied hesitantly, "Well, there's probably property line setbacks and maybe height restrictions." Rupert looked side to side to his board members, who both silently nodded their heads, neither having a better answer prepared nor knowing what the answer should be, to begin with.

Ma pointed her chunky finger in the mayor's face, "Height restrictions?! Are you serious?! Let me ask you something, are you dumb all day long, or does it wear off after breakfast?"

The mayor shook his head and huffed as he continued towards his usual center table with Daley and Doody right behind. "I don't know why you feel the need to be that way in the morning, Ma!"

"Trust me, I'm this way all day long!" She remarked to their backsides, "You were just lucky enough to get the first preview of things to come throughout the day!" She nodded her head to Sloppy Joe on his way back out of the door with his empty bread rack. He'd left a heaping of goodies, primarily of the donut kind in the pastry display along with a hand-written sales slip tucked under the cash register, and he was on his way to his next destination, smiling and shaking his head at the diner owner as he went by.

The next through the door was Constable Bob Johnson. After watching Joe leave behind him he turned back, closed his eyes, smiled wide, and tilted his head up into the air the moment the diner's door closed behind him. *"Mmmmm, mmmm!* It sure smells good, there Ma." Johnson's keen sense of smell for anything edible could also make out the aroma of home fries sizzling right next to the sausages and bacon on the kitchen's grill.

The diner's owner continued to lean on the end of the counter bar, looked up at the lawman, and with the same expressionless stare, "I'm surprised the mayor and his illegitimate twins beat you here this morning."

Bob stretched his neck out over Ma's head to see the pastry display, which her body was blocking him from fully observing, and also blocking his way to his favorite seat at the end of the counter bar nearest the donuts. "I was busy this morning. Corky Flander's goats got into Wanda McCracken's flower garden again just after daybreak. Wanda was ready to beat them with a willow branch when I got there." Ma stepped aside before Bob had a stress and panic attack and he sat down, reached over, and grabbed the first, second, and third donuts from the display that he felt was required to go with his breakfast as Ma held up the glass display cover for him. She chuckled and shook her head as she lowered the glass back down.

As soon as the lawman leaned back and stuck a chocolate-powdered into his mouth, his radio spouted, *"...Dispatch to Puddleducksquirt One, the mayor of Skunksville wants you to deliver his overdue Field and Stream magazines back to the library for him..."*

Bob's expression was one of disgust as he reached to key his microphone that was clipped to his shirt collar with a curling wire that extended down to the radio mounted somewhere under his belly on his duty belt. He managed to get powdered sugar all over the mike as he keyed it and replied with donut-filled cheeks, "Ten-fowa.   *Errrr*...ETA will be forty-five....no, an hour...*ummm*...I'm tied up on a call on the east side. Cows in the road at the Maple farm again."

"...Bullshit. You're stuffing your fat face at the diner in Puddleduck again, aren't you?..."

"No, I ain't! And the library doesn't even open for two hours! I have plenty of time!"

"...He asked you last week..."

"I told you, I'm tied up with cows!" Bob turned his head away from the mike, and from the corner of his mouth, he uttered the worst impression of a cow ever heard. *"Moooooooh!"* Turning his head back to the keyed mike, *"See?!* Cows! I'll get back to you!"

"You're full of..."

'Click!' Bob had reached down with his donut-free hand and turned his radio off as he sat up straight on his barstool and glanced at Ma, who was

still leaning against the counter and smiling back at him. Bob gave a confident nod toward the breakfast cook.

Cilla walked behind the bar and set up Bob, as well as Wally and Joshua McIntyre who'd just entered the diner and parked their butts on their usual home on the barstools at the counter just down from Bob. On their way, they'd each retrieved a donut from the pastry display and shoved them into their mouths. They both politely removed their baseball caps and tipped their heads to Cilla and then tipped their heads to Ma, who returned with a scowling nod to the boys as she slid over in front of the constable and stuck her pudgy pointer finger into his face.

"Now look here, birthday boy, you got your choice today," as she watched the lawman stuff the third donut into his mouth. "You can either have your usual cupcake with the lit candle later after lunch or..." Ma pointed at the pastry display, "...you can have one more donut for nuthin!" She swung her finger back into the officer's face, "What's it gonna be?!"

Bob looked nervously, very nervously, at the glistening glazed donuts under the glass, then back at Ma and his brow began to sweat just a little. He looked back at the cholesterol castle, and Ma frowned as she noticed him trembling a bit, his shoulders shrinking, and he leaned in towards the pastries as if an invisible set of hands were pulling him towards it. Finally, he looked back to Ma once again and whined through the powdered sugar that surrounded his lips, *"Jeese, Ma.* I can't make tough decisions like that. You know I can't. It's not fair to ask me stuff like that. You pick for me! *Please?"*

Ma leaned in closer to his face and spoke softly as if she was talking to a child, "Boy, this is one of those difficult decisions you need to make on your own. Life is full of them." She reached over and placed a hand on his shoulder. "You need to make the choice, no one else can do it for you. One choice is right, and one is wrong. I know it's tough, but it's yours to decide."

Cilla, Wally, and Joshua were all smirking.

With her hand still on his shoulder, the two stared at the pastry display together, and then back at each other. Bob nearly had tears in his eyes as they both looked at the display once more and the lawman opened his mouth to speak in a soft voice, "The cupcake and candle?"

Ma reared back, "Good choice! I'm proud of you! You didn't need another donut. Plus, you got breakfast coming."

"Hey, Ma!"

"What?!" She blurted and turned to her husband.

"Sausages are burning," El remarked casually as Ruby Red poured him a fresh cup of coffee, beginning her rounds throughout the diner with the fresh pot.

Ma's eyes widened and her smile turned downwards as she darted towards the kitchen. *"Sonovabitch!"* A moment after the kitchen doors swung behind her the same voice yelled out, *"They're fine!"* Ma appeared back at the window opening between the kitchen and the dining room, metal spatula in hand, and she pointed it outward as she watched Cicely and Smirnoff stroll in for their breakfast before opening the general store for the day. Smirnoff stopped briefly to grab a muffin from the pastry display as Ma called out, "Does anyone want anything other than the usual?!" The "usual" consisting of two eggs made to order, bacon or sausage, home fries, and white toast. Having served the townsfolk for so many years she knew just how everyone wanted their eggs without asking, and whether they preferred sausage to bacon. Ma scanned the room with her squinted eyes, seeing only the shaking of heads. Realizing it was to be the "usual" for everyone, she nodded and disappeared back to the grill.

Puut strolled into the diner, having parked his old Jeep Willey in the line of cars outside. Today, Puut was wearing green, gray, and tan khaki fatigues, his usual attire. As he walked by the counter bar heading towards his usual corner booth, and after grabbing a bear claw from the pastry display, he nearly tripped over his own two feet when he saw Red in her waitress outfit from behind where she was speaking to Cicely and Smirnoff at a window booth. Ruby was bent over just a bit as she set down a small bottle of tobasco she'd retrieved from her pocket for Smirnoff, as she knew that he enjoyed the hot sauce with his eggs. As Puut walked by Red with a childlike grin on his glazed-over face, she turned, and he found himself staring straight and wide-eyed at her cleavage. *"Oh, dear Lord thank you,"* he whispered. Ruby rolled her eyes as she walked away towards the kitchen, and Puut slid into a booth across the table from where Runyon had rested his backside earlier and was waiting for a hot, home-cooked breakfast. Puut was still staring behind himself as he landed on the wooden bench seat.

"What's the good word today, Puut?"

Puut's head slowly came back around to his friend, and he stared, uttering in his heavily French-accented voice, "Melons. Melons is a word that comes to mind at the moment. Blueballs is another." Runyon smiled and tipped his head, and his coffee cup to his friend before taking a sip.

"Frenchman!" A yell came from the kitchen window as Puut snapped back to reality and looked Ma's way. "Do you want anything other than the usual?!"

"How about a big stack of pancakes?!"

Ma frowned and shook her head as she receded back into the kitchen, saying softly to herself, "There always has to be one."

At the center table, the mayor perked up from the huddle and note-taking he was having with his board members. "Constable!" Bob slowly turned on his barstool and stared out over the mayor's head to the empty space above it. The mayor stretched his neck out, "Do you know what the setback requirements are for an outbuilding over there in Skunksmell?" Bob continued to stare out over the mayor's head as Rupert frowned and yelled, "Constable?! *Johnson?!*"

Bob's eyes moved down to the mayor, who shook his head and shrugged at the lawman in a "what?" motion. An expressionless Bob paused a moment before responding, "I think I should have picked the donut instead of the cupcake." The mayor, realizing that Bob was going to be of no assistance in the matter, disgustingly frowned while returning to his huddle without the answer he was seeking.

Several minutes later of idle chatter in the dining room and Ma humming to herself at the fryolator, and she began to set full, hot breakfast plates on the windowsill for Cilla and Red to pick up and distribute. Joshua spoke to the frowning woman when she appeared, "Corky Flander's old farm truck blew a seal in the transmission again. It'll take us all day tearing into that."

Ma answered his comment as she waited for Cilla to grab two full plates and make space for more on the windowsill, "It doesn't surprise me, he drives around in it like it's a race car. Every spring he sloshes manure all over the road when he's moving it down to his potato fields driving that truck way too fast." Ma pointed her spatula, "And I don't know what he feeds them cows, but the air in late May is putrid and makes me gag every time I go down past the farm, especially on cloudy days when the air's laying down low!"

"Maybe he feeds them your daily leftovers that you put out in the garbage!" Smirnoff was attempting to be amusing. Cicely stared across the table and gave her husband a "Really?" look.

Ma pointed her spatula at the tall man and yelled, "Keep it up and I'll put something in your eggs that'll make your shit stink! And your asshole hurt for a week too!" Smirnoff smiled and blew Ma an air kiss in response before she retreated into the kitchen again. Smirnoff's wide smile was wiped away by his wife's gaze from across the table when he glanced back at her.

The mayor sat back up and looked around the room as if he'd missed something in the conversation taking place, decided he hadn't, and then went back to his huddle. Daley and Doody hadn't moved since beginning their meeting, their heads down, taking notes and agreeing to everything the mayor was telling them to agree to.

"Thanks, gorgeous," Runyon said to his wife as she sat his breakfast plate down and then slid in beside him to share a bite of it, swirling a sausage in the maple syrup before taking a bite and feeding the other half to her new husband.

Ruby set Puut's pancakes down in front of him, along with a bottle of locally-made maple syrup. Puut looked up at his fantasy woman and smiled, "Thanks, dear." He motioned his eyes to the empty space beside himself on the bench seat in an effort to have Ruby join him.

"Keep dreaming," was her sarcastic response as she turned to walk back and retrieve the next plate that Ma had deposited on the windowsill. Puut, staring as Ruby walked away, was required to be brought back to attention when Cilla reached over and snapped her fingers in his face.

Ma dropped two more plates on the windowsill as she noticed her next customer strolling in. Ma barked at Father Winkin while waiving her spatula at the sky pilot, dripping a little extra grease onto the meals that were placed below and waiting to be distributed. "Hey, Dago Red! What's up with you always being late for breakfast?!"

The father spoke as he walked past the counter bar with his head tilted back and cocked a bit sideways in his usual pompous demeanor, "I was busy praying." He stopped briefly to grab a cannoli from the pastry display. Holding it up, he gave the fresh-baked goodie an extra look, as to him it resembled more of an éclair.

"*Bullshit.* You were probably busy spraying holy water on your tulip garden in hopes to make them grow better! Now sit down while I fix your plate!"

"*Hmphh.*" The preacher kept his nose in the air as he slid into the booth across from Elmer, who tipped his head to the preacher while shoving a forkful of bacon between his lips. Red arrived with a coffee pot ready to pour as the father held a hand over his cup and said as politely as possible, "Tea, please."

Marmaduke was the last of the breakfast crowd to wander into the establishment that morning just a few minutes behind the preacher. The exhaust from his latest jalopy wafted through the front windows, preparing everyone for his entrance. The old man strolled in wearing his usual aging and hole-worn T-shirt, faded blue coveralls, and well-worn tan shitkickers. On his head this day was a badly aging straw sunhat chock full of holes, and his unlit corncob pipe was extending from his snowy white beard. As he targeted his side-wall window booth he heard a familiar voice echo from the kitchen. "What'll it be for you, old man?!"

"The usual. No need to make things difficult." As he passed by the counter bar he stopped, turned back around, and returned to the pastry display, snatching a plain glazed that Bod had his eye on. Bob nervously watched as the baked goods were quickly being whittled away by others. Marmaduke teased the officer by waiving the fried dough in front of him and cracking a smile before moving on.

As the old man walked by the center tables the mayor perked up again, "Hey, Marmaduke. Do you recall the setback requirements for putting up a tin shed?"

"Ayah. All none of them. It's a tin shed, not the Taj Mahal." Marmaduke continued and eased himself into his booth and placed his empty pipe on the table, but not before pointing the stem at the mayor, "Don't make more out of something that it ain't just because you three haven't had a thing to do in quite a while. As long as it ain't in the middle of the road, leave Stella alone. She's just looking to put her garden tools away." The mayor responded to his words by shaking his head in disgust, and once again he rejoined his huddle.

Ma reappeared at the kitchen window, pointing her spatula out and shaking it in the direction of the three wise men seated center. She'd obviously overheard the conversation, as her ears were trained to hear everything in her diner just in case anyone was talking about her, or she detected any other chatter that she wanted to comment about. She yelled out to the mayor, "Exactly! Leave Stella alone! What do you want anyway, everyone to have their shit strewn everywhere all over their property?! Do you want everyone's place to look like Marmaduke's for *Chrissake?!*" Motioning her spatula in the old man's direction.

Marmaduke responded to the would-be insult by displaying no emotion as Ruby set him up with a fresh cup of coffee. Cilla was also on her feet again and she skipped over to meet Ma at the kitchen window, and the chef reached through and handed Cilla a large plate full of sausages and bacon. "Take these around to everyone that's been served and see who wants seconds while I get more ready. Even if they don't want seconds, give it to them anyway. I made too many." Ma was fibbing, as she'd done this on purpose. You see, Ma always makes certain that every customer leaves with full tummies, and rarely did anyone turn away extras, especially Bob who smiled wide as Cilla began with him and the boys at the counter before making the rounds to the remainder of the patrons.

When she got to Marmaduke he tipped his head to Cilla and accepted the additional breakfast goodies to go with his morning meal yet to come. He spoke up again in a direction towards the mayor, remarking in his monotone, French-accented voice, "Not to mention, Stella had that shed put up two weeks ago."

"What?!" The mayor snapped up straight from his huddle again and looked Marmaduke's way, this time with Daley and Doody joining him.

The old man chuckled as he sipped his coffee, "That's right, Ray Charles. You're pretty good at missing things happening in your town, ain't ya? The McIntyre boys put that there shed together for 'ole Stella two Saturdays ago."

The mayor frowned, spun in his chair, and glared over at the McIntyres, who both turned their heads around in stereo when they heard the reference made to them. Bob turned his head as well. The mayor was visibly agitated when he called over to the boys, "Why didn't you two say anything about putting that shed up?! And without checking on having proper permits! We've been talking about this for more than a half-hour now?!"

Wally and Joshua looked at each other and then back to the mayor. Joshua responded, quite casually, "You didn't ask." All three at the counter bar turned back to their breakfast meals. The mayor shook his head in disgust, crumpled up the notes he'd been scribbling all this time, and threw them on the tabletop before firmly planting his fork into a sausage link.

El spoke up from behind his coffee cup, "You could always fine her for puttin' up a tin shed without a permit and see how that works out for you. Bob over there can serve the paperwork for you." Percible smiled and winked at El while sipping his tea, acknowledging his amusement at the suggestion.

Joshua McIntyre chimed in, "Do you really expect Johnson here to serve up the summons on her? You know that ain't going to happen. He'd be too scared that old Stella would whoop his ass with his own pen when he handed it to her to sign the citation that she'd rip up in front of him."

Bob hadn't overheard the comment, as he was busy staring at the pastry display with deep concern.

"I'd say you've lost this battle, Rupert," the Reverend Winkin offered as Ruby set down his breakfast plate and Cilla, right beside her, plopped the remaining extras onto his plate. The father looked up, smiled, and tipped his head to the diner's employees as he addressed the town council again, "It looks like you'll need to focus on something else at the meeting tonight."

Ma's sarcastically smiling face appeared again as she set more plates on the windowsill. "Well, you better make sure whatever you bring up at the meeting is just as important. Like whether or not to have Cowboy Bob here give a traffic ticket to the nesting turtles that cause a roadblock each time they cross Main Street in late spring."

In response to her suggestion, the constable threw a concerned look Ma's way. He whispered over the counter and through the kitchen window before continuing to stare at the pastry display, *"Psssst.* Hey, Ma. I don't think I can give a citation to a turtle." Ma returned the comment with a frown and shake of her head to the fact that the policeman had taken her idea seriously. The McIntyre boys, both also having overheard the officer, each slowly turned their heads his way and briefly stared in disbelief.

Still chuckling, Marmaduke threw another question to the mayor and his select board, "Well now, what's that leave left for your monthly agenda?"

Jacob Daley checked the list he'd started scratching on his pad of paper as he held it up in front of him and sighed, "Just dealing with Ma's modifications to our town sign at the end of the road, as usual. The same item that's on the agenda every month." All three shook their heads as he laid his notes back down on the tabletop and took a bite of toast.

"Talking about that is about as useless as a three-legged-ballerina," Paul Doody remarked quietly before slumping back in his seat. "We might as well cancel the meeting if that's all we got."

"We can't cancel the meeting," the mayor whined as he stared down at his breakfast, "the town charter says we have to hold the monthly meeting regardless unless we vote the meeting before not to have one, and we didn't do that last month."

Marmaduke tipped his coffee cup to the three and laughed out loud.

"Listen up! I've told you all before, you ain't taking down my sign!" Ma barked as she marched straight into the dining room, "If that sign keeps just one foreigner out of this town, I've done my job! And you know as well as I do that I'll be at that meeting to bitch about it if you three try anything!" She parked herself in the middle of the room and looked around while wiping her hands on her apron, taking note that every patron had a breakfast plate in front of them. "Does anyone need anything else?!" Her head scanned the room again as she heard a number of satisfied customers say, "No, Ma," and "No, thank you," and she spied everyone shaking their heads in satisfaction at the good, hearty breakfast they'd all received. "Alright then, pay up when you leave. No rush. The kitchen's officially closed until lunch unless someone need's something and asks nice! Coffee's available all day long, as usual, just stroll in and help yourself!" Ma gave a stern nod and turned to return to the kitchen to clean up. She stopped herself momentarily at the end of the counter bar and looked to Bob, who was grinning at her, his usual "thank you" for the good meal he'd received. Ma looked down at his empty plate, sighed hard, and looked over at the pastry display. She lifted the glass and reached in to grab the last remaining donut, tossing it onto his empty plate. "Happy birthday."

Bob's grin grew wider on his chubby cheeks. That is until he had a thought, his grin disappeared, and his eyes widened. He mentioned in a low voice to Ma as she pushed open the kitchen's swinging half-doors, "I still get the cupcake later, don't I, Ma?"

Ma just shook her head, let out another audible sigh, and let the doors swing shut behind her.

CHAPTER 14

Another Day at the Diner

(Une Journée au Diner)

Ma wiped her hands on her apron as she peered out over the dining room from where she was standing just in front of the kitchen's swinging half-doors. She was fairly satisfied that everyone had what they needed for the moment. Bob Johnson was seated next to the McIntyre Brothers at the counter bar, and they appeared content with the boys each chowing down on their grilled ham and cheese sandwiches while Bob gorged on his free bowl of chili. Rupert was enjoying an equally hot bowl of beef stew at his usual center table. Smirnoff was seated across from the mayor and enjoying two hot dogs wrapped in toasted buns, and a side of fries. In a corner booth were Puut and Marmaduke, seated across from each other and enjoying casual conversation. Marmaduke had ordered fish chowder while Puut was nursing a cup of coffee.

El was seated in the booth nearest to the counter bar and he'd been snacking on a plate of cold fries and stale coffee for some time. And truth be told, Ma didn't really care if he was all set or not, only the other paying customers. Well, minus Bob anyway. And, if El needed something he could get up and get it himself, she thought to herself.

Ma had the lunch hour under control, from what she could observe on this warm summer's day. She did notice that Rupert was having difficulty with his pepper shaker, so she wandered over and grabbed one off the next table nearest him and set it down in front of the mayor. Rupert looked up and smiled in thank you, however, Ma hadn't paid any attention to him. Her frown deepened as she noticed something else that was immediately eating at her over in the corner booth.

"Speak English when you're in my diner!" She pointed and waived her pudgy finger towards Puut and Old Marmaduke when the conversation they were having in French struck Ma's eardrums. She stormed over to their booth and stood at the end of the table with her fists firmly perched on either side of her hips. Puut looked up and smiled while Marmaduke sipped his coffee, staring straight forward and avoiding eye contact with the old woman.

"Whatsa matter?" Puut asked through his cheesy grin that caused his graying handlebar mustache to cock upwards on each side of his face.

"Speak English in my diner! I can't understand a word either of you are saying when you're talking that funny foreign language!"

"Who says you're supposed to be listening?"

Ma's eyes widened, "I say! It's my diner, you dumb Canuk! Plus, you might be talking about me!" Releasing one hand from her hip and pointing at herself, "If you're talking about me, I want to hear it!" Ma glared at Puut for a moment more and then turned to walk away.

"La toute petite araignée a grimpé le long de la gouttière," Puut voiced behind her back. And when Ma spun her pear-shaped body back around he quickly turned his head to Marmaduke, who chuckled into his coffee cup through his snowy white beard.

"Hey! Are you deaf?! I said cut it out!"

Marmaduke placed his cup back on the table and casually responded back to Puut, "La pluie est tombée et a emporté l'araignée."

"She's gonna kill them both in about two seconds," Bob said under his breath towards Wally and Jacob just before shoveling another spoonful of chili into his mouth.

"Cut that crap out! I mean it!" Ma blurted and turned to Rupert and Smirnoff, whose table she was standing nearer, "What are they saying about me?!"

Rupert turned and looked up at the angry woman, "I dunno, Ma. I don't speak French neither." The mayor was fibbing. He did, in fact, speak just a little French. At least enough to have the ability to recognize the children's rhyme, "Itsy Bitsy Spider," that the two were quoting, and teasing the old woman with.

Ma glanced at Smirnoff, who was smirking, and barked, "What about you?!"

The Ukrainian-born man looked up and smiled, shaking his head as if to poke fun, as well as agitate Ma just a little bit more. Pretending to not understand, he replied, "Ani ja nehovorím po francúzsky, pokiaľ viete," confirming to Ma that he wasn't going to be of any help by remarking in Slovak that he didn't understand French either, as far as she knew.

Ma's left eyebrow began to twitch, and her face flushed. The McIntire boys began to giggle even though they didn't understand what anyone had said in their foreign, native languages. They both realized it was all about how to agitate Ma, and get her goat. Constable Bob was truly worried, believing Ma was going to kill someone soon and he may be required to perform an official investigation, not to mention fudge a report in an effort to keep her out of prison. Rupert was also a bit concerned, seeing that he was sitting within Ma's reach, and if she were to lash out, she probably wasn't overly concerned about who her target was to be and he just might take a hard hit if she were to start swinging. He contemplated moving over to Elmer's booth for safety reasons. And by the way, Elmer was still sipping his stale coffee and slowly shaking his head, staring straight forward, and realizing how upset Ma was becoming and knowing he'd most likely be required to deal with it all day long and possibly into the night.

"Et la toute petite araignée a regrimpé le long de la gouttière," Puut looked up and said out loud with his grin still wide on his face, completing the nursery rhyme that Ma didn't understand, and was currently taking personally.

Ma forced herself to remain calm and an arrogant expression took over her face as she cocked her head a bit and looked over to the Frenchman. "Fine. Be that way, you assholes. Go ahead and talk about me in your fancy foreign languages. I don't mind. It doesn't bother me at all. We'll just wait and see what's in your food the next time you order something and have forgotten all about this." Ma's demeanor changed back, and she scowled, pointing to everyone in the diner, "Because, I won't forget it!" Once again she forced her demeanor to change as she addressed the entire diner, smirking, "Dessert, anyone?"

Puut's smile disappeared, as did Smirnoff's when they thought about her comments, and both men's faces turned to ones of concern. Marmaduke's expression didn't change. Bob smiled behind his spoon as he inserted more chili into his cake hole. The McIntyre's, after glancing at each other, both looked down at their lunch plates with a bit of worry as if they'd already been poisoned. Elmer just continued to shake his head, truly wishing he had fresh coffee in his cup and realizing he'd be dealing with Ma's attitude far after the lunch hour was to be over this day.

*   *   *   *

Ma was under the hairdryer at Ruby Red's salon. Next to her was Val Daley with her head also stuck under the adjacent hair-drying machine. Ruby was lounging and slowly twirling herself in the cutting chair, filing her nails as she used her high heels to spin the chair around while waiting patiently for the two ladies' hair to dry and set. Ma was holding a small textbook up to the lights as she squinted through her reading glasses to make out the words as she flipped through the pages.

"Whatcha looking at, Ma?" Val called out over the sounds of the dryers.

"Huh? Oh, it's a French-English translator book." Ma turned the paperback cover to read the title to herself.

"Why do you want to learn French? You hate it when someone speaks a foreign language around you," Ruby observed, still filing her long, self-painted fingernails, and slowly going in circles.

"Just for that reason!" Ma lowered the tiny textbook and spoke to the two ladies, "Last week Puut and Marmaduke thought it would be funny to speak French in front of me in my own diner! They thought it was cute because they knew I couldn't understand them! Every time those idiots get together in the diner and know that I'm listening, they say something that I can't figure out. I'm making sure it doesn't happen again!"

"Good idea, Ma. How long have you been studying?" Ruby asked, not bothering to look up as she worked on her nails.

"I just got this here book in Skunksquirt at the library. About three hours ago."

Val's eyebrows lowered. "Just three hours? How long do you think it'll take you to learn French, Ma?"

Ma looked up with an expression that reflected a bit of surprise at the question, "About three hours!" She said confidently, "I'm about done."

"You read that textbook in only three hours?" This time Ruby stopped twirling and looked up with concern on her face, "And you think you've got it all fixed in your memory?"

"I've read enough of it! How difficult can it be? It's just French. Wee-wee this and bonjour that. I've memorized a few things, enough to get me through. If I keep reading it'll just confuse me!"

"I can't argue with that," casually said Ruby, who went back to her nail filing and chair twirling.

Ma closed the book, "I know the basics, that's good enough."

Val raised her eyebrows and flashed Ma a look that told her that she felt she was wrong. The diner's owner obviously didn't pay any attention.

*　　*　　*　　*

Ma flashed Puut a deviant little grin from the end of the counter bar where she was standing as he strolled into the diner just after six o'clock in the evening. Puut used a bit of caution as he passed by, wandering over and claiming his usual corner booth. It was beginning to look like a fairly busy supper time in the diner with many of the usual locals seated throughout. Luckily for Smirnoff, Cicely had left him in charge of the store and she was helping out with the evening hours here at the diner, so he wasn't going to be part of the battle this evening.

Not yet anyway.

Old Marmaduke wasn't far behind as he entered, and he too encountered Ma's demeanor as she greeted him, "It's a bit busy this evening, why don't you join Puut over there," motioning to the corner where Puut had just parked himself. Ma knew, as well as she was hoping that the two would test her patience this evening if they were seated together, and she felt she was prepared for them.

Ma glanced around the room, as always her first priority was her customers. As Cicely wandered over to get Puut and Marmaduke set up with fresh paper placemats and clean silverware, Ma noticed that Rupert and Eleanor were good at their center table, and Bob was content at the counter

213

bar. Paul and Mattie Doody were at a window booth seemingly enjoying their meals and El, Runyon, and Cilla were seated at the first booth nearest the door, sharing a fish fry for three. A few other townsfolk were seated about, providing Ma with a full house to watch over and take care of.

"What's Ma up to?" Runyon inquired, turning to look up at her, attentive to the obvious fact that she was acting a bit more skeptical than usual this evening.

"She thinks that Old Marmaduke and Puut are going to challenge her intelligence and speak French in front of her. She's got it in her head that she knows what they're gonna say," El remarked while sipping his coffee and not paying any attention to how his wife was acting.

Runyon turned back., "How is she planning on doing that?"

"She glanced at a textbook that translates French to English. Truth be told she probably never got past the copyright page."

Ma called over to Cicely, "What do the two idiots in the corner want?!"

Cicely yelled back, glancing at her notes, "Marmaduke wants a hamburger plate and Puut would like ham steak and gravy."

Ma decided to make the first move and to take the opportunity to give the two Frenchmen a preview of how prepared she felt she was for them this evening. She walked behind the counter bar where the McIntyre boys had just seated themselves next to Constable Bob. Ma called to her evening cook, Stanley Winkin, through the open window between the bar and kitchen with a bit of cocky in her voice, "One ham steak plate and a…" Ma quickly retrieved the small paperback textbook from her apron pocket and flipped through the pages as she faced the window, while Stanley confusingly stood at the fryolator waiting for the rest of the order. "*…Asshole a` hamburger!*" Ma extended her arms to move the textbook away from her eyes and squinted, hoping it would help her see better, then whispered loudly to herself, "*Dammit.* Hamburger is hamburger in either language! *Heh, heh,* I kinda like the asshole part, though," clearly not realizing that she'd completely mispronounced the French translation.

"*A what?!*" Came from the kitchen.

"Asshole…asshoile, de`..!" Ma, disgusted, looked up from her tiny textbook. "Just get the asshole a hamburger!"

Puut and Marmaduke looked confusingly towards each other, as did others in the diner who'd overheard Ma's loud voice. El, Runyon, and Cilla giggled to themselves, which luckily for them Ma hadn't immediately noticed as she was focused on other things.

"Why are you being mean to them tonight, Ma? Did they do something to you earlier?" Bob inquired of the diner's owner.

"Shut up and eat your...!" Ma quickly turned around and frantically thumbed through the text, again holding it away from her face and squinting hard through her reading glasses. She turned back and said loudly, attempting to impress the patrons in the corner booth, "...Raggedy de buff!"

Bob cautiously glanced down at his beef stew, somewhat afraid to take another bite and wondering just what the ingredients consisted of. Marmaduke, the wise old man that he is, had a hunch on what Ma was up to and he reminded Cicely in a low tone as she turned to call back out to Ma, "Marmaduke says not to forget his French fries!"

Ma threw a scowl back his way.

El turned back from where he had been glancing in Ma's direction and raised his cold coffee back to his lips, looking across the table to Cilla. "This isn't going to end good."

Ma looked to the McIntyres, who were each staring at her, both holding their menus in their hands. "Well?!" Ma asked in a sarcastic tone with her eyebrows raised.

Joshua snapped back to reality first. "Huh? Oh, *ahhhh*, how about a grilled ham and cheese please, Ma?"

Ma turned away, bent down, and quickly thumbed through the book. Standing up straight again as she yelled towards the kitchen, "Jam, jamboon...jambooboo...jumbilia...grille...*ahh*...*ehhh*, from, fromhomage!"

Marmaduke nearly spit the coffee out that Val had just poured for the old man as he and Puut laughed at each other. Ma spun back around and flashed a cheesy grin to the room, obviously proud of herself.

"*What?!*" Came the voice from the kitchen again.

"You heard me!"

"*I heard you, but I don't understand a word you're saying!*" The young man echoed back.

"*Sonofabitch.*" Ma said under her breath as her head fell forward and then said in a louder voice, "A grilled ham and cheese!"

"*Why didn't you just say grilled ham and cheese?!*"

Ma's head snapped back up, "Shut up!"

Rupert and Eleanor attempted as best they could to keep their eyes on their food and shoveled it in quickly, not wanting Ma's attention to come their way and both truly wanting to leave and go home unscathed. Bob had a dumb smile on his face, as he usually did regardless of what else was going on around him. That is until Ma glanced back at the lawman, and he wiped it away. Ma turned to Wally and pointed angrily.

"Ummm, how about knockwurst?"

"Are you shitting me?" Ma said quite sarcastically.

"No, that's what I want. A hot knockwurst on a toasted bun and potato chips," Wally remarked quite casually, completely oblivious to anything that was taking place other than his stomach growling and calling out for one of Ma's hot sausages.

Ma shook her head and didn't even attempt to hide the book as she looked the word up. Holding it nearer her face this time in both hands, she lowered the textbook after finding the word and shook her head, staring up into space. "Knockwurst!" Ma's tone came with obvious disappointment when she learned that knockwurst, is still knockwurst, in either language.

"I understood that one!"

"Goddamit."

"Hey, old woman!" Ma's head snapped to the corner where Puut had called out to her, and she scowled, squinted, and crinkled her nose to hear him better. Puut stuck out his neck and said loudly, "Vous êtes français est nul. Peut-être que vous devriez simplement vous en tenir à l'anglais."

Ma's eyebrows raised. Others in the diner nervously awaited her response, which many believed just might be in the form of a shotgun blast if she were to, in fact, have one mounted under the bar counter. Ma contemplated looking into the textbook, except for the fact that she'd already in a matter of a brief moment confusingly forgotten what Puut had just said. Ma picked her brain for some of the words she'd memorized earlier in the day and threw a few together, truly believing she was correctly responding to the man. Confidently, she replied in her best, terrible French, "Peut-être que oui, mais ton cul est plus poilu que mes aisselles."

Marmaduke's eyebrows raised as he stared straight ahead out over the coffee cup that he'd been holding in both hands. A few in the diner who understood French began to giggle and covered their mouths with their napkins. Those who didn't understand French even knew that whatever Ma had just said probably wasn't a politically correct response. Puut pointed at the proud diner owner, "There's no need to get personal there, old woman!"

Cicely quickly trotted over to the counter bar, grabbed Ma by her apron as she went by, and dragged her into the kitchen through the swinging half-doors.

"Whadcha do that for?!" Ma barked as the two stood face-to-face in the center of the kitchen.

Cicely, being a bit taller, had to bend down a bit to be directly in Ma's face. She pointed and whispered loudly, "You just told him that his ass has more hair on it than your armpits do!"

Surprised, "I did? Well, it's probably true." She then frowned, "Wait! You speak French?"

"Yes, I do! A little, anyway."

"What'd he say first?"

"He said your French sucks and you should stick to English!"

Ma turned her head to scowl out through the kitchen window into the eating area, speaking to Cicely through the back of her head, "How come you've never spoken French in the diner before?"

"Because you don't like it," Cicely responded while looking over Ma's shoulder out into the dining room.

Ma smiled. Then she thought, stroking her chin, and looking at the floor before turning back to Cicely. "I'll show them!" She pointed her stumpy finger, "You come out with me and stand close by. You can tell me what to say to those two morons in the corner. We'll stand behind the bar. Just talk real quiet. The boys and Bob won't let on, and, if they do, I'll whack them with a spatula! That'll keep them quiet."

Cicely followed behind Ma, "I'm not that fluent in French, Ma. What if I tell you to say the wrong thing?"

"You know more than me! C'mon!" Ma exited the kitchen with Cicely in tow and they both walked behind the counter, facing the McIntyre boys, Bob, and the rest of the diner. Ma stood straight with an overconfident grin on her face.

Puut looked across his table to Marmaduke, "Elle est de retour pour plus de punition. Slle ne peut tout simplement pas en avoir assez, n'est-ce pas?"

Marmaduke simply smiled, "Vous devriez lui donner une pause."

Ma whispered to Cicely out of the corner of her mouth, "What did they say?"

Bob responded, whispering just loud enough for Ma to hear as he stared straight down at the counter, "Marmaduke told Puut to give it a rest after Puut said you were back for more."

Both Ma and Cicely looked down at the officer seated in front of them, each frowning in disbelief, and Ma whispered disgustingly, *"Jeesus,* does everyone other than me in this place know how to speak French?"

Cicely leaned to Ma and said softly, to which Ma repeated out loud, looking straight at Puut and pretending to glance into the useless textbook that she still had in her hands, "Tu es la chose la plus laide que j'ai vue depuis longtemps et tu sens comme l'ours qui visite chaque mercredi."

Runyon glanced over to Elmer with a bit of surprise in his expression, "That sounded pretty good. What'd she say?"

Cilla leaned to her new husband and answered, "She said that Puut smells as bad as he is ugly."

Runyon looked to his wife with the same expression still on his face, "You speak French?"

"Yes, of course," She replied casually. El just chuckled, not shocked in the least at his new daughter-in-law's intelligence.

Puut looked a bit dazed, as well as a little impressed even though he'd apparently been insulted again. He was also aware that Ma was receiving a bit of assistance, however, he was still enjoying her efforts. Puut responded back, "Ce n'est pas mal, vieille femme".

"What'd he say?" Ma whispered, looking straight at Puut.

"He said, ce n'est pas mal, vieille femme."

Ma disgustingly looked down at Wally and then reached out and smacked him in the head with her textbook, "I meant in English, you idiot! And I wasn't talking to you!"

"He said you're French is getting better," Cicely whispered to Ma, leaning into her and attempting to appear casual.

'Ding, ding, ding!' Stanley Winkin struck the call bell on the windowsill between the kitchen and dining room with his greasy, steel spatula. He'd just plopped down four steaming dinner plates. "Orders are up!" He cried out, startling both Ma and Cicely. The diner's owner spun around and frowned at the young chef, however again, patrons come first so she motioned to Cicely as she herself grabbed Joshua and Wally's meals. She turned around and flopped their plates down in front of them remarking in the worst French accent ever, "Ne vomissez pas sur mon comptoir," which she truly thought

to mean, "Do you need anything else?" In reality, she had told the two not to puke on her counter. It didn't matter, neither Joshua nor Wally knew what she'd said anyway. Bob flashed Ma a funny look, though.

Cicely walked Puut and Marmaduke's meals over to them, glaring at Puut as she set the plates down. It was apparent that she was on Ma's side this evening and she didn't bother to ask either of the men if they required anything further. Puut flashed his cheesy grin back up to her and then commenced eating. Marmaduke didn't budge from his position of holding his coffee cup up to his lips in both hands with his elbows planted firmly on the tabletop.

"Psssst! Ma!" Bob muttered quietly, staring straight forward however moving his eyeballs from side to side as if that would allow him to see out of the back of his round head. Ma noticed and bent down to the lawman as he quietly said, "Say this; votre âne a eu des relations avec un chêne les jours de pluie." Ma inadvertently repeated the words the lawman had uttered, out loud and without thinking, which she probably should've done first.

"Oh, my Goodness," the mayor sighed, burying his head in one hand. Marmaduke spit coffee back into his cup as both Cicely and Puut slowly turned their heads in Ma's direction, each with a bewildered look on their faces.

"What did I say to him?" Ma whispered to the police officer.

"I think you told him that he's acting like a jackass."

"You *think?*" Ma's tone turned a bit fowl, and she now regretted her decision to immediately repeat the constable's words out loud.

Cicely scurried back over to Ma and once again dragged her into the next room by her apron. They faced off in the kitchen, "Why'd you say that?!"

"What?! What did I say to him?"

"You just told him that his mule likes to screw oak trees on rainy days!"

Ma's eyes widened, "I did?! Well, it wasn't my fault! That stupid constable told me to say it! I thought he knew French?!"

Cicely flashed Ma the, "you should have known better," look before glancing back out over Ma's shoulder into the dining room. "You need to stop this before you really embarrass yourself!"

"No way! They started it and I'm going to finish it! I'm tired of people insulting me in a foreign language! They need to learn to insult me in English!"

Cicely reflected a bit of frustration in her response, "Okay, fine. If you must! Go out there and say this; si vous arrêtez de vous moquer de mes français, j'arrêterai de vous moquer de votre anglais. Sinon, plus de repas pour vous dans mon dîner.

Ma quietly repeated the phrase back as best she could and inquired, "What does that mean?"

"Basically, it means to stop poking fun at your French or you won't serve them ever again in your diner."

"Okay, that's good. I like that." Ma remarked and whispered the phrase again, attempting to memorize it to the best of her limited ability. Cicely assisted by saying the phrase once again before the two strolled back out into the dining room. Ma mumbled the words to herself all the way out of the kitchen. They both stopped at the diner's front door when they noticed that Smirnoff had shown up as he'd closed the store for the evening and was anxious to get a good, hot meal in his belly. Smirnoff was standing just inside the diner's front door when his wife and Ma exited the kitchen. Ma stopped and scowled up at the local business owner.

Smirnoff, being oblivious to the verbal battle that had been taking place just moments earlier, thought he'd be cute when he greeted Ma. Speaking in his native tongue in one of many languages he was fluent; "Добрий вечір, старенька. Як їжа сьогодні ввечері?" A phrase that translated to; "Good evening, old woman, how's the food tonight?"

Ma's eyebrows grew wide, and her face flushed. Her expression turned down to a deep scowl, and she nearly growled as she backhanded Smirnoff in his gut with the back of her hand.

"*Ooomph!*"

Ma continued behind the bar counter as Cicely, with an equally agitated expression on her face, stood in front of her husband and gave him an additional backhand to his gut.

"*Ooomph!*" The tall man grabbed his midsection and doubled over. "What?! What did I do?!"

Cicely grabbed onto Smirnoff's shirt collar and dragged him to a booth, nearly throwing him onto the bench seat and barking at her other half, "Sit down and shut up!" She reached into her apron and slammed clean silverware down in front of her husband.

Ma peered over to the corner where Puut was sitting straight, the same ridiculous grin on his face and waiting for Ma's next phrase of wisdom in a language that she didn't understand. Ma lifted her head high, displayed an evil grin on her face, and opened her mouth to speak. Only then to realize that she'd forgotten the phrase that Cicely had taught her just moments ago. It was too late now, she thought to herself, she needed to ad-lib something. Ma thought hard for a moment, quickly dropping down and flipping pages in her little textbook in search of words, and also taking what she could from memory. When she straightened back up, this is what came from her vocal chords in the worse accent that she'd ever attempted; "Si jamais vous parlez Français à nouveau dans mon dîner, je vais me déshabiller après vous avoir attaché et vous forcer à me regarder faire une lap dance! Je vais twerker partout sur ton cul!"

Puut's smile turned down and he slumped into his booth seat, his face turning a shade of pale green, and a lump formed in his throat. He looked straight at Marmaduke whose normally emotionless expression turned to one of worry from out over the top of his coffee cup. Constable Bob, having been fully prepared to put another spoonful of beef stew into his mouth, slowly lowered his utensil back down into the bowl. He'd immediately lost his appetite as he picked up his napkin and patted his lips. Rupert threw his napkin down on the table and reached for his water glass, whispering, "Oh, that's disgusting." Cilla began to giggle as El and Runyon glanced over to each other, both wondering what Ma had just said.

Mattie Doody, who'd been thoroughly enjoying the show from her window booth this evening, and who also knew how to speak French, looked to her husband seated across from her, and she uttered, "Well, that'd certainly be a new picture for the memory wall, now wouldn't it?" Referring to the photo board on the diner's wall reflecting a pictorial history of the restaurant.

Cicely turned back away from her husband just as Ma had uttered her sentence, wide-eyed. And, for the third time, she quickly scurried back over to drag Ma into the kitchen once again. As she reached behind the counter and grabbed Ma's apron she noticed the Reverend Percible at the diner's door. He'd stealthfully entered just in time to also hear the deadly phrase, and he too knew a bit of French. As soon as it hit his eardrums he'd gone into one of his usual defensive stances with his arms up to his chest and a nervous look on his face. When Cicely grabbed onto Ma and began to pull her towards the kitchen, they both stopped in front of the preacher momentarily. His demeanor changed back to one of pompousness as he looked down at Ma through his reading glasses with his head cocked slightly and tilted back,

"And you claim that I'm the sick one!" Ma's eyes widened as Cicely yanked her into the kitchen.

Moments later everyone in the diner room heard the words echoing from the kitchen, *"I said what?!"* And they all sat, each a bit stunned, none knowing exactly how to react and waiting for whatever was to come next.

Runyon leaned to Cilla, "What'd she say?!"

All present that didn't understand the French language, and even the ones that did, looked to the newlywed to answer the question. Cilla looked around the room, and then back to her husband, saying softly, but loudly enough for the quiet patrons to overhear, "She told Puut that if they speak French around her again that she…*ummm*…she would tie him up, strip naked and…and provide him a lap dance. She said, *ummm*…she said she'd twerk all over his ass." Cilla ended with a half, fake smile, and nervous laugh. Runyon's expressionless face began to turn as green as Puut's had become moments earlier.

"That'd be a first," Elmer responded quite casually as he stared into his plate and munched on a cold French fry.

Ma burst back into the dining room with Cicely right on her tail. Ma, not wanting to show any embarrassment, scowled deeply as she stood at the end of the counter-bar. She gazed out over the sea of patrons, stopping when her eyes arrived at Puut, who had a bit of fear on his face as he stared blankly back in her direction. He pleaded, after a big gulp to move the lump in his throat, "I promise, Ma! No more speaking a foreign language in the diner! Just please, keep your clothes on!"

Ma was taken back a bit as she peered over to Marmaduke, who gave her a nod in agreement with Puut's statement. She then glared back over to where Cicely had thrown her husband into a booth. Smirnoff also provided a cautious nod to the old woman. Ma hadn't immediately realized that the threat of seeing her in the buff and dancing around the diner would have such a psychological effect on her patrons, however, it did produce the effect she'd been seeking. Continuing her scowl, she squinted and waved her chubby finger in the air and addressed the diner in general, however mostly towards Puut, yelling out, "And I meant it!" She stuck out her tongue and threw her hips sideways in a pathetic attempt at what she believed a twerk might look like before storming back into the kitchen.

Most everyone in the diner experienced a slight head rush and a severe, stabbing pain in their brains as a result of the visual that Ma had painted for them in French.

And from that point on, no one ever spoke any language other than English while dining at Ma's, and in earshot of the owner.

CHAPTER 15

It's That Time Again...Bucksnort Two

"The Lollipop Guild had better mind their own business!" Ma blurted from her second-row seat at the annual town meeting, pointing, and waving her stubby finger between the mayor and his two councilpersons. Mayor Wiggleswort, Daley, and Doody were all seated at the front of the room at the board's folding tables. "This isn't an agenda item, and it's not up for discussion!"

At this year's annual meeting, Constable Bob was seated in his usual metal folding chair off to the right of Daley. In the audience was El, seated next to Ma, and directly behind them were Cicely and Smirnoff. Opposite in the same row were the McIntyre brothers. Father Winkin was seated up front, Ruby Red and Myrtle Watson were generally in the middle of the small crowd, and in the last row was Marmaduke, lounging back with his arms folded and head tilted down. His head and snowy white beard rested on his chest.

"We just don't think that you outta do that this year, Ma," the mayor whined. "It isn't a good representation of the town. Plus, you damn near killed us all with that hot chili concoction you fed us during last year's competition. Speaking for myself I can't use a public urinal anymore without having flashbacks of what happened to me."

"You're just still upset that you didn't win!" Ma barked as she stood up, still pointing at the mayor, "I'm holding the contest again and that's that!" Ma turned to address the room, calming herself a bit as she continued, "And I'm changing it up a bit this year. It'll be held outside of the diner, so's not to contaminate the joint like it did last time. We'll hold it in the parking lot on a Saturday. Rain date will be Sunday." Ma looked at Constable Bob and pointed again, squinting, and looking over her reading glasses, "And I've decided that the torch will be passed down! Whoever wins gets the free chili for a year, not life! And if you lose, Johnson, you'll lose all of your free meals!"

Bob, who'd been lounging in his chair staring at the floor with his arms wrapped around the front of his belly, twiddling his thumbs, raised his eyebrows and looked up with a panicked expression on his face. The mere thought of losing his daily free lunch caused him to perspire, more than normal. He started to respond, "But, Ma…"

"No butt's about it!" She continued to point at the lawman, "You'd better enter the contest again, and if you want to keep your free ride, you better plan to win!" Ma spun around and pointed down to Smirnoff, sitting directly behind her. "And I'll throw in an extra free breakfast monthly for a year to the winner!" The store co-owner smiled at Ma and blew her an air kiss.

"*Hmmm*, a free breakfast too?" The mayor whispered, looking downward and not realizing he was talking to himself, "That's certainly an incentive." His selectpersons, overhearing their town leader, looked at him in awe that he'd apparently forgotten all about his objections to Ma's second annual Bucksnort contest and was now considering being a participant once again.

Daley spoke first, "But Mister Mayor, don't you remember how it turned out last year?! Everybody got stuck in the diner's doors trying to escape the terrible smell! It was horrible! The three of you clogged up the plumbing in that bathroom for days! Even one of the ambulance attendants passed out!"

Doody was next as the mayor turned to him. "And you and Eleanor ended up in the hospital! Don't you remember that?!"

The mayor's eyes raised, his expression pleading with Doody as he whined again quietly, "Yes, yes, I remember. I'm still trying to pay off the emergency room bill. But she said a free breakfast to go along with the chili this time!"

"I already said it will be outside this year!" Ma yelled, still standing, "No chance of stinking up the diner!"

"It's repulsive!" Mattie Doody mentioned out loud, "Simply disgusting!"

Ma pointed in her direction while still glaring straight at the board. "You see? She remembers how popular it was!"

"What are you serving this year?" Smirnoff inquired in his heavily accented voice.

Ma turned back to the big Slavic man, "I figure we'll start with a big heaping helping of sauerkraut, followed by cowboy beans chock full of bacon and a side salad with plenty of cucumbers, cauliflower, broccoli, and green peppers." Cicely's expression, in listening to Ma's flatulent-based menu, continually grew worse as she squinted and unintentionally leaned further backward in her seat in an effort to avoid the gruesome description being hurled in her direction. Smirnoff just smiled and nodded.

Bob was still twiddling his thumbs, staring down, and rocking in his seat, continuing to contemplate the idea of losing the contest and his daily free meals. He also contemplated seeking a therapist in his panic-stricken state.

The mayor perked up again, quite obviously excited at the concept of an additional bonus breakfast for the winner. "Hey Ma, why don't you hold it on the stage across from your diner?! There's lots of fresh air out in that field! Plenty of room for an audience, too!"

Ma began to park her butt back down in her chair while responding, "That ain't a bad idea. The spectators will probably be mostly downwind. Might work out just fine." As she sat, she looked over to El, "We can put the judges up on the stage off to one side." El responded by simply tipping his head to his wife, remaining expressionless as she continued. "We could run that microphone and speakers up there so everyone gets a good earful of the entries!" Ma looked back to the mayor. "Same as last year, loudest and longest toot wins! And bonus points if you let go from both ends and let out a nice, loud belch along with the butt trumpet!" Ma swiveled around, her ass cheeks assisting in the rotation, and looked back to Old Marmaduke, "I expect you'll be judging again this year, won't you?"

"Ayah, glad to help out." Marmaduke never looked up as he replied in his monotone voice.

Ma swung her head to Mattie who had words of her own to say, making her statement to the general audience while glancing up at the board members and purposely not addressing Ma directly, "I don't want anything to do with this disgusting display this year! I will not be one of her judges again! The entire idea is revolting!"

"Chicken shit!"

Mattie took this comment personally, swung her head back, and glared. "I am not chicken shit, Wilomena! I just don't want anything to do with your filthy contest! It's not ladylike to judge a contest based on the loudest fart! The whole idea is inhumane!"

"Scaredy cat! Yellow belly! Sissy, wimp, pansy…wuss!" Ma blurted, *"Cream puff!"*

Mattie's face flushed as the challenge of Ma's words began to get the better of her. She glared for a moment at Ma in silence, finally responding, "Oh fine!" She blurted loudly, "I'll do it!"

"Heh, heh." Ma chuckled under her breath and turned to El, "I knew that would work." She then looked over to Ruby Red and pointed, "And you're judging again this year, too!" Ruby gave Ma the "who, me?" look in return, wide-eyed and startled. Ma then swung back to the mayor and glared, squinting.

The mayor, realizing what Ma wanted from him, began to whine again, "I dunno, Ma. I don't think I want to participate this year. That chili was awfully hot, and I had the squirts for a week afterward."

"Awe, buck up, Buttercup! You didn't die! I'll rent portable crappers this year to put in the field. No urinal this time! You know you want to! Just think, if you win, free grub! Plus, the bragging rights!" The mayor, looking down with a sad, sorry expression on his face, nodded hesitantly. Ma then swung around to Smirnoff and stared at him.

"Oh, no!" Cicely blurted out, holding her husband tight by the arm in warning as he opened his mouth to speak. Smirnoff did a double take, looking Cicely straight into her burning eyes as she continued, "You aren't doing that again! You weren't allowed in the bedroom for over a week last year when it was over! And we lost business for days because you couldn't control yourself around the customers!" Cicely looked straight at Ma, "He had the walking farts for days! Do you know what that does to business?! We aren't going through that again!"

Smirnoff looked at Ma with an "I'm sorry" expression displayed on his face. He was officially out of the competition.

"Oh, fine!" Ma yelled and turned back in her seat, folding her arms in disgust. "I'll get Voisine to enter! He smells like a fart all day long anyway!" Ma then perked back up and said sarcastically to the preacher seated in front of her, "What about you, Bubblehead?! Are you game for a little friendly competition?"

Father Winkin, still looking straight ahead and out over his reading glasses at the mayor, as if he'd asked the question, said pompously, "Don't be ridiculous. I'll have nothing to do with your smelly, rancid event."

Ma leaned forward and spoke in a low, sarcastic tone to the back of the preacher's head with an evil smile on her lips, "Whatsa matter, preacher? Afraid you'll blow a hole out the backside of your robe? Afraid that your followers will see their spiritual leader as less of a religious icon if he toots in public? *Hmph!* I never saw you as a coward. I guess you fear more than just the big man upstairs, dontcha?"

The preacher stared straight up into the air. "It's not working, Wilomena. I'm not going to be one of your putrid contestants."

Ma leaned back and re-folded her arms, speaking normally, "Well then, I guess while we're waiting for the contest to begin I'll just have to make small talk with the newspaper reporter that'll be there. You know, talk about this and that. The weather and such. Or maybe about how our church leader likes to play 'ride the pony' with his church organist. Or maybe how he helped kill an old woman in the local diner."

Father Winkin's expression changed as he began to turn his head and move his eyes to the side.

"Or maybe how he likes to show dirty movies to the children's choir on Sundays."

The preacher's head, and body, snapped around and he growled, "You wouldn't!"

"Oh, yes. I would. With subtitles!"

Father Winkin lowered his head and closed his eyes in defeat. "Fine. I'll take part in your disgusting competition."

"Perfect!" Ma perked up again, clasping her hands and blurting out. El looked at her and shook his head in disapproval. Ma just gave him a look back, disregarding his concerns.

"Did we make any important decisions about the town tonight?" The mayor whiningly inquired of the room in general, beginning to raise his gavel and looking back and forth to his select board. Both Daley and Doody shook their heads. He then looked to Constable Bob who also shook his head, and the mayor gaveled down. "Meeting adjourned!"

* * * *

The atmosphere in the field resembled a small, local carnival. It was warm and the sun was shining down through thinning clouds onto the field across from Ma's Diner. Lawn chairs and blankets were strewn about in front of the stage. Ice-filled coolers with various refreshments littered the ground. It all had the resemblance of a decent-sized tailgate party. Off to one side of the stage, four portable toilets had been delivered and set up. A sign tacked to a post in front of them read, "Not for use during the competition," to make certain they'd be available solely for the contestant's needs. On the stage were two folding tables to one side for the ill-fated participants, and two additional tables opposite for the judges. Ma had set up her 'Other Diner' in the field and Val and Cilla were busy serving hot dogs, hamburgers, and other goodies. Although the contestants themselves weren't allowed to consume any other snacks before the challenge. Their menu had been pre-determined.

Close to Ma's snack shack Elmer and Runyon had set up a campfire. Chained to a steel tripod above the flames hung a large cast iron kettle containing Ma's special recipe of cowboy beans, and steam floated from the pot while the fart-makers simmered. She'd added a few extra ingredients including a big helping of jalapeno and red habanero peppers. Ma was busy stirring the concoction with a big, wooden ladle as if a Salem witch were stirring her pot of evil brew. Elmer sat close, making use of an old rocking chair he'd brought along for the occasion. He was dozing, waiting for his cue to help dole out the deadly meal.

The four contestants, Mayor Wiggleswort, Father Winkin, Puut Voisine, and Constable Bob were seated on the stage. Each enjoying their precursor of salad, heavy on broccoli and cucumber. Rupert had on his best, bright velvety dress clothes and suit coat, complete with his top hat on his balding head. Father Winkin was in his traditional black frock and white collar. Puut was dressed all in khaki, ready for battle, complete with face paint. And Bob had his clean, white uniform on. The odds were again in Bob's favor, and he was still the favorite to retain his title. The three judges, Old Marmaduke, Mattie Doody, and Ruby Red were seated opposite, all looking bored as they waited for the official start of the competition. Ruby was filing her long, painted fingernails. Mattie was fanning herself with a colorful, Chinese bamboo hand fan, and Old Marmaduke, dressed smartly in his blue coveralls, white T-shirt, and tan work boots was leaning back in his metal chair and stroking his long beard. Each had their hand-written stack of cards, numbered 1 through 10, placed on the table in front of them ready to judge the entries. Between the contestants and judges were a podium, microphone, and speaker.

The local volunteer ambulance service was standing by just in case their services were required again this year. And once again, a local newspaper reporter from the Saint Sagacious Sentinel was present. However, Ma wasn't taking any chances this year and she'd asked Myrtle Watson to film the event on her fancy digital camera and then was instructed to take it to the library in Skunksquirt where they have a public computer, and post the video to the internet and e-mail it to the three local networks in hopes one would put it on the evening news.

Ma glanced over to Cilla where she and Val were in the food shack. Her daughter-in-law checked her watch, held up her hand, extended her fingers, and mouthed the words, *"Five minutes."* Ma stopped stirring the simmering pot of beans and kicked El's rocking chair, startling him awake, his hint to begin to get ready. Ma yelled up to the stage, "Johnson!"

"What?!" Bob was mid-forkful of salad in one hand and the salad bowl was in his other hand up to his mouth, as he'd been shoveling salad into his face when Ma yelled to him.

"It's almost time to officially start!" Ma pointed her chunky finger up at the lawman, "Do you need to fart before we get going?!"

"Nope, I emptied out earlier."

"Fine!" Ma looked at El and pointed to the kettle, his cue to start filling bowls. She then waddled past the small crowd and climbed the stairs to the stage. Ma approached the podium and whacked the microphone three times with her hand, making certain it was on and creating a loud banging sound through the speakers which caused the crowd to take notice. "Okay, folks, it's time to get started! The contestants have warmed up with their salads, now it's time to pass out the main course and see who shits themselves the loudest!"

There was low applause from the audience of twenty-five or so, and as Ma smiled wide and scanned the crowd she noticed many grimacing faces looking back at her, most displaying the *"Ewwww"* expression. Ma turned to the judges, Marmaduke was smiling while Ruby and Mattie both appeared to be quite repulsed. Since this year's event was outdoors, no nose protection had been distributed. Ruby wished she had one, though, believing they were far too close to the contestants with only about twelve feet of open air between them.

"I hope the ozone isn't low today," Red said in a low voice as she attempted to check the direction of the breeze. Marmaduke just chuckled in response to her comment and Mattie looked around as if the ozone would show itself.

Ma then glanced over to the contestants to make certain they were ready. Her smile turned to a frown, and she squinted and crinkled her nose when she spied something in Rupert's hands. Ma pointed, "That isn't Pepto, is it?!" The surprised mayor attempted to shove the bottle of pink liquid back into his coat pocket as Ma marched over to him and held her hand out. "Give it up!"

"I don't have anything."

"Give it up!"

The mayor shook his head disgustingly and removed his hand from his coat pocket, handing the stomach-settling medicine to Ma, and she responded, "Cheating could get you disqualified!"

"I don't care!" Rupert whined, "I have to have something! Last year you nearly murdered my colon with that hot chili mixture you made us eat! I went through two entire bottles of Monkey Butt before the pain and chaffing even started to go away!" Ma disregarded the mayor's comments, tossed the bottle out onto the ground, and returned to her podium.

El finished filling four heaping bowls with steaming-hot cowboy beans and Runyon carried the tray to the stage, placing a bowl in front of each contestant as Ma returned to the microphone. "Okay, same rules as last year. Contestants will begin eating and when they feel the urge they'll raise a hand. Everyone else will put a plug in it! Absolutely no tooting while someone is submitting their entry! The distinguished judges will base their scoring on decibel level and longevity. Extra bonus points for anyone managing a loud belch along with their fart at the same time!"

More semi-pathetic clapping from the audience, accompanied by many strange, revolted expressions.

Ma turned to the contestants, "Okay, spoons up!" Bob and Puut raised their spoons high. Rupert and Percible simply held their spoons in hand, not quite as enthusiastic as the other two. Ma turned back to the crowd, "Alright now, the portable toilets are hereby closed to the public!" Once again she turned to the contestants and pointed, "Go!"

Ma's words didn't exactly invoke a race as the four each hesitantly scooped a spoonful of the deadly bean dish, and slowly brought the potentially explosive edible to their lips. Bob was the first to take his taste as he closed his eyes tight and inserted the spoon into his mouth. As good as it tasted, he knew what the outcome would be only moments from now. Puut was second, not having partaken in the previous year's event as he swallowed the hot beans. Rupert held his nose with one hand as if that was going to make it any better. The reality was that the beans smelled just fine. It was the after-effect he was certainly afraid of. Percible was last, having looked to his left and right, watching others carefully taking their first spoonful. Finally, he ate his portion without initial incident. Ma's eyes were wide and her smile the same as she waited for the fallout, the anticipation growing inside her gut while something else boiled inside the contestant's tummies.

The beans were hot, but not without their positive side, and as usual Ma's meal was tasty. The hot beans did manage to make each contestant break a sweat. However, the first indication was that it wasn't nearly as bad as the chili served at the previous year's event. Runyon brought their fully carbonated sodas to each contestant as they all took their second spoonfuls, and it began to turn into a competition for the prize. Bob was shoveling spoonful after spoonful into his face as he wasn't about to lose his title or his free daily meals. Percible began acting as if he'd been marooned on an island without food for years as he greedily gobbled down the beans. Puut was eating rather normally, enjoying the meal as if were any other day in the diner. It didn't take long before Ma had to waive a hand to Cilla, an indication to help Runyon bring more beans to the contestants.

The mayor, as suspected, was having the most difficulty. The jalapeno and habanero peppers were beginning to take their toll. He required taking a short break to remove the suit coat and his pain began to display on his face. *"Jeesus, Ma,"* he whined at one point, "this is killing me! Can I please have the Pepto? Just a little?"

Ma, with her evil grin and giggle, "Nope. Drown yourself in soda pop if you're colon needs extinguishing!"

Bob was sweating terribly, however, he was mentally blocking out the discomfort as he now had his bean bowl in both hands and was almost drinking from it.

Ma glanced down and around the crowd who all seemed to be enjoying the excitement and anticipation. She felt it was similar to watching an auto race simply to see the inevitable car accidents that you knew were going to occur at some point. She looked over to El, who was still in his rocking chair watching and waiting with the others and she said, "This is going to be good!" El simply, and without emotion, gave the "thumbs up" to her.

The spectators included Cicely and Smirnoff who were seated down front in their lawn loungers just a safe distance from the stage. Smirnoff himself had a cold beverage in hand and a smile on his face as he watched the competition, relieved by the fact that he wasn't directly involved this year. Moments later he was also the first to notice as he glanced over to the tree line on the northern edge of the field and saw the big black bear swaggering towards the aroma it had detected from somewhere deep in the woods. Smirnoff said a bit nonchalantly and pointed, "Hey, Shithead's coming." All heads on the ground turned to see the big bear slowly approaching, his hairy backside swinging as his nose twitched in the air, and in his mouth was Ma's chewed-up red hairpin. Ma and the judges finally noticed and looked over to see the big bear about the same time that Val leaned out of the food shack to also get a glimpse of the infamous animal that was approaching.

"It's Petey!" Ruby gleefully called out and waived to the bear, as if the animal was going to return the gesture. Puut noticed Ruby's chest bounce in her tight V-neck, and he completely ignored the bear as he swallowed another spoonful of beans.

"It's Shithead, not Petey!" Ma yelled out, and then mentioned to herself, *"Huh,* he must've smelled the beans." The contestants now glanced over to see the big black bear approaching. No one necessarily feared the animal, however, everyone remained a bit cautious and equally dubious as to what the bear's intentions were to be. The McIntyre brothers, seated closest to the simmering bean pot, got up and stood behind their lawn chairs as if the tin-foil thin metal and vinyl webbing would protect them from the big bear if he were to turn ugly towards them. El, not fearing the animal, just kept rocking as the furry creature passed by him.

Ma looked at the contestants to notice they'd all stopped eating and were staring at the approaching animal. She frowned, "Keep eating!" Her words received the attention of all four, as they looked back. Ma then pointed directly at Puut who was just about to stand up, "And you stay seated! Don't even think about *shoosting* my bear! He's just curious!"

Puut slowly sat back down, disappointed. "Nobody invited the bear," as he shoved yet another spoonful in his mouth.

Percible's expression was one of concern. He looked down from the stage through his bean-splashed reading glasses that were seated on the bridge of his nose. "What's that bear intending to do?"

"Doesn't matter, keep eating! We got a farting contest to finish! Don't be paying any attention to the animal! He's harmless! Just another spectator, that's all!"

Bob, seated at the end of the table closest to the edge of the stage where the bear was approaching, cautiously watched while he continued to shovel the beans into his pie hole. Rupert remained somewhat oblivious as he was suffering the most, now in tears with his eyes shut and sobbing uncontrollably. His gut was churning.

"Hey, look! Another one!" Joshua called out and pointed to the wood line where a large bull moose had now appeared. Everyone turned to see the creature emerge from the trees where the bear had just come from, however, this animal wasn't approaching any closer. It was simply standing and staring.

Ma stretched her neck out to see her undomesticated nemesis and then turned to look down at the McIntyre brother, pointing her plump finger in the direction of the diner's parking lot. "Joshua! Go get my gun! It's behind the seat of the truck!"

"Oh, no!" Puut called out, spitting beans from his mouth, "If I can't *shoost* the bear, you can't *shoost* the moose! Fair is fair!"

Ma glanced back over at the moose. *"Dammit,"* she whispered loudly and shook her head.

The bear approached the simmering kettle of beans, and he laid the hairpin down on the ground. With his big snout pointing up and twitching, he sniffed the sweet aroma emitting from the simmering pot. The bear was careful to remain outside of the rocks surrounding the fire as he reached over and tipped the kettle just enough to get a good helping of beans all over his big hairy paw and shoved it into his mouth. He obviously approved and just as carefully he leaned over the kettle. Using his paw to tip the cast iron pot, he dipped his snout into the beans and began to gorge.

"Ma! He's eating our beans!" Bob cried out.

Ma looked at the bear, then over to Bob, and back to the bear again. "Well, what do you want me to do about it?! Go over and push him away?!"

"We've got to do something!"

"Val! Throw some hotdogs at him to make him go away!" Puut yelled.

"Are you stupid or something?!" Val cried out from the food shack, "I'm not throwing hot dogs at a big black bear! It'd just make him mad! I don't need him tipping this trailer over with me in it!"

Apparently, the thought of an additive caused Bob the lawman to forget about the seriousness of the current situation with the bear. "Hot dogs would be good in these beans, Ma," the constable said quite casually.

"Shut up, you idiot!"

Rupert began to slump in his chair, now at a full bawl and bean juice dripping down his chin. At that moment Percible raised his own hand. Ma did a double take and then scowled at the preacher, *"What?!"*

"I feel the need to break wind."

"Contestant number one is ready!" Ma immediately turned her attention away from the bear, who lifted his bean-covered snout and looked towards the stage as if now to be interested in the competition. The crowd also, cautiously, redirected their attention to the contestants again. "Go ahead preacher, let it out!"

Percible closed one eye, squinted with the other, and tensed. He grunted a bit and a *"Pooooffft"* blew the rear end of his frock outwards. A fairly tame and quiet butt burp had emitted from the preacher's backside.

Ma shook her head and grimaced. "Oh, for *Chrissake!* Here we go again! Is that all you got?"

Dismal applause came from the audience as the judges each held up cards displaying the number '2' on them. The bear gave a little grunt, shook its snout, and went back to eating from the kettle seemingly disappointed in the effort. A disgusted Ma glanced back over to the wood line, having to perform another double take as she spied along with the moose, at its hooves were a red fox, a gray squirrel, a woodchuck, and a turtle. Perched on its back was a spotted hoot owl. Ma squinted to make sure she wasn't hallucinating and then looked down to El, who glanced over and saw the same. Responding to his wife, "What'd you put in those beans, Ma? You're attracting wildlife like the Pied Piper." Ma replied by shrugging her shoulders.

"The mayor's getting naked again." Runyon's words redirected Ma's attention as she looked over to see Rupert removing his necktie and unbuttoning his bright yellow, sweaty, and bean-stained dress shirt.

Ma inquired, "You're not going to get all undressed and run through the field like you did at the fair, are you!?" The mayor, still sobbing uncontrollably and with eyes tightly shut, was unable to answer.

"Pooooft!"

Ma looked at the other contestants. "Who did that?! Who farted?! Who was it?!" Puut, with a cheesy grin on his face, raised his arm up. "You're supposed to announce your intentions so the judges can judge!" Ma scolded and then snapped her head to the experts, who all held up cards with the number '3' on them. More pathetic applause as Ma shook her head in objection.

The bear kept eating.

Ma pointed and waved her finger at the contestants, "No more farting without advanced notice! The judges weren't ready! We're down to only two left!"

"Ma!" The old woman snapped her head to Val, who was now pointing at the bear. Ma looked over to see that Shithead had completed his meal and was sauntering past the front of the stage. The McIntyre's moved back and Cicely and Smirnoff scrambled to their feet to do the same. Others behind them also cautiously put a bit of distance between themselves and the bear. Ma looked over and spotted the newspaper reporter perched on top of her vehicle, snapping photos. She then looked to the wood line for no apparent reason and saw an additional whitetail deer, a coyote, and a weasel standing beside the moose. Ma's eyebrows raised and her head shook as she glanced back to watch Shithead as he sauntered by the front of the stage, rounded the side, and around to the back where the stairs were located. Everyone on the stage, Ma included, stared wide-eyed as the bear climbed the stairs and stopped in the center of the audibly creaking stage between the judges to one side and contestants to the other. The bear sat back on his hind end, lifting his snout and he let out a grunt. Ma stood silent at the podium closest to her furry friend.

"What's he doing?" Myrtle asked in a low voice as she, and everyone else, was too frightened to move. And, due to the fact that the bear was essentially blocking their escape, nobody had the ability to leave the stage without jumping off the five-foot-high platform. And no one, other than possibly Ruby, was in any shape to attempt that acrobatic move.

Marmaduke spoke in a casual tone and chuckled, "Looks to me like he's entered the contest."

"That's not fair!" Constable Bob protested to Ma, seemingly disregarding the fact that he was within reach of a huge black bear. "He isn't an official contestant!"

"Shut up! You're just worried you'll lose to a bear and no more free lunches!"

Bob continued, standing halfway up and now entirely ignoring the fact that there was a big black bear on the stage along with the rest of them, waving a finger at the bear while yelling at Ma, "It's not fair, I tell you! He already gets free waffles every Wednesday! This isn't right!"

"All's fair in love and flatulence contests!" Ma blurted back.

Bob turned to the mayor, intending to protest to the highest court when he noticed that Rupert wasn't in his seat anymore. Bob looked around, as did the others, only to find that Rupert had jumped from the stage and he was running butt-naked out of the field towards the diner. Behind him was a trail of bright-colored velvety clothes that he'd shed. His wife, Eleanor, was chasing behind her husband while trying to scoop the clothing back up.

Ma scowled and turned back to Bob, waving her stubby finger behind her in the direction of the diner. "There! You see?! We lost a contestant! We had four to begin with so the bear needs to be his replacement so we can keep going!"

Bob continued the argument, "I still say it isn't fair! A man has the right to know in advance who he's competing against!" Pointing at the bear with his spoon, "He just showed up in the middle of the competition! Who's to say he didn't eat something before getting here that'll make him more gassy?!"

"There wasn't any sign-up sheet! Anyone can enter the competition! You're just pissed because you know the bear can fart louder than you!"

Father Winkin, still a bit nervous about the fact that a big black bear was sitting very close to him, raised his hand. Ma took notice, "You've already gone! Only one entry per contestant!"

Pompously, the preacher responded, "I don't need to expel gas again. I just want to know, since I've completed my required task, may I go?" The preacher's eyes motioned to the bear as he tilted his head.

"No! You stay seated and be courteous until everyone's submitted their farts and the judges make a decision!"

"Hey, Ma!" It was Smirnoff's voice this time as Ma turned to see what he was yelling about. When she looked down she saw him pointing up toward the bear. Ma turned to see that Shithead was waving one paw in the air.

Mattie turned to Marmaduke, "What's he doing?"

"Maybe he wants to submit an entry," Old Marmaduke responded.

Ma, keeping an arm's length between her and her furry friend, "I think you're right." She turned and blurted into the microphone, "Contestant number…*errrr*…three is ready!"

All eyes were on Shithead the Bear as he lifted his hind end just off the stage floor and balanced on one foot, waiving both paws out in front of himself with his snout in the air. He gave two or three small grunts and then one big yell before letting out a rather loud and respectable bear fart that lasted nearly four seconds. When he was done the bear sat back down and waived one paw as the audience responded with equally respectful applause. A smiling Ma looked over to the judges. Ruby and Mattie scored a '7', while Old Marmaduke gave the big bear an '8'.

A gleeful Ma gave a wink to her furry friend before turning back to the podium. Through the applause, she declared, "I do believe we have a win…!"

"…Oh no!" Bob stood back up and cried out, pointing at Ma. "I'm not losing my free meal to that stupid bear! You have one entry left! *Mine!*"

Everyone now looked to the big lawman, even the bear who lowered his paw and turned his snout. Ma's eyebrows raised as she watched Bob crouch slightly, tucking his arms to his sides and clenching his eyes shut. He let out a groan and took in a deep breath. And, as if history were meant to repeat itself, he let out a ripper that sounded like an elephant blowing his trunk that lasted several seconds before emitting a loud explosion that blew his metal chair backward and off the stage. Bob's eyes remained shut as the force caused a rippling effect that blew dried leaves off the ground behind him into the air, followed by shockwaves that rocked the food shack and made small shrubs in the field behind the stage bend over backward. Bob held tight to his sides and kept the action going with a sound that resembled a two-stroke outboard engine at full throttle. With his eyes still clenched shut, and as the flatulence began to wind down, he grabbed with one hand into his uniform shirt pocket, pulling out a cigarette lighter. He reached around to his backside and sparked the Bic while giving one more big push and flames exploded out of his ass with a big, *"Bang!"* A fireball flew up into the air. And just before he relaxed, and not a moment before the show was over, Bob opened his eyes and burped out the bonus belch that he'd been holding in his gut all afternoon.

"Oh, dear Lord," Ma said as Bob collapsed to his knees on the stage floor, resting his head on the folding table. Applause erupted from the spectators as she turned to see all three judges holding up cards with the number '10' on each one. She briefly glanced down at El, who shrugged his shoulders back at her. Ma looked back to the Bear, who was hiding his snout in shame with his bean-stained paw. She slowly walked around the table to the lawman, took hold of one of his arms, and held it up in victory.

It was purely bad luck that at that moment the breeze which had been blowing northerly experienced a shift from an incoming front and turned south just before Bob's fart dissipated into the tree line, and it forced the foul air back toward the crowd. It hit everyone on the stage first before dipping into the trough and striking the spectators. Bob was pretty much unconscious already when everyone began coughing and retching. Mattie passed out at the judge's table and Val quickly dropped the food shack's fiberglass awning in an attempt to escape the toxic fumes. Many tried to run off the field to get away, however, there were few survivors as the breeze had gusted too quickly to allow anyone to escape, and most dropped to their knees before reaching the roadway. Even Shithead the Bear, upon being struck by the foul gale, let out a loud yell and bolted off stage and back to his safe area in the woods along with the other animals, but not before taking the time to snatch back up in his jaws his favorite red hairpin as he darted away.

As usual Old Marmaduke simply sat still, arms folded, and head shaking as he watched others suffer. He chuckled and said under his breath, "Bunch of pansies."

Luckily the air cleared quickly, and festivities resumed as the celebration of a successful second annual Bucksnort contest continued throughout the afternoon. However, Bob, Puut, and Percible would end up spending a considerable amount of time in the rented crappers. The reporter also experienced minor injury when she was thrown from the top of her vehicle when Bob's foul gale blew past, and she required a bit of attention from the ambulance crew.

The mayor wasn't seen or heard from for three days. However, Eleanor did buy up the Smirnoff's supply of Monkey Butt later that afternoon.

*　　*　　*　　*

Ma's contest did make the Saint Sagacious Sentinel in a paragraph nearer the back of the paper after all. Details were a bit lacking as the reporter only described it as an "eating competition" more similarly resembling something similar to a hot dog eating contest rather than what it was in reality.

Unfortunately, Myrtle Watson didn't know how to use the internet. As a result, rather than sending the video to the local news channels, she ended up uploading it to Sloppy Joe Morgan's Bakery website where she'd taken a moment to peruse his specials of the day while attempting to download her video. With viewers thinking it was an advertisement for his donuts, he lost business for the following several weeks until he finally noticed the video and removed it.

And Ma gave Shithead the Bear extra waffles covered in lots of syrup on the following Wednesday, feeling a bit sorry that he hadn't won the competition.

But, hey, there's always next year.

CHAPTER 16

Once Again…the Last Chapter

Ma entered the diner scowling as she stopped at the end of the counter bar, leaned forward, squinted, and crinkled her nose. She was searching her establishment for the 'foreigner'. Moments earlier she'd spied the strange vehicle that displayed out-of-state license plates in the diner's parking area when she pulled the back in with the Chevy, having been away on a short errand just before the lunch hour.

Ma scanned the dining room and fairly quickly her expression eased and her face formed a little smile when she spied the man seated at a center table. He was facing her, holding a newspaper up with both hands as he reclined back in the chair. Ma immediately recognized him as the man who'd certified her world record just two seasons earlier when it was determined that her pickup truck had been struck by more animals in the road than any other in "history," none of the animals were necessarily harmed, and the truck remained operational.

The smartly-dressed gentleman looked up over his paper, smiling back at the diner's owner and Ma walked over and sat down in front of her new, old friend. "Mister Palin. What are you doing here so far away from your home? London, isn't it?"

"Yes, my dear lady," The Guinness representative stated in his distinguished English accent as he lowered his paper and folded it, obviously pleased as he'd been waiting to speak to his favorite Puddleduckian. "It's so good to see you again." He reached over and rested his hands on hers.

"Well, what brings you here?" Ma leaned into the table, and her expression turned a bit to one of worry as a terrible thought occurred to her. "Wait, you aren't here to tell me that I lost my title, are you? Someone didn't break my record, did they?"

Mr. Palin leaned back and waved his hands at her, "No, no. Of course not. Your record still stands, and will for some time, I'm sure it's safe to say. No, my dear. I was on my way to Alberta from New York where I needed to certify two separate record attempts and I decided to make the drive myself, specifically, just so I could visit my favorite little Maine town." He shook a finger in her direction and winked, remarking with sincerity in his voice, "And my favorite record holder."

Ma's face shined and she smiled at the silly man, leaned back, and spoke up, "Well, what can I get for you? Something to eat? Anything at all, you just name it."

"How about a nice cup of tea?"

Ma's eyes grew and she pointed politely, "Tea? You got it! Tea it is!" She turned her head, "Val!"

"Yes, Ma?"

"Some fresh, hot tea for my friend here. The best we have! And coffee for me."

"You got it."

Ma turned back, pointed, and winked. "It's coming right up!"

"Now, what have you been up to since that joyous day when last I saw you?" Mr. Palin adjusted his chained eyeglasses and relaxed back in his chair.

Ma sat up, fiddling with the napkin on her side of the table. "Well, let's see. Plenty goes on around here for a small town, that's for certain. We got through that pandemic thing without too much trouble."

Mr. Palin smiled and nodded.

Ma perked up, "And I took my first vacation ever!"

"And where did you go?" He asked in the most endearing of tones.

"Oh my, it was far, far away in the Caribbean somewhere. We went on one of those big cruise ships. And oh, was it hot there."

Mr. Palin tilted his head back and chortled, "I bet it was. You certainly deserved it. And did you have a good time?"

"I sure did. We visited some beautiful places. Oh!" Ma's eyes lit up, "And my boy, Runyon, he's gone and got himself married. To a fine lady, too! You'd like her!"

"You don't say?! You approve of her, I take it?"

"Oh, yes! A fine woman! Levelheaded, too!"

"That's wonderful. And what about that fantastic truck of yours? Is it still in operation?"

"Oh, my goodness, yes! *Heh, heh*. Not all parts are the same color, though. And a funny thing," Ma squinted, nodded, and pointed, "after that day you were here we never had an animal jump out at it again. It's like the whole record-breaking ceremony thing just made them all stop and think. No more dents or dings."

"That is remarkable."

"What about you, Mr. Palin? What have you been doing all this time?" Ma's question had the sincerest of tone. She was thoroughly interested.

"Oh, you know, my dear lady. Traveling here and there. Visiting the various countries and watching people try their best to do ridiculous things in an effort to get their names into our little book." Mr. Palin leaned back in and grinned with an air of pompousness in his tone, "However, none of them as fun and interesting as what you did." Mr. Palin winked, "Yours has been my favorite ever since."

Ma's smile grew. She even blushed.

And the two friends from opposite ends of the ocean for the next hour or so, reminisced, talking about their individual lives and enjoying each other's company while sipping tea and coffee. Val set out some fresh-baked oatmeal chocolate chip cookies and the two laughed as they spoke of everyday life, and they never ran out of conversation. And Ma truly appreciated her time with the "foreigner" from far away that was in this moment seated inside her diner and enjoying her company.

*   *   *   *

Mr. Palin checked his watch and sighed, "Well, my good friend, it seems it's time for me to be on my way."

"Are you sure you have to go? Are you sure you won't have something to eat? A decent meal for your trip?" Ma asked, disappointment reflecting in her tone.

Mr. Palin sighed again, "Ah, if only I could. But, I have a long drive ahead of me and I must be going if I want to arrive at a decent hour. By the way, what do I owe you for the tea and those delicious cookies?"

Ma closed her eyes and put up a hand, "Not a thing, my friend. Put it in your gas tank, it's all set. It's the least I can do for your time and trouble."

"You are most gracious. It was no trouble at all. And I can't tell you how much I've enjoyed our little visit together. I'm so pleased that you had the time for me today."

Ma nodded confidently, "So have I. Thank you so much for stopping in." The two stood up and Ma reluctantly began to walk the Englishman to the door.

"I wouldn't have missed this opportunity for the world," Mr. Palin replied before stopping at the exit and he turned to Ma, smiling, and taking her hand in his once again. "You will take care of yourself, now won't you?"

"I will. And you as well. Please drive safely." And, as her friend turned to leave, "Oh, and Mister Palin…" He turned to face her once more, "…If you ever find yourself in the neighborhood again…"

"…I won't hesitate at all, my good woman. Good day to you." With one last endearing smile and a tip of his head, Mr. Palin turned to leave the diner.

Ma stood at the door, watching her friend as he slid into the driver's seat of his rented sedan. She stared and unconsciously waived as she watched him drive out of the parking lot. And, when he turned out onto the road she leaned out of the front glass door, stretching her neck to watch him disappear down the roadway. When he was finally out of sight Ma leaned back and let the door close. She shook her head just a bit and grinned, thinking to herself how much she had enjoyed her visit with the funny Englishman whom she barely knew, however thankful he'd taken the time to visit their quaint little town just to spend a few minutes with her. She thought about how he'd taken the time to make time. How he'd made time to be there. Finally, after a moment lost in her thoughts, both happy and sad, she shook it off and proceeded to return to taking care of her patrons, and her diner.

And as she turned away from the door, the smell located her nostrils, and as she crinkled her nose, her scowl returned to her face once again.

"*Jeesus Ke-riste*, Constable! *Again?!* Did you really feel the need to do that again in here?!"

"Sorry, Ma."

"Val! Open all the *goddam* windows! That idiot lawman just farted in my diner again!"

The End

ABOUT THE AUTHOR

David Wilson is a career law enforcement officer, born in Bangor, Maine, and has lived in the Pine Tree State throughout his entire life. Having grown up in the north woods at his family camp, he's versed in the Downeast way of life and how Mainer's live, work and play. He enjoys using his home state as the backdrop for his novels and creating the nostalgic Maine feel in his humor-fiction novels.

David's writing style is to incorporate humor into everyday events. In his first book, a memoir about becoming a police officer in rural Maine entitled *Peanut Butter Memoirs*, he used satire as a means to express his thoughts and actions in dealing with high-tense situations.

In his sister novels, *Two Seasons* and *Ma's Diner*, David commonly used real-life events and memories, adding humor to enhance the situations that his characters find themselves a part of.